GRANITE

GRANITE

Pat Mattaini Mestern

DUNDURN PRESS
TORONTO

Editor: Barry Jowett
Copy-editors: Barry Jowett and Allison Hirst
Design: Erin Mallory
Printer: Webcom

All characters, businesses, and situations in this book are fictional. Any resemblance to places and actual people, either alive or dead, is purely coincidental.

Library and Archives Canada Cataloguing in Publication

Mestern, Pat Mattaini
      Granite : a novel / by Pat Mattaini Mestern.

ISBN 978-1-55002-843-0

      I. Title.

PS8576.E79G73 2008   C813'.54   C2008-904876-8

1 2 3 4 5   12 11 10 09 08

 Conseil des Arts   Canada Council
du Canada   for the Arts

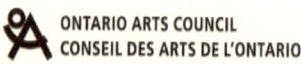 ONTARIO ARTS COUNCIL
CONSEIL DES ARTS DE L'ONTARIO

Canadä

We acknowledge the support of the **Canada Council for the Arts** and the **Ontario Arts Council** for our publishing program. We also acknowledge the financial support of the **Government of Canada** through the **Book Publishing Industry Development Program** and **The Association for the Export of Canadian Books**, and the **Government of Ontario** through the **Ontario Book Publishers Tax Credit program**, and the **Ontario Media Development Corporation**.

Care has been taken to trace the ownership of copyright material used in this book. The author and the publisher welcome any information enabling them to rectify any references or credits in subsequent editions.

J. Kirk Howard, President

www.dundurn.com

Dundurn Press	Gazelle Book Services Limited	Dundurn Press
3 Church Street, Suite 500	White Cross Mills	2250 Military Road
Toronto, Ontario, Canada	High Town, Lancaster, England	Tonawanda, NY
M5E 1M2	LA1 4XS	U.S.A. 14150

Dedicated to
Bill Dumas
whose candor is refreshing,
and whose friendship is cherished.

Also dedicated to
Glen Graham
who through an unfortunate accident
cannot read this book,
yet provided inspiration for it.

Author's Notes and Acknowledgements

In the 1950s I had the pleasure of spending a number of summer vacations in Northern Ontario. During one of these holidays I met an Ojibway elder who, among other stories told around a camp fire, related the Legend of CAT.

In the ensuing years, while doing research for a number of projects, more tidbits of information surfaced, keeping the legend alive in my fertile mind.

When considering a locale for the story, I came to the conclusion that there is no place in Southern Ontario more appropriate than Niagara Escarpment country in the beautiful Hills of Mulmur in Dufferin County.

The Village of Seven Springs, the Valley, and the characters that inhabit the area are figments of my imagination but representative of scores of mid-twentieth century rural communities and residents throughout North America where individualism reigned supreme.

While reading the book, keep in mind that many people have the same dream. It's how each individual interprets the reverie that makes it unique, and allows a person to realize their potential and to make something of it. One's ability to achieve is bound only by imagination, courage, and tenacity.

Once again I must thank my husband, Ted, for his patience and kind attention while I spent hours at the keyboard.

A Place Forever Sweet

There is a place
Forever sweet,
Where past and memory
Seem to meet.

Beyond
Today's care,
In a softer light
Some loving memory there.

What do we
Remember best?
Perhaps thoughtfulness
And being treated fair,

The changing years,
The sacrifice of parents,
The passing of individuals,
The honest person.

When fortune smiled,
Youthful hopes,
A burden lifted,
When somebody cared.

There is a place
Forever sweet,
Where past and memory
Seem to meet.

— O.B. Glenn

Prologue: Hunter's Mark

A lush valley, bounded on the south by a limestone escarpment and on the north by steep ridges that folded into distant horizons, remained where once glacial meltwater roared through primaeval landscape.

Upland rivulets and streams, now channeled into a river, fell in a burst of energy through a slash in the high escarpment. In the narrow lower trace, the water rushed around obstacles in its path, from one side of the glen to the other, before flowing placidly over a gravel bed in the middle of the wide, fertile valley. The river's journey ended on the sandy shores of the Big Bay on the Lake of the Hurons.

On higher ground, maple, beech, elm, and oak with an occasional stand of birch and cherry grew on the rich loam. Clearings were the habitats of wild gooseberry, raspberry, bramble, and choke-cherry. The river's bank was lined with cedar, willow, and stands of elderberry. Swamps and bogs were yellow and purple with water irises in early summer, red with cranberries in the autumn.

Where the raging torrents of meltwater had scoured the land to its underlay, craggy headlands were bared to the elements. Huge piles of scale rock lay at the base of limestone bluffs. Glacial granite erratics were strewn throughout the valley floor, some half-buried in the rich loam. Others stood like sentinels, monuments to past, present, and future events.

The only signs that humans knew of the valley were an ancient Indian trail that tracked along the river's edge and a log cabin that blended so well with the landscape one would have to be told precisely where to look to find it. The structure nestled in a stand of trees on the heights of the southern escarpment. When the owner walked to the overlook — The Knob — he had clear views to west, north, and east. Miles of virgin forest lay behind him to the south. This was The Mark: Hunter Logan's land. His bluff, his hills, valley, and forest. The landscape didn't much resemble that which he'd left behind, but Logan had no plans to return to the undulating valleys and hills of Upper New York. That area was now part of the new republic and held memories Hunter tried hard to forget.

CHAPTER 1
Early Summer, 1798

The legend says that the lights
That arc across the northern sky
Are spirits of those gone before.
On autumn nights with auroras so bright,
And crackling from the heavens,
Three animals dance through the borealis.
A wolf, a bear, and a cougar,
They whirl — they growl — they circle.
The wolf is cunning.
The bear is strong.
The cougar is forever.

Early in the morning on a warm June day, Hunter Logan and his dog, Moon, were trailing a deer on the west ridge, where the valley was at its narrowest point, when Moon's sensitive nose caught the smell of humans on the wind. Hunter's keen sense of sound detected voices. Hurrying to a vantage point where he could see everything from the safety of the heights, Hunter scanned the valley. Along the trail, by the river where a wild raspberry patch thrived in a clearing devoid of elders and bank willow, an Indian man talked earnestly to a woman who had a papoose cradle strapped to her back. She accepted a small pouch from him before he turned again to walk upriver. The woman followed but at a distance behind the brave.

The pair hadn't walked far when two men jumped from behind a clump of tag elder and attacked the man. The woman turned and ran back down the trail, then veered off into the patch of raspberries. She finally disappeared into the brush cover beyond. Hunter saw the Indian fighting for his life then witnessed the blow of the axe that killed him. While the brave lay on the ground, his lifeblood running into the pebbly soil, the pair threw his meagre possessions around. The last thing taken out of his pouch was a small copper pot, which the larger man, a blond-haired brute, turned upside down and shook. When he threw it to the ground, the pot bounced and rolled toward the river's bank then came to rest beside a large stone.

The pair turned their venom to the dead Indian. Rolling him over, they cut the straps of his quiver, dumped the arrows onto the ground, and searched through them. The shorter, dark-haired man cut the thongs that held the brave's medicine bag. Dumping the contents on the dead Indian's chest, the pair knelt and sorted through the oddments. The taller man removed a tobacco pouch, stuffed it into his pants, then spat on the corpse while the shorter fellow stood and viciously kicked the dead man's rib cage.

"Damn Ingin," the taller one said. "What'd he do with the gold?"

"Mub'by gave it ta' the squaw," said the shorter one.

Only when mention of the woman was made did the two look around for her.

"Damn, she's bolted."

"What'd yu expect? Yu said not to kill the woman. He was the one we wanted."

"Well, she can't get far. She's luggin' the papoose."

An angry discussion ensued that culminated with the pair deciding to split up to search the area. The shorter man retraced his steps back down the trail while the other started across the valley toward Hunter's lookout.

"Moon, it's time we left," Hunter said to the big black mongrel dog lying obediently at his feet. "We don't want that pair to know that we saw what happened."

Hunter and Moon retreated, leaving few tracks in the mouldy leaf-covered ground in the old growth forest. Hunter covered a half mile before he swung left and made his way down the ridge. At the river he took to the water, walking upstream, away from the slaughter. What is so valuable that they'd kill a man to get it? he wondered. The pair had obviously laid in wait for the couple.

The Indian must have suspected, or heard, something shortly before the ambush. As he talked to the woman, he reached to gently caress the cheek of the child in the cradle on her back before handing her the pouch. When he turned again to the trail, the woman seemed to purposefully lengthen the distance between them. As quickly as the men jumped on the brave, she knew that she must run into the dark, hushed forest reaches where she could disappear in the overgrowth and windfall.

Several hours later Hunter stood on the Knob and looked over the valley. As he suspected, the woman hadn't found his cabin. His reckoning was that she would keep below the bluffs and wouldn't go far from the body. She'd find some place to hide then go back to mourn her man. If the woman tracked along the bottom of the escarpment, there were a number of good places to hide. At least until dark when bear and cougar roamed the area, she'd be safe in any of the crevice caves, whose entrances were partially concealed by scale rock. There were cubby holes in windfalls that could provide cover.

Hunter scanned the valley for signs that the men were still in the area. The beggars have probably high-tailed it back to civilization, he thought. They'd be fools to hang around a dead body. "Moon. Come to heel. We've enough time before gloaming to find the woman," he said.

It proved difficult to find the woman's path, after she left the raspberry patch where not even broken brambles marked her way. Eventually, Hunter found a spot where her mocassined feet had slid on rotting leaves and left distinctive marks in the dark compost. Bending down, he examined the ground then commanded the dog, "Scent, Moon."

Moon sniffed then, nose to the ground, led the way through the forest. Not an animal to bay or bark, the dog paced himself to his master's stride. Hunter noted that the scent led neither to a tree fall nor cave. It ran by the side of a rill whose source was a spring that gurgled from the base of the escarpment a mile away. Where the bank was muddy, the woman, always going upstream — away from the bloody scene — left distinct footprints. A half-mile up, she'd crossed the rill, walked toward the ridge on the opposite side of the valley, then forded the river. Keeping a fair distance away from the waterway on the west side, and under the cover of thick brush, she then made her way downstream again, heading toward her fallen man.

Hunter was sure though that the woman wouldn't return to the site of the killing for some hours. She'd hide until she felt that the threat of danger to herself and the baby had passed. Moon finally tracked her to the middle of a dense cedar copse that was so thick Hunter didn't fancy following her into the maze. He figured that she might be carrying a knife. The woman would be distraught enough that she wouldn't hesitate to use it. He circled the copse. There was only one way in.

"Go to her, Moon. Stay clear." Hunter said. The dog entered the tangled mass. Hunter could hear him breaking through the thicker areas. Then there was silence. Hunter tried calling to the woman in several Indian languages. He then tried French. None of his efforts were successful. Moon didn't reappear.

Guess the only thing to do is to leave Moon in there for a while to wait her out, he thought. Hunter sat, his back against a beech tree. Perhaps an hour passed before he whistled for Moon and listened as the dog scrambled through the thicket. Moon came to lie beside his master. Hunter lay his hand on the dog's back.

When sometime later there was still no sign of the woman and child, Hunter took some hard biscuit and dried meat from his pack. Tying them in his handkerchief, then securing the cloth around Moon's neck with the leather thong that held his knife at his waist, Hunter sent the dog back into the copse.

"Go back to her, boy." Hunter said. Then, he sat back and waited results. Within the half-hour his generous act paid off. Moon came out of the copse, followed by the young disheveled woman, bent low to avoid the sturdier branches. She had taken the baby out of the cradle and held it tightly to her chest to protect it from the lashing greenery. At the edge of the copse she stood tall, alert, and perfectly still, ready to bolt, not knowing what would happen next.

Good Lord, Hunter thought. She's no more than sixteen. "Come," he motioned with one hand, while at the same time holding the other out, open-palmed, to show that he was not holding a weapon. "Come here. I'll take you home."

The word "home" seemed to register. With cautious steps, the woman approached Hunter, Moon walking by her side.

"Follow me," Hunter said, pointing to the west. Taking a chance that she wouldn't knife him, he turned his back and took several steps then looked back to see if she was following. She hadn't moved.

"Come," Hunter said again. "Moon, heel."

The dog started toward his master, stopped, looked around at the woman, then started again. He did this several times before she capitulated and took a few steps toward Hunter. Moon circled and fell in behind her as though he was herding sheep.

Hunter, respecting the fact that the woman was carrying a baby, walked at a slower pace than he normally set. He looked back occasionally to make sure she was all right. Alert always for the killers, Hunter avoided the river bank where her man had fallen. He retraced his steps and forded the river where the water flowed over a wide gravel bed then waited on the other side for her to follow.

When the woman hesitated, he walked into the water again and offered his hand. She didn't accept it but when their eyes met, she quickly lowered hers to concentrate on her footing and the babe she was carrying. Hunter chose the easiest way up the south escarpment: an area he called the Slide.

The log cabin, dwarfed by its surroundings, was in a small clearing several hundred feet back from the Knob. The building, with a lean-to hung precariously on one side, faced a smaller outbuilding that Hunter used to prepare furs for sale. His cozy home consisted of one large room that measured no more than twenty feet by twenty-five feet. Furnishings were spartan, reflecting the life of a man who spent much of his time away, on his traplines.

It took the woman a moment for her eyes to adjust to the cabin's interior. A stone fireplace took up one wall while an arrangement of poles, rope, woolen blankets, and fur skins, occupied another. A rocking chair with a black bearskin rug on it sat in front of the hearth. A wooden table with hardwood stumps for chairs dominated the middle of the room. Wooden pegs held clothing. Rough shelving was stacked with baskets and crocks, the white man's books, and tin lanterns. Two dry, salted deer hams hung from the rafters. An iron frying pan and cast-iron cooking pot shared space on the hearthstone with a large clay crock.

The woman stood near the door, ready to run, but Moon lay across the opening and made retreat impossible. Hunter motioned that she should sit on the bed. When she ignored him, Hunter took the best course of action and pretended that she wasn't in the cabin. Moon would protect him if necessary.

Hunter busied himself lighting a fire. He stirred the coals — blew on them — added tinder to the glowing embers. Gradually, he added wood from the pile by the door until he had a good fire blazing in the hearth. "I won't hurt you." Hunter talked softly to put her at ease. "You and the baby are safe here. Do you understand?"

The ensuing silence was broken by the baby's crying. Hunter was glad to hear the child's lusty howl. The babe had been so quiet he'd thought it might be dead. The woman slid along the wall and lowered herself onto the bed. Eyes on Hunter, she lay the baby on the bed then slipped the empty cradle from her back.

"It's a hungry wee devil," Hunter said. He turned his back to the woman. Obviously, the baby needed to be fed and she wouldn't like someone to watch the process. He had to trust his own instincts and Moon's reflexes. The dog never took his eyes off the woman.

Hunter had built the cabin over a spring, accessed by a trapdoor in the south corner of the floor. He commanded Moon to stay by the door before he retrieved a crockery jug, opened the trapdoor, and disappeared into the hole. Hunter reappeared a few minutes later with a jug of water and was pleased to see that the babe was being fed.

Reaching up, Hunter sliced a chunk off a deer ham, threw it into the cooking pot, added water, and pulled it toward the heat.

Out of a cloth bag hanging from a peg under a shelf he took some hard biscuits and tossed them in with the meat. Then, he sat in the rocking chair and pretended to watch the pot, while at the same time he remained alert for sudden movement near the bed.

When the woman finished feeding the baby, she came to the fire to stir the pot, showing some familiarity with the utensils and being around a hearth. Hunter, seeing her action as one of acceptance, left the chair and busied himself by placing bowls and spoons on the table.

Hunter did all the talking while they ate. His command of Indian languages left something to be desired so he spoke in English. "We'll have to bury the body. By-the-bye," he said looking at the woman. "I'm Hunter Logan, if you're asking." Hunter pointed toward the dog. "Moon. The dog's name is Moon."

"Nibish," the woman said, pointing to herself.

"Well I'll be damned. You do understand English."

"Nibish," the woman said again. "Me speak little English." She pointed toward the bed. "Him, Manchild. You not hurt us?"

"A little English is better than none. I certainly won't hurt you," Hunter smiled at the woman. "So, you're called Nibish. 'Leaf,' I think that means, doesn't it? We'll get along just fine, methinks."

When Hunter retrieved a blanket and went for a shovel, he indicated that Nibish should put Manchild in his papoose cradle and follow him. He decided to take the same route, the Slide, into the valley to the site of the ambush.

The pair made their way down the hill and kept to the forest until they reached the trail. Moon ran ahead, nose to the ground, ears alert to intruders. When they came to the disturbing scene, Nibish ran to the corpse. She knelt beside the body, touched the bloodstained cheek and dark, matted hair. Her fingers ran quickly over the gash that killed her man, disturbing swarms of flies that buzzed around like a black shroud. She wept quietly, murmuring his name over and over again: "*Hoshaphat ... Hoshaphat ...*"

Hunter came to stand beside the body. The brave must have been a handsome fellow. Even in death, his features were striking. He was clothed in buckskin leggings, cotton shirt, and beaded vest. "The poor devil didn't stand a chance," he said. Hunter didn't want to disturb Nibish, but time was short. He placed the blanket on the ground, and indicated that he was going to roll the body onto it.

Nibish left the baby in its cradle near the ever-vigilant Moon while she retrieved her man's bow, arrows, quiver, and medicine pouch. She carefully gathered a few small items scattered on the ground and tied them in her cloth girdle. That job completed, Nibish stood by her man, ready to help Hunter. The body had begun to stiffen and wasn't easy to move, but the two managed to shift Hoshaphat's remains onto the blanket. Hunter did what he could to properly bind the body in the wrap.

Hunter looked around for the best place for a grave. As the river had a gentle bank that flooded easily, the body needed to be dragged several hundred feet to a small rise dominated by a large, odd-shaped rock, several cedar trees, and the rotting stump of an ancient oak tree. This would be no small feat. Nibish looked so young that Hunter figured she wouldn't have much strength. "I'll drag the body to that stone," he said, pointing to the granite boulder.

"I will help," Nibish said.

Lifting, pulling, and tugging, Hunter and Nibish managed to get the blanket-wrapped body to the rise. This woman is no fading violet Hunter thought. But then, grief gives strength to improbable people. It didn't take long to dig a hole deep enough to ensure wolves and bears wouldn't plunder the grave. Nibish worked alongside Hunter, digging with a curved stick she'd found. She stopped several times to tend the baby when it cried.

After the body had been placed in the pit, Nibish lay the bow, quiver, arrows, and girdle on it. The grave was backfilled and rocks were piled on top. When the pair turned toward Hunter's cabin, Nibish took the papoose cradle from her back and held it to her breast. Halfway up The Slope, she stopped and called softly to Hunter. When he turned, she handed the cradle to him. Without a word, she turned away and ran toward the river. Moon started after her.

"Heel, Moon! Let her go." Hunter watched Nibish disappear into the undergrowth. "She's off. She wouldn't leave the babe with me unless she was planning to come back. God knows where she's running to, or what she's going to do."

The sun was setting behind the hills when Hunter reached the cabin. Nibish appeared out of the dark several hours later clutching the small copper pot. In mourning, she had hacked her hair off, and slathered her face with mud.

"So, she does have a knife. I figured as much," Hunter muttered. He was thankful that she hadn't slashed herself with the blade as was sometimes the custom. He tried not to look at Nibish in her agony or to go to her to touch her or to comfort her. That is not their custom, he told himself. Let the woman grieve in her own way.

It was Nibish who solved the problem of sleeping arrangements. She took a blanket from the bed, wrapped herself and Manchild in it, and lay down by the hearth.

"No. No," Hunter said, indicating that she should use the bed, but Nibish chose to ignore him by turning her back to him. Hunter stoked the fire and spent a few moments replenishing the logs. Impulsively, he took the bearskin from the rocking chair and covered Nibish with it.

Hunter lay on the bed fully clothed. "Moon. Guard!" he said quietly.

The dog positioned himself between the woman and the bed. The dog's allegiances were with his master. If the woman chose to attack, Moon would protect his owner. If she chose to leave, Moon would let her go.

Hunter slept lightly. The child had cried during the night. Hunter was aware of dog and woman padding around the cabin but didn't hear the bolt removed from the door. Early in the morning, he smelled frying salt-hind and opened his eyes. Nibish was working at the girdle tending the meat. The kettle, on its crane, boiled merrily over the flames.

The feeling that Hunter had at seeing Nibish at his hearth was akin to the one he had experienced while digging the grave. He had been running and hiding too long. The further Hunter dug into the fertile loam, the stronger his realization that it was time he stopped roving and put solid roots in the soil of Upper Canada. The deeper he dug the grave for a man he didn't know, the more the man emerged that Hunter knew he had to once again become. Memories came over him like waves, bringing thoughts of gardens and ploughed fields, family and kin. They were feelings that he'd never expected to have again. Hunter had been surprised that a few tears mingled with the sweat of his brow. How many years had it been since he'd wept or thought of family and a permanent home? Too many, far too many.

When Hunter woke on the second day, Nibish wasn't in the cabin but the baby was tucked in beside Moon on the floor. When she did return, Hunter could see that she had been crying and had again slathered her face with mud. He surmised that she'd gone once more to the grave so kept his chattering to a minimum, respecting her time for grief.

By the fifth day, Hunter was quite accustomed to a woman sharing the cabin with him. His days seemed shorter for having human company. He enjoyed watching the babe, although he hadn't attempted to pick Manchild up, knowing that might be perceived as a breach of trust. The more he spoke English around Nibish, the more Hunter realized that she *understood* it a lot more than she could, or would, *speak* the language.

On the seventh day, Hunter said, "Hoshaphat was a good man that you grieve so, but you must not haunt his grave. His spirit is not there. It travels on the wind. It dances in the lights in the northern sky. You must believe that, just as I believe that my beautiful wife's spirit is birdsong at morning light. You have a child to raise. You must not let grief take hold of your life."

On the tenth day, Nibish took the initiative and handed Manchild over to Hunter while he sat in his rocking chair by the fire reading his Bible. When Moon turned his eyes to his master, Hunter rested his free hand on the dog's big head and said, "Don't worry, Moon. I haven't forgotten you, my friend."

What more can a man ask for? Hunter thought. He had a fire on the hearth, a babe in arms, and a faithful dog by his side. Perhaps he desired the healing of his heart and a wife by his side?

On the twelfth day, Hunter broached the subject of Nibish's future. "You can live here if you wish. I will take care of you and the babe. If you decide to stay, I have to bring in more supplies: flour, potatoes, salt. You don't need to be concerned about me," he said. "I'm not looking for a woman. To think, you're the age of my daughter, if she was alive."

Hunter got his answer the next morning over their meal when Nibish indicated to him that she wanted to stay near Hoshaphat's grave. She and the child could never go to his home. Nibish had no idea where Hoshaphat lived in the north.

"Do you not wish to return to your family?" Hunter asked.

"No, because of Dago:ji' I must remain near Hoshaphat," Nibish said.

"I have to go for supplies, then." Hunter sopped his bowl with a biscuit, somewhat relieved that she had decided to stay. Her plight had lain heavy on his mind.

After he'd readied himself for the trip to the lake, he gave Nibish one more round of instructions. "You'll be fine here by yourself. The cabin's so isolated there's never company." He indicated by lifting lids and giving a running commentary where food was stashed, although he already knew Nibish had found most of his stock. He opened the trapdoor and indicated she must go down into the cellar if anyone came to the cabin. "Hide in the hole, Nibish."

Nibish nodded that she understood and said, "Mishoomis Gazhagayns. Talk Gazhagayns — Dago:ji'."

"I should talk to Mishoomis Gazhagayns?" Hunter asked. "Who's Dago:ji'? Where is Gazhagayns?"

"On the high bluff near the big water," Nibish said.

Well, that describes half the landscape near the lake of Ontario, Hunter thought. "I'll be away seven or eight days," he said, walking the right fingers across the left palm. "When I come back, I'll bring an answer with me as to why your man died, if I can. Do you understand?"

"Lady Wilcox, my friend," Nibish said. "Find Henhawk. Henhawk is bad man."

"Then, I'll look for Henhawk." Hunter gathered his blanket roll, powder horn, gun, and food pouch. He called to Moon and left, but not before explaining to Nibish one more time that she should secure the door with a heavy piece of plank each night and that she shouldn't go far from the cabin during the day.

"Fool that I am," he said, walking away from the cabin. "She can probably lose herself quite nicely in the forest. She's not as vulnerable as you think, Hunter Logan. When that child is old enough to travel, they'll go home."

* * * * * * * * *

On the third night after Hunter left the cabin, Nibish was awakened from a light sleep by a wind in the chimney that was so strong it set little tongues of flame leaping from wood in the cook-fire. She drew Manchild closer to her and set the rocking chair to motion. Strange, she thought, that the wind would blow on such a warm night. Even stranger was the fact that she was here by the white man's fire when her life's path was to have been so different — so far away.

They were headed north, Hoshaphat promised, to the great expanse of land beyond the big lake of Superior that his family called home. Hoshaphat had found CAT. He was taking Nibish and babe home before turning his steps toward a land where the snow never fell, to return CAT to his ancestor's people. Hoshaphat was fulfilling a promise, ending a dream that had haunted him, a dream that now bothered her.

"What do you want, CAT? Everyone who has touched you has known death." Nibish spoke to the fire, believing its heat and light were the embodiment of CAT. "Why do you haunt me now? Why do white men kill for you, CAT?"

Receiving no answer, Nibish closed her eyes and let tears she'd held back for so long flow freely. A good number of them fell on the baby. "Hoshaphat, what am I to do? I am not as strong as you but should I continue your journey? Am I to stay here with the man, Hunter? What will happen to your child, flesh of your flesh, if I die because of CAT?"

At the sound of yowling, Nibish's eyes flew open. Fearfully, she looked to the window, then at the barred door. The animal was close but still not a threat. The cabin was secure. Except for using the necessity, when she kept the baby tied to her, and glanced furtively around, ready to run for her life if necessary, she felt like a prisoner in the Hunter-man's cabin when he was not there. Hunter-man was kind, protective. She trusted him.

The rocking motion of the chair soothed Nibish's sore heart, and spoke to her fatigue.

Swosh, swosh — sleep my Nibish, the rockers whispered as they swept the wood floor. Exhausted, Nibish fell into a light sleep then dreamed that she was riding an antlered deer through a forest when suddenly she was confronted by a golden cat that stood high above her on a rocky ledge ...

"Come closer," CAT said. "Come closer and listen to me. I will not hurt you, woman."

Nibish did as she was told, mesmerized by the cat's blazing yellow eyes that reflected the sun's light back into hers. So fast did the deer move toward the apparition that Nibish thought she was flying through the air like a bird. When she was before the animal, she saw that it was tied to the rock, that all four feet were tethered by vines.

"You see them," CAT said. "I've been tethered so that I can't go home."

Nibish nodded that she saw he was a prisoner. She noticed that his claws glowed like the sun and his coat sparkled like the stars.

"You know that CAT needs to be free."

Nibish nodded again. The animal's eyes now seemed to shoot fire and to look through her.

"Then free me, woman. You have it in your power to do so."
The eyes were not shooting fire now but looked like the end of the
barrel of a gun — ringed with metal and black but with the power
to kill.

"I can't break your bindings. Hoshaphat must do that."

CAT's voice was now soft, almost like a warm, gentle wind.
"Earth-child. I cannot live in captivity. I can't live as a hunted thing.
I can't live in a golden body or a copper pot. My spirit must be free so
that I can roam this land, if I cannot return to my ancestral home."

Nibish didn't look at CAT again for fear its eyes would shoot
fire and kill her.

"You can free me. You can keep me free, forever, so that no one
else needs to die to imprison me again."

"But your true home is far away," Nibish said. "You will not
be happy here."

"I will claim this as my own," CAT said. "Woman, do you hear
me? Free me!" CAT stopped talking, opened its golden mouth, and
let out a bloodcurdling scream.

Nibish's eyes flew open. Disoriented, she grasped Manchild
tightly and looked quickly round the room, expecting to find the
cat with the golden fleece sharing it with her. The cougar's cry
reverberated in the clearing. From the opposite side of the bolted
door, there was the sound of wood being ripped by claws.

Nibish was out of the chair, grabbed a poker, and made for the
door. CAT was trying to get into the cabin. Banging on the door
with the poker, Nibish let out a series of loud whoops. When the
scratching stopped, Nibish ran to a window and looked out, just
in time to see a lean, tan body slink into the underbrush. Hunter-
man had warned her about cougars. He said that they were bold
enough to come right into the clearing to look for food.

A dream? Reality? Whatever it was Nibish experienced, she
shook like an aspen leaf from fear, exhaustion, and grief. She

rechecked the door, then lay Manchild on Hunter-man's bed. She removed a small leather pouch from around his neck and tucked it into the small copper pot on the mantel. Crawling onto the bed beside her babe, she held Manchild against her chest, drew a blanket up to her chin, and closed her eyes. She had much to think about.

For two more nights Nibish had the same dream and after each she implored Hoshaphat to tell her what she must do. "It is your CAT, Hoshaphat. You are Ojibway. I am Seneca. You had the dream that you must find CAT and take it home. I have only had a dream to free it here. I will stay near you, my brave man, but where must CAT be? Tell me what is right."

On the fourth morning at the crack of dawn, Nibish bound Manchild to her, removed CAT from the pot and its pouch, and walked to the high bluff. Standing well back from the edge, for fear CAT might push her over, Nibish threw the golden idol as high and far as she could.

Nibish watched as CAT arced, glinted gold as it caught the rays of the rising sun, then fell into the tops of the trees below the ridge. "I have freed you, CAT. No one will disturb you until you wish them to, by making yourself known again. *The wolf is cunning. The bear is strong. The cougar is forever.*"

* * * * * * * *

As he entered the Horn-of-Plenty, Hunter's quick glance took in his surroundings. Several small windows and the open door provided the only light for the inn. A huge hearth dominated an outside wall. A man and woman sat on a bench near the fire enjoying an ale. Hunter knew there was something not right about the situation when Moon growled. "Steady on boy," he said when he saw the objects of the dog's attention, two rough-looking characters seated at a corner table. The pair looked up briefly then went back to quaffing their ale.

"Well, I'll be damned," Hunter muttered, recognizing them. Hand on the dog's back, he said "Not now, boy." He made his way across the room, plank flooring echoing the sound of his boots.

"What's your pleasure?" the innkeeper asked.

"A tankard of ale and bowl of that mutton stew I smell in your good woman's pot. You're new here. Where'd Jus go?"

"Take a seat an' I'll serve you and answer yer questions," the innkeeper said.

Hunter chose to sit where he could keep his back to the wall so that he could face the table where the two men finished their ale. He put his belongings on the floor near Moon.

Besides the two tables occupied, another four surrounded by an odd assortment of chairs made up the Inn's furnishings. The innkeeper's wife scurried around preparing food at the hearth, wiping her brow occasionally on a large apron that had once been white.

The innkeeper pulled a wooden gate across the bar, locked it, drew the ale, and, coming around the cage, set the tankard on the table. "My wife will dish your mutton stew. I don't trust the buggers. I rarely place trust in people from away."

"My good man, I'm the last person you need to be concerned about."

"I'm not referring to you."

By the time the steaming bowl of savory stew and thick slice of brown bread were brought to the table, the two men had left.

"My name's Wil Barnes," the innkeeper said, bringing another tankard of ale. "Nice dawg ya got there. He's a big 'un. Mean bugger is he?"

"No meaner than he has to be. So what happened to Jus?"

"He left fer his ol' home. Jus got word from his brother that his mother was ailing. He figured that everything's settled down Maryland way and he'll be all right now," Wil said. "He thinks that folks will forget what side o' the rope he threw his hat over in '77."

"I figured by the way he was talking the last time I dropped in that he was homesick," Hunter said. "He wasn't married and didn't bring family north with him. That's hard on a man."

"He'll be back, afore ye know it," Wil said. "He put roots here, had a woman, ye know, a widow lady from England. She refused to go south with Jus. He'll be back, I wager. Things aren't the same over there now an' he was really stuck on the lady."

Hunter smiled. He remembered the power that some women could wield over men. When his thoughts suddenly turned to his dead wife, Hunter shook his head and swatted at the swarm of flies that arrived with the food. "Many people come through today?"

"Nope. So, what's your name, just in case someone asks?"

"Hunter Logan. The dog's name is Moon."

"Well, it looks like ye come a distance."

"Two days north and a half west, off the Carrying Place Trail and up the Indian Fork passage to Huron," Hunter said. "Can you spare a crust of bread, a sacrificial offering for these damn flies, and a bone for the dog? We've been eating hard biscuits and roast squirrel the last couple of days."

When Wil returned with bread and bone, he sat down beside Hunter. "Do you want company up Huron way? We're thinkin' about movin' in that direction but heard it's purdy uncivilized yet."

"I'm squatting on wild land because I like solitude. There's been no survey done yet," Hunter said. "There's weeks at a time that I don't see anyone but Indians on the trail. If you're thinking of running an inn, you're better off here, or down toward the head of the bay until more folks move north."

"Well, if it wasn't for the good folks sittin' over there quaffing ale, you and the other two gents, I'd not have a penny in my coffers today. It cain't get much worse. I'm a farmer by trade. Hard work's what I'm used to."

"Do you know the pair that just left?"

"Henhawk's the name o' the tall one. Tom Delaney is the short fellow. They work for Squire Wilcox."

"The Yankee Wilcox — from near Albany?"

"Believe so. He came up after the Revolution. Bought land and set up shop. I don't think he's too settled, though. He has a few fence-sitting callouses gotten during the war. People don't trust him."

"I know what you're talking about. Where does he reside now? The last that I heard was that he lived in Newark near Niagara," Hunter said.

"Five miles east of here, a big wooden house, right on the lake. Ya cain't miss it," Wil said. "You sound like a Yankee yerself."

"I may be," Hunter said. "But I'm not about to go into my personal history today. Can I still stay in the loft? There are few places around here to spend a couple of nights that don't cost a bundle of hard-earned furs."

"Yep, the loft is your'n, and anyone else's that needs a place to lay their head."

"Fair enough. Tell your good wife that her cooking is better than Jus's was. Tell me, have you heard of a man or place that goes by the name of Mishoomis Gazhagayns or Dago:ji'?"

"Nope," Wil replied. "I'll ask around for you."

"If you'd do that, I'd appreciate it."

* * * * * * * *

By late afternoon Hunter, a glass of good whiskey in hand, Moon by his side, sat on Squire Wilcox's porch looking over Lake Ontario.

"So I finally get to meet Hunter Logan, legend of Canajoharie and the Valley. I'd heard you'd buried yourself in Upper Canada after you lost your wife and children."

"Heard you came this way to take advantage of the business opportunities," Hunter countered.

"You don't wish to talk about the massacre, then?"

"No, I don't. Suffice to say that when I lost everything that was near and dear to me, I turned my back on the horror that caused it."

"Fair enough." Squire Wilcox refilled both glasses and settled into his chair. "So, why are you here? To what do I owe the pleasure of a visit?"

"Do you have a couple of fellows by the names of Henhawk and Delaney that work for you?"

"I do. What have the scoundrels gotten into now?"

"Henhawk killed a man up my way. Struck him dead with an axe."

"Who?" Squire Wilcox turned his full attention to Hunter.

"An Indian by the name of Hoshaphat."

Wilcox's glass stopped midway to his lips. "Hoshaphat's dead? What happened to Nibish and the baby?"

"I'm not talking about a woman and child. I'm referring to a strong young man cut down in the prime of his life for no apparent reason. And don't give me the hogwash about his just being an Indian. I respect Indians a lot more than I do white men. There are no finer men than Brant and his warriors."

Squire Wilcox looked genuinely upset. "My dear Mr. Logan, I liked Hoshaphat and Nibish. I'd never want to see them dead. However convoluted it may seem, there might be a reason why they were attacked. Henhawk probably believed that Hoshaphat was carrying a pot of gold," he said.

"You'd better start at the beginning of this tale." Hunter filled his glass. Stretching his long legs, he made himself as comfortable as possible amidst the cushions on the chair.

"Hoshaphat and Nibish came here shortly after Manchild was born. I found them camping in a lean-to by the creek in April. Hoshaphat explained that he was looking for some item that was important to his ancestors. As they weren't disturbing anyone, I said that they could stay. My missus and Nibish became quite attached. While Hoshaphat was away, Nibish spent a great deal of time with my wife and the servants. She learned to hearth-cook, was taught some English. The girl's only sixteen, you know."

"I noticed," Hunter said. "Did Hoshaphat explain what he was looking for?"

Wilcox leaned forward to retrieve the bottle. "He came from way north of the Lake of Superior to look for a pot that his great, great Ojibway grandfather had buried while being pursued by the Iroquois."

"What was so important that Hoshaphat had to find it?"

"If I recall, it had something to do with an Indian legend of some kind — something about a cat that shone like gold that was buried in a small pot."

"They arrived here in April. It's the end of August. What happened in the meantime? You said that Hoshaphat spent a lot of time away."

"For days on end the fellow would be upcountry searching river banks for the treasure. He had an idea of what kind of territory he was looking for — asked questions about the land

and rivers that flowed north and west of here, looked at some maps I have."

"'Tis obvious that he found something," Hunter said.

"Last week, he came back in a great state of excitement. Hoshaphat told me that he'd found the burial place, a cave," Wilcox said. "It appeared to me, from his description of the area, that he'd been in the Gore District. He said that he'd found the golden pot and left wampum in its place as he'd been instructed in a dream to do."

"Are you sure he said a gold pot?"

"I heard that, as plain as day. When I asked to see it, he wouldn't show me. He was talking to me in the stable. I'm sure that Henhawk and Delaney were close by," Wilcox said. "Shortly thereafter, Hoshaphat and Nibish packed and left. Wait a moment .... " Wilcox left the room but returned several minutes later. "Hoshaphat gave me this."

Hunter examined a hunting knife with an eagle feather attached to the horn handle.

"You must have been a special friend that he'd give you an eagle feather."

"And Nibish made this for my wife." Wilcox handed over a beautifully beaded talisman on a leather thong.

"You didn't see the pot or an idol of some sort?"

"No, and I'm personally not inclined to believe Hoshaphat's story about there being one, either."

"Would he have known the difference between gold and copper?"

"I'm sure he would."

"Would Henhawk and Delaney know the difference? Might they think that the pot was made of gold?"

"They'd be stupid enough to think anything," Wilcox said.

Brows furrowed in thought, Hunter paced the porch, his

eyes on the body of water that separated him from the land of his birth. "Do you think that if the pair actually believed that Hoshaphat found gold, they'd follow him and kill the man for it?"

"I think that if the idiots had been drinking, that's precisely what Henhawk, and that fool that hangs around with him, might do. The pair came across the border with me, but let me tell you they're not sterling of character. Are you sure that it was Henhawk who killed Hoshaphat?" Wilcox came to stand beside Hunter.

"I saw him strike Hoshaphat dead and recognized the man again at an inn not far from here. His identity was confirmed by the innkeeper."

"No court will convict them," Wilcox said. "The victim was, after all, an Indian, as you've said. What's next?"

"The victim was a human being and I do expect restitution for the woman and child from you."

"What kind of restitution? Financial?"

"A milk cow and calf, a nice fat piglet, a bag each of corn seed, and potato eyes," Hunter said. "I'd also appreciate a promise that you'll get Henhawk and his cohort off the trail by not mentioning the murder or Nibish in front of them."

"You want me to set you up as a farmer? Are you blackmailing me because I have two fools working for me?"

"If Nibish is going to stay around, she has to be fed. I've not got the money to buy seed, let alone a cow and pigs."

"You know where she is?" Wilcox paced the length of his porch, pausing occasionally to glance Hunter's way. "What if I choose to ignore the entire situation? After all, I didn't kill the Indian."

Hunter was ready with his counterattack. "I do know where she is and I've not asked for much. Giving me what I have requested would be the cheapest thing you can do as payment for a stupid act by two of your henchmen. If you choose not to give me these items, I'll let it be known around York what your true dealings were with the Revolutionary Army of the Republic. You, sir, are inclined to make money by whatever route is easiest. I'll wager that you haven't yet severed all your financial ties with the Republic across the border."

"Sir, I've heard that you also maintain first-class connections south of the line, even though you've chosen to hide yourself in the bush. How would those connections feel if they knew you were trying to blackmail me?" Wilcox said.

"It wouldn't matter to them. I don't call my request blackmail. I will also state that if you thought gold was involved, you would not hesitate to turn your henchmen loose on an Indian — just like you encouraged, nay paid, your group to loot and burn any Loyalist homes in the Valley, including mine."

"You can't prove that."

"Yes I can," Hunter said. "Look, Wilcox. What's the price of one milk cow, a piglet, and some seed against a list of those interests you supported during the Revolution? Knowing that you were partially responsible for the events that led to my family's massacre makes me seek justice by unusual and un-gentlemanly means."

"I have a right to freedom in this country," Wilcox said.

"True, but there are people here with long memories and sharp knives," Hunter said.

Wilcox paced, hand stroking his beard, weighing his options. "Do I have time to consider your request?"

"I'll give you two days to say yea or nay. Send word to the Horn-of-Plenty. If you don't know where the tavern is, ask Henhawk. If you choose to give me what I request, I'll be leaving in three days time. I'll expect to see everything at the Horn," Hunter said. "Bring them yourself. And let me warn you, don't let one of your options be to send Henhawk and Delaney out on the trail to end my days, or Nibish's, like they did Hoshaphat's." Hunter gave Moon a pat on his huge rump. "We'll handle them if you do, won't we boy?"

"I had nothing to do with Hoshaphat's being killed. You must believe me. But I must say that I place no credence in Indian legends and superstitions. There was no gold. He came south on a wild goose chase perpetuated by a dream."

Although Hoshaphat may have been naive about Squire Wilcox, Hunter wasn't. "Regardless of whether you believed his story or not, I know you'll now do what's right for the woman and child," Hunter said. "You don't want your reputation ruined around here, do you? And your good wife, she'd want you to do that much for Nibish, would she not? As you say, the two women were friends."

"Look, Logan, about your family — the circumstances. It was a war, for Lord sakes. We did what we had to, to achieve results — to win. Who knew that a bunch of Gawd-damn men would seek revenge for a raid on a fort?"

"You didn't lose your wife and children, Wilcox. On whose side did you work to achieve results? The way I heard it, you worked both sides against the middle," Hunter said. "I've had to come to grips with my loss. I'm still bitter at times but at least, like some people, I didn't choose to support whatever side was winning, then run for cover when things got nasty. I've one more question: have you heard of someone or a place by the name of Mishoomis Gazhagayns or Dago:ji'?"

"I never heard the name. I don't know the man. or the place. Why do you ask?"

Noting the blank look on Wilcox's face at mention of the names, Hunter felt that the man was probably telling the truth. "I just wanted to do a little socializing while I'm out of the bush. I'll be expecting your decision tomorrow, then?"

* * * * * * * *

Hunter's next stop was at the mill in Ancaster and the docks on the lake where he knew a large number of people usually congregated: Indians hawking wild game and fish, housewives eager to exchange fresh produce for flour, newly arrived immigrants seeking work or information on land availability.

By asking around, Hunter learned that Mishoomis Gazhaga-yns, Grandfather Cat, could be found on top of the escarpment near the site of an old Iroquoian village. With that information, Hunter returned to the inn and consulted with Wil, who was familiar with the terrain inland from the lake for some miles.

"You can see where you're going from here. There's a rough path up the escarpment that crosses the government road. The path goes up and o'er the top, down into a valley and back up again" Wil explained. "The second time ye climb to the top, go right and follow the trail toward a big bare bluff face. Ye cain't miss seeing that bluff from the valley. You might want to spend some time up there, just lookin' around."

"Would your good missus pack some food for me? Enough for two-three meals? I'll leave right away."

"It's not that far away," Wil said. "Ye can be up and back in a day. There's nowt out there tonight but 'squitoes so big they'll carry you away."

"Please don't take my departure as an offence to your good company," Hunter said. "I need some time to myself to do some thinking."

On top, Hunter chose his bivouac with care. He and Moon hunkered down for the night behind the trunk of a huge maple that had fallen in some long-forgotten storm. All evening,

Hunter mulled over the situation that put a young Indian woman with her baby in his care. For years he'd lived in self-imposed exile. After his wife and babies had been senselessly massacred in the Valley of the Hudson, he'd turned his back on humanity, preferring a dog for companionship and the solitude of the Canadian wilderness. On the occasions when Hunter did return to civilization, it was only to sell his furs and purchase supplies. He did allow himself the privilege of purchasing books — all he could afford.

A near-fatal accident on last winter's trapline forced Hunter to think about his solitary circumstances and to acknowledge that there was possibly more to life than exile. He was a schooled man who in his youth had been surrounded by family, friends, music, and books. Was he missing music? Was he missing friends ... companionship? This spring, after experiencing several bouts of severe loneliness, not something he usually allowed to interfere with his exile, Hunter bought writing supplies and began to put his thoughts and dreams on paper.

Hunter rose before first light and shared the last of the inn's salt pork, cold potatoes, and biscuits with Moon. Their thirst was quenched by the waters of a spring that bubbled to the surface thirty feet from their camp. Tracks left in the soft mud showed the reason that Moon had been restless during the night. It appeared that a large cat had drunk from the same water source.

Hunter sat now, his back against a tree near the edge of the bluff. Interesting land, this Upper Canada, he thought. This unique escarpment land-feature which snakes its way across the land, east from the falls at Niagara then north from the Head of Burlington Bay, becomes part of the Mark before it ends at the tip of the long peninsula at Lake Huron. He'd walked most of its northern reaches tending his trapline.

Below the ridge, to left and right, stretched an endless plain that he surmised had once been the floor of the lake. Now it was lush with old growth forest, cleared fields, swamp lands, and bog. As Hunter reveled in the beauty of the dawn, his calloused hand stroked Moon's big head, a gesture that made both feel content with the day.

Sunrises, with their ever-changing palette of colour and cloud, never ceased to impress Hunter. Today, morning began as a magenta streak in the eastern sky that turned the lake into a series of blood-red ribbons. As the sun rose higher, the sky's eastern colour became a mass of gold and orange, which broke sharply into pink clouds that folded into purple from the southern horizon to the black northern sky. Eventually, as the sky coloured blue, the dark north horizon turned a soft grey.

"Moon, we've enjoyed a lot of sunrises together, just you and me. I think that's about to change. We've been alone long enough. What do you think, Moon? Are you ready to share our life with a woman and child?"

It is strange how life repeats itself and changes so quickly, Hunter thought. Through one dastardly deed, he lost his family. Through a second murder, he found himself involved with Nibish. She was so young that his heart went out to her the moment she stepped from the copse, with a babe in arms. His first thought had been that this young woman should not suffer the same fate as his wife and family, for Nibish would surely be killed if the pair of ruffians found her.

"You like her, don't you Moon? You took to her right away." Hunter played with Moon's ears, stroked his neck. Of course, he had no guarantee that Nibish would stay. There was the possibility that she would be gone before he reached home. But she's a child yet. She'd not be foolish enough to leave with the babe, would she?

If Nibish stayed, Hunter knew that he couldn't spend weeks on his trapline during the winter. By asking Wilcox for seed he'd acknowledged that changes to his life would include clearing the land and sowing crops. "Why not?" Hunter asked. "I was willing to do that before ..."

Hunter looked at his hands — big, ham-sized hands that were used to work. He was a strong man, young-looking for thirty-nine years, six feet tall with a thick shock of blond hair and beard. He was still capable of putting his back to the plow. He was knowledgeable about crops and animal husbandry.

"So, we agree, Moon, that if Nibish is at the cabin when we get back, we'll settle down to some serious farming? If she's not, we'll have a milk cow and piglet to dispose of before we go back on the trapline this winter."

The fleeting fragment of a dream crossed his mind. Hunter frowned as he thought again of the details of the strange recurring reverie, the one he'd had ever since Nibish entered his life. It was always the same: a big antlered buck, harnessed to a plow with a shiny grinning cat on its back — a golden cat with big eyes, the ugliest cat that Hunter had ever seen.

The sun rose enough that the lake and sky blended together like a deep blue mantle, split only by the outline of a Durham boat, a small white streak in the seamless aqua landscape, pushing its way up the lake from Newark to York.

"It is time to find Mishoomis Gazhagayns," Hunter said. "By my calculations, he shouldn't be more than two miles downwind."

In response, Moon licked his master's hand.

* * * * * * *

Mishoomis Gazhagayns, although bent with age, still possessed a powerful frame. It appeared that the wisdom of generations lay on his blanket-covered shoulders. He sat on a deer skin near a small fire. His legs, comfortably crossed, were covered with dirty leggings. Smoke from a long pipe curled round his head as he looked over the endless green expanse of fertile plain, and beyond, to the sparkling waters of the lake.

"Approach," Gazhagayns said. "I heard you come long way back."

"And I thought that I was being quiet," Hunter said.

"Not as quiet as Gazhagayns. Not so much as one of my feet will turn clumsy white."

Hunter approached, his hand on Moon's back. Respectful of the old Indian's age and according to custom, he placed a packet of tobacco in the elder's lap. Then, not looking directly at Gazhagayns, Hunter waited for an invitation to sit.

"You must wish to see me badly," Gazhagayns said. "Like the otter, I'm not easy to find."

"I must speak with you about Nibish and Hoshaphat. Someone has killed Hoshaphat."

"Kitchi Manitou holds Hoshaphat gently in his hand? Sit. Talk."

Hunter folded his long legs under him and sat beside Gazhagayns. Three eagles soared on the updraft so close to Hunter that he could clearly see their eyes.

Seeing Hunter's preoccupation with the birds, Gazhagayns observed, "They see and know all. I see to the end of the horizon and know little."

"I see to the end of the horizon, and know nothing," Hunter said.

"Why do you travel with a bear-dog? What is it you must ask

me?" Gazhagayns tucked his gift into a pouch, signalling he was willing to talk.

"I trust Moon better than any man. As for why I came looking for you, Nibish said I should find you. I figure you must have information that she thinks is important."

"Speak then," Gazhagayns urged.

Without mentioning that Henhawk and Delaney were involved with the killing, Hunter explained the circumstances that caused his visit. "Do you know why Hoshaphat was killed? What's your connection to Nibish?"

Gazhagayns drew heavily on his pipe and took time to form his reply. He didn't know Hunter but from what he perceived of the man seated before him, Grandfather Cat felt that he should respond truthfully.

"I understand why you hesitate," Hunter said. "But I'm not responsible for Hoshaphat's death. I'm sheltering Nibish because she might be in danger too."

Gazhagayns's silence lasted several minutes. "Long time ago," he finally said. "I was Seneca of the Iroquois Nation. I had the name of Dago:ji' — 'Cat.' I fought on the western front, on Ohio River. After war I went north to Otchipwe-Kitchi-gami to trap furs. Met Ojibwa woman there by name of Nigoaimes. I became her man. She called me Gazhagayns — 'Cat' in Ojibway. We had family. Hoshaphat is my grandchild. After Nigoaimes drowned in lake, I came south and fought with Thayendanegea — Joseph Brant. I went to reserve land on the Grand River." Gazhagayns pointed west toward the horizon. "I couldn't live on reserve so came here to old Iroquois village to spend my last days."

"Hoshaphat came south to find you?"

"Hoshaphat came to find CAT and me too," Gazhagayns said.

"He was looking for a cat and you knew where he should look?"

"I am more than eighty corn-moons. I know much from Nigoaimes. There runs a legend in the north, told first by Nigoaimes' grandmother. She spoke Spanish and came from very far away. She was a spoil of war that Ojibway warrior took for a wife. She carried with her to the north a small charm, and it brought nothing but trouble."

"A copper pot that shines like gold?" Hunter asked.

"No," Gazhagayns replied. "You do not listen. It is not a copper pot. Ojibway knows copper. They find pieces in rock, carry them around as if gods. They hide pieces in secret places and speak to them. They pass these pieces from father to son. It was CAT that Hoshaphat found. With these two eyes, I saw it."

"Saw what?"

Gazhagayns lowered his head and pulled his blanket tighter around his shoulders, pondering whether he should say more.

Knowing it would not be right to disturb the old man's thoughts, Hunter waited for an answer. He knew what the elder was thinking. Why trust this stranger? Why speak the truth to a white man?

"I saw a four-legged creature, very small." Gazhagayns finally said. "It was a tiny statue, very ugly Dago:ji' — CAT that shone in the sun. Hoshaphat wrapped CAT in rabbit fur and carried it in copper pot."

Hunter mulled over Gazhagayns' information. It was odd that the old man mentioned a very ugly cat. His own strange dream involved a feline. "Are you sure it was made of gold?"

"Gazhagayns knows gold, like coins. It was a gold Dago:ji' — CAT, living in the small copper pot."

If what this elder is saying is true, and Hunter had little reason to doubt him, Henhawk and Delaney didn't find the booty. They'd checked the pot and tossed it aside. It was now on the hearth in his cabin. The two men also searched Hoshaphat's body but came up empty-handed. Nibish may, or may not, know about the whereabouts of the object. "Hoshaphat was CAT's guardian?" Hunter asked.

Gazhagayns nodded. "Long ago, another warrior had a dream. While that man was travelling south, the Iroquois threatened attack. He protected CAT by burying it in the copper pot. Then he turned north to Superior. Before he left for the south again to complete his dream journey, the brave was killed."

"And what was the dream?" Hunter asked.

Gazhagayns closed his eyes, the better to separate details of the dream from the legend ...

"There is much illness and hunger in the camp. Camp has high stone walls all round — a stream runs through — bark wigwams in a row on one side — warrior sits by fire and dreams of a cat that shines in the sun. CAT tells the warrior that his clan is hungry and sick because of it. CAT says that it is tired of dancing with the bear and the wolf. It is tired of the cold. CAT says that no one will go hungry and illness will go away when he is returned to his home — far south of the big lake — far south of the big river."

Gazhagayns looked at Hunter to make sure he was listening.

"The warrior leaves camp, riding a big buck-deer. He holds the antlers as he rides and carries pot with CAT in it." Gazhagayns used his arms and hands to illustrate his story. *"On his way — to this long, long trail to the south — the warrior gives what he has to those with hands out. Their eyes are dull with hunger but his pack is never empty. Sometimes, the warrior takes something of himself and gives it, too."*

Gazhagayns shook his head. That part was not clear to any who had the dream. Was the warrior giving bits of his life, or clothing, or words from his mouth? "That is why the first warrior ancestor left the north; he had the dream and followed it."

"This warrior rides an antlered buck — a deer?" Hunter asked.

Gazhagayns nodded. "Hoshaphat's people were ill. He also had a dream. Hoshaphat's dream was that he must find the pot and continue the journey — return CAT to its home. If Hoshaphat did that, CAT would be happy and Hoshaphat's clan would never be sick again."

"You have had the dream?"

"No. Hoshaphat came to me because I know the land," Gazhagayns said.

"Did this dream tell him where to find the pot?"

"No. But the legend did — a legend handed from ancient ones to grandfather, to father, to his son, to Hoshaphat. The legend said that to keep CAT safe from the Iroquois the warrior buried it in a small copper pot in a cave on the bank of a river that roared through a high canyon on way to the Lake of Erie."

"Hoshaphat found the pot and came to you again?"

"After months of looking, he came to show me. I saw CAT. I counselled him to speak to no one about it. I warned him it was dangerous to talk to white man. He left my fire to get Nibish and Manchild, to take them home before turning his moccasins south."

"Did he know where he should go in the south?" Hunter said.

"No," Gazhagayns said. "Hoshaphat said that another dream would tell him where CAT lived. Hoshaphat said that he would not leave the north until he had the second dream."

Hunter found it hard to believe that his personal reverie had so much in common with those of the others. "I don't profess to understand dreams," Hunter said. "I have enough difficulty comprehending what takes place in my waking hours. The statue must have held some importance to the slave woman. Does the legend say what CAT represents?"

"To everything there are four seasons," Gazhagayns mused. "To life there are four seasons. There is a beginning — a birthing; there is a nurturing — a growing; there is a time of reward — a harvesting; there is an end — death. Only the cougar is forever."

"Perhaps, like Hoshaphat, she was guardian of CAT," Hunter said.

"Hoshaphat is dead and that saddens me, but he did not die in vain," Gazhagayns replied. "You're here for a reason and that is not to find gold. That reason is Nibish and her child. Your life and hers now lie in your children and their children unto generations."

"My children? Are you not dreaming now yourself?" Hunter asked.

"I saw this not in a dream. I may be toothless and old but I'm wise. Don't question. I know this will be," Gazhagayns said. "You have buried Hoshaphat?"

"We did," Hunter answered. "He lies by a large boulder that should protect his grave forever."

"Then Nibish will stay close by. She will stay near Hoshaphat. Every day she will speak to the sun and ask it to smile on his grave," Gazhagayns explained. "And I say that the ground where Hoshaphat is buried must remain sacred. He will be an ancestor to your children's children. He will guard CAT. You will guard the grave. One day, someone will dream the dream and know what must be done."

"If Nibish knows where CAT is, what should she do with it?"

"A dream will tell her what to do," Gazhagayns said.

"And if she never has the dream?"

Gazhagayns shrugged. "Someone will have the dream, maybe you."

"Your counsel is wise," Hunter said.

"It was meant to be, my friend. You did not tell me your name."

"Hunter Logan. Do you live here alone?" Hunter asked, looking at the flimsy bark structure behind Gazhagayns. "What will you do during the winter months?"

"Listen, Hunter-man, when the berry moon rises and you come out of hills for flour, I will go home with you. I must be buried with Hoshaphat. I need to see my children, Nibish and Manchild. I am nearly an ancestor. You'll take care of me. You and that bear-dog."

"You want to live with me?"

"Look about you, Hunter-man. Behind are forest and village where ancestral voices still speak. In front is big land where white man's houses begin their march to the north, west, and east. See, below, smoke from cabin chimneys. I did have a dream. I saw many, many chimneys, many, many white men's buildings to all horizons. Only here, on the bluff, was nothing."

Hunter could certainly see signs of habitation — smoke from chimneys, an axe ringing from a clearing, the narrow government road.

"Listen to me, Hunter-man. Indians did not need a piece of paper to say this was our land. My ancestors hunted wisely, walked lightly, and held this earth in their hearts for their children and them for us, unto generations," Gazhagayns said. "Why? Tell me why a paper is needed that says our lands are theirs now? All can share Mother Earth."

"I can't answer your question, Gazhagayns, but to say that we Europeans are an insecure race that we need to see, in writing, what we own," Hunter said. "We squabble and fight over land, if we do not have paper proof that it is ours; even sometimes if we do. Knowing what one owns will be important when many people come to live here. Perhaps this is not the best way but it is our way."

"But the land is not the white man's to give. It is ours. And you, Hunter-man? Do you have a piece of paper for your land?"

"When I came to Upper Canada, I couldn't bring myself to live near people," Hunter said, patting Moon's big head then glancing toward Gazhagayns. "I had a great burden in my heart and needed solitude. That's why I squatted in the middle of nowhere in the bush, closer to Lake Huron than Lake Ontario. I have no paper. I haven't had the need for one — yet."

"It is sometimes good to be alone. Sometimes bad," Gazhagayns said.

"I'll have to acquire my land, be it from your people, a land company, or the Crown. At the moment, the Crown owns the land I'm squatting on, but I'm not sure how they obtained it. I've been on the Mark for so long that I could claim it by squatter's rights," Hunter said.

"I come live with you. I give you a paper saying that the land belongs to me but I gave to you to hold in your heart and in your keeping unto generations," Gazhagayns said. "When I die, you bury me with my medicine bag and pipe beside Hoshaphat on *my* land."

"I don't think a piece of paper signed with your 'X' will satisfy the Crown." Hunter smiled at Gazhagayns. "You've never lived on my land. You don't even know where I live."

Gazhagayns swept his arms toward all horizons. "This is our land, my land, hunting grounds for many, many ancestors. My paper will say so. I do not sign with an 'X.' I can print my name. Brant taught me to do so."

Hunter understood Gazhagayns brand of logic. "We'll talk about the paper later," he said. "You're welcome to share my cabin, Gazhagayns. I'll make a bed for you. If Nibish is still there, she will welcome you. In fourteen days time, when the berry moon appears in the sky and mirrors in the lake, make your way down to the Horn-of-Plenty with your possessions and wait for me. I'll tell Wil to expect you."

"And if you do not come?" Gazhagayns asked.

"I will keep my promise," Hunter replied. "Even if Nibish is not at the cabin."

"Do not worry, Hunter-man. Nibish will be there for you," Gazhagayns assured him. "Bring bear-dog to the Horn. He needs to find a she-dog to make more puppies like him. He will pull me on litter over the trail if legs fail to carry me."

"I'll carry you on my back if I have to," Hunter said, realizing that he had just taken on the responsibility of another human being. The thought of sharing his daily bread with Gazhagayns, and having spirited conversations with the elder, somehow seemed pleasant, leading Hunter to believe that he had made the right decision about re-engaging himself in the world outside his little bit of chosen territory.

* * * * * * *

Half expecting that hustling a cow, calf, and piglet over hill and dale had been fruitless, Hunter was relieved that Nibish came out to meet him when he approached the cabin. She appeared as pleased to see him as he did to lay eyes on her. It hadn't been an easy trip home. The cow balked at having a cage and sacks tied to her back. The calf managed to get lost. Piglet squealed in her cage most of the way.

"I might be a bit touched in the head, but I thought it was time to do a bit of farming," Hunter explained, as Nibish helped take the ropes off the wooden cage. "The cow sure hated wearing that load. I had to carry the calf a couple of times through the muckiest parts of the trail. But we made it without too much trouble. There's salt, tea, oatmeal, corn, and wheat seed. We can shut the piglet in the fur shed until I get a root fence built. The cow can be tethered and put in the shed at night to keep her safe from cougar and bear."

When Hunter realized he was blathering like an idiot but Nibish hadn't said anything, he stopped talking and carried the sacks into the cabin. He was pleased to see that she had been working on a basket near Manchild, who was asleep on a blanket on the floor, surrounded by white ash strips.

While Nibish worked at the hearth, stirring a pot of oatmeal gruel on the crane, Hunter told of his exploits. He spoke slowly, interspersing the talk with a few Indian words, wanting Nibish to understand most of what he said. When he mentioned Gazhagayns and the fact that the old man would come to live with them within the month, she turned bright eyes to him.

"Mishoomis come? Live here?"

"He wants to come, says he needs to be near you and the babe. He'll be a good fellow to have around. Maybe he can help me with the fencing and do a bit of gardening. I'll have to build a couple of cots over there in the corner — one for you, one for him. Perhaps an addition to the cabin would be in order? It will be cosy in here come wintertime."

"Mishoomis is very old man. I will help," Nibish said. "And when Manchild grows up, he helps too."

When Hunter first asked about the copper pot that sat on the mantle, and the golden cat figure that had been inside, Nibish turned frightened eyes toward him. "I'm not interested in it," Hunter explained. "I just wondered what ... CAT looks like."

"I don't know what you talk about," Nibish said.

The second time Hunter questioned Nibish, he decided to initiate the discussion in a roundabout way. "Nibish, do you have dreams? Do you believe that dreams can come true?"

Again, Nibish turned frightened eyes on him.

"I know nothing," she insisted. "Know not about Hoshaphat and Dago:ji'"

With that statement, Hunter knew she very well did know everything about CAT, but he didn't press the issue. She was obviously afraid that he wanted gold — if that's what the idol was made of. He'd have to show Nibish that his intentions were honest. The best thing he could do was to drop the subject of the pot and CAT. Sooner or later she'd tell him about it.

Nibish worked alongside Hunter as they built an outside root cellar and a corral for the livestock. They cut and bundled swamp grass for winter feed. Nibish picked and dried wild berries. She tidied the cabin and made the meals.

Every morning Nibish stepped outside to face the rising sun, to invoke the spirits to take care of herself, Manchild, and the man who'd taken her under his wing. After Mishoomis came to live, both he and Nibish walked to the edge of the bluff — to the Knob, to salute the rising sun as it rose above the undulating hill country.

At night, by the light of the waning sun, she and Mishoomis sat quietly as Hunter read aloud from a copy of *The Scotsman*, a favourite book, or the Bible. It was questionable if they understood, or believed much. They listened, Nibish cradling Manchild in her arms. Sometimes when Hunter wrote in his journal, Nibish sat beside him to watch the ink flow over the paper. Hunter taught her to write her name.

Eventually, when an itinerant minister passed through, Hunter persuaded Nibish to take marriage vows. Wil Barnes and his wife acted as witnesses. Wil had packed their meagre belongings several months after speaking with Hunter at the Horn-of-Plenty and moved with his wife and several sheep dogs into the valley on the opposite side of the river to the Mark.

LINEAGE

Hoshaphat and **Nibish**
|
Issue: *Manchild* (1798)

* * * * *

Hunter Logan and **Nibish**
|
Issue: *John* (1799)

John married Isabella Barnes
|
Issue: *James* (1821)–Mary (1823)–Jenny (1825)

James
|
Issue: *Hunter* (1841)– Rebecca – Mary

Hunter
|
Issue: *Joseph* (1865)–Isabella

Joseph
|
Issue: *Thalia* (1884)

* * * * *

Wil Barnes & his Good Wife Esther
|

Issue: *William* (1799)– Isabella (1801) married John Logan

    William
     |

    Issue: *Charles* (1829)–William– Deirdre

        Charles
         |

        Issue: *John* (1849)–James–Anne–Mary–Dianne–
            Harriet

            John
             |

            Issue: *James* (1892)–Margaret–Susan

                James
                 |

                Issue: *Charlie* (1912)– Elizabeth (1910)–
                    Joan (1914)–Henry (1920)

CHAPTER TWO
Beginning Late Spring 1962
The Week of June 17–23

Thursday, June 20

Lish packed as much as she could into three suitcases and several cardboard boxes. She put personal papers including a battered card box in her father's old leather briefcase and paid her landlord, Dino Dimato, in advance for three months rent.

"Why are you leaving?" Dimato asked. "You've got a nice apartment. Are you looking elsewhere for a job? You don't like the city anymore? You're not thinking of accepting that job in Detroit?"

"I need a long vacation," Lish said. "If you could collect my mail and keep it for me, please? I won't have a forwarding address — for a while. I promise that I'll be back." Whether she would live in the city again depended on a lot of things — the first one being what she was going to do with the information she had at hand. The last thing that Lish put in the car was an old canning jar full of dirt with a label, handwritten by her father.

While an attendant filled her car, a '60 Chevrolet, with gas at a station on Yonge Street, Lish checked a road map, looking for villages with vaguely familiar names. Names that she'd heard her grandmother and father talk about when they thought she was asleep; names that were on the label of the jar.

"Taking a vacation," the attendant, with the name *Lyle* stitched on the pocket of his coveralls, said as he handed her change. "Are you having trouble reading the map?"

"I'm just ... looking for some peace and quiet," Lish said. "How do I get to this road from here?"

Lyle looked at the map and gestured in the direction she should go. "About twenty miles up that way — north. Watch for the road sign pointing to Orangeville then turn west." Lish paid little attention to the sprawling new housing developments sprouting in former farm fields. She avoided thinking about the depressing sight of several small crossroads communities, where dilapidated buildings waited for the onslaught of some developer's greedy plans. Lish desperately needed to be where sanity still prevailed, where history still complimented nature, and built heritage counted for more then fodder for a wrecking ball.

She'd been so deep in thought that Lish missed the sign. She stopped to ask a woman who was collecting her mail from a rural box where she should have turned toward Orangeville.

"Three miles back, watch for the barn with the big BA Gas sign painted on it. There's a frame house, surrounded by big maple trees, right on the corner. Turn right," the woman told her. "About a mile down that road there's a general store if you're needing groceries."

Lish spotted the barn, turned right at the corner, and drove for some miles before, lured by the sight of hills in the distance, she turned the car north again, past red brick farmhouses, sturdy weathered barns, and cattle up to their bellies in grass. Views were framed by cedar rail fences and distant stands of maple, elm, and oak.

The road, except for low areas where it skirted natural sinkholes or bogs, ran as straight as a pin, due north, up one long hill after another. The hills were high enough that from the top Lish could see broad valleys with the deep grey-green outline of hills for miles beyond. These must be the Hills of Mulmur, she thought. Mulmur was one of those names spoken quietly by her father and grandmother.

Lish stopped to buy a bottle of cold soda at Stanton General Store, hunkered by the side of the road as if trying to hide among the shrubberies that surrounded it in case someone viewed the vestige of a former community as an anomaly and decided to remove it. While paying she noticed a note pinned to the cash register.

"Do you know this person?" Lish asked the motherly looking woman behind the counter.

"Everybody knows Mrs. Russo. She's looking for some company and a bit of help around the house. She lives near Seven Springs. I think that she'd like to hire a young local girl who's looking for a summer job, though. She doesn't take much to strangers."

"Do you mind if I take the note?"

"Go ahead. I've got a couple of copies."

"Is there a village called Hunter's Mark around here? I can't find it on the road map," Lish said.

"Hunter's Mark isn't a town. It's the tract of land owned by Mrs. Russo, the woman who's looking for summer help."

To contemplate her next move, Lish shared a bench by the store's front door with an elderly fellow whose face was wrinkled and leathery from years of working the fields. His pants were held up with a pair of wide black braces with a curious diamond pattern in white that crossed a red plaid shirt.

"Do you live around here? It's a lovely area," Lish said, as the man first turned watery eyes to look at her, then established permanent eye contact when he liked what he saw.

"Nope, I don't live here," he answered. "Yep, there's nothing prettier than Seven Springs. I was born on flat land northeast of here. I never went more than fifty miles from home after I come back from the war. A small world, isn't it, when all the pleasures in life can be found so close to home?"

"You must have been a man content with his lot."

"Hell no, excuse my language, young lady. Afore the war, I al'ays wanted more. I was a wild one, I'll tell you! But after the rhetoric — and the fightin', and the dyin', I got most of what I wanted not far from the old homestead: a farm, good friends," the old man continued. "There's a big difference between *want* and *need*, yah know. I didn't need it, but al'ays wanted one of those cars that yer driving. That didn't happen, though. Until eleven years ago, I drove a Model T."

"All things come to those who wait," Lish said, thinking that the words sounded hollow, given the man's apparent age.

"Including the grim reaper," the fellow said wryly. "And sooner ruther than later in my case. S'alright. I hitch a ride whene're I need one. Who were you plannin' to visit?"

"I'd like to speak with ... Mrs. Russo at Hunter's Mark."

"Well now, Thalia does own the Mark and lives at *Granite*. There's none prettier than her cottage of lilacs and laughter. You'll recognize the place by the stone house and lilac bushes."

"Is it far?"

"Nope. Where the bowstring bridge crosses the river — up that way a bit — that's where the Mark begins. You'll get there just in time fer the last of this year's lilacs. If Thalia is feeling her oats there'll be plenty of laughter aroun' the place. If she's in a snit, duck an' run."

Back on the road again, car windows open to enjoy the smell of freshly mown hay, Lish passed through Mansfield's cluster of buildings, a church and general store on the left, service station and garage on the right. Cresting the hill into the Pine River valley she caught a glimpse of lush fields, the meandering river, and, through a dense tangle of cedars, a bridge. A sign nailed to a telephone pole announced, Seven Springs — Turn Left.

Lish turned onto a gravel sideroad lined with rail fences and mature trees. She lowered her speed to compensate for the meandering byway that followed the river through the valley, twisting and turning but always going west.

As Lish rounded a curve, the sound of the motor startled a deer grazing in the ditch. She braked hard as it leapt across the road in front of the car and disappeared into a tag elder and cedar copse. She heard the deer crashing through the undergrowth, then became aware of the trill of bird song and the trickle of running water.

A quarter mile ahead, a bridge with delicate soaring concrete arches spanned the river. Upriver the valley narrowed until, in the far distance, it folded into forest framed by a limestone escarpment. In the near distance, midway up one of the hills, there appeared to be a stone house surrounded by a mauve-coloured mist. Could that be the cottage of lilacs and laughter? Lish wondered.

Lish drove closer to the bridge, parked by the side of the road, and walked to the centre of the span to take a closer look at her surroundings. Mud swallows, in a complicated air-ballet, swooped around the bridge's understruts to the tune of water flowing over the riverbed. The water was so clear that every stone could be seen on the bottom. Here and there along the river's edge and in surrounding meadows, huge boulders lay bare to the sun.

Lish could almost hear her father's voice. In his precise way of speaking, he would explain that the rocks were left eons ago when the valley was formed at the end of the last ice age. He'd know the composition of the rocks, the species of every tree growing in the valley, the names of all the wildflowers ...

"Dad, you realize that even after all these years have passed, I miss you." Lish spoke to the wind. "Why was this part of the country so important to you that you included some of its earth in your memory jar?"

Lish's eyes were drawn upriver, to the left, to a large clearing where a partial cedar rail fence protected an odd-shaped rock. From the clearing, a swoop of lilac bushes curled their way up the hill toward the stone house, which sat on a fold of land, backed by the heights. How delightful! She'd forgotten in the hustle and bustle of the city that such tranquil places still existed. She'd been so busy travelling to faraway places that she had overlooked the beauty of Ontario's rural landscape.

Like the hills around it, the house was solid and seemed to grow from the ground. Anchored by huge chimneys, its stone walls defied nature's nastier elements. Typical of architecture in the Scottish tradition, second floor dormer windows reflected the late-morning sun and seemed to wink at Lish — to beckon her to come closer.

The place, with its front porch, kitchen tail, and woodshed, appeared larger than most rural houses. It would be the perfect home in which to raise a large family. To the left of the dwelling the remnants of a driving shed leaned west to east. A thunder-shack was almost obliterated by lilac bushes, its crescent-mooned door now open to the elements.

Lish did notice when pulling away from the bridge that, when she put the car into gear, there was a hesitation. Not knowing much about mechanics, it didn't give her cause for concern. As the car rounded a gentle bend in the road and Seven Springs came into view, Lish was reminded of a scene from a postcard. Two meandering streams flowed like ribbons through lush vegetation, one on each side of the village that sat mid-valley. An odd assortment of buildings lined the main street and an intersecting gravel road.

Lish drove slowly, looking at the buildings: the red brick churches, two log cabins, a number of wood and brick homes, a white clapboard store, a garage, several small barns. All were surrounded by lilac and honeysuckle bushes. Children played in the schoolyard. Several women leaving the church waved at her, as though they recognized the car.

On impulse, Lish turned right onto the first narrow gravel road west of the village. She wanted to see the stone house at close range. From the bridge it had appeared to be on the heights on this side of the village. The byway, lined with ancient maples whose branches interlocked to create a tunnel over the road, twisted and turned up a steep incline. Just as the car crested the hill, Lish heard a loud grinding noise coming from under the vehicle. She took her foot off the gas and steered toward the narrow shoulder where the car rolled to a stop.

"Great," she muttered. "Out in the middle of nowhere, and the car goes on the fritz. I don't know a soul around here." Lish thought over her options. She could walk back toward Seven Springs — can't be more than four miles — and hope that someone would pick her up along the way. She could stay with the car and pray for someone to come along. She might walk up the road and hope to find a farmhouse with a telephone.

"When you're sold a lemon ...," Lish thought as she looked around. There was not a farm house in sight, nor telephone lines. She drummed her fingers on the steering wheel. "I'll give it half-an-hour, then I'll walk toward Seven Springs. I may as well enjoy the scenery while I wait."

Lish lounged against the side of the car until the engine cooled, then made herself comfortable by sitting on the hood, her feet on the bumper.

What was that? Rustling in the bushes? A rattling? No. The sound was coming from down the road. Something was coming up the hill.

"Sounds like horse hooves and wagon wheels and jangling harness, just like the rag-and-bone man's cart in Perth," Lish said aloud. The rustling of leaves, as a westering wind passed through the trees, accompanied the clip-clop of hooves. There was one other sound that carried on the wind — possibly the cry of a cat, so faint that it was almost indiscernible. In what seemed like a scene from the turn of the century, an old-fashioned buggy, drawn by a rangy old black horse and driven by a handsome dark-haired fellow, came into view.

"Beggars can't be choosers and it pays to be a lady in these circumstances." Lish slid off the hood, adjusted her skirt, and ran her fingers through her hair. She waved her other hand and called, "Hello! Can you help? My car quit on me."

For a moment it looked as though the driver wouldn't stop. He looked past her, then directly at her with coal-black eyes, and finally said, "I don't have any tools, but if you want to climb in, I'll drop you off at a place up the road."

Why does this man look familiar? Lish thought. She retrieved her purse, briefcase, and the jar of dirt, then climbed into the buggy. "My name's Lish MacPherson. Do you live around here?" she asked.

"Yep. Come on, Juniper. Off with you, now. Walk on."

"Thanks for stopping. I never thought for one moment that I'd see a horse and buggy on this road. Do you own a farm up here?"

"No."

"You like to drive a horse and buggy?"

"Sometimes, when Juniper cooperates and needs a run."

Lish smiled to herself. I'll count this as my first unusual adventure this week. I'm in a horse-drawn buggy, in the middle of nowhere, with a man who doesn't talk much. I have no idea who the gentleman is. Where he's taking me is a mystery. Can it get much more interesting than this? "You have a name, oh man of few words?"

"Maybe I do today; maybe I don't."

Lish's attention was drawn to an odd noise. Where was it coming from? The bush at the side of the road? It sounded like ... screaming? Yowling? A human? No. A cat? "Do you hear a cat?" Lish asked, scanning the roadside ditches.

The driver gave her a peculiar look, then said "I don't hear anything but the birds in the trees."

There it is again, Lish thought. Is it one of the buggy wheels? No. The noise hasn't frightened the horse. She looked again for an obvious source, this time scanning the fields. "Are you sure you didn't hear a sound, something that a big cat, a cougar, might make? I heard one once — in a zoo," Lish said, glancing toward the driver. Where had she seen this fellow before?

"I would have said I heard it if I did ... today."

"Well, I have been accused of having a vivid imagination more than once."

"If that's the worst you've been accused of, you've not much to worry about," the fellow said, stopping the wagon at the end of a dirt laneway that was no more than two tracks with grass growing between. Lilac bushes lined both sides and spread across the hill, obscuring the view of what lay beyond. "Thalia lives here. She can summon someone to help you."

"Thanks. I appreciate you stopping for me."

When he made no attempt to help her out of the wagon, Lish awkwardly stood and turned to face him while her left foot searched for the step. "Well, thank you, Mr. ..."

"Noah," he said, not looking directly at Lish. "It's Noah to my friends. Tell Thalia that I picked you up on Lavender Line, near the sugar bush. Here you are, don't forget your jar of earth." He handed the purse, briefcase, and jar to Lish.

"You do look familiar," Lish said.

"I never saw you before," Noah answered, turning slightly to look at her, the hint of a smile on his face.

"I should tell ... Thalia ... that you found me on Lavender Line, near the sugar bush," Lish repeated. "Do I owe you something for the ride?"

"No. Just do a good deed for someone else someday," Noah replied. He waved his hand in the direction of the drive. "Hike up the laneway to the house. I'll see you around sometime."

It was only after Noah and his wagon pulled away, taking the smell of horse and barn with them, that Lish caught the heady, sweet perfume of lilacs. She stood in the middle of the lane, dwarfed by old gnarly bushes. Branches, heavy with last-of-the-season blossoms, hung over the road. Bushes swept down a grassy hill toward the valley and along the crest of the hill.

"*I wandered today to the hill, Maggie ....*" Was someone singing? Was a radio playing?

Halfway up the lane, the back wall of a house came into view. The closer Lish walked up the gradual incline, the more detail was visible on the building. The stone wall now seemed to sparkle in the sun.

It was the quavering voice of an elderly woman singing an old ballad. "*The young, the gay, and the best in polished white mansions of stone ...*"

Several cats appeared, curled round Lish's feet, then ran ahead of her along the track.

"*They say I am feeble with age, Maggie, My steps are less sprightly than then ...*"

When Lish reached the top of the lane, a voice called out, "I'm over here, by the garden. Come to the left, my dear. You'll see me once you pass the corner of the drive shed."

Lish looked to her left and saw, in an overgrown flower garden, an older woman seated in a kitchen chair, a large straw hat on her head. The cats twisted around her feet and rubbed themselves up against her legs.

"I'm afraid that you've caught me at my worst time. I wasn't expecting company. I like to sit here in lilac time ... smelling the blossoms ... singing ... admiring the view ... thinking." The older woman continued, "I think many situations through, sitting here. Adam and Eve always let me know when someone approaches. Come here so that I can take a good look at you."

"Adam and Eve?"

"The cats, my dear."

As Lish walked toward the woman, she gasped at the scene that lay beyond the house and garden. Behind her a high limestone escarpment ran from horizon to horizon. Below, water flowed placidly through the valley and under the bowstring bridge. On the far side of the river, a red-brick house basked in the early afternoon sun, backed by a large grey barn with a tin roof. Both were surrounded by orchard, gardens, and farm fields. Old growth forest — maple, elm, oak, beech, and wild cherry — covered some of the lower loam-rich level and spread along the base of the limestone ridge.

"Is this Hunter's Mark?" Lish asked.

"Yes. Pretty isn't it?" the woman replied. "I never tire of the view. That forest has never been defiled by an axe or saw, and will never be in my lifetime. The only thing that I ever allowed was the tapping of maple trees each spring up on the Line. "

"It is magnificent, Mrs. ..."

"I'm Thalia, as in the Muse of Comedy. Thalia Logan Russo. And who might you be? Better, how do you know about Hunter's Mark and how did you get here? This is rather an isolated place."

Thalia looked suspiciously from the briefcase to the jar, then to Lish. "You're not selling something ... or buying something ... or collecting something, are you?"

Russo, Lish thought. This is the woman who advertised for help at the General Store. "Let me assure you, Mrs. Russo, I've no intentions of selling — or buying — anything. I just prefer that personal papers stay with me," Lish explained. "As for knowing this is Hunter's Mark, I heard it mentioned in Stanton."

"Just call me Thalia, my dear. No formality is needed around here."

"Lish, as in a short form for Licinius MacPherson. A man by the name of Noah dropped me off at the end of your lane," she said. "I was touring the backroads when my car died. Noah was kind enough to pick me up. He said you'd be able to help me."

"Noah stopped for you?" Thalia mused. "My dear, that is significant. That man keeps pretty much to himself. He does a few jobs for me and takes his meals here once in a while, though."

"At first, I thought that he was a Mennonite — driving a buggy, you know. I thought perhaps that he had left the Waterloo area to establish a new community."

"I expect he's enjoying a holiday," Thalia said, not wanting to delve into Noah's reasons for being in the area — not that they were very clear to her at the moment either.

"Noah indicated you had a telephone that I could use," Lish continued.

"I do not like intrusive modernity. I imagine that Noah meant I had a means of communication." Thalia smiled. "I can certainly summon people, but not by phone. See that bell mounted in the tower over there, near the brow of the hill? The meal bell? Ring it three times. Someone will come."

"Three times?"

"No more. No less. Two rings means I'd like a ride out for groceries. Three rings means come when you can, the problem is not serious. Continuous ringing indicates that I'm in trouble. Watch for someone to wave from the farm across the valley." Aided by a sturdy shepherd's crook that had been hooked onto the back of the chair, Thalia rose.

Lish was surprised to see how tall the woman was. From the way Thalia sat in the chair, she expected a shorter person to stand before her — someone that somewhat resembled her grandmother. Thalia Logan Russo must have once been a real beauty, Lish thought. She still has a striking presence: suntanned skin, clear eyes, full lips, an aquiline nose. The woman's clothing was peculiar. Her skirt and blouse were reminiscent of the 1930s. Her straw hat was a relic from the '20s.

"Ring the bell, my dear," Thalia said. "Then we'll have a cup of tea while waiting for Charlie to arrive. He has to come around by the bridge. He'll be clever enough to see your car on the Line and realize there's a problem."

Dutifully, Lish rang the bell — three times — watched for someone to appear across the valley, waved to him, then followed Thalia, who walked slowly with a bad limp and an exaggerated swaying of the right hip, toward the house. The cats trailed behind, sniffing the air, checking for a four-footed meal in the high grass.

"A man waved." Lish held the porch door for Thalia.

"That's Charlie. I'd better cut a pie. He'll expect pie," Thalia said as the cats scurried to check their food dish. "Now, you two biblical felines, don't trip me up."

Thalia's porch was enclosed. Windowsills were lined with potted geraniums and tomato and pepper plants. Fern stands overflowed with greenery. Several wicker chairs sported crocheted throws and plump cushions in a riot of colours. A grey woolen army blanket in a cardboard box near the door was obviously a favourite sleeping place for the cats.

Watching Adam and Eve check their food dish reminded Lish of the sound she'd heard while riding in Noah's wagon. "Mrs. Russo ... Thalia ... I'm sure that I heard a cougar today. I didn't think they were around anymore. I read somewhere that the last one was killed years ago."

Thalia stopped partway through the kitchen door and turned dark eyes on Lish. "You heard CAT?" she asked. "Are you sure the noise was that of a big cat, not a sort of sing-song sound?"

There was something in the way that Thalia's eyes searched Lish's face that caused her to look away, embarrassed. "As plain as day," Lish said. "It sounded just like the cougar in the Buffalo Zoo. It's odd, though. The sound didn't scare the horse — or me. And Noah said that he didn't hear it."

"Well, well." Thalia stepped through the door. "There aren't many that hear CAT. You're a special one, Lish MacPherson."

"I can well understand how a cougar can live in this area, especially in the woods up there." Lish pointed toward the forested land. "Maybe they're moving south again. The same article mentioned that there might be some in Algonquin Park and north of Sudbury. Perhaps someone kept one as a pet and let it loose."

"Perhaps," Thalia said, taking the kettle from the stove to the sink.

"I thought you said that you abhorred modernity," Lish said, eyeing an electric stove. "You need hydro wires for electricity."

"Oh, I have made a few exceptions. Five years ago, when Charlie insisted that I get electricity, I capitulated. But I just can't be bothered with a telephone or a newfangled-looking record player. Really, I haven't had the need for those — yet. I'm stubborn enough to hold out, too. I don't like being told what I need and what I don't need. I like my privacy."

"You do have a radio," Lish said. "I hear it playing in the background."

"Oh yes, I love my radio. I leave it on all the time for company. I have Charlie and his sister Joan. They have a phone — and a television set too, if I want to take a look at something silly," Thalia said. "Set your things down and sit at the table. Then you can peek around while I work and chat. You won't find another kitchen for miles around that looks like this one. At least, that's what Joan says. She's always at me to buy a Mixmaster or an electric kettle to electrify the place more than it already is. But I say, enough is enough."

While Thalia busied herself setting the table with cups and saucers, plates for pie, a pitcher of milk, and a sugar bowl, Lish looked around the spacious kitchen, bright with colourful wallpaper, scatter rugs, and waist-high wood wainscoting. The room had a cosiness to it — a warmth that seemed to encompass all the good conversations and meals that had taken place within its walls.

A huge black Crown Huron stove dominated the room. There was a woodbox beside it and two rocking chairs conveniently placed in front where a good book on a cold winter's night might be enjoyed. Another woolen blanket on the floor by the stove provided a second bed for the cats.

"You do spoil Adam and Eve," Lish said. "I imagine that they luxuriate in the heat from the stove."

"They are the devil incarnate," Thalia said as she filled the kettle.

Lish noticed that the sink had both modern taps and an old-fashioned hand pump. A small electric stove and refrigerator were in direct contrast to an old Hoosier cabinet with three pies cooling on its metal counter and an old pine sideboard that held dishes. A wringer washer, its skinny green legs showing beneath a canvas cover, stood in a corner, partially hidden by fern stands.

"If you could get some linen napkins Miss Mac... Lish. You'll find them in the top, right-hand drawer just inside the butler's pantry — through that door. My mother insisted on having a fancy pantry between her kitchen and the dining room. Can you imagine such a thing as a butler's room in a rural farmhouse?"

When Lish sat again at the table, she noticed her jar of dirt had been moved slightly.

Meanwhile, Thalia's thoughts as she scurried to and fro were definitely on Lish MacPherson. If the young lady heard CAT, she was meant to be here at Granite, just like Noah. The trick was that she now had to find a way to keep Lish on The Mark until a few things could be sorted out.

Thalia's ruminating was interrupted by the appearance of a huge man standing in the doorway. He was preceded by a large dog that loped past him to greet the two women.

Never had Lish seen such a hulk of a man or such a huge dog. My Lord, she thought, he's a giant. He must be more than six feet tall, is barrel-chested, with a shock of hair and beard that matches his red shirt. And the dog looks like a bear.

"Charlie. I didn't figure you'd be too long arriving after you saw a young woman standing by the bell. Come in. Meet Lish MacPherson. Lish, this big, sloppy animal is Luna. She won't hurt you, neither will her master." Luna made herself comfortable on the cats' blanket.

"Are you the one that drives the '60 Chevy that's sitting a bit askew down the Line?"

"I am," Lish said, feeling quite intimidated by the man, whose bulk overwhelmed Thalia, who was standing beside him.

"Well, you ain't goin' far soon," Charlie said. "I figured there was a problem just by the way the car was parked, if you want to call it that. You left the keys in the vehicle, my lady. I'd say you've got a transmission problem. A big transmission problem."

"Oh my gosh!" Lish exclaimed. "I was so rattled by being offered a ride on a wagon that I forgot to remove the keys and to lock the doors."

"There's nowt to fear around here," Charlie assured her. "Pie! Do my eyes see rhubarb custard pie?"

"That they do, Charlie. Sit down." Thalia couldn't believe the good fortune that had been delivered in Charlie's words. Now, if she could only play the scenario correctly. "You say that it's a bad situation with the car?"

"Yep. It needs to be towed to a garage. Parts will have to be ordered. Up this way, that'll take a day or three. Another day to do the job and you're looking at three, four days, not counting today. I can't tow the car to the boddon until tomorrow morning, earliest." Charlie forked pie and smacked his lips. "You'll need somewhere to stay, Miss MacPherson, and there ain't no hotel aroun' here."

"The boddon?"

"Down the hill, to the garage in Seven Springs," Thalia explained. "You are most welcome to stay here, Lish. The Lord knows that I have bedrooms to spare. You can have your pick."

"I did want to spend a few days in the area and was going to look for accommodation," Lish said.

Thalia tried not to sound too eager. "I put a little notice up at the Stanton General Store for summer help. To be perfectly honest, Lish, I would enjoy the company of a young person around the house. I could use two extra hands for some small jobs. There will be occasions when I won't be good company. I'd be ... preoccupied. Oh my goodness. I'm running on like a gramophone now."

"Well, Miss MacPherson, what will it be, bunk and work, or hike?" Charlie asked.

"Hike to where?" she asked him.

"There's the rub." Charlie laughed. "It's a good twenty miles to the nearest woman-friendly hotel or tourist house."

"And you say it's going to take at least three days for the car to be repaired?"

"Yep, maybe more," he replied.

Lish looked from Charlie to Thalia, then around the kitchen. She could do worse, she thought. This could prove to be exciting: an isolated place, no telephone, interesting company. "I did see your note at the store. I couldn't resist its message — 'if you're interested in puttering for the summer in a somewhat unconventional household contact the Bird on the Hill,'" Lish recited. "I turned down the road to Seven Springs because I was going to look you up. Somehow fate, in the form of a broken-down car, delivered me to your door. Yes, I'll accept your offer to lend a hand around Granite. That is what you call this place, Mrs. Russo?"

Thalia smiled and nodded, thrilled with the turn of events. "Fate does have a fickle nature, all right," she said. "If you're going to stay, you must remember to call me Thalia."

When Charlie rose from the table, the dog came to his side. "I brung your suitcases but locked the cardboard boxes in the trunk. I just know'd for sure you'd stay. It don't pay to leave things in an unlocked car overnight, even if it is in the middle of nowhere."

"Well, now that I'm going to have company, Joan will have to do some grocery shopping for me tomorrow. I'll need some staples: milk, flour, sugar, coffee," she said.

"Can I do the shopping for you?" Lish offered. "If this gentleman picks me up tomorrow, I'll get a ride into the village, buy what you need, and get a ride back with him."

"Do you like to ride on a tractor?" Charlie asked. "I'll be towin' the car with my tractor."

"I can sit in the car on the way to the garage, and ride the tractor with you on the way back."

Charlie roared and slapped his knee. The woman didn't know that he'd be towing the car backwards. "Okay by me," he said. "Whatever suits yah." He could hardly wait to see the look on the faces of the regulars at the crossroads as he cruised by. "See ya tomorra' around nine in the morning then?"

"Before you go, would you carry Miss MacPherson's — Lish's things upstairs to the south bedroom and open the windows, if you can? They haven't been lifted in a while."

When Charlie came back into the kitchen, Thalia was at the back door. She took his arm, leaned over, and whispered, "Charlie, she heard CAT. This afternoon."

"Ya don't say!" Charlie looked back at Lish, who was busy clearing the table.

"And, if my eyes didn't deceive me, the young lady's jar of dirt has the name Hunter's Mark written on the label — along with several others," Thalia told him. "I have to wonder why. She's a smart-looking city girl for sure, but she must be one of us, Charlie. If she doesn't like working for me, we've got to think of something else that will keep her here until we find out for sure."

"Well, we can make her into a country girl soon enough," Charlie said. "I get the feeling, based on the amount of luggage our Miss MacPherson has, that she was planning on taking a rather long vacation."

"We'll just have to be clever, won't we, Charlie? Say hello to Joan. We'll see you in the morning."

"Don't mind all the house plunder," Thalia said, leading Lish through the hall. "There are generations of collecting and history in this place. I don't have the heart to throw anything away."

"I'm sure it gives the house character," Lish said.

"That it does." With great difficulty, Thalia climbed the stairs to show Lish to a bedroom. "You can understand why I sleep on the first floor. When going to bed became this difficult, Charlie turned my library on the main floor into a bedroom. It was closer to the outdoor privy. Indoor plumbing was installed five years ago — downstairs."

Thalia fussed around the bed, straightening the spread, plumping pillows. "The sloped ceiling makes the room look cosy. You might hear a squirrel or two throwing chestnuts around the attic. Although Charlie says that he's caught all of them, I don't believe him," Thalia said. "There's no electricity in the bedrooms. I never had it installed on the second floor. If you want to stay up late reading, you'll have to use the coal oil lamp. You do know how to light one of those, don't you?"

"Thalia, you should open your house to summer guests. I'm sure that city people would pay well to spend time in a rustic country setting," Lish suggested. The room was furnished with a spindle bed covered with a gorgeous cream-coloured hand-crocheted spread, a heavy chest of drawers, a wardrobe, hooked scatter rugs, and lace curtains at the windows.

"Goodness, I'm an eccentric old bat with an overwhelming penchant for privacy who, long ago, saw threescore and ten slide by. "I don't have the patience to run a tourist home."

"I thought you might be sixty!" Lish said, looking at Thalia's dark hair held neatly in a bun at the back of her neck.

"Like my mother, I've aged well, just like rat-trap cheese." Thalia laughed. "There'll come a time when I'll take a turn for the worst, just like that." Thalia snapped her fingers. "It happened to my mother and to my husband. It'll happen to me. One day I'll be vibrant, eccentric, and lucent, the next I'll be feeble and quite mindless."

"I can't imagine such a time," Lish said.

Thalia smiled. "It happens to the best of us, my dear. Make yourself at home. I'll be downstairs, in my hidie, doing some ... writing," she said. "Shall we say six o'clock for dinner? Cold chicken and more of that rhubarb pie with real whipped cream is on the menu. Oh yes. Don't forget to name the bedposts."

"I should give the bedposts a name?"

"It's an old Logan custom. On your first night in a new bed it brings good luck to name the posts," Thalia explained. "Male or female names. It's your choice. Be sure to take a good look out the windows, too. There isn't a vista so great or a mountain so high that I can't wrap my heart around. I'm sure you'll feel the same way when you see the views from this room."

As soon as Thalia left the room, Lish, impressed by her hostess's poetic bent, went to a window. The view down the valley toward the farm and bowstring bridge was spectacular. Just a moment... What was that in the fenced corner where the lilacs ended? — down by the big odd-shaped rock that sparkled in the afternoon sun. A deer? A large cat? And someone that looked like the mysterious Noah was walking on the river bank.

Thursday, June 21

The smell of hot coffee lured Lish downstairs very early the next morning. Doors and windows were open to let lilac-scented breezes flow through the house.

Thalia was at the kitchen table, her hands in a mixing bowl. She looked up from her work, smiled, and said, "I didn't want to wake you. Not everyone gets up as early as I do." She waved flour-covered hands. "Coffee's in the pot on the stove. Cream and sugar are on the table. Would you fill the cat dish with milk again? They are hungry beggars this morning. I'm making buttermilk biscuits for breakfast. There's nothing that can beat hot scones dripping with butter and homemade berry jam."

Lish helped herself to coffee, filled the cat dish, and made herself comfortable at the table. She figured, and rightly so, that Thalia was the mistress of her kitchen and would ask for help if she needed it, but not a moment before. As soon as she sat down, the larger of the cats, Adam, an orange and white tabby, jumped into her lap.

"I do hope you like cats," Thalia said. "These two are independent devils that come and go as they please, unless there's someone to pet them. They are good hunters — keep the mouse population down around the house. They are good judges of humans, too. They won't go near Reginald. He'd kick them if they did. They respect Luna, though. Cozy up to her when she lets them. Luna's a little touchy at the moment."

Lish liked animals. The last cat she could remember was one that she'd had twelve years before. She never considered owning a pet in the city.

"Did you sleep well last night?" Thalia turned the dough onto a floured board to knead it. She counted ... one ... two ... three .... "Fifteen kneads only for biscuits or they bake tough and nubbly."

"I did have a good sleep, which is surprising because I haven't been sleeping well lately. I have too much on my mind."

"Well, it is peaceful here. There's not much physical labour to do, which leaves plenty of time for thinking through problems — clearing the mind of garbage, I say." Thalia cut the dough with an upturned drinking glass and placed each piece on a baking sheet. "Four hundred degrees for twelve minutes," she said. "We'll have breakfast in twenty minutes."

"When we chatted last night, you said that you lived here all by yourself." Lish stroked Adam under his chin, causing him to flip over onto his back on her knee. "Aren't you lonely, especially in the wintertime?"

"Sometimes," Thalia said. "But a person can be just as lonely in a city, surrounded by people. I keep busy. My eyes are good, so I can still do needlework, knit, read ... scribble. I've got Charlie and Joan, Luna, my cats, my memories. Memories can consume precious moments if you let them. An active mind can fill hours of time. When I'm really feeling cabin-bound, I go across the valley and stay with Charlie and Joan. Charlie comes every day to check the house."

"I guess I've not spent much time in an isolated place recently," Lish said.

"My dear, you're a lot younger than I. You've a right to expect more from life. You want to be around people, near friends. You mentioned that you were twenty-nine? That's a wonderful age. You're in the prime of your life. The world is yours to enjoy. I'm so pleased that you've accepted the offer of a ... job here."

"I might not be suitable," Lish said. "You haven't mentioned what that job might be. What is it that you have in mind for me to do?"

"Oh, not too much. If you don't mind doing a bit of work in the garden, some cooking and cleaning, shopping, and perhaps a little typing. You're sharing space with an eccentric old woman, but you're most welcome to stay as long as you like."

"What if we're not ... compatible?" Lish asked.

"We are taking a chance, aren't we? I'll tell you right off that I'm the one that might be difficult to get along with. I can be a bit of a recluse," Thalia said. "I'll let you know quickly if things won't work out."

"We're both mature women. I'm sure that we have much in common. I'll respect your privacy. I'm a bit of a recluse, too ... at the moment."

"I don't know what your situation is, but let's try the arrangement for the summer, if you have it free."

Lish smiled. "To be honest, the decision to leave my job was rather sudden. I have no intention of going back to Toronto anytime soon."

"Then the decision to stay here does make sense. The price is right: free in exchange for a bit of work. You can type, can't you?"

"I can, and take shorthand too, if necessary," Lish replied.

"To tell the honest truth, Lish, at the moment I could really use a third hand. Joan and I are working quite hard to meet a commitment. I just don't have much time to cook, get the laundry done, and plant a garden this summer." Thalia bent to put the tray of biscuits in the oven. Now, that was easier than expected, she thought. I had anticipated a much harder time persuading Lish MacPherson to stay on The Mark. She almost invited herself.

"I won't commit myself for a definite period of time," Lish said. "I rent an apartment in the city."

"Not to worry, my dear. If your career or life eventually does take you away from the cottage of lilacs and laughter, I will understand that you must go."

"That is interesting," Lish said. "An old man sitting in front of a store on the highway used that same term. He said that there was none prettier than Seven Springs and the cottage of lilacs and laughter."

Thalia, looking out the window to the western hills, felt the hair rise on the back of her neck. "What did this man look like?" she asked, a hand to her fluttering heart.

"He was dressed like a farmer and said that he owned a Model T. His son always drove him to the store. The man wore wide black braces with something embroidered on them. There was something unusual about his face. Might you know him?"

Thalia's heart gave a flutter. "Yes. I think so." She hesitated a moment, then turned to look at Lish. "Would you help me set the table for breakfast? I seem a bit light-headed at the moment. When did Charlie say he was coming?"

"Around nine o'clock," Lish said, lifting the cat off her knee. "Sit down and I'll set the table and see to the biscuits. They should come out of the oven in ten minutes?"

Thalia made small talk while Lish worked around the kitchen. "The house is open to you, but I ask that you respect my privacy and not enter my hidie, the study. That's my private domain. I usually keep the door locked."

"Of course," Lish agreed. "Everyone needs their quiet room."

"There are a few things you might enjoy while you're here. The day after tomorrow, Charlie's taking me, Joan, and Noah fishing. That evening there's a community box social and dance in Hornings Mills — an early summer fling. There's good music to dance to, not that newfangled music they play on the radio these days — Elvis and that Orbison fellow. There'll be nice people to meet. Noah says he'll go with us."

Seven Springs

Charlie let Luna out of the car first, then went around to open Lish's door.

"At least you are gentleman enough to open the door for a lady in some distress," Lish said, trying to step out with some attempt at grace and dignity. "When we drove past the crossroads with me in the driver's seat, the dog as my slobbering passenger, I must have looked ridiculous."

"Waul, the old boy's club on the porch at the General Store sure had their laugh for the day," Charlie agreed. "You were the one that said you'd ride in the car, even after you saw the back end jacked up and hanging from the back of my tractor."

"There wasn't much choice for either me or Luna, I think. Before we spend any more time together, Charlie, what's your last name? Just in case someone asks, or says it, and I don't know whom they're talking about. I assume you have a last name?"

"Barnes," Charlie said. "Charles Wil Barnes."

The pair stood in front of a shabby-looking one-storey building with new BA gas pumps outside. JEFF'S GARAGE, a sign stated and, barely discernible beneath, almost like a shadow, was the word *Blacksmith*. Two grime-streaked windows faced the street. Luna had already put her weight against the door and, with her tail wagging, disappeared inside, where an older man in coveralls sat behind a messy desk. One half of the building was a repair shop. Even with the garage's bay door up, the interior was dark. One bare bulb hung from the ceiling. Another light in a wire cage lay on the front fender of a car where only the torso and legs of a man were visible. The rest of the body was obscured by an open hood.

"It's a one-lighter garage for sure," Charlie said. "That's Len Grant behind the desk. He was the blacksmith. It's the passing of an era, for sure. Len's father is getting out of the business, so the son, Jeff, is takin' over. Don't let the lack of lights fool you. Jeff's the mechanic and a damn good one too. He's a little slow sometimes, but a good man to have on the job. That's him hammering on something under the hood."

Although Lish was a good driver, and knew enough to keep the fuel tank full, she knew little about how cars ran, and nothing about repairs. Most of the cars that she had driven belonged to the company she worked for. They took care of the mechanical problems. Checking the oil level and tire pressure was not her cup of tea. "Maybe you should talk to this Jeff fellow about my car," Lish said to Charlie. "I don't want to appear entirely stupid. Assure him that the bill will be paid."

"Cash," Charlie said. "He won't accept a cheque. Cash, or credit, if he knows you as a local. Put on one of those charming smiles and show a little leg an' he'll float you credit. He was burned once by someone from away."

"That's unfortunate," Lish said. "I hope he managed to collect his money."

"The guy that burned him was one of them big-mouth gawkers from the city. The beggar came up here scouting for cheap land and had car trouble. Jeff trusted him. When the fella didn't pay, Jeff couldn't find hide nor hair of him to extract the money for the bill."

Realizing that he had company, Jeff extricated himself from under the hood and came toward the door. He wiped greasy hands on his coveralls then ran them through his hair. "Don't ever have to worry about cooties. They cain't live in grease." Jeff smiled at Lish. "I'd offer my hand, but it's not fit fer a lady to shake."

Jeff's eyes raked Lish's tall frame — from the top of her head to the tip of her toes, from her long, dark brown hair and hazel eyes and hourglass 36"-23"-35" body to her size-six feet. He whistled long and low. "Now, lookie what the good Lord dropped at my door. Charlie, you haven't introduced me."

"Pull yer brain out of the gutter," Charlie said. "This is Lish MacPherson. She had a little difficulty with her car's transmission, so she's Thalia's guest at the moment. Now get yer dirty mind off the woman and onto the car."

While Charlie discussed the automobile's problem, Lish compared the two men. Seven Springs certainly sprouted tall, strong, handsome fellows, regardless of age. Both were more than six feet tall. Both had red hair and sparkling blue eyes.

Both were barrel-chested with strong arms, powerful torsos, and long legs.

"Taking in the scenery, Miss MacPherson?" Jeff smiled and gave Charlie a punch on the arm.

"I was thinking that you look alike enough to be father and son."

"We're uncle and nephew," Jeff told her. "My mom was his sister — Elizabeth Barnes. It's a small world in the hills around here. I was just saying to Charlie that I can do the job. Might take until the end of the week, though. I've gotta finish the preacher's car first. I'll need cash for the parts, if you don't mind. I can't float much as there's just my dad and me, and business has been slow-to-nonexistent this month."

"How much?"

"I'd say that fifty bucks would suffice."

Lish glanced from Jeff the mechanic to Charlie the farmer, who nodded slightly, indicating he thought the request reasonable.

Handing the money over, Lish realized that she only had thirty dollars left in her purse. Sooner, rather than later, she'd have to visit a bank to withdraw enough money to pay the rest of her bill. "Is there a bank nearby?"

Jeff laughed. "The closest is in Orangeville. Then, there's Fergus ... and you aren't about to drive your car anywhere. Wait a minute, I'll get you a receipt for the $50. I'll send word up to Thalia's when the car's repaired. Heck, I'll drive it up there myself, just for the hell of it. That'd save Charlie a trip. Where're you two headed now?"

"To the store," Lish told him. "I've a list of groceries that Mrs. Russo ... Thalia needs."

Jeff's eyes twinkled. "That'll be a visit worth recording," he said, before retreating into the garage again.

"I'll walk you to the store, post a letter an' then come back for my tractor," Charlie said. Not waiting for an answer, he called to Luna and set out at a brisk pace.

Lish had to take two steps for every one of his to keep up. Luna paced her. "Why does Mrs. Russo insist on being called 'Thalia'? She's old enough to be Jeff's great-grandmother."

"That's how she likes it," Charlie said. "The name 'Russo' sometimes rubs her the wrong way. If you're nice to her, she might tell you why someday. Can I ask you something? It's none of my business, but curiosity killed the cat."

"Satisfaction brought it back," Lish said. "Go ahead. Ask."

"Waul, do you preserve dirt for a living, or as a hobby? I mean, I couldn't help but notice the jar — and the names on the label — when I was enjoying my pie at Thalia's yesterday."

Lish laughed. "It does seem a bit odd to carry a jar of soil around, doesn't it?"

"I'll admit that it does," Charlie said.

"Eight months before Dad died, he drove around Ontario, to all the places that held some importance to him. He gathered a bit of soil from each."

"A strange thing to do, I'd say."

"I thought so, too. While he was invalided, the jar sat on a table beside his bed. Every so often he'd open the lid and smell the earth. He told me once that each of the place names on the label contributed to his time on earth. He called it his Memory Jar."

Not one to beat round a bush, Charlie asked, "And what was his story about Hunter's Mark?"

"I don't know," Lish said. "Dad never elaborated about his past. He spoke very little about my mother. My grandmother was even more tight-lipped. The jar was so important to him that, after he died, I hid it away because I knew that Grandmother would throw it out. I've been curious about it and the names ever since."

"If I were wearing your boots, I'd be a bit curious too, wondering about the significance of the names," Charlie said.

"I have time to travel now, and decided to visit each place that he listed, to see what I could find that was important enough to Dad that he added a bit of the area's soil to his jar," Lish explained. "He was a man of many talents. My wanderings should be interesting."

"Waul, I'm sure you'll find something out about Hunter's Mark soon enough," Charlie said. "Wouldn't you know it? The local riffraff is gathered at the Post."

The store, a two-storey frame building, was desperately in need of a coat of paint. It sat at the bottom of a T-intersection. If a car rolled down the intersecting street too fast, it would run right up the front steps. The building's second floor was the meeting room for the Imperial Order of Odd Fellows, or so the lopsided sign hanging in one of the upper windows stated. Dirty windows looked out onto a front porch, replete with an odd assortment of chairs, a table, and a checkerboard. The locals, all men, were sprawled on the steps.

"They're waiting for the mail," Charlie said. "You're going to have to run the gauntlet of prying eyes and a mind — if they possess one between them."

Lish giggled. "I'll admit the place looks like it's seen better days."

"So do most of the locals," Charlie said. "Food's good though. And company's interesting. Stay, Luna." The dog lay down in the shade by the door. "Chew any of these dang porchers who bother you." Charlie looked at the scruffy group. "Especially that one in the blue plaid shirt."

"Ain't you bein' a bit mean today?" the scruffy fellow said.

"You ken account fer most folks, and then there's Sidney," Charlie said to Lish. "You're just as likely to find Sidney lying in the middle of the road havin' a snooze as you are to find him sittin' on the porch havin' a chaw."

"Get away wi' yah," Sidney said. "See you in church, if the devil don't get yah first, Charlie."

Lish felt a dozen pairs of eyes on her until she stepped over the sill into a store that smelled of coal oil, pickles, cheese, rope, leather, fertilizer, and frying meat. When her eyes became accustomed to the dark, she saw that a counter and post office were to the right of the door. Long, narrow aisles were lined with wooden shelves stocked with boxes and tins. One old cooler held milk, butter, and cheese. Bottled soft drinks were in another.

"It just doesn't get any better than this," Charlie said. "Georgie tries to please everyone, in more ways than one."

Toward the back, Lish could see a meat counter on one side of the store, an assortment of hardware on the other. The large grate that dominated the centre of the floor was surrounded by small wooden barrels of nails, screws, nuts, and bolts. The left-hand side of the store, opposite the cash register area, was an eatery with a counter, stools, and a half dozen tables. It appeared that someone had made a half-hearted attempt to clean the windows in the restaurant area.

Charlie handed Lish a basket. "I'll tell Luna to stay on the porch. You shop — don't forget to post the letter that Thalia gave you — then I'll treat you to a cheese sandwich. Georgie's are the best 'cause she puts dill pickles on them. The woman might be a bit of a floosy, but her cookin's great."

"A floosy?"

"She likes visiting strip joints in the city when her hubby's away on long-distance hauls. He's a trucker."

Is this information that I really need to know? Lish thought. I don't want to harbour any preconceived notions about village inhabitants. With the wire basket in one hand, Thalia's list in the other, she walked around the store picking groceries. Charlie had returned by the time she was down to the last item left to find.

"Seeds," Lish said. "I can't find carrot, beet, corn, and squash seeds."

"Well, well," Charlie said as he looked at the list. "Thalia's going to plant a garden. She hasn't done that in the past seven years. Thalia must figure you're gonna help her with it. Seeds are on a rack back here." Charlie scuttled toward the rear of the store.

"What if I don't have enough cash to pay for this?" Lish asked. "Thalia didn't give me money for groceries."

"You're supposed to put them on Thalia's chit. Georgie runs a bill for her here that gets wiped at the end of each month. After she writes the lot down, we'll eat."

Seated at a corner table in the restaurant, Lish and Charlie devoured the sandwiches while examining the local livestock as Charlie described the odd group of people in the store.

"Bud and Glenn are eating pie at the counter. Glenn's the one that needs a bath and shave — the one that can't sit still. He's fast, like a gazelle. Neither time nor man can stop that boy when he decides to run. Bud's his pa."

"Where's his mother today?"

"She died some time ago. She never showed herself in public with them. She thought that she was to blame fer the way Glenn popped out."

"The poor woman," Lish said, watching as Glenn devoured a slice of pie. After each bite, he wiped his sleeve across his mouth.

"Poor because of the way he turned out?" Charlie asked.

"No, because the woman assumed full responsibility for his condition. My dad used to say that people like Glenn are special gifts, sent to special people."

"Could be," Charlie said. "That doesn't explain the Delaney brothers, over there, at the table by the magazine rack. From the left, there's Tom, Dick, Harry, and Joseph — the short bald one. Joseph is the name his mother gave him, but you'll never hear anyone call him that. Everyone around' here calls him WGD — short for 'Who Gives a Damn.' I wouldn't say that those fellows are gifts."

The Delaney brothers were all short, sinewy, and poorly dressed. They were maybe in their fifties and, obviously, no woman figured in their lives. Buttons were missing. Shirts went unironed. They all needed a haircut.

"Delaneys own the farm down the Line from Thalia. They sort of share the same uplands. The family's been there since the 1860s. The boys live in a dilapidated brick house on the property. Rumour has it that they made a deal — sold the place but got the right to live in the house until the last one kicks the bucket — or the house falls down around them."

Lish had finished her sandwich and was eyeing the pie rack. The raisin looked good.

"Sold to whom?"

"Developers. We've all been wonderin' about the details. The Delaneys aren't talkin'. There's been some really strange things go on around here recently. The village used to be quite active. Then several small businesses closed and people began to sell and move away. A half dozen homes went up for sale up the road and were snapped up, just like that." Charlie snapped his fingers to emphasis his point. "There are developers tossing big bucks around. And then there's Reginald ..."

"Doesn't anyone care enough about the village to have some loyalty, to stay and try to build it up again?"

"There are thems that *do* and thems that *don't*; thems that *will* and thems that *won't*; if you get my drift. Some would sell their mother to the devil to get ahead."

"I guess that if there's nothing to keep them in the area — no job, no family — what's the sense in staying?" Lish said, looking at the pie again. "If they can't afford to live here ..."

"There's thems that *can* and thems that *can't*; thems that *talk* and thems that *rant*."

"Speaking of rant, who are the people at the table arguing over which one is going to pay for lunch?"

"I dunno who they are," Charlie said. "They're not from around here. I'd say from the look of 'em that they are not exactly normal country folk out fer a drive. I figure that they're married by the way they're fussing. Heads up, Georgie's coming this way and she's got her eye on you."

Georgie, wearing a revealing yellow sun dress accentuated by a large dirty butcher's apron and earrings that dangled to her shoulders, sauntered suggestively toward the table. "Fed Luna a soup bone," she said. "She looked at me with those sad eyes like she was starving. I saw your girlfriend eyeing the pie. You want a piece?" She spoke to Lish but winked at Charlie as she removed the empty sandwich plates.

"The husband's away again, is he?" Charlie winked back.

"How can you tell," Georgie said. "What'll it be? Raisin? Rhubarb? Chocolate cream?"

"Raisin," Lish said, "and a pot of tea."

"The same fer me." Charlie glanced past Georgia. "Well, lookie here," he said. "Noah just walked in." Charlie waved and Noah came toward the table. "Bring him a piece of raisin pie too, and make that a big pot of tea. Are you driving the horse and buggy today, Noah?"

"I sure am," Noah replied, surprised to see the woman he'd given a ride to seated at a table with Charlie Barnes. "It's Lish MacPherson, isn't it?"

Lish extended her hand. "We didn't have time for niceties

yesterday. Did I thank you for picking me up?"

"You're staying with Thalia then?" Noah said.

"Yes. I'm there for a while."

Georgie set two pieces of pie and a large pot of tea on the table. Like the woman herself, her tea cozies were big, bold, and colourful. She made a second trip with the third piece of pie and a cup for Noah, setting them down without a word. Right after he arrived in the area, Georgie had tried her wiles on Noah. When he ignored her, she left him alone. The guy was weird enough though. He fit in really well with Charlie Barnes and Thalia Logan Russo.

"The reason I waved you over," Charlie explained, "is that we've got a load of groceries to deliver to Thalia and I'm driving the tractor. Can you give Miss MacPherson a ride back to Granite? It'd be more comfortable than her bouncing along on the tractor, trying to juggle cans of tuna and soup. Maybe you could give Luna a ride, too?"

Although Charlie hadn't consulted her about the travel arrangements, Lish wasn't too upset about being paired with Noah once again. His dark complexion and jet black hair intrigued her. And he did look vaguely familiar — as though she'd seen his ... photograph somewhere.

"If the lady doesn't mind waiting for the mail, I'd be pleased to give her a ride," Noah said, looking at Lish with deep-set, inquisitive brown eyes. What was a beautiful, sophisticated city girl, a business woman doing driving these county back roads, he wondered. "Sorry, I should have introduced myself properly yesterday, but I had a few things on my mind."

"It's not a problem," Lish said. "We can chat on the way ... home."

At Granite

Adam and Eve in her lap, Thalia thanked the sun for shining on her most treasured possession, her land. She never failed each day to address the sun, to appreciate its warmth, to request that it continue to shine on her special place on earth. Even on rainy days, when the earth's tears caressed her face, she imagined that the sun heard her.

Charlie had placed her bench right beside the bell, in the most advantageous spot in the yard for viewing the valley and hills. June was one of the prettiest months at Granite. Charlie's herd of cattle lay in a field of yellow buttercups. White daisies nodded in clumps along back lanes and around open pastureland. Mauve and purple wild phloxes waved in fencerows, at the edge of the beaver meadow, and along the river's banks toward the bridge. Swamps were full of yellow and purple flag iris. The ridge on the opposite side of the valley showed every colour of green that an artist's palette could provide.

Joan waved from the Barnes farm then went back to hanging laundry on a line that ran from the back stoop to the drive shed. Downstream, where the valley began to widen, the bowstring bridge hunkered in the shade, its delicate-looking arches in sharp contrast to towering roadside trees. The grave marker stood solitary in the crux of the cedar rail fence.

Thalia closed her eyes and let the smells and sounds of Hunter's Mark surround her. Even on the heights, she could hear the rush of water as it tumbled over ledge and rock-strewn river bed; detect the scent of honeysuckle and lily of the valley; hear robins in the bushes and mourning doves on her roof. Eve, spying lunch-on-the-hop, jumped to the ground in hot pursuit.

Thalia opened her eyes. The grave marker's embedded mineral components sparkled in the sun. "Ah, CAT," she said. "You never cease to amaze. Just when I was at the end of my tether, you sent me Noah chasing the dream. Now Lish MacPherson has entered my life with her peculiar jar of earth. What comes next?"

Absent-mindedly, she stroked Adam. If Frank was still alive, and in his right mind, he would know what must be done. But he was gone ... eight years now. His mind had vanished long before that.

Hadn't her father warned her that she, by her heritage, was the one that had to preserve CAT and The Mark, as he had done? Did he not make her promise that she would keep the trust? She, as the fifth-generation Logan, had the greatest responsibility.

Thalia watched the sun's rays play on the limestone escarpment's rock, which harboured thousands of years of earth history — here a shell, there a partial ammonite, in a crack a fossilized fern. How insignificant my life ticks in the universe's clock, she thought. But if I don't do my part to preserve what is here, there will be little left for future generations.

A long time ago, Thalia stopped listening to the rhetoric that was laid on by Reginald. He was not part of the Clan. She would *never* capitulate or compromise to accommodate his ideas. His intentions were not in the best interests of The Mark and CAT.

Friday, June 22

Lish thought about her grandmother as she worked alongside Thalia in the garden. Granny MacPherson used to say that some days on Scotland's Isle of Harris had texture to them. Lish's third day at Granite certainly had a texture to it. The morning mists, like a cashmere shawl, enveloped the two women as they worked. Lish planted seeds while Thalia sat in her chair, telling her how many to drop and how far apart. Thalia's joy at planting in the good earth, as she called it, showed on her face.

"Every year Charlie plows the garden, then he says that I can't plant it," Thalia said. "I am prone to weak spells — and there is the problem with my leg and hip. I have to be content with a few pots of tomato plants on the back porch. With you here, we can both enjoy a vegetable garden. Perhaps we can weed the flower garden, too?"

Lish pushed stray hair behind her ear. "Maybe your friend Joan can help you with the harvest if I leave before some of the vegetables mature."

"When one sows, one never knows what one ultimately reaps," Thalia said. "Perhaps I should explain about Joan. She's such a lovely person and a wonderful ... assistant. I was devastated to learn, as was Charlie, that she has cancer."

"That is such a terrible disease," Lish said. "Cancer took Dad's life, and at such a young age. I was twelve when he died. Even since I was a babe-in-arms, we lived in Perth with grandmother."

"How tragic that your father didn't see you grow into a lovely young woman," Thalia said. "Joan, my dear friend, soldiers on. But Charlie and I have to assume that she doesn't have much time left to enjoy being ... mobile."

"Dad tried so hard to spend one more birthday with me," Lish said. "That didn't come to pass."

"Perhaps, knowing Joan's circumstances, you might be persuaded to remain long enough see the fruits of your labours. You did say that you can do office work?"

"At the moment, that's my specialty," Lish answered.

After lunch, Lish was once again reminded of her grandmother's parallels between weather and cloth when she and Thalia sat on the wide front porch overlooking the valley.

The day's texture changed to that of cool silk as stray breezes blew round the corner and caressed the women, taking the heat out of their skin.

Thalia picked up some knitting. "I'm doing an afghan for the autumn church bazaar," she said. "I've got to knit six of these strips. Each of them must be eight feet long. Do you know how to knit?"

"I was taught a few stitches by granny," Lish admitted. "I haven't had knitting needles in my hands for a while."

"Why don't you try this? It's a basic knit-pearl pattern. Here, I'll show you." Thalia held the needles toward Lish. "Watch now." Vein-lined hands completed a row. "You try now. Knit twenty, pearl twenty, across the needle, turn, pearl twenty, knit twenty back to the end, then repeat the pattern."

Lish's first attempt was adequate enough that Thalia suggested, "Why don't you add a few inches and enjoy the scenery while I finish a little ... writing. I'll be in my hidie. If you need anything, knock on the window."

Lish settled into the chair, her eyes on the needles. There were worse jobs, she thought. I wonder what Thalia is writing? A large bird that flew low past the porch drew her attention away from the knitting.

A hawk, riding the wind's fickle currents, circled lazily overhead. Sharp cries from the valley drew the bird's attention. Lish looked for the source, thinking that it might be another hawk in distress. Instead, she saw Noah by the large stone. Arms out, he enticed the hawk with sharp, poignant cries. The hawk circled lower and lower until it swooped across the river, wheeled, and showed its claws to Noah as it flew over his head. The bird climbed once more on the currents.

Lish watched as Noah explored the area around the rock and fence. He went from trees to the boulder to the river bank — bending here to dig with a stick, there to turn a rotten piece of wood. Lish called and waved. Whatever he's looking for, he's so intent on the search he doesn't even hear me, she thought. He's perfectly happy scuffling in the dirt and grass.

Mulling over her own situation, Lish moved the knitting needles mechanically, not worrying about the pattern. When Thalia broached the subject of her staying as a guest, there seemed almost an urgency to the invitation. Lish liked the elderly woman's feisty attitudes and obvious eccentricities. Her time could be useful here, until she'd decided what, if anything she could, or would, do. Lish could hide at Granite, if *hide* was the right word to use.

When Noah called from the brow of the hill, Lish waved and indicated he should come sit on the porch. What had she learned in the past day about Noah? Nothing. For that matter, what did she know about Thalia? Both Charlie and Thalia alluded to a son by the name of Reginald. The elderly woman relied heavily on Charlie and his sister, Joan, to assist her at Granite, which she loved with a passion that bordered on land-worship.

"It's a hot one. Building for a doozie of a storm, I'd say." Noah's voice startled Lish out of her ruminations. He sat in the chair beside her, his long legs and bare feet spread out in front, his straw hat beside Thalia's wool container. "Sorry. Did I frighten you? I didn't realize you were deep in thought."

"I was thinking about how fickle fate puts people in the same room," Lish said, looking at the knitting.

"I'm here because of a twist of fate, too," Noah said. "No. Wrong. I was driven by a dream to find this place. And I needed a break...."

"I walked out of a bad situation," Lish explained.

"Let me guess. A marriage gone wrong?"

"I've never been married," Lish said. "Look at this. While

my mind wandered, I changed the pattern. Now, how do I correct this?"

"Give it to me." Noah took the needles. "It's not so bad. Eleven rows are all that need to be ripped out." Noah removed the needles, unravelled the work, then began to pick up the stitches again.

"Where did you learn to knit?" Lish asked.

"A long time ago, in a far distant land, a teacher thought it was a good thing for a boy to learn how to knit a scarf," Noah replied.

"And in that same place you learned how to call a hawk?"

"Heck no," Noah said. "That was a different time, another place."

"Does everyone have *another place, another life*, or is it just the chosen few that have to go through hoops to obtain what knowledge and abilities they have?"

Noah gave Lish a long, searching look. He liked what he'd seen in the wagon. He still very much liked what he saw in the young woman that sat beside him. If anything, Lish was prettier, with her hair in a chignon, a touch of colour to her cheeks. "It seems to me you're no shrinking violet, Lish MacPherson. I doubt that you'd avoid any hoops that needed jumping through, if you were pushed far enough, hard enough."

"I stand up for what's right, if that's what you mean," she said. "I saw you down near the stone, looking around. What's so interesting about that spot that you spent nearly an hour searching around it?"

"Spirit Rock." Noah fingered the knitting. "You know, it's good to keep your hands busy during a storm. There's a big one gathering to the west."

Mid-afternoon's texture had turned to that of the rough knobbly blanket Lish had slept under as a child. Thunderclouds, filled with an electrical energy that would make the fainthearted nervous, boiled on the western horizon. "Perhaps we should go in?" she said.

"Don't let a storm frighten you," Noah said. "Isn't that right, Thalia?" He stood as the older woman came to stand on the porch. "Take my chair. I'll get another. Let's watch this one together. There is nothing that can compete with a storm for spectacular free entertainment."

"I can't say that I like, or appreciate, thunderstorms," Lish said. "But if you're both going to stay outside, I may as well join you. I guess a porch is as safe as anywhere else."

"Listen," Thalia said. "Listen to the thunder. Follow the sound as it rolls through and past us. Nature gives a good show, at her worst and best. I cannot find words to describe her power!"

"Just relax," Noah said, seated now on Lish's left. "It'll be over in fifteen minutes."

Thalia sat with her eyes closed. "Hush.... If you listen sharply enough, you can hear the rain coming. First a whisper, as if it's talking to the trees, getting their permission to water them. Then you can hear the first drops as they fall on leaves — a gentle tapping, nothing more. Close your eyes and listen, Lish."

What the heck, Lish thought. It's better than being zapped with your eyes open.

"Now, concentrate, both of you," Thalia said. "Concentrate on the wind. It will tell you when the rain is coming."

Thunder rumbled in the distance then reverberated down the valley, losing strength as it slipped away past the bridge and over the village. The rain began as a sigh in the distance, then a gentle cutting as drops began to strike leaves.

"Now, open your eyes," Thalia said, "Look at the layers of rain as they wash over the valley. Can you see — over near Charlie's farm, the wide, grey finger of water almost touching the ground?

Charlie's getting a real soaker. And here, to the west, what looks like a blanket heading our way? Listen to the wind bringing it to us."

Winds picked up and drove the storm west to east. Lightning crackled, followed by tumultuous thunder that seemed to break right over Granite. Rain lashed sideways, driven by the wind. So much water fell that the eavestrough couldn't cope. Water poured off the porch roof and bounced off the ground. Lish felt a soft dampness on her skin as stray droplets breached the security of the porch.

"Isn't this dramatic?" Thalia shouted at the height of the storm. "Think of the power this storm possesses. You know that the most dangerous part of a storm is the half-hour after it blows over? That's what I've been told anyway."

Lish, frightened into silence, certainly had a new appreciation for storms. Captivated by Thalia's enthusiasm for the weather, she said, "Perhaps, you should write about your love of storms. You described this one so ... poetically."

"Oh, I have ... sometimes," Thalia replied. "Look now. It's blowing toward the east. Would anyone like a nice cup of hot tea and some peanut butter cookies? Joan makes the best cookies. Charlie brought a tin of them yesterday."

"A cup of tea sounds good to me. Can I make it for everyone?" Lish asked.

"I'll stick around for those cookies," Noah said. He settled into his chair. "If you give me a few balls of yarn, patterns, and some needles, I'll help you make some items for the bazaar, Thalia. Knitting is relaxing ... for me, anyway."

"You two get to know each other better while I putter in the kitchen," Thalia said. "I'll call for you to carry the tray, Noah."

Thalia stood for a moment looking at the pair through the screen door. For whatever reason, he-of-the-dream and she-of-CAT had ended up together — as they should — at Granite. It was now her job to keep them together until CAT made it clear why they were here. Then she would act on its advice — if it was within her power to do so. She sincerely hoped it was. For her, time was running out.

At dusk, Lish decided to visit Spirit Rock, as Noah called it. When Lish mentioned her mission to Thalia, the woman said, "My old bones won't allow me to climb back up the hill. Take your time to look around. Stay for the sunset. I'll lend you a flashlight and leave the porch lights on to guide you home."

An hour before sunset, Lish took the dirt footpath down the hill, accompanied by the cats, who ran ahead to check their mousing prospects. The moist evening air was soft with the scent of honeysuckle. Wild canaries warbled evening-song from elder bushes. The plaintive call of cardinals came from cedars along the river.

The closer Lish got to the stone, the more intriguing it became. It wasn't like other round, grey, erratic granite boulders in the valley. This stone had a blue-green tint to it. Embedded quartz glittered in the reflected light of the setting sun. It was at least six feet tall, angular, wider at the bottom, snubbed at the top as though it had once sported a tip. The stone stood alone against a backdrop of the cedar-rail fence and wild rosebushes. Was that man-made markings on its sides?

Impulsively, Lish reached to touch the stone, to feel its strength, its warmth. As her hand caressed the surface, its heat seemed to penetrate to her heart. Was it energy? Was it the sudden realization that this was the most beautiful, peaceful place on earth? Here, surrounded as she was by nature in its glory, her worries seemed to melt away.

Tears welled in Lish's eyes and a question pricked at her brain. "Have I come home?" What did her father tell her shortly before he died? *Home is where the heart is at ease, where the soul has come to rest. Hell is what you lose in life. Heaven is where you find it. Happiness can be found in the strangest places. One's personal Valhalla is as close as a door to open, or an opportunity to take.*

Her father would have loved this stone, these hills. He'd led an interesting life as prospector and trapper in Minnesota and Northern Ontario. He knew minerals and furs. He read copiously. He always wanted to write about his experiences. During the Depression he brought his new bride to southern Ontario where he'd heard that jobs were easier to find, but he told his daughter that he would forever miss the North.

Lish sat amidst the daisies, Adam and Eve lying by her side. Absent-mindedly, she stroked their warm fur. When a rabbit leapt within six feet of her, Lish clutched each cat firmly by the fur on its back to try to prevent an attack.

"Don't you dare even think about it," Lish whispered. The felines watched, but didn't move. With no obvious sign of fear, the rabbit hopped toward her and went nose-to-nose with Eve. Then, disinterested, it leapt away and disappeared into the daisies.

Although by now the sun had sunk below the horizon, the sky retained a sensuous robin's egg blue colouring in the west, darkening to inky black on the eastern horizon. Cattle lowed in nearby fields. A dog barked. And faintly, on the scented night air, Lish heard the meowing of a cat — a motherly cry, as though it was calling to its kittens. The cats heard it too. They slithered free of Lish's hands and slunk up the path.

Searching for the source of the cry, Lish looked toward the river, where hundreds of fireflies twinkled in the grassy fields. She scanned the dark, brooding forest and heights of the escarpment. Granite's porch light was on. Thalia stood by the bell, in a long, white housecoat, waving a lantern.

Lish waved and started up the path. Such an extraordinary woman. I've been here only three days, yet I feel that I've known Thalia forever. How peaceful this valley is in slow-time. It would be a very difficult place to leave.

As the lantern's light signalled a rhythmic, hypnotic pattern, Lish wondered if she had finally found in this lush countryside, her personal "place forever sweet." Take each day as a new beginning. Learn much from the people around you. Granny's advice had always proved right in the past. Lish smiled. There was possibly none better to learn from than eccentric Thalia Logan Russo and down-to-earth Charlie Barnes.

Saturday, June 23

Thalia, determined to catch a fish by hook or by crook, sat on a kitchen chair at the river's edge and concentrated on her fishing line. Luna lay at her side. Noah stood nearby, expertly casting his line upriver into a deep pool. Lish, who hadn't fished since she was ten years old, had difficulty getting her line into the water. It didn't matter how far she threw it, the weighted hook never seemed to land more then three feet from shore. Charlie aimed for the deep placid water under the bridge.

Joan was more inclined toward enjoying her surroundings than fishing. "It is so pleasant to see land that's still pristine and to know that some people still care enough to keep it as nature intended," she said as she sat on a blanket beside Thalia, who was crocheting a table covering.

"If a man walks in the woods for love of them half of each day, he is in danger of being regarded as a loafer. But if he spends his days as a speculator, shearing off those woods and making the earth bald before her time, he is deemed an industrious and enterprising citizen. Chalk that one up to Henry David Thoreau," Noah said, concentrating on his line, playing it gently every once in a while to move the lure — teasing the fish, he called it.

"Charlie, did you read Mulmur Murmurings this week?" Thalia asked.

"Darn tootin' I did. You have to read them to see whose eye is being poked this week," Charlie said.

"I liked the one about the unnamed local resident who should have known better than to take a skinny dip under the bridge. You know, the one about the fishes doing a little nibbling," Thalia said.

"I'd like to know who the dickens Hugh Dunnit is," Joan said.

"Hugh Dunnit?" Lish asked.

"A pen name for someone in the area who keeps an eye on everything, and everyone, for the weekly paper that comes out of Orangeville," Thalia explained. "No one's immune from his, or her, pen."

"Including your house guest, Thalia," Charlie said.

"That's right. I believe the words were that 'our Bird on the Hill is enjoying the company of a Lovely Damsel. Some delicate dainties were spotted on her clothesline.' The devil always refers to me as 'our Bird on the Hill,'" Thalia said. "And you, Charlie. You get pinned, too, on many an occasion."

"I got it in the neck once for going to Toronto to reconnoiter the lay-of-the-land, to see who-was-up-to-what around these parts," Charlie said.

"I didn't think you were a city person," Noah said.

"I'm not. I was invited down to one of those slick presentations," Charlie said. "Lord, I had to drive through the horizontal ooze that's spreading like a virus out each side of the place. What is it that they're called? Suburbs? Well, they can be exburbed, as far as I'm concerned."

"It's apparent you're not in favour of certain types of development," Lish said.

"How can you tell?" Charlie replied. "It can't be my acid tongue that gives me away."

"No disrespect intended, but I can imagine you felt somewhat out of place in the city," Lish said.

Charlie smiled at the thought of himself among the prim, proper, and primed developers. "More like a goldfish among sharks," he said. "Everything was laid on: food, booze, rhetoric. Those high rollers just couldn't understand the word *no*. They figured I'd jump at the deal they waved in front of me, and a few others from up this way, including the Delaney brothers. Now, that was somethin' to see."

Noah laughed. "The Delaneys went to Toronto?"

"Darn tootin', crazy beggars."

"Don't leave us dangling," Joan said. "Tell Lish and Noah what happened next."

"When they didn't get anywhere close to home base with me, the big shots upped the ante, sweetened the pot. I still said no and walked out. But I think they got to the Delaney brothers."

"They sure got to the owners of those cottages that sold quickly shortly after the meeting," Thalia said. "Three of the prettiest in the Valley — hadn't even been listed."

"Why'd you go in the first place?" Joan asked. "I told you not to."

"Waul, it's always good to know what the enemy is up to."

"What did they want your land for?" Lish asked.

"A ski resort. Northlands it was called. Yep, Northlands Development."

"Northlands," Lish said. "Do you recall anyone at the meeting with the last names of Campbell, O'Hearn, or Yule?"

"Can't say that I do, can't say that I don't," Charlie replied as he worked his line.

Lish persisted. "Yule — a tall, pale-faced man with a slight stoop to his shoulders. The miser's hump, I call it. Small eyes, fleshy face, big nose?"

Charlie laughed. "That about describes all the men in the room, with the exception of me and the Delaneys, of course. Pardon the pun, but I was like a fish outta' water. Why do you ask?"

"Please don't hold it against me, or judge me on it, but I once worked for a company that specialized in certain types of land development."

Noah gave Charlie an odd look but didn't say anything.

"Well, if you're not working for them now, that says something about your character and conscience," Thalia said. "And you do have nothing to do with Northlands Development, we must assume?"

"I swear that I don't," Lish said.

Charlie pulled his line, baited the hook again and threw it back into the water, aiming for the deepest channel under the bridge. "It's not polite fer a lady to swear, Miss MacPherson. I'll believe you," he said.

"Thank you, Charlie Barnes," Lish replied.

"There are people would jump at the chance to sell out for big money, but Charlie and I aren't interested. Our families have been on this land for generations. Isn't that right, Charlie? We're here to stay," Thalia said.

Charlie looked affectionately at the elderly woman. "Farming doesn't pay the bills some years, but it's an honorable profession and allows me to stay on the land, for better or for worse. Churchill said that we make a living by what we do and make a life by how we live. It just happens that my living and my life involve the same stretch of land."

Thalia's smile made Charlie's day. "To be honest, the problem is that Charlie doesn't have any children to pass the land and trust along to. And I have no-good Reginald, who'd sell in a minute if he could get his hands on The Mark. We're not getting any younger. Charlie is fifty years old. Joan celebrated her forty-eighth birthday last month, didn't you my friend?"

"Never married, and feel ninety," Joan answered, pausing in her work.

"You're deep in thought, Noah." Charlie worked his line.

"A man in thought is sometimes better than a man in action," Noah said, suddenly whipping his line. "A fish in hand is also better than one in the creek, if you're hungry." A rainbow trout, its colours flashing in the sun, had taken the bait.

Everyone stopped fishing to watch as Noah landed his catch.

"I'm going to let all of you take a good look at this one, then I'm going to release it," Noah said. "I don't believe in killing something for the love of it and I'm not in need of a meal tonight."

"You know," Charlie said, "If we're gonna' get all smarted up fer the social this evening, we'd better pull our lines and skee-daddle."

"Is it far to Hornings Mills?" Lish asked.

"Not the way I drive," Charlie said. "You'll like the Mills. We'll take the pretty way. It's got two churches, a big hall where the social's being held, a garage, three stores, and a cemetery with gorgeous spirea bushes at this time o' the year. Joan wants to visit the cemetery."

"I must do some shopping before the social," Thalia said. "We'd better leave a bit early. You *are* joining us, Noah? You haven't changed your mind?"

"I wouldn't miss this event, Thalia. I'll be ready at the end of your lane in my finery."

"Hornings Mills sounds like a city compared to Seven Springs," Lish said.

"Just like Seven Springs, it's got lots of water. In either place, you can just throw a shovel into the ground and you come up with a gusher. But you can't compare the Mills to any city. It's one of those villages that were once the backbone of the country. What's really keeping the Mills alive now is summer folk who built cottages in the area."

"Lose the vibrancy of villages," Noah said, "and you've lost the heart of the land."

"Well said. How true," Thalia agreed, pleased at the depth of understanding Noah had about community.

"Is there anything that you do like about the big city, Charlie?" Lish reached to help Thalia out of her chair.

"I like the way it throws a pretty young woman our way every once in a while," Charlie said. "Did that once before. Gobbled up Thalia for a while, then tossed her back into the fold. Best thing the city ever did. But that story's not mine to tell."

"What is yours to tell?"

"That I'm glad you came and pleased that you're staying fer a while." Charlie pulled his line.

"At least we didn't count on fish for supper tonight. There'll be plenty to eat at the social." Joan bundled her work into an embroidered canvas bag and accepted Noah's hand to get up.

"You lived in Toronto, Thalia?" Lish asked.

"Once," Thalia replied. "I'll tell you about it sometime. Now, if someone will be good enough to help me up to the bridge, to Charlie's car? These creaky bones don't carry me far. If it weren't for Charlie and Joan airing me once in a while, my world would consist of puttering around the house and muttering around the yard. Why, I haven't been up to the cabin for some years. I can't get around the rocks."

"I promised you that I'll take you to the cabin," Noah said, giving his arm to Thalia. "Even if I have to carry you around the rocks and through the woods, I'll make sure that you get there — soon."

"And mark my word, I'll hold you to the promise." Thalia leaned heavily on the deeply tanned arm, thinking of another time, same place, many years before. She turned to look at Noah — same profile, same winning smile, same mannerisms as the one before.

Hornings Mills

Hornings Mills' Spring Social proved to be everything that a big city dance wasn't: unsophisticated ... relaxed ... fun. The ceiling of the hall was festooned with white, mauve, purple, and yellow crepe paper streamers that cascaded from a circle around the main light fixture toward outer walls where they were affixed to a picture rail. Window ledges held canning jars and crocks full of fresh flowers. A picture of the Queen shared the wall above the stage with an honour roll that held the names and pictures of those killed in both wars.

Supper was potluck. Everyone put their offerings on a long table and people helped themselves. Introductions were made. Politicians glad-handed. Farm folk caught up on the news. Neighbours passed on local gossip.

Lish MacPherson's presence at the social was both news and fuel for speculative gossip. Word had gotten around that the Lovely Damsel was some looker and single. The unmarried women in the crowd viewed her with suspicion. Married women memorized every detail of her dress, hairdo, and mannerisms. The menfolk either ignored her completely or vied for the opportunity to say hello.

"Don't let the bach-line irritate you," Charlie said. "They'll pick you apart with their eyes. Give 'em the what-the-hell-you-looking-at glare. Most of 'em don't know what a come-hither look means."

Noah received the same inquisitive looks. He was not totally comfortable in the surroundings and made it his business to be as unobtrusive as possible in the crowd. He stuck close to Joan and Thalia, not caring to integrate bachelor's row. He'd agreed to attend because Thalia insisted he do so, and he was her guest.

"Where's Luna?" Lish looked around the hall. "You insisted that she come, Charlie."

"She's outside, guarding the car," Charlie said. "She's not partial to dancing."

"That dog won't let you out of her sight."

"She's a bit soppy whenever she's going to have pups — insists on being with me, whatever the circumstance. Did I tell you that she's descended from a long line of dogs that came to this part of the country nearly two hundred years ago? The first one was called Moon."

Lish laughed. "She's a big baby. I didn't realize that she was going to have pups."

"Don't underestimate Luna," Charlie warned. "She'll take a strip off you quick as look at you if she thinks it's warranted. Never tell her to *attack*. I always spell the word around her. Luna can smell trouble in the wind, in your sweat."

After the meal, tables were pushed against the outside walls, dishes were washed, and the lights dimmed. A few of the young people left the hall to hang around outside where they could listen to their type of music — rock n' roll — on portable radios.

A local band consisting of a piano player, two fiddlers, and a guitarist entertained inside. For the first dance, the trio played the Tennessee Waltz … "a one and a two and once round the hall with yer lover, twice roun' with yer wife."

Charlie put his hand out to Lish. "May as well let 'em see how you can cut a rug."

For his size and bulk, Charlie danced gracefully, light on his feet. As he waltzed Lish around the room, he said, "Rules of the game: you have to dance with a guy if he asks. In a small community like this he'd be the laughing stock if you turned him down. Don't go outside with any of 'em. They get fired up with liquor — keep it in their cars. Don't allow groping. Tell 'em hands off or Charlie'll kill them."

"And if I want to dance with someone?" Lish said.

"You can ask a fella to dance, if yah see one you like. Rules are that he can't say no — unless, of course, it's the Delaney brothers or old Chuckie Rue. Don't forget that I claim the first square dance of the evening with you. Did I say you look pretty tonight?"

Noah claimed Lish for the next dance — a foxtrot. "If I see you being hogged by a fellow, I'll rescue you," he said. "Otherwise I'm sticking close to the Miss and Mrs. I might ask for some time on a guitar. I can't keep my fingers from wanting to pick."

"You play the guitar?"

"In a former life," Noah said.

Jeff Grant commandeered the third dance, guiding Lish through the intricacies of a Schottische. And on it went, one fellow after the other taking Lish for a spin around the floor, until mid-evening when coffee and pie were set out and set upon.

Square dancing and polkas took up the first part of the second session. Lish was never without a partner until Charlie finally rescued her for a waltz, then led her to Thalia's table. Noah kept his word and spent his time at the table with Joan and Thalia, his back to the dance floor. At intermission he had spoken with the musicians.

"I heard you tell Thalia that you need to go to a bank," Charlie said.

"I have to pay Jeff for the work he's doing on the car," Lish explained.

"Tell you what," Charlie said, a twinkle in his eye. "If you can get one of the Delaney brothers to dance, I'll lend you my car and even fill it with gas."

"Charlie," Joan said, "that's unfair. Just give her the car."

"All's fair in war ... and love," Charlie said.

"I'll sweeten the pot." Noah got into the conversation. "If you do persuade a Delaney to dance, I'll sing a song for Thalia."

"You sing?" Thalia said.

"You bet I do," Noah said. "And I'm good at it, too."

Thalia laughed. "If Lish succeeds in getting one of the Delaney boys up on the floor, I'll dance with Charlie to that song."

When everyone looked at Thalia, she said, "You know that, because of my leg, I haven't danced in years. But I'll be safe in your arms, won't I, Charles Barnes?"

"Indeed you will, Thalia."

Lish glanced from Thalia to Charlie to the sulking Delaney brothers in bachelor's row. I've nothing to lose, she thought. And lots to gain.

"Deal. And you've all got to keep your word."

When the band struck up again, Lish made a beeline for the brothers. As she walked across the dance floor, the crowd went silent. The woman wasn't really going to approach the dim-witted Delaneys ... she was going to the ladies room. No! She was standing before Tom, Dick, Harry, and WGD. What was she saying?

The band never skipped a beat as the musicians watched the city girl challenge the country grumpkins. When there was no response by the end of the first play-through, the band repeated the song, waiting, like everyone in the hall, for the next move.

"Gentlemen," Lish said, looking from one to the other. "Who's going to dance with me?"

When no one made a move, she said. "Well, one of you is. That same person is also going to tell me all about Northlands

Development. Now, who will it be? It matters not to me who I dance with."

The brothers looked furtively at each other, then three pair of eyes focused on Tom, the oldest, the one who usually did the talking.

"So," Lish said, watching the eye-play. "It's you, sir, is it?" She stood a head taller than Tom. "Let's not waste time. You're Tom?"

"I was the last time I looked in the mirror," Tom said.

Tom made the most of the situation. He timidly put his arm around Lish's waist, then held her well away from him as he stumbled around the outside of the dance floor. "My Ma never taught me how to dance properly," he said.

Lish felt like commenting that she never taught him to wash, either, but held her tongue. Some things were best left unsaid. As the pair passed Thalia's table, Noah gave a nod and thumbs up.

"Now, Mr. Tom Delaney. You'll answer my questions even if it takes two dances."

"I don't have to answer anything," Tom said.

"Oh, yes you do, because you may have been cheated in this land deal that you're supposed to have made with Northlands Development," Lish explained. "You'd better tell me all you know, starting at the beginning."

It took three dances — one a polka that Lish and Tom sat out in a dark corner in animated conversation — before Lish returned to Thalia's table.

When she sat down, Charlie said, "Boy, you sure impressed him. He just herded his brothers out of the hall like the devil was chasing them. What'd you say?"

"I thanked him for the dances. Told him that someday I'd go over to their house and teach them all how to waltz. What else was discussed is mine to hold and yours not to know — tonight," Lish said. "Thalia, what song do you wish Noah to sing?"

"The French Song," Thalia said. She began to sing the ditty. "*Quand le Soleil dit bonjour aux montagnes, Et que la nuit recontre le jour ... When the sun says good day to the mountains and the night says hello to the dawn ....* Do you know that one Noah?"

" *... I'm alone with my dreams on the hilltop. I can still hear his voice though he's gone.* I sure do. Give me five minutes."

After a short break, the band leader said, "Ladies and gentlemen, we have a treat tonight. A young man by the name of Noah is going to sing a song requested by Mrs. Russo, who is going to dance with Charlie Barnes."

Noah was familiar with the song but it was so new that the band had never played it. When they declined to accompany him, Noah first played the tune through, to get comfortable with the borrowed guitar.

The grand old dame, the Bird on the Hill, was going to dance! Folks lined the dance floor to watch. When Noah did begin to sing, his clear baritone voice and beautifully played tune were the only sounds in the room. Even the ladies washing dishes came out of their kitchen to listen.

Charlie took Thalia in his arms. Despite her height, she looked like a delicate bird next to his bulky frame. "You didn't say this was going to be our debut in the old corral," he whispered. Are you ready to perform, my girl?"

Charlie held Thalia gently and danced slowly across the floor, careful not to aggravate her leg and hip with any excessive or quick moves. Several times, in executing a turn, he literally lifted her off her feet to swing her around.

As Charlie guided her through the dance, Thalia sang the lyrics, her voice catching on ... *I hear from my door, the love songs through the wind. It brings back sweet memories of you ...*

"Ah, Charlie, it's just like the good old days, isn't it? When your father danced with Angel and Frank danced with me."

When Noah dedicated a second song to Joan, Charlie stayed on the dance floor with Thalia. On the first notes of "Memories are Made of This," Jeff presented himself to Joan.

"Come on, my lady. You've got to have a turn on the floor too." Away they danced, the old and young; the frail and the strong, the weak and the energetic. Jeff was careful not to move too quickly. He held Joan firmly and made the turns slowly.

When the song ended, the entire room broke into applause — for Thalia, for Joan, and for the new man on the block, the mysterious fellow by the name of Noah who could sing like a bird and play the guitar like a pro. Lish was impressed. But where had she heard that voice before?

CHAPTER THREE
The Week of June 24–June 30

Sunday, June 24

Lish agreed to attend church with Thalia only because she didn't want to hurt the woman's feelings by refusing the invitation.

"To tell the truth, Thalia, I haven't attended church for some months," Lish admitted.

"Don't let that stop you from enjoying this service," Thalia said. "I promise that it won't be boring. If you don't like the sermon, just concentrate on your own private thoughts."

"I did pack several shirt-waisted dresses that are suitable for church. But I don't have a hat," Lish said. "I'm not partial to wearing hats."

"That doesn't present a huge problem," Thalia said. "I'm sure that I have one that will suit you."

Lish took extra care dressing for the occasion as she didn't want to be an embarrassment or the subject for any more gossip. She'd caused enough whispering at the dance to last awhile. At the foot of the stairs, she realized that it wasn't her that would be the standout. Thalia came out of her bedroom in a forest-green, ankle-length dress with matching hat that looked as though it might have been worn during the early 1900s. I should have expected this, Lish thought, especially after the woman had the courage to wear a 1920s dress to the social.

Seeing Lish's amused look, Thalia said, "It's so rural around here, I have to do something to liven things up, don't you think? I always try to give the service a bit of a lift. This is going to sound blasphemous but there are occasions, when the devil gets me in a corner, that I truly believe that I only attend church to observe people. If there's one thing I don't want to be accused of, it's being considered *normal*."

Lish laughed. "Normality is a state of mind. You must be the bane of the minister."

"He's used to my outrageous costumes. He knows there's not much he can do with me. I give the church enough money to pay at least half the man's salary. The congregation's used to me too. I'm sure some attend church just to see what I'm wearing. Look at it this way: if the community is talking about me, they're not gossiping about each other."

"There's some truth in that statement," Lish said.

"Today, I'll guarantee that all eyes will be on you. The entire Valley and Springs reads Mulmur Murmurings," Thalia said. "My dear, you do look lovely. That blue colour suits you. Would you like to see the hat I've chosen?" The apprehension on Lish's face must have been apparent because Thalia patted her sympathetically on an arm and said, "It's a 1940s straw number, very understated. I wouldn't embarrass my guest now, would I?"

"Where do you get all these ... costumes?"

"I follow in Mother's footsteps. She never threw anything out. Neither did Grandmother. The attic is full of trunks of clothing and other odds and ends."

"Does Charlie dress up? And Joan?"

"Heavens no! Religion is very important for them. I admire their strong beliefs. But what works for some, doesn't for others. Now, let's pack the picnic lunch and walk to the Line so Charlie doesn't have to drive up to the house. I want to enjoy the morning air. My leg isn't hurting too much today, but I'll have to lean on you quite a bit for support, if you don't mind."

Seated in the Logan pew at Seven Springs United Church brought back some interesting observations and memories for Lish. She had fleeting images of times past — sitting on her father's knee in a lace dress and dainty hat, trying hard to please her grandmother by joining the choir, tripping over a floor runner at a Christmas pageant, a minister who put more effort into expounding about generosity when the collection plate was passed than into his sermon ...

"It's difficult to separate the smell of musty hymn books from dead mice," Thalia whispered into Lish's right ear. "I cannot suppress the urge to sneeze in this building."

"The place smells more like fowl suppers and barn manure, candles, and creosote," Charlie whispered into Lish's left ear.

The minister, Reverend Harrison, seemed to be a nice young man. But, Lish thought, he certainly didn't address her personal needs. Who was he speaking to? Not the young couple one pew over holding hands. Not general-store-Georgie of the roving eye. Definitely not three of the Delaney brothers, who fell asleep shortly after they sat down.

"Do you see that family in the third pew — the woman wearing the red hat? They drive from Collingwood. Rumour has it that the man was caught in an affair," Thalia whispered.

"Perhaps he's trying to hide his indiscretion by attending church in a different community, thinking that no one knows his secret," Lish whispered back.

"Then the man's a fool," Thalia said. "Scandal travels faster than a car."

"Darn tootin' it does," someone said from the pew behind the Logan party.

As the minister droned on, Lish's mind wandered much further afield than Seven Springs. It wandered back to the city, to COY. Her former bosses made a big show of attending church. Campbell, O'Hearn & Yule donated huge sums of money to various church causes, always getting their name or picture in newspapers for doing so. Yet, without a doubt, they were the biggest crooks in Ontario.

"Pssst," Charlie said. "You might want to stand up. You're the only one sitting."

Now, that must have looked foolish, Lish thought. I wonder if that Murmuring fellow goes to church? Lish glanced around. WGD Delaney smiled at her from two pews over. Lish smiled back, then concentrated on looking at the stained-glass windows while singing the hymn, one she remembered. She was fine until the congregation launched into the fourth verse.

Seated again, Lish caught only fragments of the service. Her mind wandered back to COY. The firm didn't question certain unsavory business practices. To COY, it was progress. Profit. Wealth accumulated.

Charlie's hand slid under Lish's elbow, gently trying to lift her. "Attention," he whispered. "It's better to go with the flow around these parts, unless you're pregnant. In that circumstance, you're forgiven for sitting through the service."

"I'm on the standing side." Lish's words were drowned out by Charlie's deep baritone voice as he joined in singing the second hymn. Face the truth, Lish thought. You suspected what COY was up to three months ago. How long were you going to let the situation go? Until you met Matthew Baine, were you willing to play their game?

"And down again, my girl," Charlie whispered, with a twinkle in his eye. "I think we're getting the hang of it now. The next thing you need to worry about is the collection plate. If you don't have any change, use a little creative hand-work and pretend you put som'pin on it."

Creative, Lish thought. What did Yule say when she faced him up? "You have to be prepared to use creativity in business if you want to get ahead in the game." So, when did business start to be a game? When did it stop being trust and sincerity, honesty and hard work, to become a money-grab at all costs. If her future at COY meant cheating seniors and buying favours ...

When Charlie passed the collection plate, Lish rummaged around in her purse for some change and found a five-dollar bill. "You want me to scratch around fer some serious change?" Charlie whispered.

It was all Lish could do to suppress a laugh. What was the gist of the minister's sermon? After chickens finish scratching in the dirt and pecking the feathers off each other, they come home to roost ... a twisted parable about people who find fault with religion returning to the fold at the end of their lives. Perhaps, when Campbell, O'Hearn & Yule finished plucking unsuspecting people of their assets, like the chickens coming home to roost, their sins would come back to haunt them.

No, the sun would have set in the east before that happened, Lish thought. Poor old Matthew Baine suffered from dementia and was in no position to deal with the papers she'd been instructed to deliver and have signatured. The elderly gentleman knew not why he should sign or what he was signing. "I want to talk to my son," he said. "He'll know what to do." When Mr. Baine began to cry, Lish put her arms around the old man to console him, then made him a cup of tea. She left a blank sheet of paper on his desk and took both copies of the signed document back to the office, but didn't file them. They were in her briefcase at Granite. She found the son's name and telephone number in an address book that the old gentleman kept in the desk.

Lish was brought out of her self-examination when the small organ wheezed to life for the last hymn. The tiny organist timidly played the keys as though she half-expected that they'd bite back. The congregation, just as cautious, took up the last hymn — "The Old Rugged Cross" — only showing bravery when the familiar chorus began.

Lish glanced one more time at the stained-glass windows, especially the second to the right of the sanctuary. Was that a large cat — standing on a rock, surrounded by colourful wildflowers, feathers, a peace pipe, and quiver? Could it be a cougar? Lish felt a chill go through her. The hair stood up on the back of her neck.

"You didn't get too much out of that service," Charlie said, walking beside her up the aisle.

"I do apologize, Charlie. My mind just seemed to wander ..."

"Hypnotic Harrison does sometimes put people's mind in a state of animated suspension," Charlie said. "I've caught myself gathering wool on more than one occasion. Come on, we're off to River Bend Park."

Most members of the congregation gathered in the shady park where tables were set under mature trees and horseshoe pits shared space with a ball diamond. Several children's swings hung from the huge branches of a weeping willow.

"We make the most of our time because we can only get together during the summer," Thalia said. "Charlie says that we make chatter while the sun shines. I say that we make time while we have someone's ear. Some winters the snow is so deep, the minister can't get through to conduct the Sunday service. The Lord help anyone who dies during a week of heavy snow."

"Gossip is what they do best," Charlie said. "Just set awhile and listen. The secret is not to give any information but to gather it in. It's a matter of keeping your mouth shut and your ears open."

"Charlie's right," Thalia said. "There's always more information to be learned than given."

"Thalia's savvy enough. Stick with her and you won't get pumped or picked up by one of the Delaney boys. I'll get you ladies several chairs from the trunk of the car."

Thalia didn't have to walk around to meet people. She sat in the shade of a maple and everyone came to her, like moths to a flame, royal subjects to their queen. All the fuss was because of her young friend, Thalia said. But as time passed Lish realized they came to pay their respects to Thalia who, while making introductions, had a kind word for everyone.

"This is Maggie Webster, friend and compatriot," Thalia said of a tiny older woman who walked with the aid of a cane. "Maggie lives in the prettiest little house at the far end of the village. How are you, my dear? This is for your birthday." Thalia handed Maggie a small, thick, white envelope.

"I'm managing. I worked for Thalia, you know." Maggie turned suspicious eyes on Lish.

"My arthritis got so bad that I had to retire. Thalia doesn't forget me though. She sends baskets of vegetables and fruit down all the time. And a ham arrives for Easter, a turkey at Christmas. Every little bit helps."

"But Thalia ...." Lish received a hush-it glance from Thalia. "But I'm sure that Thalia is pleased to help you."

After Maggie hobbled away, Lish said. "You haven't had a vegetable garden and your orchard looks like it hasn't been tended properly in years, Thalia."

"Maggie doesn't know that. If I didn't make sure that she had some fresh vegetables and fruit she'd eat sweets, which she isn't suppose to have because she has diabetes now, too."

"What did she do for you?

"My little secret. Now, look who's standing beside me: Wee Jimmy."

Wee Jimmy was anything but little. Although he now looked well past eighty years of age, his hulking form told another story. He must have been a strong, handsome fellow in his prime. He too received a gift from Thalia. Wee Jimmy reached tobacco stained fingers for a sealed envelope. He spoke for a few minutes, and gave Lish a bit of advice about the meal: "If you can't make out what's in a casserole, don't take any of it." He then hobbled toward the horseshoe pits.

"How can you afford to help him?"

"How can I not?" Thalia said. "Did you notice that he shook hands with his left hand? He was in Frank's construction crew. When he lost four fingers in an accident, Frank gave him a job as hired hand around Granite. Charlie does most of my work now. Wee Jimmy lives in a cottage just down the road. I still pay him — a pension, of sorts."

And so it went. Lish was made party to information that Georgie of the come-hither look was given start-up money from Thalia for her restaurant. Georgie's mother, Mary Thomas, lived in Creemore now but also had worked at Granite at one time.

"To put it mildly, half of Seven Springs and the Valley must owe you money or are indebted to you," Lish said.

"Oh, I don't expect any of them to pay me back," Thalia said. "Let's say that I don't mind paying for privacy." Thalia waved to the minister. "I have to talk with the good reverend for a few minutes. Georgie has cornered Charlie. Maybe you should rescue him?"

"Charlie's a good catch," Georgie said as Lish joined the duo. "He's a cantankerous old goat, but he's got a bank roll, if you're interested."

"Go find yer husband," Charlie said. "I saw him down by the river with one of the Rooke girls — the cute one with the blond, curly hair." He and Lish watched as Georgie stomped toward a secluded bend in the river.

"You devil!" Lish said. "He's playing horseshoes with WGD."

"Did you learn anything?" Charlie asked.

"Only that Thalia Logan Russo buys loyalty."

"Let's just say that she finances silence."

"For what?"

"She'll have to fill you in on that one. Look at her in that pretty dress, just settin' there taking it all in. You can't help but admire a woman who can keep everything together the way she has."

"What was falling apart?"

"She'll have to tell you that too. All I'll say is that there are generations of commitments that have fallen on her shoulders. There are promises ... bargains. Let's talk about something else."

Fine with me, Lish thought. Perhaps it's best that I don't know what Thalia's all about, what game she's playing, if it is a game. "I noticed a window in the church this morning that portrayed an animal that resembled a cougar."

"The Logan window," Charlie said. "It's a tribute to those who came before and those who are still here, I suppose. It was paid for by Thalia's grandfather. Isn't it a beauty?"

"The symbols are certainly ... curious. A cougar, Indian peace pipe, and quiver?"

"Thalia will have to explain that one. We'd better rescue Joan. She's talking to the Stewarts. They're from the Lavender area. Nice people, but always lookin' for information. You get the woman talking recipes and I'll challenge Stewart to a game of horseshoes."

Joan was willing to talk recipes, but after a few minutes Mrs. Stewart lost interest and went off to find more fertile rumour ground. The flowers on her hat bobbed like they were blowing in the wind as she walked away.

"Joan, did I hear you say that you baked a couple of rhubarb custard pies for Noah? Is he coming for supper?"

"Noah is going to be at Granite for five-thirty. He wants to get back to the cabin by nightfall. He says that climbing Lavender Line and trying to navigate the path into the cabin in the dark is not a good idea."

"Where does he stay?"

"Thalia lets him use the old log homestead on the ridge above Grotto Spring."

"He keeps a horse and wagon up there?" Lish asked.

Joan laughed. "You can't keep much but yourself up there. His car is parked in our drive shed. He likes to borrow Frank's old wagon and Juniper. The horse belonged to my dad. It looks like we're going to set out the picnic. Come on. You can help me. We'll leave Thalia to her court."

"What job do you do for Thalia?"

Joan laughed. "Thalia will have to tell you that."

"Joan, I noticed there are hardly any families here. Shouldn't there be more children?"

"It's the sign of a dying village when families move away," Joan said. "Sad isn't it."

Monday, June 25 — Beginning After Midnight

Lish stood by the trash barrel at the bottom of the garden, a half dozen papers in one hand, a matchbox in the other. After looking around to make sure no one was watching, she lit the papers and tossed them into the barrel. The fire was so small that surely no one would see it.

"This is for you, Matthew Baine," Lish said as she watched the papers burn. "May the Campbell's, O'Hearn's, and Yules of this world burn in hell for their unscrupulous dealings with those who couldn't defend themselves."

There it was again, coming from the forest, the yowl of a big cat carried on the wind. Lish shivered, tightened the belt on her housecoat, and went back to the house.

After Breakfast

"The car's easy to drive and smooth on the road," Charlie said of his '53 Super Wasp as he fussed around the vehicle.

"You're having second thoughts about letting me drive it, aren't you?" Lish asked.

"It's one-of-a-kind, for around here. The other farmers drive Fords and Chevs. I bought it in Fergus, a good used model. This is the first car I ever owned. It's solid, heavy, and good on winter roads."

"Don't worry, Charlie. If the lady can't handle the car, I'll take the wheel," Noah said.

"Given what you drive, I'd be down on my knees praying you'd keep the Wasp on the road," Charlie said.

"Now, let Lish be," Thalia said. "I've packed chocolate chip cookies and a thermos of coffee, if you get hungry. Don't forget to pick up my dress at Russell's. The alterations should be done by now."

"Where're you going again?" Charlie checked the wipers.

"We're going to Orangeville and then to Fergus to pick up Thalia's dress and the windmill part that you ordered from Beatty Bros. Ltd. We've got the map that you drew, Charlie."

"The map is pretty detailed," Noah said. "We can't get lost."

"If you run into trouble, you got my number? You can always call the garage in Fergus — Howes & Reeves. Ask for Ted. He knows the car — and me."

Lish smiled. "Charlie, I've been driving for thirteen years. Don't worry. We'll take care of your baby."

"All right, then, we'll see you around suppertime. Give me a ride home so you'll know how to find me when you return. I'll give you a ride back here. Do you want to come with me for the day, Thalia?"

"I think that I'll stay home, maybe do some more scribbling."

"Do you need Joan to help? I can bring her around in the truck."

"Tomorrow would be better for me."

While driving to Charlie's farm, Lish passed a couple standing by the side of the road taking photographs of the valley. "If I'm not mistaken, that's the couple who were arguing at the General Store," she said.

"By jove, you're right," Charlie said. "What are they doin' sneaking around out here. I'd better keep an eye on that pair for sure."

"There was a dark blue Ford parked at the crossroads," Noah added, taking a close look at the man. "What's he doing with that huge telephoto lens on his camera?"

"Drop me off at the gate. I just might be tempted to walk back and have a little chat with them," Charlie said. "On the other hand, I'd better get to work on the machinery. Are you still up for haying tomorrow, Noah?"

"I sure am," Noah said.

Charlie was right. The Wasp was smooth and settled in at sixty miles an hour. Lish easily retraced her route, back out to the highway, through Mansfield, and south toward the Stanton General Store.

"You don't mind me hitching a ride with you?" Noah asked.

"There's no reason why you shouldn't," Lish replied. "Why didn't you want to drive your car?"

"I prefer that it not be ... seen," Noah said.

Lish laughed. "Is it stolen?"

"No, it isn't. There's a long explanation about the vehicle that you don't really want to hear," Noah answered. "Why are you driving at gawk speed?"

"We're passing through Stanton. I wanted to see the old man again," Lish explained. "There was something about him ..."

"Strange thing," Noah said, looking at the store. "I stopped there also to buy a soda pop and passed him on the way in. He invited me to sit a while. I asked if he wanted a cold drink and he said, "Don't drink much but whiskey these days, but I wouldn't mind a honey-dip donut or two.""

When it was obvious that the old man wasn't seated on the bench, Lish sped up again. "Did he say anything else?"

"Yep. I sat beside him slurping my drink. He asked me where I was headed. I said Hunter's Mark. I knew that it was located in Mulmur Township, but I didn't know for sure exactly where."

"How do you know about Hunter's Mark?"

"Don't ask me to explain that right now. The old guy said that I should head for Seven Springs then ask where a lady by the name of Thalia Logan Russo lived. So I did — and here I am."

"I find it strange that both of us would talk to the same man about the same thing."

"Maybe not. He might just hang around the store every day like the old beggars at Georgie's. You're a good driver," Noah said, digging into the chocolate chip cookies. "Want one?"

"How can you think of food? We just ate breakfast."

Noah helped himself to coffee, pouring it carefully from thermos to cup. "Can I turn the radio on? There must be some country music on one of the stations."

In the Hockley Valley, Lish turned right, toward Orangeville. "Nice area," she said as she negotiated the winding, shady road. "You said that you didn't want your car to be seen. Are you hiding out? Running away from someone, or something?"

"A bit of both," Noah said.

"Want to tell me about it?"

Noah's answer was an emphatic "no."

"Just wondered. How old are you? Thirty?"

"Close," Noah said, diddling the radio's knobs. "I'm thirty-four."

"That's a good age for reinventing oneself."

"That you should know," Noah said. "Why don't you tell me something about yourself?"

"Let's drop the subject. I've got banking to do in Orangeville and a phone call to make. I'll use a payphone, then we'll head for Fergus."

"I just might find a payphone and bank, too. How be that we go our separate ways and meet again at eleven at the car?"

"Fair enough."

"So, what were you burning at midnight?"

"You saw me?"

"If you don't want to be seen at your skulduggery, don't wear a white housecoat in the full of the moon, or light a fire after dark — albeit it a small one."

"I was burning ... part of my past. I was ... liberating someone from a rotten-to-the-core situation. Don't ask me to elaborate. And don't mention that I was burning anything to Charlie or Thalia, will you?"

"Got you." Noah said. "But both already know."

In Orangeville, Lish called a number in Toronto. The phone was picked up after five rings.

"Mr. Baine, John J. Baine? You don't know who I am, and you

don't need to know. Listen to me carefully. Your father, Matthew, never signed papers to sell his property."

Lish listened for a moment, then interrupted. "I know he doesn't want to sell. You don't want him to sell. Listen, regardless of what someone, or some company says, your father did not sign any papers. There are no papers, do you understand?... That's right, sir. No papers. And please get power-of-attorney over your father's affairs as soon as possible.... No, I'll not give my name. Please, it is important you never reveal that a telephone call was received.... No, I don't expect you to understand at the moment. You will, in time. You must trust me. I must trust you."

That felt good, just like old Smith & Jones times, Lish thought, when she finished the call.

"Success?" Noah asked when they were back in the car.

"A measure of satisfaction," Lish replied.

"You look like the cat that ate the canary," Noah said, giving Lish a sideways glance.

"I feel like a mouse who's found a cache of cheese. I just have to watch for both cats and traps."

In Fergus, Lish drove down St. Andrew Street past Monkland Mills, pretty stone homes, and Howes & Reeves garage. She parked in front of Fergus Restaurant.

"I've been here before," Lish said, looking around. "I remember a high gorge and a whirlpool. Come on. I'll show you."

Noah donned sunglasses, pulled his hat well down over his forehead, and trudged along behind Lish.

"I stood here on the bank, holding Dad's hand, looking at the river gorge. That must have been — twenty-five, twenty-six years ago."

"Did you live in Fergus?"

"No, but when I was a child, we must have visited Fergus on enough occasions that I have a few memories of the place."

"Let's grab a sandwich at the restaurant," Noah said.

Seated in a rear booth, Noah insisted on facing the back wall and Lish tried to make sense of her fragmented memories. "Mother died shortly after I was born. I always took it for granted that I was born in Perth until I needed a birth certificate. My birth was not officially registered."

"Now, under certain situations, that can be a tricky predicament," Noah said.

"I was in Toronto at the time. Granny took responsibility for the oversight. I was issued a birth certificate based on three affidavits: one from the minister who performed the baptism and wrote the information in the church records; one from my first-grade school teacher; and the last from a respected banker who lived next door to Granny and remembered me as a baby. He also just happened to be a close friend of the area's local provincial Member of Parliament."

"That was quick thinking put to good use," Noah said. "It doesn't hurt to have a shoe in the door."

"Granny knew everyone. She then covered all the bases with a letter explaining that Dad was so distraught over his wife's death he must have forgotten to register my birth. Granny's letter had to mention my mother's maiden name but I never saw it."

"Was there no family Bible? No marriage records?"

"I lived in Toronto for at least three years before Granny died," Lish said. "A first cousin of hers was named executor of her estate. I received a financial inheritance, but none of her personal effects or papers — not even one piece of her furniture."

"What made you finally think that you were not born in Perth?" Noah asked.

"That lack of proper birth registration and the names on Dad's memory jar," Lish said.

"Memory jar?"

"A very personal family memento," Lish said.

"When did you leave Perth?"

"Eleven years ago. I completed high school, went to business college, then moved to Toronto," Lish said.

"Is Fergus one of the names on that jar?"

"It is," Lish replied.

"Then is it not possible that you were born here? For your own peace of mind, you should consider finding out." When the young waitress came to take their order, Noah peppered her with questions. Was there a hospital in town? Where might the cemetery be? Did a family by the name of MacPherson live in the village at one time?"

"There is a hospital and a cemetery. I can't remember a MacPherson family, but I'm only sixteen. I'll get Villie — she's the owner. Maybe she can help you. "While you're warming the seats, you may as well eat. What'll you have?"

"Is the salmon salad sandwich good?" Lish asked.

"Iffy," the waitress said, wrinkling her nose. "It's made with pink salmon."

"I'll have an egg salad sandwich and a bowl of soup."

"Good choice. You want out-of-a-can tomato or chicken noodle soup? You get chopped olives in the egg salad because Paul — he's the cook — refuses to leave them out. And for you, sir? You look familiar. You been in here before?"

"Nope." Noah avoided looking directly at the waitress. "How about tomato soup and a hamburger with a side of french fries?"

"Sounds reasonable to me. The burger comes with lettuce, cheese, and tomato," the waitress told him. "I'll be back with your cutlery and a couple of glasses of water."

Lish looked round the restaurant: tin ceiling, old fashioned soda fountain and candy counter, juke box, red leatherette seats in the booths. "This place isn't familiar, but I vaguely remember Russell's store."

"While we're in Fergus, do you want to go to the hospital and ask to see their birth records?"

Lish took some time to answer. "No," she finally said. "The office wouldn't show their records to a stranger. I'll have to prove why I want to know about a birth — who I am. I'll get the address and write."

Someone put a few coins in the juke box. The first record dropped to the plate and a baritone voice wafted through the restaurant.

"Why the strange look?" Noah asked.

"For a moment, I thought the fellow singing was you ... at the dance," Lish said. "My landlord loved country music. He had a huge collection of records. I heard the songs over and over again because he liked to play his music loud but I didn't pay too much attention to the artists."

"Country music all sounds the same," Noah said. "You hear one, you've heard 'em all. You spoke of your landlord in the past tense. I can assume you've left the city for good?"

"I ... Can I change the subject? Exactly what are you doing at Granite?"

Vestiges of a dream passed through Noah's mind ... an encampment surrounded by high rock walls ... a horned buck .... Noah shook his head to dispel the images. "I'll just say that you've got to look back to see who your ancestors were before you can look ahead to see who you can become. You have to see how far they've come, to know how far you can go. You have to draw inspiration from the ... your ancestors. My family places a great deal of respect on their elders. They remember them, talk about them."

"I didn't ask for a sermon," Lish said.

"The simple answer then? I don't really know ... yet."

By the time the waitress returned to the table with glasses of water, napkins, and cutlery, the song had changed to Elvis Presley singing "Blue Hawaii."

"Who sang the last song?" Lish asked.

"I don't pay attention anymore," the waitress said. "I think it was Jason something or other. I'll be right back with your food."

"Good, I'm hungry," Noah said. "What are our plans after lunch?"

"We have to pick up Charlie's windmill part at the Beatty Bros. plant, then Thalia said that we should drive to Elora to see the Tooth of Time before heading home. Do you have anything that you need to do while we're here?"

"I noticed a fruit store on the corner," Noah said. "I need to buy some oranges and bananas. I can't live without fresh fruit. When Georgie gets any at her store, they're a week past good and ready for the compost heap."

As the pair were leaving the restaurant, Lish asked, "What is your last name, Noah?"

Noah decided to take a chance. "Curlew," he replied. "An arctic bird."

Tuesday, June 26

Adam and Eve had taken to sleeping on Lish's bed, and demanded, by sitting on her chest, to be let out early every morning. When she came downstairs to oblige by opening the back door, Lish was in for a surprise. Her car was parked near the drive shed. She trudged through dewy grass to retrieve a note, tucked under a windshield wiper: "Hitched a ride to Charlie's with Dad to help with the haying. See you around noon hour. Don't worry about paying today. I haven't figured out the bill. Jeff."

Lish took a few minutes to enjoy the view. What a gorgeous day. Charlie's silo and barn poked out of a light mist that lay in the valley like a gossamer blanket. The mist was thicker near the river, where cattle grazed in a field that faded in and out of the swirling grey. A horse neighed. Down the valley, another answered. The smell of wood smoke mingled with cedar and damp earth.

By the time Lish retraced her steps, Thalia was bustling around the kitchen. "We've lots to do before we leave for Charlie's," she said. "There's not a moment to spare. We have sixteen people to feed and only four of us to do it."

"Should Joan even be working?" Lish asked.

"Joan would never admit be being unable to help. She won't sit down for long, even if you ask her to," Thalia replied.

"It seems to me that Charlie works hard. He must have a lot of farm work to do."

"Charlie hires a farm hand when he needs one. When he took over his father's farm, he also bought his Uncle William's place that was right next door. Charlie now has more than three hundred acres, at least twenty milk cows, a beef herd, and an orchard. Jeff is supposed to be in line to run the farm when Charlie gets tired of the job, Jeff being his only nephew."

"Who's helping him today?"

"Area people. He pays well. It's hot, tiring work. They'll go till dark," Thalia said. "Wait until you get a whiff of fresh-mown hay. It smells of summer and love-making in the loft. Oh my, my ..."

"You're talking from experience?"

"Hush. Try your hand at making the molasses drink. The recipe's in the green scribbler," Thalia said. "The men need lots of salt and sugar. Georgie will keep them watered this morning. I'm in charge of desserts and a couple of hearty salads."

"Georgie's going to behave herself with all the men around?"

"Now don't say too much bad about Georgie. She's all talk and no do. She's got a heart as big as Texas and about as warm too. She's one of the few people around here not connected to the Logan or Barnes families. There's hardly a soul in the Valley not related in some way."

"I assume that the Delaney brothers are an exception, too" Lish said.

"The village needs new blood," Thalia said. "That's what Frank was, new blood. And Angel, Charlie's mother." Thalia stopped working. "My, Angel was a beautiful woman and from away. Enough said. I'm putting you in charge of the macaroni salad. I don't use a recipe, but there's a good one in the Kate Aitken Cookbook. Be sure to mix lots of cold chopped ham into it."

"Are you making cakes?"

"We don't have time to cool and ice cakes, so I'm whipping up some no-crust miracle pies — eggs, coconut, flour, and sugar. We'll pack tins of fruit from the pantry and make a fruit salad when we get to Charlie's. Joan will have plenty of heavy cream we can whip. We should leave here around ten."

Just before they left, Lish removed two sealed cardboard boxes from her car's trunk to make way for food and some folding chairs. The boxes were too high to be slid under the bed. A bedroom closet was nonexistent. Lish put the boxes in a pine clothes cupboard and locked the door.

Pickup trucks lined Charlie's laneway. The two-storey house sat amidst flower and vegetable gardens. Several dogs cavorted with Luna in the apple orchard, one a big rangy cross between a German shepherd and a collie.

"Love at first bite," Thalia said. The shepherd cross is the dad." Charlie keeps the line going. Just park over there, by the summer kitchen."

While Georgie transferred the food to the kitchen, Lish carried the chairs to the long make-shift table under the maples near the drive shed. She could hear machinery in one of the fields behind the barn; men laughing, a tractor's throaty roar. On her last trip, Charlie came out of the drive shed with a shovel in his hand. Before he shut the door, Lish saw the back fender of a large, expensive car.

Georgie was such a whirling dynamo in the kitchen, it was best to obey orders and stay out of her way. Lish was given the job of cutting bread and thick juicy slices off a huge ham. Thalia added dressing to salads, filled butter dishes, and cut pies. Joan sorted dishes. The dogs hung around the door, waiting for hand-outs. A half dozen cats sat on the woodpile hoping for charity.

Even with all the windows open, the kitchen was hot. Georgie was clever enough to wear a kerchief around her hair. Joan sported a towel around her neck to absorb perspiration. Thalia commandeered a washcloth to mop her brow.

Georgie handed Lish one of Charlie's checkered neck scarfs. "Dip it in cold water then tie it round your head, or we'll be picking you up off the ground. It might not look good, but it's effective."

As Joan and Lish set the table, Joan explained that the men would be served first, then the women could sit down to eat. "We just stand out of their way and let them shovel it in."

At noon hour, the four women stood by the table, looking at their efforts. "Have we forgotten anything?" Joan asked. "Oh dear, I hope there's enough food. They're always a hungry bunch. Lish, as our guest, you get to ring the bell. The rope's just inside the woodshed door. Ring it until you see the first men coming round the barn. Shouldn't take more than eight pulls."

Sixteen men made a beeline for bowls, soap, and towels that Georgie had placed on a table by the outdoor pump. When each finished washing his face and hands, he threw the contents of the bowl over his head. Shirts came off and were hung over the garden fence to dry.

"Poor fellows," Thalia said. "It's got to be one of the hottest days this June. Quick now. They're racing to the table."

Lish never saw food disappear so quickly. She and Georgie ran from kitchen to table, replenishing what they could. Georgie could carry twice as much, twice as fast. The fellows ate silently, falling on the food like starved cats. Only when desserts came out did they relax a bit.

"Charlie's hired a good crew this year," Georgie said, her eyes on Noah. "Look at the man," she said. "He's been in the sun. Isn't he the handsome one?"

Lish's eyes were on Charlie: handsome, strong, naked to the waist. She felt a niggling tingle of desire. How long had it been since she'd dated an honest-to-goodness man, in the true sense of the word? Too long, she thought.

By the time the four women finally sat down to eat, only Jeff and Noah were still at the table. Charlie and the other fellows were stretched out under the maples having a nap.

"The river's cool," Noah said. "I figured I'd go for a swim when the work's done. Want to join me?"

"I didn't bring a bathing suit," Lish said.

"Who said anything about wearing a suit?"

"You wish." Georgie slapped Noah's arm. "You wouldn't know how to handle hot stuff like us, would he, Lish?"

"Try me," Noah said, giving Lish a wink. "How about it, Jeff?"

"At the moment, I'd prefer another piece of pie. It's nice and sweet, less volatile, and doesn't ask for a commitment," Jeff said.

"You'd do better to have a rest." Thalia yawned. "My old bones are aching and I haven't lifted one bale."

"Do me a favour, Thalia. Keep Dad here this afternoon," Jeff said. "He shouldn't be in the field. He had a weak spell this morning."

"Gracious," Thalia said. "He mustn't work in the heat after lunch."

"He can fix my mixer," Joan added, "and the bathroom light fixture, and the cellar door."

Noah had just flopped on the grass on his back and closed his eyes when Luna sounded the alarm, bringing Charlie to his feet.

"We got company," Charlie said, "Down at the road. And they've got a camera with a bloody big lens, pointed this way."

Georgie positioned herself in front of Thalia, blocking the view of the lane and road. Noah rolled over so that his back was to the camera.

"The only reason they're here is to snoop," Charlie said. "I'm going to set Luna on them."

"Don't do that," Lish said. How interesting, she thought. It's obvious to me that Georgie doesn't want Thalia's picture taken. Noah has cleverly turned his back to the camera. "You catch more with honey than you do with vinegar. A few choice words might send them on their way. Let me talk to them."

"Don't rile them or they'll know for sure someone here really does have something to hide, and become real nuisances," Joan said.

"I wonder who might that be?" Lish asked.

Charlie called Luna to his side. "Lish has a point. We don't want to cause a ruckus. We don't want to draw undue attention to anyone. But we don't want pictures, either. We like our privacy."

"Let me see what I can find out," Lish said. "If you all just act normal, I can circle the house, go through the orchard, and accost them at the gate."

"Go for it, girl," Charlie said. "Chew them out."

"Maybe I should do it," Jeff suggested.

"You'd crack their heads," Charlie said.

Thalia added her bit to the conversation. "Let's see how Lish handles the situation."

"Am I being graded?" Lish asked.

"No, dear. You're just going to prove your nettle. As long as you have nothing to hide — or is it your picture they're after?"

Lish thought of the contents of the two boxes. Maybe it *is* me they're looking for. Does COY know files were copied? How would they know where to find me?

"Take Luna with you," Charlie said. "Command her to *stay* and she'll stop wherever she is. Say *alert* and she'll bark and growl. If you say *guard*, she'll circle and work 'em like sheep. If you say *attack*," Charlie whispered the word, "... well, you don't want to ever do that without meaning it."

"Give me five minutes," Lish said. "Jeff, would you indulge in a bit of teasing with Georgie? Give the pair something to concentrate on." Lish left the table, Luna by her side.

"I'd rather Noah join the fun," Georgie said.

"Leave me out of it," Noah said, lying on his stomach in a position that suggested he was having a nap.

A short time later, Lish stood, hands on hips, behind the photographer and his partner, pleased that she'd managed to get so close. The pair were so engrossed in the antics of Jeff and Georgie that they hadn't noticed her walk out the orchard gate and up the road behind them. It was no surprise to Lish that they were the couple that were arguing in the General Store.

I may as well make myself known, Lish thought. "What the devil are you two up to? This is private property."

Startled, the pair turned toward the voice. "No it isn't," the photographer said. "It's a concession road. We've as much right as you to be here."

"You might have a right to stand on a public road, Mr. Private Eye. But you've no right to photograph a private event, so ... bug off."

"Who says so?"

"I do," Lish said. "And Charlie Barnes, who'd rather bash your head in than talk to you. You're being paid by someone to snoop, aren't you?"

"We're just doing a job," the woman said. The photographer's fetch-and-carry, whose pockets bulged with lenses and film, was tiny and blond. She spoke with a clipped English accent. A pair of binoculars hung round her neck.

"You, lady, are snooping, plain and simple," Lish said.

"Who we are and what we're doing is of no concern to you." The photographer adjusted the lens on his camera. He was tall and thin. Big eyes bugged out of an angular face. His Adam's apple bobbed when he spoke. Thinning hair was combed creatively over a narrow head. "Are you going to stop us?"

"Yes," Lish said.

Bug Eye laughed. "You and who else?"

"Me and the dog. Luna. Come," Lish called. The dog came out of the ditch behind her. "Before I order her to *A–T–T–A–C–K*," Lish spelled the word, "would you like to tell me exactly who the subject for your lens is?"

"It could be none of you," Bug Eye said. "It could be all of you."

"Are you going to tell me who you work for?"

"That's none of your business," The Fetch said.

"Will you be leaving the Valley soon?"

"Depends," Bug Eye said. "You can't run us out of the place."

"That's true," Lish said. "But I can run you off the concession road. Luna — *alert!*

Luna barked ferociously.

"That's going to send us packing?" Bug Eye said. "It's nothing but a big noise from a stupid animal." He took The Fetch by the hand but made no move to leave.

Luna's bark turned to a menacing growl. The dog positioned herself between Lish and the couple, her eyes on the movements of her prey.

"Would you like to hand over your film?"

"You have got to be joking," Bug Eye said.

"Remember, you had the opportunity to do so," Lish said. "Luna. *Guard!*"

The dog crouched and, like a sheepdog, advanced on Bug Eye and The Fetch, growling and snapping, forcing the pair to retreat a few steps. Luna slunk in and, working them like sheep, herded them toward their car, which was hidden from the farmhouse by a clump of cedar.

"You haven't seen the last of us," Bug Eye said, not turning his back to Luna.

"You probably haven't heard the last from me, either," Lish said. "For what my advice is worth, you two are not very discreet about snooping."

"How would you know?" The Fetch said. "You'll regret confronting us."

"I don't think so," Lish said, following behind Luna. "You should thank your lucky stars that I came to the road. If Charlie or Jeff had confronted you, the end result may have been a little different."

As soon as the pair got into their car, Lish, afraid that they might hit the dog, called Luna to heel and moved to the side of the road. The car pulled away quickly, tires spewing gravel. "And goodbye to you, too," she said when Bug Eye gave her the finger.

Charlie and Jeff walked down the lane to meet Lish.

"That took guts," Charlie said. "You acted like a real pro, Lish. Good girl, Luna."

"I was always good at amateur theatrics," Lish responded.

Jeff couldn't mask his admiration. "Listen, before we get swamped, will you have lunch with me? Say Saturday, at Georgie's? You can pay me for the repairs and we can get to know each other better."

"That sounds like a nice idea," Lish said.

"It's a deal then," Jeff said. "Did they say who they were looking for?"

"No. Who do you think they were photographing, Charlie, and why? The guy had a point you know. Who's going to stop them from taking pictures, short of guerilla tactics like running them out of the Valley."

"Beats me," Charlie said. "Are you ready for the afternoon? You've still got that fresh, dewy look about you. There's clean-up, dishes, and supper to prepare afore you can go home. Make sure that Thalia doesn't work too hard, will you? And Joan? And Len, too?"

Fresh dewy look? Lish felt like a well-used dishrag: just as dirty, just as hot, just as wet and smelly. Never had she been so tired.

Thalia did what she could to help with supper, but ended up sitting in the orchard with Len. Joan went to lie down before the supper dishes were washed. Lish and Georgie soldiered on, during which time Lish gained respect for the brassy, buxom woman whose overwhelming presence masked the real Georgie of sincere heart and intelligent mind.

"I hope that you don't believe everything you hear about me," Georgie said, her hands in dishwater. "I might have a roving eye, but it's hubby who cheats regularly on me while he's on the road. Mom — she's manning the store today — says I should leave the beggar. She says I'd be better off without him."

"And what do you say, Georgie?"

"If he doesn't bother me, I don't bother him. He's a hard worker. He's bringing in a decent wage. He's on the road all the time. He can't hang around Seven Springs and twiddle his thumbs all day. You know men, and all that."

"Some men do find it hard to settle down," Lish said.

"And there's people around who mean something to me: Thalia, Charlie, Joan, Len. You just can't walk away from them," Georgie said. "Can I give you some advice?"

"Go ahead," Lish said.

"Be careful around Jeff. I saw him panting over you today. He's ... different to the rest of us."

"Point taken," Lish said.

* * * * * * *

At the end of the long day, Lish helped Thalia into the house, fed the cats, and carried boxes of empty pots and pans into the kitchen. "I'll make a pot of tea," she said.

"No tea," Thalia said. "Look in the five-gallon crock in the corner of the pantry," she said. "There's a bottle of Drambuie. A glass of that will go down nicely right about now. Surprised? Don't be. I enjoy a tipple every once in a while. At my age, it's not going to hurt. I like mine over ice."

Comfortable in the rocking chairs, with libations in hand, Lish asked, "Who do you think Bug Eye and his Fetch were photographing?"

"Everyone has their secrets, dear. I have mine. Charlie has his. I'm certain that Noah harbours one or two. I'm sure that you have things you'd rather people not know. The photographer and his lady friend probably have theirs, too. They make a living by revealing others' secrets. We all make a living in different ways. What do you work at?"

Whiskey does loose the tongue, she thought. Tonight, truth might be better than fiction. "When I graduated from business college, I had high-flouting ideas about writing the great Canadian novel. I moved to Toronto, where it didn't take long for me to realize that I needed a job if I was going to eat and keep an apartment."

"That's always a tough lesson for a young woman to learn," Thalia said, savouring her drink.

"It certainly was. My first job was in a bank. I was good at math and thought that I could work my way up through the ranks."

"But it's a fact that you are a woman," Thalia said. "I have never met a female bank manager — not that I see a lot of bank managers, mind you."

"I found working in a bank boring," Lish continued. "I was lucky enough to be accepted for a position at Smith & Jones." Lish paused, expecting comment. When none was forthcoming, she said, "Then, I went back to the bank for a short period of time. One day, I saw an advertisement for a position at a property development company — Campbell, O'Hearn & Yule. It appeared, at least on paper, to be a decent, well-paying job."

"It wasn't?"

"To begin with, it was. I started as general secretary to Mr. Yule but was soon given more specific responsibilities. The pay was good. I could afford a newer car."

"I gather from the tone of your voice that things didn't work out as planned."

"Some time ago, I was given access to the document file closet. My job didn't involve delving into old files, only working on the ones that pertained to current projects. But I am thorough and investigative. As I leafed through some of the older files, it quickly became apparent that there were discrepancies, incidents of advantage-taking ... "

"Your bosses possibly trusted you with access to the closet because they felt either that they could buy your loyalty — or that you were stupid enough not to ascertain what they were up to. If the second is the case, they grossly misjudged you, my dear."

"What bothers me is that I didn't suspect wrongdoing sooner. I'm usually more observant. At any rate, after one particularly disgusting situation where a senile old man's property was very nearly bought for one quarter its value ... I gave notice that I'd be leaving the firm. I didn't elaborate on my reasons — just eluded to wanting more time to travel ... write."

"Your bosses weren't impressed," Thalia said. She held out her glass for a second drink.

Lish obliged, but was generous with water, skimpy with the liquor. Thalia was looking very comfortable in her chair, Adam and Eve on her knee. The last thing Lish needed to do tonight was tuck the elderly matriarch into bed.

"Yule in particular was furious," Lish said. "He tried to persuade me to stay. He said that he, personally, had invested a lot of time and effort to train me to become part of their *team*. He went into a rage and ... fired me. He said that he'd personally make sure I never worked in Toronto again."

"Do you think that he realized you were a threat to their carefully contrived schemes?"

You're getting into deep territory here, Lish thought. Use some caution about what you say next. "I believe Yule suspected ... something. He'd have no idea exactly what I knew ... know. I'm just not sure how to proceed."

"I assume that your midnight fire had something to do with what you just told me," Thalia said. "You do realize that before approaching the authorities you would need absolute paper proof of this firm's wrongdoings, my dear. You can't get that by burning important documents."

"Thalia, do you know what really hurt? Hearing the word *fired*. This is the first time I've said ... *fired* ... out loud. There is a stigma attached to the word."

"But you were going to quit anyway. It's just one little misused word — out of the mouth of an unscrupulous man," Thalia added.

"That's true," Lish said. "I never thought of the situation in that light."

"I consider that leaving this company is the best thing that could have happened to you," Thalia said. "You were given the freedom to find Hunter's Mark, Granite, and me — and Charlie, and Joan, and Noah; and from the way Jeff was looking at you today ..."

"Jeff was very attentive, but one of the crew said that he has a girlfriend in Creemore, or did he say Collingwood?"

"One of his great aunts married a Chisholm from out the Valley. Like I said, every once in a while you've got to introduce new blood or you'll spawn a race of either blithering idiots or brilliant eccentrics."

"Georgie did warn me about Jeff."

"He was a good boy, was Jeff," Thalia said.

Wednesday, June 27

Clusters of tiny curls framed Lish's face as she laboured over the old Beatty washing machine. Its putrid green-painted tub was full of hot, soapy water in which Lish fished with a wooden stick for clothes. Catching one of Thalia's house dresses, Lish pulled the lever to activate the wringer and fed the garment through the rollers. With a wet plop, it landed in a wooden basket on a laundry stand on the other side.

Lish pushed stray hair out of her eyes with a wet hand and turned to look at Thalia, who was busy scrubbing unmentionables on a board in the sink. There was apparently no rest for the wicked or tired at Granite.

"Thalia, do you not think a newer model would make life easier for you?"

"As long as that one works, it's good enough for me. Charlie donated it when I finally agreed to have hydro. When that load's done, we'll fill the machine for the rinse, put a little bit of vinegar in to really take the soap out. I'll be done at the sink by then. I used to love to do the laundry. Nowadays, it's a real chore. Fortunately, I'm not a dirty person so it doesn't have to be done that often. Georgie usually does my bedding. I can't handle that — too heavy."

"Using this machine is an experience," Lish said. "I'll grant you that."

"It's a post-war model. The date's right on the tub, 1922," Thalia said. "Think of the task as fuel for the brain; grist for my ... the pen."

"Think of it as hard work."

"Did your grandmother not have a machine?"

"She did. But she also had a woman come in to do her laundry and housework."

Thalia examined a spot, applied some soap, ran the slip up and down the scrub board, and smiled at the apparition by the machine. "Just wait until you smell these clothes fresh off a line that catches the winds off the escarpment. There's nowt like it, Grandmother used to say."

"I do have to wonder who this Hugh Dunnit person is that he ogled my undies on the line last Thursday and had the audacity to write about it," Lish said.

"Some people in the Valley and Springs would like to get their hands around Dunnit's neck," Thalia said.

Lish was cautious as she put a bulky tablecloth through the wringer. She'd already caused one blow-out. The wringer had flown apart while mauling a thick towel. It was a frightening experience. Thalia had to come to her rescue.

"Touchy machine," Thalia had said, as she struggled to put the wringer back together again. "It does this all the time. It once threw parts across the kitchen because it didn't like a sweater I tried to put through. The bottom wringer bounced right off the wall over there. You can still see the mark."

"That's dangerous!" Lish said.

"Contrary, I'd say. After the laundry's done, there's strawberries to pick. In the past I've let the birds eat them. Has anyone ever told you how pretty you look with curls around your face? And you have such expressive eyes."

"I can't say they have," Lish said. She was not a beautiful woman. She was strong, broad-shouldered, but carried herself well in spite of her height. Her figure was good. Her face was "classic," according to her grandmother, the most endearing feature being her eyes. She had long arms and large hands, long legs and small feet.

"Is there not a beau in your life, Lish?"

"Not recently," Lish said. "I dated several boys during high school that caused me to look at pairing off — coupling — with a rather jaundiced view. Then there were men who, after the first few dates, wanted more than I was willing to give."

"Mother told me that what some young blades needed was a good clop on the side of the head," Thalia said.

"I haven't met the right man," Lish said. "I need someone who will take me as I am and admire me for my brain, not my looks or body. I've set some pretty high standards; money isn't one of them."

Thalia smiled. "You'll know when the right man comes along — the one you want to have children with."

"Don't you think I'm a bit old to consider marriage, let alone children?"

"Being nearly thirty is not old! You have to be careful, though. You might think a man's the right one. There'll be passion in your bones. But he won't be the one you'll marry. You have to feel love in your heart. There's a big difference between hankering after flesh and giving your heart — loving for life."

"It sounds like you speak from experience," Lish said.

"It's just the ramblings of an old lady." Thalia glanced at the clock. "Another hour and we'll be finished. That's not so bad now, is it?"

Noah walked in while Lish was rinsing the last load. The apparitions that greeted him in the steamy kitchen were wonderful. Lish was drop-dead gorgeous. Fuzzy curls and tendrils of longer hair, hanging like ringlets, framed her face. There was a luscious glow to her skin, like she'd bathed in cream. Thalia's skin appeared dewy and without wrinkles. A riot of curly sprouts escaped her hair bun and looked like a halo round her head. The pair were chatting and laughing as though they'd known each other for years.

"May I interrupt this party?" Noah melted under Lish's smile. God, he thought, I could love this woman.

"Nice timing. You can hang the last load," Thalia said. "I'll make a cup of tea. There's nothing like a hot cup of tea after a hot laundry as long as it's drunk while enjoying cool porch breezes."

"I was thinking," Noah said, lifting the basket to his shoulder. "I promised I'd take you to the cabin. Lish now has her car. If we drive to the end of Lavender Line — to the trail head — we can walk in. I can carry you over the rough spots, Thalia. What do you think?"

"Noah. I would love to go. It's been seven years since I've visited the cabin. Charlie makes sure it's kept in good shape, though. How be we pack a lunch and leave as soon as we tidy up and have our tea? I've a great pair of 1930s jodhpurs I can wear."

"Not that it's any of my business Thalia, but don't you have anything modern in your closet?" Lish asked.

"Of course I do. I have that lovely black dress with the jet beads that you brought back from Russell's store. But I laid it away in tissue. That's going to be my funeral dress."

Lish looked from Thalia to Noah. For the first time the thought crossed her mind that she was staying with someone who was not only eccentric, but a bit crazy, too.

Noah shrugged, laughed, and left to hang the laundry.

"Don't fret dear. I always dress the part, get into the mood for what I'm ... doing. And I'm not about to die on you. Heaven's no! With the exception of my confounded gimpy leg, I'm in pretty good health for a septuagenarian. I just like to plan ahead. Don't let me forget my walking stick. By the way, I'd appreciate it if you didn't mention our late night cocktail party to anyone."

After Lish parked the car, the trio pushed through elderberry and pin cherry bushes at the side of the Line, Thalia leaning heavily on Noah's arm. Old growth hop-hornbean thrived at the edge of the glade. The trio soon entered the forest proper where maple, oak, and beech with trunks so large that two people couldn't arm-girth, rose one hundred feet to provide a leafy canopy. Where a storm or age had felled a tree, it lay decaying, the life blood for fungus and fern. Large and small granite boulders, their surfaces covered with moss — God's marbles, Thalia called them — were scattered throughout the area. The scent of rotting wood and leaves mingled with the acrid smell of wood smoke.

"My cooking fire," Noah said. "I banked it before I left, but the canopy keeps the smoke below leaf level. The ground is pretty uneven right here. Do you want me to carry you, Thalia?"

"Gracious no," Thalia said. "I want to say that I did this walk on my own, just like I used to. It's not far now. My old legs will hold out long enough to get me there."

"If you can't make it back, you can stay the night."

"I'd like that," Thalia said, "but the outhouse arrangements don't agree with me. You know you're getting old when you're afraid that you'll get stuck or fall through the hole in the thunder shack."

The cabin came into view in a clearing, weathered logs in symmetry with their surroundings. A stone chimney, wild grape curling around it, anchored the building. Hollyhocks grew in front of small-paned glass windows. Overgrowth almost hid several outbuildings in various states of decay. The sun, directly overhead, spotlit the clearing. The scene was so pristine, so unique that Lish felt a lump rise in her throat.

"It never changes," Thalia whispered, patting Lish's hand. "Neither does the feeling that I get when I see it. It's timeless. Weathered logs ... smoke rising from the chimney ... the bench by the door ..."

"I doubt that much has changed inside, either," Noah pointed out.

"Before we go in, can we walk to the bluff?" Thalia asked. "I want Lish to experience the Knob."

"I hope that you don't mind, but I did clear the path to it," Noah said. "I didn't want to be responsible for you falling and breaking a leg."

"I've been through that," Thalia said. "I don't need another experience like that one."

"How did you break your leg?" Lish asked.

"I went to the aid of a cat in distress."

"A big cat?" Lish asked.

"A house cat," Thalia said. "It appeared to be hurt and was on the roof of the drive shed. I fell off the roof trying to rescue it. The cat got down by itself. I dragged myself to the bell and rang for Charlie. The accident left me with this painful, permanent limp — hip complications — and a determination not to climb any more ladders."

"Are you impressed, Lish?" Thalia asked as they stood on the Knob.

"I'm awed. I didn't realize the bluff was so high." Lish felt compelled to go to the edge of the overlook. What a spectacular view. Lish looked down to the tops of the trees below. Granite lay far to the right.

"The area where Granite was built is called The Slope," Thalia said. "You can see that it's the only place along this part of the escarpment where getting down to the valley is relatively easy. Father used to say that he was lucky to have valley pasture, upland meadows, and plateau fields."

Beyond Spirit Rock, Lish saw the arches of the bridge and the river, its water sparkling in the sun. On the opposite side of the valley, Charlie's farm and fields lay sheltered below the ridge.

"Look to the left, toward the upper reaches of the valley. Do you see the waterfall?" Thalia asked.

Where the river valley narrowed and became more pronounced, Lish could just make out a ribbon of water tumbling over the edge of the escarpment.

"I call the area right below us the Vale of CAT," Thalia said. "It wasn't too far from here that the last four-legged big cat, a cougar, *was* shot in the 1880s."

"But there has to be another roaming the area now. I hear one," Lish said. "I'm sure that I do, Thalia."

"And you may well, dear. There will be an explanation — in time — I'm sure."

On impulse, Lish picked up a small stone and threw it. All three watched as the stone arced, then disappeared into the tree tops.

"Even if the stone were painted bright red, you'd never find it down there," Noah said. "It would bounce from limb to limb, rock to rock, and fall in some obscure place."

"The pebble might catch in the crux of some branches," Thalia said.

"Trying to find it would be like looking for the proverbial needle in a haystack," Lish said.

"Don't think that, if great value was attached to the pebble, some people wouldn't try to find it," Thalia said. "That's why this area needs to be protected — so no one will desecrate its secret places. Dear me, I'm rambling. I'm anxious to see inside the cabin. I hope you like it, Lish. It's a space apart, a respite from the world. It was often my refuge in a storm."

In Thalia's log hideaway, Lish felt a warmth and security that wasn't entirely generated by the fire on the hearth. So much has happened in this place, she thought. People have loved, laughed, cried, and lost here.

"I keep the cabin as my father did ... and his father ... and his father. Everything is authentic. That is the way it must remain. The spell that this place casts must never be broken. Noah, show Lish all the little hiding places, especially the well-hole, then you can move the rocking chair outside for me and we'll enjoy our picnic."

Conversation flowed freely as the three enjoyed lunch. Thalia sat in a chair so old its rockers were worn flat on the bottom. Lish's bench was covered with carved initials. Noah sat cross-legged on a bear skin he'd taken from the bed.

Thalia explained how Granite came about. "You see," she said, "with the exception of the bottom pasture, most of the arable land on The Mark is on the top of The Slope, across Lavender Line. Hunter Logan and his son, John, lived here and walked the quarter mile to their fields."

"That would be inconvenient, given how difficult it is to walk around here, even today," Lish said.

"John realized that. When he married, he built a barn and frame house on The Slope — that's the old homestead across the Line from Granite. To John's credit, after his father died he kept this cabin as it was. He had his reasons for doing so, just as I do."

"Hunter Logan was the original owner of the property?" Lish asked.

"Yes, depending on one's beliefs," Thalia said. "But let me continue — great, great grandfather John decided a grand fieldstone house should be built on The Slope across the Line from his frame home. He began hauling stone to a site he chose for the view."

Thalia chose her words carefully; she wanted to give just enough information to be useful, not enough to influence either Lish or Noah. The chair creaked under her weight as she tried to rock. "John never saw his granite house built. He died before enough stones were picked and hauled to the site. He fell off the Knob and died right below where we were standing."

"An accident?" Lish asked.

"Well, I wouldn't say it was an accident," Thalia said. "He suffered from Galloping Consumption. I think that he just ended his life the way he wanted to. His son, James, never saw the house built, either. He ran out of money and couldn't do more than haul rock. My grandfather Hunter — aptly named, don't your think? — built the house with his son Joseph's help — my father."

"I've seen the ruins opposite your laneway," Noah added. He helped himself to peanut butter cookies then passed the tin to Lish.

"After my father died, the barn fell into disrepair. Frank wasn't much of a farmer. A big wind took it down around 1948. The house burned down early — around 1890."

"Your dad must have been a prosperous farmer," Lish said. "Unlike a lot of other farmers, it appears that he didn't have to sell the timber off his land to make ends meet."

"My dad struggled for every penny he made," Thalia said. "There wasn't a Logan born that would allow The Mark to be logged."

"The timber must be valuable," Noah said. "Some of these trees are far more than two hundred years old."

"The decision to keep Hunter's Mark as pristine wilderness was a pact made to someone generations ago ... and kept through to my generation," Thalia said.

"Know what I think?" Noah said, pouring coffee from the thermos. "No one owns the earth — the land. They are born with the right to breathe its air, drink its water, and eat from the abundance of its land, but have no justifiable claim to own any of its soil — tillable, rocky, water-covered, or otherwise. They are to hold all in trust for the next generation."

"There are a few of us who still hold the land as sacred and who believe in the stewardship of it for generations to come," Thalia agreed. "But, when pieces of paper denoting ownership of patches of land became de rigueur, it caused a complete new way of thinking about territory."

Wanting to make her thoughts known, Lish interrupted. "If it were still an as-was situation — no papers necessary — a few would run roughshod over the masses. They'd take the land, by force or intimidation, and grind those who hold it precious into the dirt."

"Well stated, Lish," Thalia said.

"Given that argument, paper ownership does have merit," Noah agreed. "It's people that have no respect for the land. They don't realize that they'll be dust one day, part of the very land they're so disrespectful of, or covet so much."

Thalia put finger to her lips to indicate Noah and Lish should be quiet. She listened then said, "What do you hear?"

Noah, closing his eyes, concentrated on identifying the sounds around him ... house sparrows twittered under the eaves ... a bluejay scolded from a tree ... leaves rustled in a gentle breeze ... a motor ran in the valley ... a faint rhythmic ... howling?

Lish let her back rest against the logs, closed her eyes, was silent for a moment, then said, "I hear yowling but I can't tell where it's coming from. Today it sounds almost human."

"I hear CAT all the time," Thalia said. "It could be whispers on the wind, a breeze howling through a knothole, the wind whistling along the escarpment, the ghost of John Logan regretting that he jumped from the Knob. Or, it could be Dago:ji'."

Noah glanced at Thalia, a strange look on his face. "You just said an Indian word for a cat."

"Yes, I did," Thalia agreed. "This forest preserve is full of wondrous things, if you know where to look for them. But how did you know it was an Indian word, Noah?"

"It's part of my life," Noah said. "I'll tell you about it sometime."

Friday, June 29

As far as Lish was concerned, Thalia was acting a little strange. After she returned from the cabin, the woman shut herself in her study, coming out during the day for meals only. She ate little, said less, and seemed anxious to get back to solitary confinement.

Lish amused herself by wandering around the house and yard. She fed the cats, made egg salad for sandwiches, and heated soup for lunch — Thalia appreciated that. For supper, Lish warmed up a pot of lamb stew and attempted to make biscuits. They were dismal failures, but Thalia ate them anyway and said nice things about her cooking.

The next day, Lish wandered into the parlour. Thalia's extensive library was housed in floor-to-ceiling bookcases that took up two full walls. Nineteenth- and early-twentieth-century travel tomes with lavish line drawings shared space with old, well-thumbed Eaton's and Simpsons catalogues. There was a large selection of history books on more recent periods. One shelf was completely devoted to periodicals about clothing. Three shelves held paperbacks — the popular love-them-or-lose-them stories that so many women liked to read. Many of these were the works of Annetta C. Nagol and Wilda G. Neves.

One parlour wall had windows that overlooked the front porch and valley. A second wall's centrepiece was a fireplace with a fancy Victorian marble surround and mantel. Above it hung a huge oil painting of Isola Bella and the seventeenth-century Palazzo Borremeo with its beautiful gardens of terraces, fountains, and statues — a scene that Lish well knew. Four years before, she had stayed at a hotel on the shore directly opposite the island.

The room's furnishings were as eclectic as Thalia's clothing. A little shiny copper pot was displayed in a glass case on a table near one of two comfortable, overstuffed Victorian chairs and a horsehair settee. A triangular curio cabinet that held an odd assortment of knick-knacks stood in a corner. Another set of shelves held a collection of china vases.

I may as well read, Lish thought. She pulled a promising title from the paperbacks — *Loralee's Last Love* — and made herself comfortable on the front porch. As these stories go, this is not bad, she mused, after reading the third chapter. After supper Lish chose another title — *Angel's Fury*. This story had a little more depth to it and some really good dialogue.

The next morning Lish rose before daybreak. She sat on the front porch, wrapped in a blanket, pencil and scribbler close by. Adam and Eve slept at her feet. Birdsong began around four in the morning, heralding the sublime quietude of the sunrise. The eastern horizon, first a mass of gold and orange, broke sharply into pale blue. Pink-tinged clouds turned to purple on the western horizon. To the north, everything was grey.

Had she been so caught up in her career that she'd forgotten how to appreciate nature, enjoy life, Lish wondered. She had climbed the rungs of success under her own steam, but forgot that some companies still owned the ladder. So, where did she stand now? Yule made sure that doors were subtly closed. Should she reconsider the Detroit offer?...

A doe, with a fawn following close behind, picked her way along the river path. Charlie walked from his house toward his drive shed. He stopped once to look toward Granite.

Even if Charlie does see me, I'm an insignificant dot on the landscape, Lish thought. I know for sure that I must never doubt my actions and abilities. What sage advice would Granny give? *There's no difference between a stumbling block and a stepping stone but perception and attitude.* I can be challenged by a crisis or challenged by a dream. What will it be?

When it was light enough to see, Lish put pen to paper. What she began to write in the scribbler gave her immediate pleasure. She began by describing the sunrise: "the morning air is so soft and still it amplifies the cat's purring to the point it sounds like a small motor running on the porch." Across the valley, Charlie was on his tractor, heading to the west field. What had Thalia said? *Charlie's days have as many hours as anyone else's. He just puts more into his than most people.*

Lish's pen flew across the page. "His strong body and quick mind hide a generous man with a huge capacity for love and life. His huge hands are as gentle as kitten's paws when necessity dictates need." Words flowed from her pen like water under the bridge. "His compliments are kisses from the lips of his heart."

Thalia, watching from her study window, noticed with pleasure that Lish was writing. But, Thalia thought, what is her connection to The Mark? Why does she interpret what she hears as CAT? There are far more questions than answers at the moment. It's best to let Granite and CAT work their charms in their own way. I must never compromise time to accommodate curiosity. I give Adam and Eve a few days to find their way home when they decide to roam. I have to do the same for people

Lish was in the middle of recording a vivid, recurring dream when she heard tapping on glass. Thalia was at the window, her hands poised as though she was eating. Lish nodded and gathered her things.

When Joan arrived around 7:30 a.m., Thalia and she retreated to the study. Lish heard the telltale click, click, click of an electric typewriter. Curiosity chewed at her but she dared not breach Thalia's private lair. As Lish dried dishes, a question surfaced. What inspired her to wake before dawn with an urge to write? Why on earth would she pen such intimate, sexy details about Charlie Barnes?

Lish couldn't settle down after breakfast to write or knit. She hiked to Spirit Rock and examined its surface once more. Although some areas of the stone looked like they'd been worked with a hammer and chisel, there was neither rhyme nor reason to the markings. They seemed randomly cut. A sharp whistle got her attention. Lish waved to Charlie across the valley. Had he stopped work to watch her? No, he was waiting for Noah, who was running across the field.

Back at the house again, Lish leafed through a few cookbooks. If it was her lot to make sure that lunch and supper were on the table, she may as well feed the masses properly. Cooking was not something Lish had done much of. Restaurants were all too convenient in the city.

Lish checked the cupboards, fridge, and pantry for supplies, then surprised herself by making a macaroni and cheese casserole for lunch and a tolerable-looking coffee cake for dessert. She was peeling vegetables for a pot roast supper when Noah arrived.

"Charlie says to say hello. He handed me the paper and said that I had to read Mulmur Murmurings before I gave it to Thalia. Jeff says to remind you about the lunch date at Georgie's. By the way, you're looking terribly domesticated," he said, settling into a chair by the table. "The cake looks good."

"Don't even think of wanting a piece," Lish said. "Joan and Thalia are so ... involved, I needed something to keep my mind off ... to keep me busy. What's so important about the column?"

"I'm not sure," Noah said, opening the paper. "Let's see, 'at evening choir practice this week a bat entertained the idea of landing in Minnie G.'s hair bun to prove once and for all that the lady can hit the high notes when she wants to.'"

"Dunnit doth have a sense of humour," Lish said.

"Oops," Noah said. "This hits close to home ... in more ways than one. 'Rumour is that the call of a rare and seldom seen Curlew bird was heard in Hornings Mills on Saturday night.'"

"That's an odd way to say that you sang at the social."

"Someone is prodding with a little stick to see what might flutter out," Noah said. "You're mentioned again. Listen to this: 'At the same shindig, the Lovely Damsel proved her worth by endeavouring to dance the night away with all manner of Valley and Springs scoundrels. None complained about the attention."'

"The writer piques my interest," Lish said. "The way Thalia's clothesline is situated, binoculars would be needed to scope things out. We know one thing for sure: he — or she — was in Hornings Mills."

"Half township was at the social," Noah said. "I wonder what the ladies are up to? Should we breach their moat to deliver the paper?"

"I've tried several things," Lish said. "When I knock, Joan answers. The way the door opens, you can't even get a peak inside."

"Is there a reason for all this domesticity other than the need to feed the ladies?" Noah asked, picking up a carrot.

"It keeps my mind off a dream that I had last night ... about walls and an antlered deer," she replied, tossing potato peelings into a compost pail. "This isn't the first time I've had the same dream. I started to write it down this morning but was interrupted. Now I'm not sure that I should record it. It's so personal."

Noah bit his lip, then chose his words carefully. Lish had shared his dream! He didn't understand the significance of it. Obviously, Lish didn't either. The dream haunted him, drove him to distraction. "If you talk about it, I might be able to help. What exactly do you remember?"

"You have to promise not to laugh," she said.

"I will take what you say seriously," Noah said.

I've nothing to lose, Lish thought. "In this dream, I sat at a fire near a crude shelter in a place that was ... maybe a canyon? A stream ran through it. I saw fish jumping. There was a garden. I remember seeing corn ..."

Noah was so nervous he had to do something. He got up and filled the kettle. My God, he thought, Lish is having my dream. "Go on."

"I leave this place in the strangest way. I climb on the back of an antlered deer. I don't know where I go or how long it takes. During the ride, I give things away."

"What? What do you give?" Noah's voice sounded strained.

"I don't know. It fit into the palm of my hand. Maybe it was part of me?"

"Were you taking it out of a pot, or a pouch?" Noah asked.

"I can't remember. Why do you ask?"

"You're going to think this incredible but I have the same dream. I think that I finally hand over a small ... stone, but I don't know to whom."

"How long have you been having the dream?"

Noah shook his head. "Perhaps six months? There is an old legend .... Let's just say that eventually I spoke with my father about a legend he told me years ago that involved a deer and a cat. Last month I found myself in some ... difficulty and decided that it was a good time to follow the legend's trail."

"I've not heard, or read, any legend or myth about such a dream," she said. "I do think that this place is influencing my thoughts."

"The odd thing is that last night I could have sworn that a large cat-like animal was right outside the cabin door. Thalia's always talking about CAT. I wonder if she has the dream?" he asked.

"Come on. Let's try to tempt the ladies with a pot of tea and some cookies. There's more at work here then pure chance. I think it's time for a little chat," Lish said.

She fixed a tea tray then knocked on the study door.

Joan answered and peeked around the door.

"Could we have a word with Thalia?" Noah asked.

"Now is not a good time," Joan said. She closed the door, then opened it again. "That was rude of me. I'll take the tray.

Thank you for thinking of us. Perhaps Thalia will talk with you both, later?"

"Let's walk down to Spirit Rock," Lish said. "That's where I heard the cat really close by. For the amount of time you spend around there, you seem fascinated by it, too."

"I'm sure the stone is important," Noah said. It appears in my dream frequently."

Thalia, taking a break from her work, noticed Lish and Noah in the valley examining the stone. "Joan, I can't put the inevitable off for too long. I'm going to have to talk with them soon."

"Are you not taking a chance, Thalia? What do you know about those two young people that pertains to The Mark?"

"Not much, but I suspect a lot," Thalia said. "You know me, with my very active mind. I'll leave it up to Lish to discover if Noah has any secrets. I'll trust Charlie to find out if Lish is being dishonest. I'll give them all another few days before answering any questions. Where were we?"

"We're almost finished editing chapter ten," Joan said.

Saturday, June 30

Feeling the eyes of the regulars on her, Lish fidgeted with her wristwatch. Jeff was late. He didn't seem like the type of guy who'd stand a girl up. What should she do, order lunch? Wait another ten minutes then go look for him? To make matters worse, Bug Eye and The Fetch were seated in the corner table, just waiting for her to say something.

"He's coming," Georgie said as she undulated past Lish's table in one of her most revealing sundresses to deliver the tab to the pair. "I saw him in the parking lot just now."

Jeff entered the store, looked around, and made a beeline for Lish's table.

"You're running late," Georgie observed, heading back to the counter.

Standing with his back to the corner table, Jeff said, "Stick around a minute, Georgie. I need a diversion so that I can check a car. I don't want the pair behind me to leave the store before you see me at the window."

"Got yah," Georgie said. "You want a ruckus to draw attention away from you breaking into a car."

"Correct."

Lish only had time to say, "I don't believe I heard that," before Georgie turned on her, raised her voice several octaves and said. "So, you heard me. I don't want you hanging around my husband."

"Me, hanging around with ... Hank?" Lish stammered. "You've got to be kidding." But as the words left her mouth, she realized that she was the fall guy in the ruckus. From the corner of her eye, she noticed that Jeff had left. Bug Eye and The Fetch were gathering their gear. Lish stood and backed toward the door to cut off their escape route. "Well, if you'd pay more attention to hubby, maybe he wouldn't graze greener pastures," Lish said, raising her voice to match Georgie's.

"If you weren't such a pussycat, he'd not take a second look at you." Georgie was in a fine theatrical fettle.

"Me, a pussycat? At least I don't flaunt my goodies to half a county of willing oglers. While the cat's away, the mouse does play," Lish said, basing her lines on what she'd heard about Georgie.

"Meow, meow," Bud said, causing the Delaney brothers, who were enjoying the free show, to laugh hilariously.

"Stay outta our fight." Georgie circled so that she could position herself closer to Lish. That pushed Lish toward the counter, her back to the Delaney brothers.

"Well," said WGD, getting into the ruckus "If you weren't such a slut, Hank wouldn't have to go looking for better."

"Who are you calling a slut, little man?"

"There's you, her, and the lady in the corner," WGD said. "Do your own figuring."

"He does have a point," Lish said.

"You lily-livered little city witch. Where do you get off thinking me a slut?"

"Wait," Lish said. "WGD called you a slut, not me. But if the shoe fits." This ruckus is getting just a little too personal, she thought. I detect some malice in Georgie's voice. She glanced toward the window, looking for Jeff. "So, what are you going to do about me, sis?"

Georgie reached behind her for a missile. The pie rack was handy, with a full selection of sticky desserts. "If you think you're so sexy, wear this!" Georgie, who pitched for the local women's softball team, grabbed the nearest pie and threw it with both force and accuracy.

Lish's reflexes were quick. She ducked, just in time. The pie sailed over her head and hit WGD in the face. Except for the ticking of the clock, the room was silent. Bug Eye and The Fetch sat, their mouths open, in disbelief at what they were seeing.

Georgie, hands on her hips, waited. Either the entire assembly would erupt into a pie fight or they'd see the humour in the situation. She could feel the hot breath of the porchers, who'd crowded through the door, on the back of her neck.

WGD stuck his tongue out, licked his lips, and said. "Damn good lemon pie, Georgie. Too bad it went to waste." Tom, Dick, and Harry roared. Glenn laughed so hard he started to hiccup.

Lish saw Jeff at the window. "Truce," she said, holding her hand out to Georgie. "Most men aren't worth fighting over."

"Darn," Bud said. "It's over? I ain't had so much excitement since I went to see a Three Stooges movie down in Orangeville."

"Well, maybe it wasn't you I saw with Hank." Georgie shook Lish's hand. "Good show, eh? I didn't really mean anything that I said."

"Neither did I." Lish put her arm around Georgie and said quietly. "Whatever Jeff was doing, he's finished."

"A round of pie for everyone," Georgie said as she headed for the counter. "All but WGD. He's wearing his slice. Didn't your mother show you how to eat pie properly, my man?"

"I dang well can't remember if she did." WGD licked his lips.

"Did I miss something?" Jeff asked innocently as he came through the door.

* * * * * * *

Later, at the garage, Jeff shared his haul with Lish. "Those two must be working for some publication," he said, looking at Bug Eye's business card. "They're trying to build a story."

"About whom?"

Jeff pulled a couple of packets of photographs out of his pocket. "It appears to be Noah they want in their lens. All of these pictures are of him. I'll bet that he didn't know they were being taken, either. Have a look. Noah and you on the street in Fergus, Noah holding your hand in Elora, Noah at the stone, Noah crossing the bowstring bridge in the wagon. But why Noah?"

"Perhaps we should ask Noah," Lish said. "What are you going to do with the pictures?

"The same thing I'm going to do with the roll of film that I took out of their camera."

"You shouldn't have broken into their car."

"I didn't break in," he said. "They left it unlocked. I just helped myself. Besides, you're the last person that asked them to hand over their pictures. They'll suspect you did it."

"They'll know that it wasn't me. They'll take into consideration the fact that the pictures were in the car when they went in for lunch, gone afterwards. They know that they came into the store after I did. I didn't leave before them. I was being verbally abused by Georgie, in plain sight of the pair of them."

"Boy, you've thought your position through quite thoroughly," Jeff said.

"Should we figure a way to give the pictures back?" she asked.

"Hell no," Jeff replied. "Snakes don't deserve a second chance. I'll just chop, chop, chop them into little pieces and burn everything in the trash barrel. Or, just maybe, for fun, I'll cut the faces out of the pictures then mail 'em back to the address on the business card. After we find out what those two are up to, for sure, someone should run them out of the Valley. Let's go see what Noah has to say for himself. Are you coming?"

"I wouldn't miss this adventure for love nor money."

* * * * * * *

Noah's afternoon nap was interrupted by someone shaking him. When he opened his eyes, Jeff and Lish were seated on his bed.

"So, my friend, why are people spying on you, taking rolls of clandestine pictures?" Jeff lay the photographs on Noah's chest.

"I guess the cat's out of the bag," Noah said, rubbing his face then running his fingers through thick black hair. "Have you ever heard of a country music singer by the name of Jason Curlew?"

164

"I knew it!" Lish exclaimed.

"You're Curlew, the country and western singer?" Jeff said. "You cut a couple of real good records. Your career was on a real roll. You were invited to go down Nashville-way to play a few gigs."

"One and the same. Noah's my middle name."

"What's the last thing I heard about you?" Jeff scratched his chin. "You finished a gig in Toronto and had one in Hamilton the next night then a weekend at one of the big hotels in Buffalo. But you just dropped out of sight. Your publicist said that you were called away suddenly on ... family business. That was about three weeks ago. What are you doing here?"

"I'm here because of a damn dream," Noah replied. "And letters that Thalia wrote to Jimmy Curlew, my grandfather."

"Letters?" Lish said.

"Letters about CAT and hallowed ground, letters about land and an old deed, one letter about something Jimmy did that really hurt Thalia ..."

"Did you bring them with you?" Jeff said.

"I didn't. I'm not sure anyone should read them," Noah said.

"Fair enough," Jeff said .

"Shouldn't you tell Thalia that you have them?" Lish said. "There's nothing in them that she wouldn't know. She wrote them."

"Thalia doesn't know that I'm Jimmy Curlew's grandson," Noah said. "That might be a shock."

"Perhaps we'd better speak to Charlie," Lish suggested. "He'll know what to do."

Jeff agreed. "I'll drive us over to his farm."

* * * * * * *

Charlie sat, feet on the porch rail, a bottle of Scotch by his side. "I'll be damned," he said. "So, Jimmy Curlew was yer granddaddy. He was quite the lad. From what I understand, he blew into Seven Springs, knocked Thalia right off her feet, then blew right out again fer the north. Thalia got him out of her system and married Frank Russo."

"But she wrote to him *after* she married Frank," Noah said.

"Well, it's up to Thalia to tell her story," Charlie said. "I've blabbed too much already." Charlie poured himself a dram, drank it, then passed the bottle and his glass. "Whiskey'll kill the germs. Have a slug. It helps the arthritis, not that you young people would need to worry about that."

Noah and Jeff took Charlie up on his offer.

"How be I talk to Thalia first, say tomorrow, after church?" Charlie offered. "I ken tell you som'pin though. You're interested in the boulder over the river there, aren't you? I'll fill you in on that. It makes a good story."

"The rock is intriguing," Lish said. "It appears to have been moved to the site. It's such a prominent landmark."

"It does have a unique shape," Noah agreed.

"You're reading too much into the stone," Charlie said. "It's always been there, one of God's little unexplained surprises. Blue Heathen, it's called. It isn't like other stones in the Valley. But there are plenty small ones like it up on top of the escarpment. Over the years, a few of those have fallen from the bluffs."

"I've never seen a large Blue Heathen," Lish admitted. "But if I recall, Dad told me that it is a very hard granite, not the type of rock that anyone could easily etch on."

"How would he know?" Jeff inquired.

"Dad was a prospector," Lish explained. "He knew his rocks. He had boxes of samples that he showed me."

"The rock probably got the marks a few thousand years ago, if you can believe what the scientists say about how this part of the continent evolved. What's important about the spot is not what's on top — not the stone. It's what's underneath — beside the Heathen."

"Someone's buried there?" Lish asked.

"More than one, as a matter of fact," Charlie replied. "Jeff, you've heard all this before. The stone marks a burial ground: hallowed ground, ancestral land. There's a bit written down about the burials. I understand that there are three Indian graves: two men, Hoshaphat and Gazhagayns, and a woman by the name of Nibish. Hunter Logan's buried there too, close by his dog, Moon."

"It's an Indian burial ground," Noah said. "I should have guessed."

"Blue Heathen marks the grave of heathens," Jeff said.

"Jeff, hold yer tongue or some day it'll git you into trouble," Charlie said. "They're Noah's ancestors. If Noah is related to Jimmy Curlew, he has Indian blood running through his veins."

"So, the singer Jason Curlew is a full-blooded Indian," Jeff said. "That would be big news to your fans."

"I am Ojibway-Cree with strong Seneca-Iroquois blood running through my veins, and proud of it." Noah glanced toward Lish. "You haven't said much, Lish."

Of course, she thought; the black hair, dark eyes, respect for the land. That should have given his lineage away. "I'm just amazed at the little surprises this valley possesses," she said.

"Oh, you'll be amazed when you do find out just what secrets these hills hide," Charlie assured her. "Thalia has mentioned Hunter Logan? Hunter's mate was Nibish, after Hoshaphat was ... died. Nibish raised two boys, Manchild, who was Hoshaphat's child, and John, who was Hunter's son.

John is Thalia's ancestor. Manchild is your ancestor, Noah — same mother, different fathers."

Charlie avoided all mention of a murder, a copper pot, and a golden idol called CAT. It was up to Thalia, the elder, to tell that story. He wasn't sure that Jeff had ever been made party to the information. "After Manchild left the area, no one knew what happened to him — until Jimmy Curlew came along, that is. That information is going to have to satisfy you until Thalia feels like talking. Don't pressure her at the moment. She's real busy with a ... deadline."

CHAPTER 4
The Week of July 1–July 7

Sunday, July 1

"It is a special day with a potluck planned to celebrate Dominion Day, but I can understand why you're not coming to church with me," Thalia said. "If I was capable of doing it, a hike along the river would be preferable on such a pleasant July day. The trudge to the cabin aggravated my leg. I've had to take some pretty strong medication to deaden the pain."

"I thought that I'd pack a lunch for Noah and I," Lish said.

"It's nice enough for a swim," Thalia suggested. "There's a wonderful swimming hole up near the glen. I'm sure that Noah in his wanderings has already found it."

"I didn't bring a swimsuit."

"I might be able to help with that situation."

Thalia rooted around in a dresser drawer, then handed Lish a 1920s woollen woman's bathing suit. "I just knew that it would come in handy one day. It's scratchy to wear though. Do have fun. By the time you get back, I'll be in my study. I'd appreciate not being disturbed."

"When can we sit down and chat ... seriously?" Lish asked.

"I promise we'll do that in a day or two. But I've a lot on my mind at the moment. I really am under some pressure, my dear."

Lish saw Thalia, Charlie, and Joan off to church — Thalia in a classic 1950s summer suit, complete with feather hat. The older woman leaned heavily on Charlie's arm, her hip sway very pronounced.

With Adam and Eve trailing behind, Lish hiked down the trail to meet Noah at the rock. The four-legged snoops soon lost interest in Lish and went off to hunt lunch.

Noah took the food pack, added it to his own haversack, and suggested they walk to the bridge, then hike up the other side of the river to the shallow ford. "Charlie wants you to see the wildflower meadow up close. He says that at this time of the year, it's beautiful."

As they followed a well-worn path downriver, through a large raspberry thicket, Lish said, "Thalia told me that this was an old Indian trail that went from Lake Huron to Lake Ontario. She and Charlie are trying to preserve the section of it that runs through their properties."

On the other side of the river, Noah and Lish walked the bank and crossed Charlie's cow pasture. They traversed the bottom of a hayfield, beyond which lay a meadow where Lish stood in acres of nodding white daisies, Queen Anne's lace, black-eyed Susan, soapwort, mauve and white mallow, tansy, wild dill, purple status, and ox-eyed daisies.

"I've never seen anything as pristine as this," Lish said. "Father would have loved it."

"Charlie doesn't let the cattle graze here. It hasn't been ploughed in years. It's his salute to The Mark. Thalia loves wild-flowers. Look. Over there. The Knob." On the opposite side of the river, the limestone bluff loomed above Vale of CAT.

"The tops of those trees are the ones that we looked down on from The Knob," Lish said.

"Consider what this entire valley looked like before man

cleared it," Noah said. "Imagine trees as ancient as those as far as the eye could see — from the river to the bottom of the escarpment, from one end of the valley to the other, and up on top of the ridge, too."

"How destructive man can be," Lish said.

"People have to eat," Noah said. "The only way they can is to clear land, plant crops, and harvest them."

"I can understand that. But I can't understand wanton destruction that is not related to food production, but has a lot to do with making money."

"We do think along the same lines," Noah said. "Come on. The ford's just over there."

Noah helped Lish cross the river, pushed through dense growth, and led her by the hand through a stand of mature arborvitae, the air fragrant with their scent. "Just think, my ancestors probably snapped lower branches off these trees to use them as fire starters," he said. Damp ground was thick with moss. Squirrels scolded the intruders. Cedar Waxwings flitted from tree to tree, uneasy in the company of humans.

The path meandered through the majestic old growth forest toward the escarpment. "One never leaves footprints in Thalia's Vale of CAT," Noah said, bending to touch the soft spongy layer on the forest floor.

"It's like a cathedral, Noah. Even the lighting reminds me of one, so much so that I feel we should whisper. Look. Only the tops of the trees are affected by the wind. Although there's excellent timber here, I can understand why Thalia's family never allowed this to be cut, even if, at some point, they needed the money. Look at the size of the trees — hundreds of board feet of valuable timber."

"Now you're sounding like a slash-and-burn lumber baron," Noah said.

"I don't mean to," Lish said. "I was just making an observation. Think of this, Noah, if Thalia is in financial difficulty ...." Her voice trailed off as a familiar sound echoed through the forest. "Listen! Do you hear that? It's a cat, meowing as though it's calling to its kittens. Listen."

Noah listened. "Maybe one of Thalia's cats followed us."

"I don't think so. It wouldn't cross the river," Lish reasoned, looking around.

"Do you know what this reminds me of?" Noah said. "A sacred grove where my ancestors would have gone to speak with Gitche Manitou. The smell reminds me of the north. I want you to see the spring, Lish. It's at the base of the bluff, directly below The Knob. Well, look at this." Noah pointed to recent scratches on a tree.

"What would make those?" Lish asked him.

"The scratches are about the right height for either bear cub or large cat," Noah answered. "If it is a big cat, we won't see it. It will slink into the shadows and disappear. Do you see where that shaft of sunlight is striking the rock? That's the spring."

Before approaching the spring, Noah checked the ground for prints. "There are so many tracks, I can't tell what-from-which." Water, bubbling from the ground, filled a large natural rock bowl. Light beams from the noonday sun, directly overhead, danced on the water. The spring sparkled as though its surface was strewn with diamonds.

"Charlie calls this Grotto Spring. The first time I saw this place, I felt the need to pray," Noah said. "Do you know how long it's been since structured prayer entered my life?"

When Lish looked into the spring, she didn't feel the need to pray. She had the feeling that eyes were watching her. She stared into the water for a moment then turned to look into the forest. What was that flash of tan? A deer ... a person ... the photographer? "Noah, we should go back to the river. I'm not so sure we haven't been followed."

Noah looked around. "I don't see anyone, but if you want to go, we can. You're not impressed with the Grotto?"

"It's beautiful but ...." Lish found it hard to put her feelings into words. "I don't think that I was meant to be here — not just yet. There's something about the spring that ... that bothers me. Now, that statement must have sounded stupid."

"Not at all," Noah said. "Sacred places demand their own time of a person. I don't believe that we've been followed but I do think that we should enjoy a cool dip. There's a great swimming hole upriver a bit. I brought a bathing suit. Did you?"

"Thalia was thinking for me — and you. She gave me one to wear." Lish replied. "She said that you'd probably found the spot. The Lord alone knows what the suit will look like on me, though. Her clothing tastes run from interesting to outlandish. She is an amazing woman, Noah."

"We could bath nude."

"Not on your life!" Lish said. "Wouldn't that make a juicy bit of news and picture? Jason Curlew bathing nude. We can't dismiss the fact that Bug Eye and The Fetch are still trying to get you on film."

"More like, Jason Curlew bathing nude with his girlfriend," Noah said. "We would have seen them if they'd followed us this far upriver. It's not the easiest place to find. Let's just try to enjoy ourselves today. I'm up for that dip. Are you?"

Later, the two lolled on lush grass near the river. "What more can we ask for," Noah said. "We've enjoyed good company, a nice swim, warm sunshine."

Peace of mind, Lish thought but said instead, "I've had a lovely time, Noah."

Noah rolled to his side and threw a stone toward the river. "Are you going to tell me why you're here, Lish? You know far more about me than I know about you."

Lish told him basically what she'd divulged to Thalia. The word *fired* was far easier to say the second time around.

"So, the bastards gave you the big kiss-off. You feel badly about it. You shouldn't. You didn't compromise your principles. They did. You're now free to pursue whatever you want to in life. You don't need their type of people, Lish. Things happen for a reason."

"But I didn't really answer your question. Why am I at Granite? You already know about my jar of dirt. Why didn't I end up at any of the other names on the label — Algoma Mills, Sault Ste. Marie, Port Arthur, Armstrong, or back in Perth? The answer is simple. I don't know ... yet," Lish said. "On a different tack, would you listen to a theory I have?"

"Run it past me, Lish."

"Thalia said that she had a lot on her mind. Charlie told us not to disturb her as she had a lot to think about. I wonder if her dilemma has something to do with Northlands Development."

"She's so attached to the land, so negative about Northlands," Noah said.

Lish sat up, moved closer to Noah, and spoke in confidence, as though the land had ears. "How does Thalia keep The Mark? How does she financially assist Maggie, Wee Jimmy, Georgie, and half the other people in Seven Springs?"

"She gives the impression that she has money," Noah said.

"What if she doesn't? What if she's in financial difficulty and really under pressure to sell this land. If a company like Campbell, O'Hearn & Yule is in any way involved with Northlands ... COY is expert at pressuring older people into parting with their land. What if Thalia wants to preserve The Mark but is forced to sell certain parts of it because of all her obligations?"

Noah pulled himself up to sit beside Lish. "If you're right, I don't think there's much we can do about it. It's not our problem, Lish."

"I'm not so sure about that."

"Don't draw too many conclusions, or ask too many questions, Lish. The answers might be hard to take."

Lish felt Noah's closeness and half-hoped that he would put his arm around her. She needed human contact; a gentle touch, a friendly gesture. "You walked away from obligations, Noah. You were obviously looking for something. Have you found *it* yet?"

"Whatever *it* is, I'm more comfortable with *it,* and myself, at the Hunter cabin than anywhere else in my rather structured life."

"You simply walked off the stage one evening and ended up here."

"Yes," Noah said. "An unusual move, Lish. I love singing and am at the pinnacle of my career. Bolting the way I did was uncharacteristic. I just felt that I needed ... time."

"To do what?"

"To sort out a few things," Noah said. "Would you believe that I've taken up painting again? It's been ten years since I painted a picture. When you and Thalia came to the cabin, I hid my work so that you wouldn't ask questions. I suppose that I'm expressing myself on canvas as well as in words. But you wouldn't believe what's beginning to haunt my pictures: an antlered deer and an odd-looking cat."

"You feel the need to paint the dream?"

"It appears that way. And another thing: the cabin has inspired me to write songs, too. It's got to be the cabin. It just reverberates with inspiration. Look, let's change the subject — it's a touchy one with me at the moment. Tell me what you can about Northlands."

"If I remember correctly, it's a massive land investment project that involves a large ski resort. I didn't realize that Northlands was proposed for this particular area until Charlie mentioned the name the day we were fishing."

"Jeff says that Northlands has met with some success purchasing land around here."

"From what Tom Delaney told me, the developers need all of Thalia's holdings and Charlie's, too. Tom says that they're desperate to get their hands on The Slope."

"That would put ski runs right through Granite, Spirit Rock, and the graves. Remember, Charlie said that he attended a meeting in Toronto," Noah said. "You don't think that he's saying one thing but doing another ..."

"Although such a large development does need people who are willing to sell their land, and people who are willing to buy into the project, I find it hard to believe that Charlie would sell Thalia short," Lish said. "But what about Thalia?"

"Thalia is devoted to The Mark, but, as you say, pressure might be on her to sell. She's elderly. She's alone."

"Thalia's eccentric, a little unusual, thinks along different lines, loveable, got a solid head on her shoulders," Lish said. "I'm intrigued by her."

"I've never met a person quite like the lady." Noah draped his arm casually over Lish's shoulders. That was, he decided, as far as he wanted to push his luck. Another time; another place .... "What's the situation with her son? Is he trying to dislodge her from Granite by telling people that she's crazy, incapable of taking care of herself? She's never talked to me about him. She seems appreciative that both of us are around. She treats us like a son and daughter, rather than guest and summer help."

"Given the age difference, we're more like grandchildren," Lish said.

"If we're into theories," Noah said, "think about this in terms of Thalia's son. Thalia Logan was sweet on my grandfather, Jimmy Curlew. Could there have been a little hanky-panky while he was here?"

Of course, Lish thought. That was a distinct possibility. Thalia's ancestry certainly influences her keen appreciation of her land. What is bred in the bone is born in the blood.

"You'll have to ask Thalia about her relationship with Jimmy Curlew. She promised to answer a few of our questions in a day or two. I'm sure she'll have a few of her own to ask. We'll have to be patient, Noah."

"Patience is one of my lesser virtues," Noah said.

"What are Thalia and Joan doing locked in the study? Writing letters? Planning for a future without Granite? Trying to figure out how to save The Mark? She also locks the door to her bedroom. Keeps the keys around her neck."

"You didn't break her trust by trying the door?" Noah asked.

"What do you take me for?" Lish replied. "Of course not!"

"I've one more question, Lish. It needs asking and it's not exactly a nice one."

"Well, ask it," Lish said.

"Given that you have a connection with COY, which might have a connection to Northlands ...." Noah hesitated then said, "Who says that you're not working for them? Perhaps you've been sent here to do some serious damage? I mean, can the collective *we* really believe that something as simple as a jar of dirt brought you to Seven Springs?"

Lish had been expecting the question for some time. She thought Charlie might be the first one to ask it. "Thalia, Charlie, and you will have to trust me, Noah. I *did* once work for COY. I have no intentions of re-establishing contact with the company."

"Fair enough," Noah said.

"I have a question for you. How does the collective *we* know that you're not here to institute a land grab yourself, on behalf of your ancestors? As you say, you believe the land should belong to no one."

"I have the best interests for The Mark at heart," Noah said.

"Ah, but do they include Thalia and Charlie?"

"I have to trust you. You have to trust me," Noah said. He checked the angle of the sun and began to collect towels. "Look, I'm expecting a call from my agent around three o'clock. I gave him Charlie's number. Would you like to go for a buggy ride afterwards? Charlie likes Juniper to have a run every once in a while. We can do a concession road or two."

"That beats hanging around Granite wondering when to make Thalia supper; or horror-of-horrors, feeling a need to do the dusting."

"I'd say our lady of the cottage of lilacs and laughter has you totally domesticated."

"Where did you hear that name?" Lish asked

"From the old man at the store. You know, I was out that way with the buggy the other day. I thought the old fellow would like to take a ride. When I asked about him, the only thing I got was a blank look from the chick behind the counter. The girl said that she sees the old guy around the place occasionally. He likes to sit out front of the store and watch the cars go by. She thinks that he lives upcountry a bit."

Lish packed the picnic leftovers in Noah's haversack so that he could enjoy at least one meal without having to put a fire in the hearth at the cabin. "You surprise me, Noah. I half expected some hanky-panky this afternoon from a well-travelled man of the world like yourself."

"I'm not that sort of guy," Noah said. "Maybe I'm used goods. Maybe you deserve better."

"Maybe in the end you'll have to leave that sort of decision up to the woman. And personally, before you bring up the subject of your Indian ancestry being a factor, that doesn't matter to me," Lish assured him. "If I love someone, I love them unconditionally."

"I wish my former wife had felt the same way," Noah said. "Come on. Let's see if Charlie's home from the potluck."

Monday, July 2

It began to rain at daybreak — a cool drizzle that turned the valley into a study of grey. When Lish woke and looked out the window, she could barely make out the bridge and Charlie's barn. Cattle grazing in the front pasture faded in and out of the fog. She stretched, yawned, then returned to her warm bed, snuggled deeper under the covers and fell asleep again. Pots banging in the kitchen woke her the second time. She looked at the alarm clock then groped for her bathrobe. "Eight o'clock! How could I have slept in?" Dressing quickly, she hurried downstairs.

"I woke you, didn't I, dear? I didn't want to disturb you but a stack of pots fell off the shelf," Thalia explained. "I've already eaten breakfast. There's oatmeal in the small pot on the back of the wood stove. I managed to get a fire going to take the dampness out of the kitchen."

"I'm supposed to make you breakfast," Lish said. "I'm sorry. I don't usually sleep in."

"There's always a first time," Thalia said. "Could you carry a cup of coffee to the study for me? My leg is so aggravating this morning, it's put me right off being a independent woman. I found out the hard way once that sway-hip and hot coffee don't go well together. It's a good rain though — the kind that puts inches onto the corn. It's the sort of day that you should bake a spice cake. Charlie loves spice cake. Maybe you can knit some inches too?"

Lish laughed. "You're telling me that you expect Charlie, and he expects spice cake."

"For sure. He always does when it rains like this. You'll have to add wood to the stove now and then. Open the kitchen door if you get too hot. Adam and Eve like to sleep on that blanket when the stove's on. Watch you don't step on them."

"You'll call if you need anything," Lish said, following Thalia into her study with the cup of coffee.

"Don't notice the mess. Just put the cup on the desk by that portfolio — not by the typewriter. Now, away you go before you get too ... nosy."

Dutifully, Lish made a spice cake then did a bit of clean-up before she made herself comfortable in the rocking chair to knit a few more inches onto a piece for the afghan. Last night she dreamt a shifting succession of vignettes, all of them with some connection to The Mark. Rocking and knitting were good for thinking; this time about one vignette in particular — delicate pastel ribbons that were tied around her waist floated on breezes toward the front door of Granite, taking her along with them. She hadn't gotten too far with her ruminations before Charlie arrived.

"You smelled the spice cake," Lish said.

"Maybe," Charlie said. "I brought the mail, too." He wiped his feet at the door and strode into the kitchen. Luna shook herself on the porch and padded along behind him. "Helluva a day, isn't it? My dad used to say there ain't piddling yah can do on a day like this but mend harness."

"I thought rain was good for the crops," Lish said.

"It all depends on what you've got to do around the farm, how you take the weather. Where's my cutie-petootie this morning? I picked the mail up at the store because there was a package for her that wouldn't fit in the box at the end of the lane."

"Thalia's in her study," Lish told him. "I'll put the coffee pot on."

"Spice cake, you say. It doesn't smell too half-bad. But proof is in the eating." Charlie clumped into the hall, leaving a trail of wet bootprints behind. He banged on the study door, and shouted, "Mail! A nicely wrapped box for you today, Thalia."

When Lish stooped to pat Luna, the dog looked at her with big, sad eyes. "What's the matter, girl. You're not yourself today. Do you want me to dry you off?"

"She's a little piqued," Charlie said from the hall. "She's near time to pop her puppies. Thalia? There's a letter from Rotten Reggie." The last comment brought instant results. The door opened. Thalia reached for the package.

"I almost forgot," Charlie said, coming back into the kitchen. He pulled mail from a pocket. "I've got two letters for you, Lish."

Lish noted the return addresses: one from Fergus, one from Port Arthur. She ripped both open and read each over several times.

Luna waddled over and lay on a corner of the blanket. Adam and Eve eyed the dog suspiciously, but didn't give up their cozy bed.

Charlie made himself comfortable at the table. "Do you mind if I help myself to cake? You're suddenly quiet, Lish. Something wrong?"

"A strange twist to my tale," Lish responded. "Do you know where Noah is today?"

He hitched a ride into Seven Springs with me. He and Jeff are chumming around. He said they'd be back around suppertime. Jeff'll drop him off here. Do you need him for something?"

"I sure do."

"Can I help?"

"Not this time, Charlie."

Charlie had been watching Luna, who was inching across the blanket, giving Adam and Eve something to think about. "Lish, girl. Do you know anything about birthin' puppies?"

"Not a thing, Charlie. Is Luna ready to have them now?"

"Soon," Charlie said. "She's got that look about her. She's been moping around this morning. She likes to pick her soul mate for the occasion, usually a woman. The last time, she chose Georgie and stayed with her for a couple of weeks."

"Oh my!" Lish said. "I'm not sure I could handle that."

"Charlie!" Thalia came down the hall, her cane thumping on the oak floor. "That wretched Reginald wants to come here. To talk. Says we need to meet face to face."

"You don't have to see him. You know that," Charlie said, pushing a chair away from the table for Thalia. "You can tell him to go to hell, if you like. You washed yer hands of him long ago, threw the bath water out with him in it."

Thalia ignored Charlie's offer, and stumped instead to the rocking chair beside Lish's — her thinking chair. As soon as she sat down, Luna whined softly then licked Thalia's outstretched hand. Adam and Eve, seizing the opportunity for a graceful exit, climbed onto Thalia's knee.

"It's nearly time, isn't it, Luna, my lady. You know where to find a woman's company in your time of need, don't you. I know how you feel."

"Anyone for coffee?" Charlie got tired of waiting for someone to pour him a cup and decided to help himself. "From the look of this cake, I'd say you're learning fast that the way to a man's heart lies through his stomach. Can I cut it?"

"Go ahead," Lish said. "You say that Noah should be here around suppertime?"

"That's what he said." Charlie removed the percolator from the pot, blew on his fingers, then poured three cups of coffee. "He and Jeff are off to Collingwood for truck parts."

"If he gets back tonight, I did promise that we would talk," Thalia said.

Lish tucked her letters into a pants pocket. "I really have to talk to Noah first. Perhaps we can all talk tomorrow night?"

Charlie sliced the cake — a huge piece for himself, a small one for Lish, and a smaller one for Thalia. "I make a good butler, and I even come with references. The only thing I don't do is iron newspapers," he said, passing plates around. "Don't tell the guys at the store that I have a feminine side to me. I'd never live that one down."

"You're tough as nails when you have to be," Thalia said. "I don't know what I'd do without you. What am I going to do about Reginald?" Thalia rocked, her right hand rubbing her forehead in rhythm with the chair.

"You're doin' that worry thing again," Charlie said. "You're gonna rub the skin right off yer forehead." Charlie turned to Lish "The mealy mouthed little rat has the ability to make Thalia fret for days. She's scared to death of him. He'd have nearly killed her once, if it weren't fer Frank ..."

"I hadn't told Lish anything about Reginald," Thalia said.

"Waul, maybe now's a good time to say something, at least about the bit I just mentioned."

Thalia put a hand on each cat and set the chair to rocking. Closing her eyes, she began, "It was the last year of the war ... later in 1945."

"Did Reginald serve overseas?" Lish asked.

"Not overseas. But he did serve his country, in a way. I believe that he worked in Hamilton, in one of the steel mills. In the office — finance," Thalia explained.

"He'd have been exempt from service if he worked on the farm with his father," Lish said.

"Hell!" Charlie said. "He never worked a day of his life on any farm — Frank's or mine. Too damn lazy."

"Charlie is right," Thalia said. "But in truth, by then, we weren't doing too much heavy farming. We had a big garden, beehives, a greenhouse and bedding plants, the orchard, a large flock of laying hens. We did a good business in eggs."

"If the beggar had shown the least interest in farming, he could have helped at my place," Charlie said.

"True," Thalia said. "But let me continue. During the Depression, Frank and I scrimped and saved, knowing that the only way we could keep The Mark in our old age was to save money for bills and taxes. We would never sever land or sell timber rights. We did whatever was necessary to make a few dollars. We lived frugally. The war years were a different story. Everything was in demand."

"While Thalia and Frank were struggling, Rotten Reggie didn't bother his mother," Charlie said. "He left home when he was eighteen years old and didn't even bother to come home for Christmas after he hit the big city."

Thalia rocked, her feet rhythmically beating the floor, her thoughts turning like pages in a book. The pendulum on the clock ticked time to the squeak of the rockers. How much to divulge, she wondered. "Reginald decided he wanted us to advance some of his inheritance. His attitude was that we had money, didn't we? He was our responsibility, wasn't he? That was always his logic: give it to me because I'm the only one you raised and I'm going to get it anyway. Why do some children inherit the worst of both sides?"

Charlie dragged his chair over to Thalia's side, shooed the cats off her knee, and took her hand. "It's hard for you, I know. But the story needs to be told."

"When Reginald asked me, I said no. He approached Frank, who also said no, then somehow either showed, or gave, Reginald details about the bank account. Frank was getting a little confused at times. To make a long story short, Reginald forged Frank's signature on a cheque and withdrew a substantial portion of the money we'd saved." Thalia choked up. "I can't go on, Charlie."

Charlie took up the story. "The bastard had the nerve to show up at Granite again after he'd done the deed, thinking that Thalia wouldn't do anything about it, He said that Frank gave him the cheque. After all, wasn't the account in Frank's name? Wasn't it Frank's money."

"I wonder why he needed the money?" Lish said.

"I think that he got in with the wrong crowd, perhaps a gambling debt? Hamilton's a rough city," Charlie said. "To get back to the story: when Thalia demanded the return of the money, or she'd lay fraud charges against him, an argument ensued in which Reginald tried to stab Thalia with a paring knife. Frank stepped in and was the one that got hurt, a big cut ..."

"Charlie," Thalia said. "I think that you've said enough."

"Well," Charlie said, "the upshot was that Reginald was ordered off the property. Thalia didn't lay charges. He never paid the money back. Rotten Reggie did receive a registered letter from Thalia's lawyer stating that he had been written out of the will; that he had by forgery and ill gains, gotten all the inheritance he was going to receive."

"He stayed away?" Lish asked.

"Oh no," Thalia said. "He came back several times ... once for Frank's memorial service. He never came near Granite that time. And he was here, one other time."

Fragments of a conversation niggled at Lish's memory. Under what circumstances had she heard snippets of a similar story? Was it at a reception in Toronto? "Reginald didn't change his name, by chance?"

"He'd be capable of doing that if it served his purpose," Charlie replied. "I wouldn't put it past him. Rotten Reggie would do anything for a dollar. He hates Thalia with a passion. Why do you ask?"

"No reason but curiosity," Lish said.

"He signed his letter Reginald Russo," Thalia said.

Lish reached for Thalia's hand. Poor woman. Her only son a lousy cheat; and her living in fear of him all these years. She smiled and gently squeezed the hot hand. "I promise that if I'm still here, you won't have to face your son alone. I'll stand by you. So will Charlie."

"We'll let Luna take care of him, won't we, Thalia" Charlie said. "She knows exactly what to do — and when." When Thalia resumed her rigorous rocking, Charlie indicated by a finger to his lips that they shouldn't disturb her rhythmic ruminations.

When she spoke again, Thalia said, "It's difficult for me to get much work done with Reginald on my mind. I'll have to see him. I'll give him an hour of my time, then order him out of my life forever. But I won't face him alone, not ever again."

"He'll want money," Charlie said.

"He won't get it."

"He'll want land."

"You know that he'll never get his hands on The Mark. Lish, you are very kind and considerate, but are under no obligation to me. Having said that, if you are here when a meeting is set up with Reginald, I do think you'd be a good person to have in attendance. You're very observant — ask good questions ..."

Lish had the feeling that those delicate little ribbons she'd dreamed about were tightening around her, binding her closer to Granite. "As far as I know, I'm a neutral figure in the situation," she said. "That would help."

Thalia squeezed Charlie's hand. "For me, The Mark and my beloved Granite have always been a refuge from the storms. I really don't want Reginald invading my calm preserve, taking away my precious memories of my place forever sweet."

"We'll set the meeting up for my farm," Charlie said. "That

way Rotten Reggie won't leave a stink behind at Granite after he leaves."

"When should we schedule the meeting?" Thalia asked.

"I'd leave it as long as possible," Charlie replied, "At least until after Luna has had her puppies. We want her in fine fighting form. Let him sweat for a while afore you answer. Let him think that you're not going to answer. The Rotter has been outta your life for a good long time. Another month or so isn't going to matter much to him. You don't really need to see him. You made that clear."

"I'm not getting any younger, Charlie. I'll talk with him one more time. It's the right thing to do." Thalia struggled to get out of the rocking chair. "I should get back to work, try to keep my mind off the situation."

"Do you want Joan today? She's feeling a bit better, maybe she can do a couple of hours of work?"

"Yes, I could use her," Thalia said.

"I'll go get Joan and bring Luna's dog food at the same time. She's not going anywhere soon." Luna had stretched herself full length on the blanket. "I'm afraid that you've got her for the duration."

"Charlie, I don't know what to do with a dog that's going to have puppies," Lish said.

"You don't have to do anything. You can hide in your bedroom if you like. But Luna does like someone to talk nicely to her when she's in misery. That's why she's here. She wants your sympathy, Lish. Isn't that right, Thalia?"

Thalia didn't answer. She'd already shut the door of the study.

Tuesday, July 3 — After Midnight

Thalia went from the supper table to her study and then to bed around eleven. Luna's sad eyes kept Lish in the kitchen. She sat, back propped against the wood box, the dog's big head in her lap. With the exception of the clock's ticking, Granite was so quiet a mouse could be heard skittering across a wooden floor. "I'm not going to ring the bell and scare Charlie and Joan half-to-death," Lish said. "I guess that it's just you and me, Luna. I won't be of much help."

Charlie appeared at the back door around midnight. "I saw the kitchen light on and figured that you needed company," he said. He sat in one of the rocking chairs, cozy by the heat of the stove.

"Noah didn't come for supper," Lish said.

"Jeff decided to stay in Collingwood," Charlie told her. "I can understand his logic. Jeff figured that it was so foggy he didn't want to attempt the drive home. I spoke with Noah, too — told him that you wanted to chat with him. He'll be back tomorrow. Waul, I guess later today," Charlie said, looking at the clock.

"Thanks for talking to Noah, Charlie. It is important that I see him."

"I'm sorry that pooch is keeping you up late. You know, at her age, Luna shouldn't be havin' pups. This will be her last batch, if I've anything to do with it. But then, I said that about the last litter."

"Thalia was in no condition to stay with us. She's in a lot of pain, although I'm sure she won't admit it. And she's still fretting over Reginald's request."

"She'd need to fret," Charlie said. "The other half of the story is that when she ended up in hospital in Orangeville with her broken leg, Rotten Reggie violated her privacy and took up residence here. He decided that she wasn't coming home and staked his claim to the property — squatters right. Began to ...." Charlie cleared his throat. "WGD alerted me to the fact the Rotter was here. Luna took a round outta him."

"She attacked him?" Lish said.

"Waul, she nipped at him all the way down the lane until he went ass-over-tea-kettle. Then she drooled over his private parts until I picked the bastard up and marched him off the property. I told him that if he *ever* set foot on The Mark again, I'd put a bullet through what was left of his personal baggage. He lit out for Len's garage quick enough."

"He's that bad? Why would he go to Len Grant's place?"

"Len always had a soft spot for the kid. Reginald was a nice little boy, you know. But somewhere, somehow, he went off the rails. There's always one bad apple in the barrel. You cain't do anything about it but toss the rotter out or it'll taint the rest of the batch."

"Grandmother's favourite saying was that there's none as evil as a man so preoccupied with money he can't see the beauty of the day." Luna sighed mightily and licked Lish's hand. "Charlie, what do you say to a dog? Push?"

Charlie smiled. "You just pat her, let her know you care. It won't be long now afore we'll have our first wee pup. Did Thalia tell you about Luna's lineage?"

"She told me a bit," Lish said, feeling so sorry for the dog that she wanted to cry. Was it the dog's situation or her own? She hadn't cried in months — no, in years. Not since her father died.

"Hunter Logan's dog was named Moon. Wil Barnes came up this way with a brute named Belle. The pair got on famously and littered the County, so to speak. If it weren't for Moon, John — the son — would have been killed by a cougar when he was a babe-in-arms. The Logans and the Barnes have kept the line alive, this batch being the latest to carry on the tradition. I personally have no idea what Moon looked like, just hearsay, you know."

"No wonder all the dogs in the village look the same," Lish said, watching Luna's stomach rise and fall with her heavy panting.

"Well, lookie here." Charlie got down on his knees as a wet mass of fur began to make an appearance. "It's a black one. Do you see that, Lish?"

Lish couldn't help herself. She started to cry. Big tears rolled down her cheeks and dropped onto her sweater.

"What's the matter, my girl?"

"Oh Charlie, it's everything. Luna ... Dad's death ... Granny's death ... my situation ... this place."

"Hush now." Charlie crawled around the dog so he could put his arms around Lish. "Shh. Don't cry. It's all right. You've come to the right place. You're safe in Thalia's cottage of lilacs and laughter. There's nothing, or no one, will ever bother you while Charlie Barnes is around." Charlie's big calloused hand caressed Lish's hair. He kissed her forehead then wrapped his strong arms around her.

And that's how Thalia found Lish and Charlie at five-thirty in the morning. Luna lay quietly guarding two puppies — one jet black, one with distinctive collie dog markings. Charlie sat with his back against the wood box, with Lish, sound asleep, snuggled in his arms.

Charlie winked at Thalia and whispered. "See the reward I got for staying up all night? How often do I get to cradle a lovely damsel in my arms these days?"

If Thalia was surprised, she didn't show it as she limped around the kitchen, busy with breakfast preparations.

After breakfast, Lish locked herself in her bedroom to sort through the boxes she'd brought with her. She sat cross-legged on the floor, surrounded by her mess. Her legs and back ached but she wasn't going to give up until she finished the job. Those papers she deemed interesting or pertinent she set to her right. Those that were probably not important went to her left.

Lish justified the fact she had the material by reminding herself that they were copies, not original documents. She had xerographed them with one purpose in mind: to prove, if necessary, that COY was involved in unethical land transactions. Lish was also looking for a firm link between Northlands and COY.

When Charlie came to the door to see if she was all right, Lish answered his knock. She assured him that she was fine and impulsively kissed him on the cheek. "You're a good fellow, Charlie Barnes."

Charlie blushed, touched his cheek and said, "It's been a long time since a woman kissed me. I'm not so good as just tolerable. Do you want a cup of tea?"

"Charlie, I'd love a cup of tea and a couple of cookies."

A half-hour later when Noah knocked and asked what she was doing, Lish called to him that she didn't want to be disturbed but would see him later. She had one question: "Did you happen to see Bug Eye and The Fetch around Seven Springs in your wanderings? Did they follow you and Jeff?"

"I found out that they're staying in the area," Noah told her. "That makes it almost impossible for me to be seen in Seven Springs or Hornings Mills. What are you doing in there?"

"Trying to make sense of some information. I'll see you this evening, at Spirit Rock. There should be a lovely sunset tonight."

"Well, you're worrying the hell out of Thalia and Charlie."

"Tell them not to worry. I'm not doing anything very ... wrong."

After going through the boxes, Lish spent several hours making notes. She re-sorted the piles, put everything away, and went downstairs to see Luna and her pups.

"My goodness, you must be hungry," Thalia said. "You worked through lunch."

"I have to go into Seven Springs. I'll get a sandwich at the store. Do you need groceries?" Lish fussed over Luna as Thalia made a list.

"You will be home for supper?" Thalia said.

"I'll only be gone for an hour or so. I'll make supper when I get home."

At the store, Lish gathered groceries and information. Georgie said that the odd couple hadn't been around since the scene in the restaurant but they had set up housekeeping "of sorts" in one of the recently vacant cottages down the road. "Why are you asking?"

"Just wondered if they'd been scared off."

"I don't think so. They're probably laying low for a week or so. I heard they were cruising the backroads the other day. That wouldn't have done them any good yesterday. Fog was so thick in the valley you could cut it with a knife. I didn't have a hair of business cause no one could see to get here."

Lish drove slowly past the vacant cottages and kept a sharp eye out for signs that one was inhabited. Luck! A blue car was parked in the drive at the second one. Boldly, she pulled into the driveway and blew her horn. The Fetch appeared at the side door.

"I want to talk to both of you," Lish called. "I've got a job for you and it pays well. Don't worry. I don't have the dog with me today."

The Fetch — her name turned out to be Gloria — motioned that Lish should get out of the car. The photographer — his name was Bernard — came out to talk with her.

"I have a list here: dates, names, addresses. I need to know the age of each person listed, and if they had any debilitating medical problems on the date given or within two years before that date. I don't want to hear about aches and pains. I want to know if they were in the early stages of senility or were pressured in any way to sell their property. Can you do that?"

"For a good buck," Bernard said.

"Money's no object," Lish said. "But you have to give me a ballpark figure. I also want you to find out as much as you can about a man named Reginald Russo, other than the fact that he once lived around here."

"One hundred bucks a name and expenses."

"Fifty dollars per name if you've accumulated good information on it. No expenses," Lish said. "I'm sure that you have a permanent residence in Toronto that you can use while in the city. Take it or leave it."

"Sixty and meals."

"Fifty-five dollars. No meals. Pack a lunch."

"Fifty-five and an interview with Jason Curlew."

"Fifty-two and I'll work on Noah."

"Deal," Bernard agreed. "Give us at least three weeks."

"Two weeks."

"Where can we find you?"

"Leave word with Georgie at the store that you're around and want to see me," Lish said.

"You drive a hard bargain. What's this all about?"

"None of your business. Just get me the information. Get an affidavit if necessary about the health issue — a signed letter would be great."

"That'll be another twenty-five smackers a head."

"Ten dollars per letter, one letter per head," Lish said. "And you're out of the area for two weeks."

"Give us three weeks."

"Sixteen days," Lish said, thinking how pleased Noah would be that he could move about the area freely for the next few days — and how her bank account would suffer if the pair were successful with even half the names.

"By the way," Gloria said, "you owe us $52.00. We pay a fellow by the name of Reginald Russo for the use of this cottage."

"Son-of-a-gun!" Lish exclaimed. The Rotter had already begun to accumulate land at the base of the hill.

At sunset, Lish and Noah sat with their backs to Spirit Rock to watch the sun set behind the hills in a blaze of red. Clouds picked up the colour and spread, deep pink, across the southern and northern reaches. The scene was so spectacular that neither spoke until hundreds of fireflies flickered in the meadows near the river.

"You're sure a secretive one," Noah said. "You had Thalia really worried when you locked yourself in your bedroom. She thought it had to do with something that Charlie did."

"There's no need for her to worry," Lish said. "There's more need for you to sweat a bit."

"Let me get this straight," Noah said. "In return for information that will help Thalia to keep The Mark, this Bernard guy wants an interview with me."

"That's right," Lish said. "You're going to have to give an explanation for your absence at some point. You may as well benefit Thalia's cause, and do it sooner rather than later."

Noah spent some time thinking over his answer. He finally said, "Okay, when you're satisfied that you received useful information, I will give the Bernard fellow an hour of my time. But not here, and not at the cabin. I don't want him to pollute my private space — my hideaway."

"That's fair enough," Lish said. She understood fully how Noah felt about the cabin, The Mark, and Granite. "We can set the interview up for Georgie's store, or somewhere in Toronto, at Jeff's garage or the middle of nowhere, if that's what you want."

"Is this why you wanted to talk to me?" Noah asked.

"To begin with, no." Lish looked to the sky for inspiration. The western horizon was now a slit of electric blue, fading to sapphire then deep blue in the eastern reaches. Life was almost as complex, deep, and mysterious as the sky. "Remember our chat in Fergus? I said that I'd write for information about my birth and mother?"

"Yes."

"Well, I did write the hospital and enclosed information to prove who my father was. I also wrote to a woman in Port Arthur, someone who used to correspond with Dad. She was able to provide information and says that she'll keep in touch."

Noah leaned toward Lish, very interested in the turn the conversation was taking. "Port Arthur," he said. "I was in a residential school up that way."

"Does the name Agnes Whitefish ring a bell, Noah?"

"Agnes." The name took Noah back to his childhood.

"Agnes Curlew Whitefish," Lish said.

"My grandfather, Jimmy, had a sister named Agnes. She went to residential school, then found work in the Fort William area. She never returned to the reservation. Grandfather eventually lost track of her when she was, maybe, thirty years old."

"Agnes had a child by a man whose surname was Whitefish. That child — Jessica — was my mother. My father met Jessica when he was in the north. Jessica Whitefish MacPherson died of a ruptured appendix shortly after I was born. She's buried in Belsyde Cemetery in Fergus."

"Wow! We're cousins. We're both connected by blood-trace to Thalia Logan Russo."

"Because you're such an interesting, charming fellow, Noah, we're more closely related than I'd like to be," Lish said.

"So, we have an ancestral link; but why did we end up here — together — at this time?"

"Heavy-handed fate," Lish said.

"Fickle-fingered fortune," Noah said, thinking of his grandfather's link to Thalia. "Agnes would know about this area because I'm sure her brother would have mentioned it. But what brought Jimmy down here years ago? Curiosity? We've got to talk with Thalia."

"Thalia said that tomorrow at ten a.m. would be the best time for her."

"Listen! Do you hear that, Lish?"

The sound that Noah was referring to made the hair stand up on the back of Lish's neck. A big cat's plaintive yowling filled the valley.

"That's got to be a cougar, Noah."

"It sure sounds like one," Noah said. "It's a yowl one can't forget easily."

"Do you feel safe walking to the cabin with a cougar roaming around?"

"I'm not afraid of it, but I don't feel that I want to confront it alone at the moment," Noah said. "Maybe Thalia has a spare bedroom?"

"Noah, we have to be realistic. There's not been a big cat around this part of Ontario for years."

"What is it then?"

"I don't know," Lish said. "How come everyone can't hear it? Thalia hears it. I bet that Charlie hears it. You hear it. I hear it."

"Jeff swears that he doesn't know what I'm talking about — yowls, scratches on trees, all that sort of thing. He doesn't hear it."

Lish stood. Turning toward The Mark, she paid homage to CAT by way of a nod. She had no idea why she did so. It was a spontaneous act that even surprised her. How many people in Seven Springs *do* hear the cat? If Jeff doesn't, he's not one of *us*. Since when were we divided into *them* and *us*?

Wednesday, July 4

If furniture could talk, Thalia thought as she glanced round the kitchen table, what this table hasn't seen and heard in its lifetime isn't worth writing about. "Where to begin?" she said. "Of course, Joan and Charlie know the story. They can fill in any of the details that I miss."

"I thought perhaps Jeff would be here," Lish said.

Charlie cleared his throat, looked over his coffee cup toward Thalia, then said, "Waul, he had some business in Orangeville this morning. Besides, he's not too connected ..."

"The Barnes' connection to The Mark is through marriage?" Lish asked.

"'Breathes there a man with soul so dead; Who never to himself hath said, This is my own, my native land! Whose heart hath ne'er within him burn'd, As home his footsteps he hath turn'd.' Chalk that one up to Sir Walter Scott. I'm a man of the land. I'm not goin' anywhere soon. I'm loyal to Thalia."

Ah, Lish thought. Charlie Barnes's outer facade masks a much deeper inner man. "Well said, Charlie."

Joan, looking pale, said, "For a simpler answer, one of our ancestors married John, the son of Hunter Logan and Nibish. Thalia, perhaps we should forget family ties for the moment and explain why we spend so much time in the study?"

"Thank you, Joan. That is a good place to begin," Thalia agreed. "But I have to stress that what is said around this table goes no further than those who are seated here today. Agreed?"

When all nodded agreement, Thalia said. "As you now know, Lish and Noah, Reginald nearly bankrupted Frank and me. As Frank was really in no condition to work, that left me to find something lucrative to pay the bills. I always enjoyed writing. On a whim, I penned a novel, set in early 1900 — one of those Edwardian bodice rippers. Totally unlike my own life, but I always had a good imagination and do enjoy the finer details of history."

"Let me guess," Noah said. "You and Joan are currently working on a manuscript."

"That's right," Thalia replied. "Let me explain how things fell into place. After I submitted the manuscript — to the first publisher, mind you — it was accepted. I was asked to go into an agreement for another, which turned into another ... and another. The more I wrote, the more money came in.

"I admire your tactics, Thalia. Solving your financial difficulties with your pen meant that you didn't have to leave Granite, or compromise The Mark," Lish said. "You managed to combine the best of two worlds."

"But I did have to compromise," Thalia said. "I do love to read and always thought, like William Styron, that a great book should leave me with a number of experiences and quite exhausted by its ending; that I should have led several lives while reading one. I never thought that I would write books that didn't meet my personal criteria. But the royalties pay my bills ..."

"Your books must fill the needs of some people or they wouldn't sell," Joan said.

"I browse shops but can't recall seeing your name on any books," Lish said.

"I use a number of pen names: Shirley Scalil, Annetta Nagol, Wilda Neves .... Copies of all my books are in the parlour. You've read several, Lish. Nagol is Logan ... Neves is Seven ...."

"Of course!" Lish said. "Both were better written then most novels of that sort. Where do you get ideas and form plot lines? From the looks of your personal shelf in the parlour, you've written so many titles."

"To get into each time period, I wear my ideas, float around in them, live the moment, make up a lot, remember my wild times, listen to Georgie's exploits .... "

"Trunks full of old clothes, Thalia's old-fashioned way-of-life here ...," Joan said.

"Let's just say that although the type of books I write don't garner big awards, they are accurate to detail," Thalia said.

"If her books did win awards, that would interfere with Thalia's desire for anonymity," Charlie said. "Once, we took a chance. The publisher did push for a picture. We got Joan all dolled up, had professional photos taken, and sent them off."

"I enclosed a little note stating that I preferred not to be portrayed because I lived in a rural area and appreciated my privacy. The company didn't push the issue, didn't publish the photograph."

Joan laughed. "I'm sure that they thought I didn't quite portray the look they wanted."

"And what if they had published a picture?"

"I was prepared to live with the consequences," Joan said.

"You see, Joan and I work closely on each book," Thalia said. "She can speak as well as I about each plot and the process of writing it."

Noah was on his feet, coffee pot in hand, filling cups. "Why hide?" he said.

"I get fan mail — forwarded from the publishing house," Thalia said. "To a person, the writers assume that I'm a young woman." She put her hand over her cup. "No more coffee, Noah. As it is now, I'll shake all day. In many different ways, readers make it known that they appreciate the fact I'm young because older women writers harbour a few hang-ups that don't allow the freedom-of-mind to pen such sexy, romantic novels. If they only knew ...."

Lish laughed. "In other words, you feel that if readers knew, or saw, how old you were, they wouldn't buy your books. The upshot would be that the publisher wouldn't accept any more of your manuscripts."

"I've a few readers that are, what do the young people call them these days? Noah, you'd know."

"Hangers-on ... heel puppies ... fixation fixtures ... pains in the butt ... in-your-face groupies," Noah ventured.

"Who wants to be bothered with older people these days?" Thalia said. "We're written off as being senile. I'm positive that if readers found out I'm seventy-eight years old .... There are lots of younger writers that the publisher could foster."

"So, no one knows who you are?" Noah asked.

"Only those now seated around this table, a few people in Seven Springs — those I help financially, when I can. I do owe them a lot for their loyalty. Of course, the publishing house knows because they *do* pay me," Thalia said. "My fear is that one of those avid readers will do a little investigating. No one has — to date."

"That's why Georgie stood between the camera and you. She thought that the guy was scoping you," Lish said.

"Something like that," Charlie said.

"Until recently, royalties from these books were the one constant thing that I could count on to allow me to keep my beloved home and The Mark," Thalia said. "I will not allow anyone to interfere with my efforts to preserve both places."

"You're trying to maintain historical roots," Noah said.

"Far more than that," Thalia replied. "But before I go any further, you must have questions."

"Does the elderly gentleman at Stanton store, the one who spoke with both Noah and I, have anything to do with The Mark?" Lish asked.

"He's a friend, someone who knows me well."

"What about Jimmy Curlew?" Noah asked.

"Ah yes, the letters that were written to Jimmy Curlew."

"I'm sure Charlie told you that I was his grandson," Noah said.

"He did, confirming something I've known since the day after you arrived. You look just like him." Lips pursed in thought,

Thalia sat back to assess the situation. Charlie had indeed connected Noah and Jimmy, and he'd mentioned letters. How to proceed?

"There are no secrets between Thalia and me," Charlie said.

Thalia smiled at both Lish and Noah. "Perhaps before the chat goes any further, you both should read Hunter Logan's journal. It may explain a bit. Joan has typed a copy for each of you. Shall we say, we'll meet around this table again the day after tomorrow — Friday morning — at ten o'clock?"

Thursday, July 5

Obviously, Thalia and Charlie had something important to discuss that they didn't wish Lish to hear. It was Thalia who suggested that she go for a walk.

"I'll be busy for the morning," Thalia told her. "You must have much to think about. Why don't you hike the uplands on the home farm. From the top, the plateau stretches to the horizon."

"More like until it drops into the next deep valley," Charlie said. "You should see it, Lish. The weather is perfect for a leg-jaunt. Be careful that you don't step in a groundhog hole and break an ankle. You can't get lost but if you're not home by lunch hour, I'll come looking for you. I'll walk you down the lane."

There was nothing for Lish to do but take a ramble. She crossed the Line, opened the farm gate, latched it again, then waved to Charlie who waved back, turned, and headed back toward Granite. She kept to the narrow overgrown lane, watching all the while for snakes, another of Charlie's cautions.

A third of the way up, Lish came across the ruins of the barn. Its upper structure's huge log beams had collapsed into a stone foundation that still looked in reasonable shape. Several of the valley-facing windows still had glass in them. A door flapped on its hinges. To her right, a pile of blackened, rotting wood was all that was left of the farmhouse. A tangle of weeds, bushes, and overgrowth hid stone cellar walls.

When Lish finally stopped to catch her breath and turned to look toward Granite, she was once again visually reminded why Thalia, Charlie, and Joan were so attached to the land. The scene that stretched before her rivalled any that Lish had seen during her vacations. "You explore your own backyard last," she murmured as she turned to the path again. As she got closer to the top, Lish noticed two men walking the fenceline.

"Hi-up," one called. He turned and walked toward her. The other loped beside him, looking this way and that without regard to where he was putting his feet. "It's Bud. I saw you at the store. Have yah seen a cow on your climb?"

"I can't imagine how a cow can graze this steep slope," Lish said.

"If they're hungry enough they'll graze anywhere." Bud came up beside Lish and doffed his hat. "It helps if they have adjustable legs, though. Low on one side fer when they need 'em." He chuckled. "So, you truly ain't seen a cow down that way?"

"No, I haven't," Lish said. "You've obviously lost one."

"Glenn was following the cows to pasture after milking. One bolted and came this way. I didn't realize that there's a break in the wire fence needs mending. If I didn't know better, I'd say it had been cut," Bud said. "Look at him go!"

Glenn, who'd continued down the path, veered left toward the ruins of the house.

"He's just like a weasel," Bud said. "He cain't set still ... not for one minute."

"Aren't you afraid that he'll get hurt in the rubble?" Lish asked.

"Maybe. But I can't tie him down. You know, after his ma died, some folks wanted me to put him away, inta one of those mental places. I won't do that. He's all I got. He's not a mental case. But he can't farm, can't be trusted aroun' machinery. Are you goin' to the top? I'll walk with you."

"Thanks. I'd appreciate the company. Charlie scared the life out of me with tales of rattlesnakes," Lish said.

"You can't be too careful. They be aroun'. There's a couple of hay bales we can sit on up there till Glenn's finished his romping. I'll check 'em for varmints and slithery things afore we sit."

Bud gave Lish a few minutes to enjoy the view before he asked about Thalia. "She doing okay? She's good to Glenn, always gives him birthday and Christmas presents."

"Are you related to her?"

"Nah. I'm not, not even indebted to her because I take charity from no one — not that she's offered any. But I know what she does an' I won't rat on her."

"You're a decent man, Bud ..."

"Henderson. William Henderson. Got the nickname 'Bud' in the army. Served with Charlie in the same SAS unit. He watched my back; I watched his."

"So, where is your farm, William?"

Bud smiled. His mother was the only one *ever* called him William. "Part of it used to back onto Delaneys. My barn, house, and 150 acres are on the back concession. I'm a flat-lander, not a ridge-hugger."

The pair lapsed into silence as they watched Glenn run from the house ruins to the barn. He circled the foundation a couple of times, then squeezed in through a doorway.

"Don't yah worry, Miss MacPherson. He ain't as dumb as he looks. He's done that afore. There's spaces in the ruins he can explore. He's probably looking for kittens — brought two home once from there."

"I'll try not to worry about Glenn, but what about that?" Lish pointed downhill, to a forested area on her right where smoke rose above the treetops. "Is there a fire?"

"Nah. That's just the Delaney boys burning lunch. You ever seen where they live?"

"The day that my car quit on the Line, I didn't notice a house or I would have walked to it. Charlie showed me where the lane was the next day. It must be long and curved, because I've never seen buildings."

"You don't want to. The place is fallin' apart aroun' them. I blame their ma for their peculiarities. They weren't schooled much — didn't git off the farm much. To tell the truth, the family was not well liked around these parts — some old feud."

"Overprotective, was she?" Lish asked. Thinking of the restrictions her grandmother imposed on her during her teenage years, Lish could sympathize to a certain extent with the Delaney boys.

"Tom and Dick joined and fought during the war."

"Probably to get away from their mother," Lish said.

Bud laughed. "Darn tootin'! Harry, WGD, and his ma managed during the war. They sold maple syrup and grew wheat on the valley land, t'other side of their hill. They worked my plateau land, too. The valley land has gone to bush now. When Tom and Dick got back in 1946 they were pretty well shattered. They worked in Orangeville and Collingwood but eventually drifted back to the farm.

"Like a lot of young men," Lish said.

"Yep," Bud agreed. "Most got on with their lives. Those two boys didn't, or couldn't."

Just the sort of people that COY picks on, Lish thought. And Reginald Russo knew their story well enough that he did some serious cajoling. What was it that Bud said that bothered her? A question begged to be asked. "You said that your land used to back onto Delaney's property?"

"Yep. Part of it did. I was a little hard up for money to pay taxes and sold the back fifty two months ago. The deal is I can still farm the land though, just like I still own it."

"Who bought the land?"

"Jeff — Jeff Grant, Charlie's nephew. He said that when he married he wanted to build a big house on the heights for his wife. It's going to be a surprise so he hasn't told his father — or her."

A yell from Glenn brought Lish and Bud to their feet. He was coming up the trail at full gallop, shouting and whooping with each bound. "Looka what I found. Looka what I got."

"He's onta something for sure, this time," Bud said. "I've never seen him so excited."

Glenn, bouncing foot to foot, handed several soda bottles and a small brown bag over to his dad. "And looka this!" He reached into his pocket and gave his father a small metal object.

"Good lad, Glenn," Bud said, examining the items. "Somethin' with little teeth had a good feed on the donuts. The ants are still sucking up sugar, so the bottle ain't been there too long."

The metal object glinted in the sunshine, causing Lish to take a close look at it. "Could it be a cigarette holder? I'd say by the look of it that the mice around here must do a good job of polishing silver," Lish said.

Bud laughed. "Truth be, it is a fag-holder. I saw Frank Russo with this one many a time. It's got his initials on it. See, right there on the front lid: FR. But it's in too good a shape for the time it may have been lying in the ruins." Bud handed the holder to Lish. "Mrs. Russo should have this."

"When did Frank die?" Lish asked.

"Well ...," Bud said, giving Lish an odd glance, "some eight years ago maybe, I'd say. Has Mrs. Russo never told you about Frank?"

"She hasn't said much. Nothing about when, or where, he died," Lish said.

"You'd best speak with Thalia. Ask her about Frank's supposed disappearance from the area. Glenn, are you ready to go look for the cow again — over Delaney's way? By the look of that smoke, they just might be cookin' her up for lunch."

Glenn was already loping toward Delaney's bush.

"You said 'supposed' disappearance," Lish said.

"There's some folks think that Thalia, or Reggie, knows where he is. A couple of people think that he's in one of those old folks' homes down country a bit. See yah around, Miss MacPherson ... Lish. Nice chattin' with you."

"And it's been nice chatting with you, William."

Not giving Lish the opportunity to ask any more questions, Bud turned to follow Glenn.

Friday, July 6

After a sultry night, the wind came up. Thunder rumbled in the distance. Ugly black clouds boiled to the west. By the time Lish came downstairs, Noah was at the kitchen table. "I figured I'd better come early," he said. "I don't like the look of this one. I battened down the hatches at the cabin. I'd hate to be there if a tree fell over it."

Thalia was at the stove making a pot of oatmeal porridge. "It was so muggy that I couldn't sleep. I've been up since five o'clock working on the manuscript. Weather like this gives me a headache. You might want to check to see if Luna is ready to come in. Noah let her out ten minutes ago to do her business."

Before Lish could reach the door, Joan came in, Luna by her side, Charlie behind her.

"We saw the lights on and figured breakfast here was just as good as breakfast at the farm," Charlie said. "We may as well have our little chat early so's I can get back to work, if'n the storm moves off quickly. I brought the paper in with me. It was in the mailbox early today."

"My dear, let's hope that this doesn't turn into something far more dangerous than a thunderstorm. Lish, can you help me with bowls and cups? The weather is sure aggravating my leg this morning."

"I read somewhere that some scientists think atmospheric pressure has something to do with pain," Noah said.

"You don't have to be a scientist to know that," Charlie said. "I ken al'ays tell at least twelve hours before a storm's due that we're in for bad weather. My knees ache."

Joan, a cushion behind her back, sat by Noah. "There was no sense leaving the radio on this morning because it just crackled, so I couldn't hear much. But I did hear one of your songs being played, Noah, and the announcer saying 'that's the late, great Jason Curlew.' Then the fellow said, 'that's not true folks. I hear he's been sighted near Toronto.' Unfortunately, I couldn't catch the rest."

"Bother!" Noah said angrily. "The last thing we need is for a half-dozen reporters to show up in Seven Springs looking for me. Who's tattling? Jeff, any of you, those two snoops that were on the road?"

"Don't worry, Noah. I'll handle the reporters if they come," Charlie assured him. "The only way into the cabin is up Lavender Line, or up the bluff. We can put a gate across the Line, right past Thalia's gate if necessary, with a 'No Trespassing' sign on it. You can hide out. We'll feed you. Speaking of food.... " Charlie lay the paper on the table and held his bowl up for porridge.

Lish circled the table, filling bowls. Knowing Charlie's appetite, she also sliced a loaf of bread, putting the butter dish and several jars of jam within his reach. "Don't keep us in suspense, Charlie. Who is Dunnit picking on this week?"

"Here's a good'un. 'Our favourite dog has presented the Springs with two healthy pups. This time she chose the companionship of the Lovely Damsel rather than Gorgeous G or the Cagey Farmer.'"

"Who was at Granite to know that Luna had two pups?" Joan said.

"I'm sure that information is known in Seven Springs," Lish said. "I chatted with Georgie when I went for groceries yesterday afternoon. Maggie was at the store. She said that you told her about the pups, Charlie."

"How about this'un," Charlie said. "The Gunns are going to be gunning for sure with this little tidbit. 'Nettie and James Gunn are pleased to announce the marriage of their daughter Caroline to David Byely, who's from away. The wedding took place at Trinity United on June 22. The couple will live away — a good decision on the part of Miss Caroline who always had a head on her shoulders that was far too big for the Springs.'"

"Ouch," Noah said. "Has anyone tried to find out who this person is?"

"Many a time," Joan said. "Go on, Charlie. What else is there?"

"You're mentioned again, Lish. Listen to this one: 'The Lovely Damsel recently enjoyed the breezes on the hill in the company of Bud and the galloping songster. Let's hope that is the only thing she enjoyed while in his company. We can't recommend his apple pie.'"

"I walked the hill yesterday morning," Lish said. "How does the paper get the news so quickly? Who knows that I met Bud up on the hill but the people seated around this table?"

"Anyone with a good pair of binoculars," Charlie said. "Wait till you hear the second half of that rant. 'We can, however, say that the General Store's lemon pie is better eaten than worn. From what we can ascertain from those in the firing line, feathers, fur, and insults flew. So did pie.'"

"This is getting very personal," Lish said. "Who knew about the ruckus at the store?"

"The regulars, the porchers, then everyone in the Valley who heard about it by tongue-telegraph within a half-hour of the pie flying," Charlie said. "Wee Jimmy asked me about it when I went to see him yesterday afternoon to drop a package off from Thalia."

"Fortunately, there are still many things that no one knows about the old hill bird," Thalia said. "We have a lot to talk about today. As usual, I assume the information will go no further than this table? Where should we start?"

"I think you'd better explain what happened to Frank," Lish said, sitting beside Joan.

"You've alluded to him suffering from memory loss, but you've not said if he died or if you had to ... if he went somewhere." Lish fingered the cigarette holder in her pocket, waiting for the right opportunity to give it to Thalia.

Charlie chuckled. "Oh, he went somewhere. No one's sure about the *where* though."

"There's nothing to joke about," Joan admonished her brother with a stern look and a slap on his arm.

"We've lived with it so long, perhaps it is time to laugh a little about the situation," Thalia said, rubbing her forehead. "It's just sometimes difficult to talk about."

"Another time then?" Noah suggested.

Thalia took a deep breath, sat up, and placed her hands around her coffee cup. At least clutching the cup, they weren't worrying her forehead — and Charlie. "Our first years together were fine. But as time went by, it was obvious that Frank had a problem ... that he suffered from creeping dementia. The situation got progressively worse. Eventually, I had to keep an eye on him twenty-four hours a day."

"I helped when I could," Joan said. "So did Wee Jimmy and Georgie's mother, Mary. Georgie did her best too."

"We all did what we could," Thalia said. "That sickness is so insidious. It's terribly difficult to deal with. The mind is a wonderful thing until you lose it. Then, it turns on you, like an enemy."

"Too true," Charlie said. "Especially for some of the guys who came home from the war. You two young'uns wouldn't know too much about that, though."

"We all know people with their own personal demons, my agent being one of them," Noah said. "Every time a car backfires, he ducks for cover."

"Can you all give me a minute to gather my thoughts?" Thalia asked.

Noah was first off the mark. "Anyone for a warm-up?" Before he could reach the coffee pot, lightning crackled across the sky. Thunder rattled the windows. Lightning flashed again; the lights flickered.

"Geez! That one was close!" Charlie leapt to his feet. "I'm going to take a look." He disappeared into the hall, heading for the front porch.

Lish took advantage of the break to pat Luna, who seemed fretful. Thalia sat quietly, Joan beside her, a hand on her arm.

"There's nothing wrong that I can see," Charlie said, coming back into the kitchen on the tail of another clap of thunder. "It could be that one of the big trees got a whack. At least the hydro's not out — yet. There's nowt we can do but sit it out."

With everyone settled at the table again, Thalia continued. "It's just like Frank to cause a disturbance. It's as though he doesn't want me to talk about him. But the story needs to be told, no matter how difficult it may be." She took a deep breath. "Frank basically vanished."

"We don't know where he is, what happened to him," Joan said.

"To begin at the beginning," Thalia said, "one night in April — April 14, eight years ago, Frank got out of bed and left the house. I should have been more diligent about watching him. I did keep the door locked."

"Now, Thalia, you know that locked doors never stopped Frank," Charlie said. "And you couldn't stay awake twenty-four hours a day. His disappearance was not your fault."

"I checked Frank twice after midnight," Thalia said. "Twice, and sound asleep he was, both times. I fell asleep and when I woke up around 4:30 a.m., he was gone — vanished."

"Thalia checked the house, saw the back door wide open, and realized he was outside. She ran to the bell and rang it — woke up the whole Valley, she did," Joan said. "Everyone came to see what was wrong. And they all looked for Frank — even the Delaney brothers."

"Rain began to fall around eleven a.m.," Thalia said, "yet everyone stayed. They scoured the countryside, the hill farm, Seven Springs. They drove the backroads, checked the ditches ..."

"We called the police," said Charlie. "They came and searched too. As young as Luna was, she was given the scent. Because of the rain, she couldn't follow it, except that I thought she picked something up at the edge of the forest, down that way." Charlie called to the dog. "You tried to find Frank, didn't you girl? You tried as hard as you could."

Luna, who'd been looking at her master, ears up, whined softly.

"Luna and Frank were inseparable," Thalia said. "She was four months old at the time, even slept in our bedroom. But the evening that Frank disappeared, she disappeared, too. Luna turned up at the farm. Charlie found her when he went home to get food for the searchers."

"She was muddy ... bruised ... wet," Charlie said. "When I brought her back to Granite with me, Luna walked from the bedroom to the kitchen door and from the door to the bedroom over and over again."

"To make a long story short," Thalia said, "we put photographs in all the local papers. We did everything we could to find Frank. The police figure that he simply wandered away and ..."

Charlie reached for Thalia's hand. "There's so much bush and forest around here — on the uplands, on The Mark, along the bluff. Frank knew the area. There's no telling which way he went and where he ... stopped. Maybe he followed the escarpment on top, or bottom. It goes for miles in either direction."

"But we checked everywhere — twenty miles each way. We did what we could," Thalia said. "Eventually, Frank was declared officially dead by the powers that be. I just can't think of him as gone."

"Have you a picture of Frank?" Noah asked.

"I'll get the picture from your bedroom," Joan said.

Lish took a very close look at the photo Joan brought back, then handed it over to Noah, catching his eye as she did so. "I noticed a scar on his face," she said. "Was that the result of Reginald's attack?"

"It was," Thalia said.

"Might he have ... arranged a ride with someone?" Noah asked. "I mean, was he cognitive enough to make himself disappear so that you could collect his insurance?"

"Oh, dear me, no," Thalia said. "You sound just like the police, Noah. Frank's mind was so far gone that he couldn't have thought up a scheme like that."

But his son could have, Lish thought. "A question that you might think odd, but do you know what Frank was wearing when he disappeared?"

"Now, you definitely do sound like the police, Lish," Thalia said. "I do remember. His pyjamas were on the floor. The clothes that he wore the evening before were missing — a plaid shirt, dark work pants, and, oh yes, his favourite set of wide braces." Thalia rubbed her forehead.

"Do you know what was in his pockets?" Lish asked.

"There'd probably have been his favourite whittling knife — a pearl-handled pocket knife — a lighter, his cigarette holder ..."

"Thalia, you don't know for sure," Charlie said. "When the police asked, Thalia looked around for the things he usually carried. She couldn't find the pocket knife, his cigarette holder, and lighter. His wallet was missing, too."

Lish's hand closed around the cigarette lighter. There are more questions that need to be answered before I show this to anyone, she thought. Only Bud knows I have it. I'll have a little chat with him on Sunday.

"Of course, Reginald came as soon as Maggie called him. He was in the house and possibly took some of his father's things, including the wallet. I was so distraught, I wasn't thinking straight, or watching him closely at the time," Thalia said.

"That would be something the man was quite capable of doing," Joan said.

"Maybe we'd better get off the subject of Rotten Reggie." Charlie gently pulled Thalia's hand away from her forehead. "Worrying again, my girl? Why don't you tell Lish and Noah how you met Frank."

"Yes, that would be a good idea," Thalia said, clutching her hands in front of her. "During the summer of 1911, Frank was part of the crew that came to build the Valley bridge. With father's permission, a camp for the men was set up in the meadow below the house."

Noah chuckled. "Talk about fate. Your beau ended up right in your own backyard."

"After the crew boss got complaints about the camp food, he spoke to mother about cooking the noon meal for the crew. When she agreed, Frank was sent to build tables in the drive shed where they could eat and rest."

"Let me guess," Lish said. "You took a liking to Frank."

"Yes. Frank was a charming man. I'd lived a somewhat sheltered life here. Father asked only one question about him: 'Can he hear CAT?'"

"*Could* he hear CAT?" Noah asked.

"I was so smitten that I didn't care if CAT was part of Frank's life. That was a mistake."

"Then he couldn't," Lish said.

"For the time and the place, I will admit that I was a loose woman that year. The same summer Jimmy Curlew walked into my life. He just took up residence in Hunter's cabin one day. Jimmy heard CAT and had as much right to the land as my family. To be quite blunt, I fell for him, too."

"He was a married man," Noah said.

"As I later found out. I believe that Frank was the man I needed to help me on The Mark. I'm sure now that he didn't hear anything, but he believed me when I spoke of CAT. Frank talked about cougars, and forests, and the need to keep places just like this pristine and untouched. I loved him for that. He worked hard to make Granite — The Mark — a place that paid for itself ... until his mind went."

"And my grandfather?" Noah asked.

"I feel that Jimmy was what I needed to understand my emotional and psychological ties to The Mark. He spoke about the legend of CAT. He felt that its resting place, and that of his ancestors, must be preserved. I loved him for that. Is it possible to love two men at the same time?" The question was directed at Lish.

"I don't know," Lish said. "I haven't had the pleasure of loving even one man in my lifetime for long."

"What I did know is that by September I needed to leave Seven Springs for a while," Thalia said.

"Thalia, you weren't ..."

"Of course not. I wasn't *that* loose a woman! I'd never been off the farm, you know. Always here for Mother and Father — never a life of my own. That doesn't mean to say that I wasn't a free spirit. I made my own fun," Thalia said. "Both relationships were getting a bit heated. I had to go away to think things over."

"Which I assume means that you weren't as conventional as most young women your age," Lish said.

"'Thalia never had two men fighting over her at the same time before' is more how the story should be told," Charlie said. "From what I hear, Frank and Jimmy actually got to fisticuffs at one dance."

"I went to Toronto, found a room and a job at Eaton's. I didn't tell either Jimmy or Frank what my plans were — just walked out of their lives one day. Jimmy found me first, and I found out that he had as many problems as crows in a tree. He was a married man with a wife in northern Ontario."

"And what about Frank?" Lish asked.

"Mother eventually let Frank know where I was. He began to court me in earnest. Eventually, we returned to The Mark."

"How long were you in Toronto?" Lish asked.

"Almost three years," Thalia said. "I liked the hustle and bustle of the city. Frank and I lived in a little apartment in an old house on Bloor Street. But eventually I knew what had to be done. I had to come home. I had obligations here."

"Frank wanted to stay in Toronto?" Noah asked.

"Frank said that he could live anywhere as long as he had his little family. Our union worked. We were so different that we complimented each other. And yes, we loved each other."

"And the baby?" Noah asked. "You came home with a baby, I gather."

"Yes." Thalia coughed.

"You never saw my grandfather again?"

"Never. I wrote to him about The Mark. I needed to know what he thought must be done to ensure its future. I asked if he had a child who might be interested in assisting me."

"He never answered the letters?" Noah asked.

"Never," Thalia said. "Perhaps we should talk about the legend. We know from Hunter Logan's journal that Nibish must have trusted Hunter enough that she told him what she did with the idol. I can understand why she needed to free CAT. From what Jimmy Curlew recalled of the legend, CAT was blamed for a number of bad circumstances among Hoshaphat's people."

"The legend that Dad related to me is much the same as that told to Hunter Logan by Gazhagayns," Noah told them. "It tells of a golden cat that demands to be returned to its home, be it in the southern states, Mexico, or South America. Hoshaphat was a brave man to take on the task of finding it. So was the warrior who began the first journey."

"We can assume that the idol was brought north with a slave captive — the spoil of an old war between the Ojibway and a southern tribe. We don't know what supposed magical qualities were given to this statue but it must have meant something to the woman that she carried it with her," Thalia said.

"She must have been an important member of her tribe that she was guardian of CAT," Noah added.

"We don't know where, or how long, Hoshaphat spent looking for CAT," Thalia said. "There were miles of limestone escarpment and gorge to search, even with what oral information the man had about where the idol was hidden. Hoshaphat must have met Nibish down this way at some point during his search."

"That Hoshaphat found the idol at all was quite an achievement," Joan said.

"Over the generations, many details are lost, or embellished, in the retelling of legends. But, during the late-eighteenth century, Hoshaphat must have had a reasonable idea where to look," Noah said.

"I imagine Hoshaphat spent some months in Niagara and also along the Grand River, which is where he may have met Nibish. She had the babe, Manchild, before they turned up at the squire's house on Lake Ontario," Thalia said.

"Noah and I have walked in The Mark," Lish said. "No one will ever find CAT in that jumble of rocks and ground cover."

"Not that people haven't tried," Charlie said. "Rotten Reggie has tramped every inch of the place looking for it."

"I didn't approve of him looking for CAT," Thalia said. "But my entreaties fell on deaf ears. I feared what would happen if he found it."

"You see," Joan said, "an artifact like an ancient golden idol from South America would be worth a lot of money today."

A niggling thought crossed Lish's mind. Thalia is a writer. She could have written the journal recently and had Joan type her notes. Where is Logan's original document?

"Did Reginald know of the legend? Has he read the journal?" Lish asked.

"Personally, I never told him," Thalia said. "As far as I know he's never read the journal. Any knowledge Reginald has is what he may have heard Frank and I discuss."

"Who else was around when you and Frank talked about The Mark?" Lish asked.

"I'd have to say Maggie, but we tried not to chat when she was around."

"Despite Hunter Logan's journal and the Ojibway legend, do we even know for sure there was a ... slave woman brought north and a golden idol?" Lish asked.

"There are grounds for that part of the legend," Noah said. There are towns like Espanola with Spanish names on the north shore of Huron. My great-grandmother spoke a fractured Spanish language. There are Ojibway words that sound Spanish."

Charlie took up the story. "Hoshaphat was killed for the gold, not for the importance of CAT to the Ojibway people. Because of a dream, Hoshaphat planned to return CAT to its rightful place, wherever that might have been. Nibish was also influenced by a dream — to free CAT on Hunter's Mark. Hunter Logan believed enough in Nibish and the legend that he requested his descendants respect CAT and preserve The Mark."

"In so many words, Charlie is correct," Thalia said. "I'm sure that many people do not agree or even believe me, or the legend. I must state emphatically that I am devoted to protecting this land."

"This land — The Mark — is one of the few wilderness areas left in Southern Ontario," Joan said.

"What will it take to preserve Granite and The Mark?" Lish asked.

"A dedication to the legend; a commitment to the land and a ready supply of money in the bank," Thalia replied.

"And you know for sure that Reginald does not have the commitment and dedication to keep everything as is?" Noah asked.

"Let me tell you, he would let this house rot," Thalia said. "He would sell the timber rights to The Mark. Excuse my language, but he doesn't give a damn about this place, Seven Springs, Lavender, or Terra Nova. He has absolutely no emotional ties to this land. He sees dollar signs in every blade of grass."

"What made him like that?" Noah asked.

"He was never a child of the land. I have to think, now, that he was dropped into my life to make it hell-on-earth. He was a decent child, but as he grew into an adult, he hated living here."

"That's why he spent a lot of time with Len Grant," Charlie said. "Seven Springs wasn't a big place, but Rotten Reggie thought that it did have more going for it than the farm."

"Reginald told me that there was no future here," Thalia said. "He hated Frank, especially after his mind began to deteriorate. Reginald didn't understand that the man needed care, love, and attention. He didn't realize that I needed moral support, a little help ..."

"Sounds like a right rotter to me," Noah said.

"He cannot understand my rationale for preserving the integrity of this land."

"Thalia, to your credit it is apparent that you have always believed there is truth in the legend," Noah said.

"There has always been a CAT here, be it human, four-legged, metal, or a figment of one's imagination," Thalia said.

"If one believes CAT is not flesh and blood, they must at least believe in the power of myth, legend, and ghosts," Noah said.

Thalia smiled at Noah. "Well said!"

"Given that Reginald is trying to destroy The Mark, and The Mark includes Granite, you do have a big problem, Thalia," Lish said.

"Thalia is astute enough not to let Reginald get his hands on the property," Joan said.

"Well, Joan, unless I can ...," Thalia spoke directly to both Noah and Lish. "Let me just say that I must believe both of you — Lish, Noah — when you say that you hear CAT. You are, if my information is correct, both descendants of Nibish and Hoshaphat."

"But isn't Reginald a blood descendent too? Your ancestor is Nibish."

"We have to work our way around that situation ... somehow." Thalia's voice was lost in a thunderous barrage. Then the lights went out.

Saturday, July 7

"It's nice of you to come with me," Charlie said. "It's no fun driving around without Luna. Now, looka' that. Some land gawkers." He pulled the old truck as far as he could to the side of the road and waved a car past. "I don't recognize the folks," he said. "I wonder what they're doin' on these back roads."

"Maybe they're lost," Lish said. "I didn't know there were still roads like this in southern Ontario."

Charlie laughed. "We don't call 'em roads, just interesting cow paths. If those folks get stuck in the corduroy washboard up ahead, they won't relish the walk to the nearest farm house."

In the crossroads community of Lavender, Charlie turned left. "I don't know why the place is called Lavender," he said. "There's nowt that resembles that flower growing wild around here. I drove this way so you can see Sanity Hill."

"Perhaps the name refers to lilacs. Every house seems to have a few bushes."

"Here an' I thought that Granite had a stranglehold on them," Charlie said. "Close your eyes, now. Promise not to peek until I say you can."

Lish did as she was told. "What's so special?"

"You'll see." Charlie parked the truck at the side of the road on the crest of a hill. "You can open those blinkers now."

"Charlie! How magnificent!" Far below lay the lush, forested valley of the Noisy River. Beyond, green hills folded to the horizon. Those farm structures that could be seen appeared as miniature buildings. "The Mark is beautiful in its own right. But this is so ... majestic. Look! The land beside us must be the highest in the area."

"And it's mine," Charlie said.

"You own it?"

"My dad bought it for back-taxes some time before the war," Charlie told her. "He wanted to provide a farm for both his sons. This is good plateau land, above the escarpment."

"You have a brother?"

"I had a brother," Charlie said. "He signed up before me and was killed in Italy. After the war, I came here — a lot. I had to have something to visually remind me about what exactly it was we were fighting to preserve. Come on. We're going for a little walk."

Charlie led the way through a high pasture to the top of the hill, where not even trees blocked the view. "Farmer Brown did me a favour by dumping his picking-pile right here," Charlie said. "Have a seat on my Thinking Stones."

Down in the valley, Lish could just make out the roofs of a few houses in the village of Dunedin. An ant-like tractor worked a field on a far hill. Lish could hear nothing but birdsong that carried on a gentle breeze.

"Do you like my little piece of heaven?" Charlie asked.

"I do," Lish said. "Charlie, you're always thinking of others. During all our chats with Thalia, you've not said much about yourself."

"There's not much to tell," Charlie said, leaning against the warm stones.

"Sanity Hill ... Thinking Stones ... quoting Sir Walter Scott," Lish said. "There's more to this man than meets the eye. Bud told me that you and he served together."

"We were pals in the SAS — Special Air Service. Reconnaissance in both Italy and France."

"Then you must be able to speak, and understand, French, Italian, and German."

"An' Dutch and Farmglish too. It took me a year to get back into the swing of speaking Farmglish, so's I'd feel at home again. Did Bud tell you that I was married?" Charlie asked.

"He didn't say a thing about that."

"Well, I was." Charlie tucked his hands into overall pockets. "My wife was Bud's wife's best friend. I was demobbed in early '46. She was going to follow, even had a bunk on the Samaria with a few hundred other war brides. I was to meet her in Montreal."

"She didn't come?"

"Nope. I got a telegram saying that she'd changed her mind, and that a letter would follow. Of course, Bud's wife knew the story. It seems everyone knew the story but me."

"Oh, Charlie!" Lish put her hand on Charlie's arm. "How terrible."

"It appeared so at the time. The gist of her wanting out of the marriage was that her former fiancé appeared on the scene. She thought that he had been killed in action. He turned up after the war ended. It turned out he'd been a prisoner of war. She decided to divorce me so that she could marry him."

"A British or Dutch girl?" Lish asked.

"British," Charlie said. "A London girl. Farm life wouldn't have suited her, anyway. I heard from her lawyer. The divorce was finalized quick enough."

"There were no children?"

"Nope. Not from lack of ...." Charlie coughed. "Nuff said about that. Bud's wife came over and adjusted pretty well until Glenn came along."

"So, this was where you came when you needed time for yourself. This is your refuge-in-a-storm."

"Yep," Charlie said. "Sometimes the nightmares were so bad. Sitting up here, like I did — still do sometimes — made me realize that there were things I needed to get on with —life being one of them."

"Thank you for sharing your life story with me."

"Not a problem," Charlie said. "I figure that you need to understand there's more to save then just Thalia's little patch of ground. There's this!" Charlie stood and flung his arms to the horizon.

There are humans need saving, too, and more than one life to get on with, Lish thought as she accepted Charlie's hand to get up. She continued to hold his hand as they walked back to the truck.

"How be, after we pick up the chop in Glen Huron, we take the back roads again to Collingwood and Wasaga? Do you want to see where I spent my summers trolling for girls?"

"I'd love to, as long as somewhere along the way we stop for lunch."

Charlie drove through Dunedin and turned onto the Glen Huron Line before he said, "I don't think he will, but if Rotten Reggie happens to be in touch with Thalia — or shows up at Granite when I'm not around — will you let me know right away? She's deadly afraid of that man."

"I'll ring the bell or put Thalia in the car and drive away. I can't believe there's such animosity between mother and son."

Charlie shifted gears as the truck climbed the steep ridge road. "You might not have noticed, but Thalia never refers to the Rotter as her son. Maybe it's because she doesn't want to believe that he's as crazy as an outhouse rat. Dang," he said, as he ground the gears. "I'm losing my touch with this old rig. Must be the distracting company I'm keeping today."

"Can I ask a serious question, Charlie?"

"Fire away."

"Do you really hear CAT?" Lish looked at Charlie so seriously he couldn't meet her gaze.

"I try to," he said. "An' sometimes I think that I do. It might sound stupid, but all through the war I told myself I had to survive, to come home to save CAT. That's what kept me going ... kept me sane. That's what holds me to this land today. Maybe that's what CAT is all about: dedication ... loyalty? Jeff says it's a myth gone mad."

"Did you know that Bud sold Jeff some of his land?"

"I knew it, and that bothers me, considerably," Charlie said. "Do me a favour, Lish. You be careful around Jeff. He's my nephew, sure enough, but he does have a girlfriend. And lately, he's got some strange ideas."

"He's not asked me out since our lunch at Georgie's," Lish said. "I gathered from Noah he's currently pretty stuck on a woman in Collingwood."

"I think she's a secretary, works in an office. I have her name in my pocket." Charlie pulled to the side of the road. "Nuff said about that. Now, out we get to take a look back over the valley — back to where we were, just so you'll remember how precious this countryside is."

CHAPTER 5
The Week of July 8–14

Monday, July 9

Charlie knew by the way Lish drove her car up the laneway that something was wrong at Granite, but he didn't expect the situation would involve Luna.

Lish was out of the car before he managed to reach it. "Luna's gone! Her puppies are gone! I would have rung the bell, but thought I should check the road. Noah's walking the riverbank."

"Now, that is out of character for Luna," Charlie said. "When did you last see her?"

"Just after ten o'clock last night. When I came down this morning, she and the pups were gone."

"Did anyone check the buildings on the home farm and the drive shed?"

"No."

"Did you hear anything during the night?"

"Nothing. Thalia said that she slept lightly and would have heard if something was amiss," Lish said.

"How did Luna get out?"

"Once, when Thalia got up in the middle of the night to let Luna out, she tripped on a floor mat. We began to prop the back doors open so Luna could come and go as she pleased," Lish said.

"It was Thalia's idea. She figured that as long as Luna was with us, we didn't have to worry about Reginald."

During the conversation, Charlie's eyes searched the garden, the barnyard, and near fields. "No doubt that she's all right. Luna just might be bringing the puppies home the hard way. I'll tell Joan to be on the lookout, check the out-buildings and barn here, then cut across the fields. She'd probably cross the river at the ford and come up the back lane."

"I'll drop in at Delaneys' on my way back," Lish said. "They can be on the lookout, too."

"Good idea," Charlie said. "That's something they wouldn't mind getting involved in."

"And Bud?"

"I'll call him. He can check his property, although I can't imagine why Luna would go that way. Will you stop in at Georgie's and ask her to pass the word?"

Charlie couldn't help but feel sorry for Lish. He put his arm around her shoulders. "Don't worry now, girl. Luna will be fine."

"Charlie, do you think that Reginald might have something to do with her disappearance?"

"Nah," Charlie said. "Luna would have put up a real fight if Rotten Reggie went near her. I'm pretty sure that she just decided she wanted a change of scenery. I'm going to get Joan up so she can watch at this end."

By mid-morning, fields and buildings had been checked, but Luna was not to be found. Charlie, Noah, Lish, and Thalia stood by the bell. Charlie and Noah swept the valley with binoculars.

"Luna's gone to-ground," Charlie said. "She did this once before, but not with pups. She doesn't want to be found."

"We can leave food on the back porch and rig the door," Lish said.

Noah laughed. "That's an open invitation for all racoons to have a feast at Thalia's expense."

"Luna is quite capable of taking care of herself and the pups in the wild. She's a smart dog. She'll make her whereabouts known when she's good and ready to do so," Charlie said.

"You're probably right," Noah agreed. "I can sympathize with the pooch. Maybe she just wanted some peace and quiet."

"Perhaps she's protecting her pups," Thalia said. "But from what?"

"Let's just leave be for a while and try not to worry about her," Charlie said. "Lish, would you give me a ride home? Chores don't take a holiday. I'd better check on Joan, then get back to work."

The Delaney boys were checking the ditches on both sides of the road when Lish drove past their property. She stopped near Tom and rolled down her window. "Thanks, Tom. Thank the others too."

"Yeah, thanks," Charlie said. "It's good of you to help."

"You're welcome," Tom said. "By the way, Miss MacPherson ... Lish. Thanks for the pleasant time we had yesterday."

As Lish pulled away, Charlie gave her an odd look. "I saw Tom talking to you after church. Then you begged off the picnic. You spent the afternoon with a Delaney?"

Lish laughed. "I can tell by the tone of your voice that you don't approve."

"Nah. Let's just say I'm surprised."

"Well, so was I when Tom asked if I could give him and Dick a lift to Collingwood. They wanted to visit an old chum of theirs who's in bad shape — near death, I understand. The other two would have come along, but Harry needed WGD to help him fix their car."

"Tom and Dick are not bad guys, just a little misguided,"

Charlie said. "No girls were good enough for the Delaney boys, by their mother's standards."

"Tom told me that she came from a really poor Irish family. Bud indicated that they were never made to feel welcome in Seven Springs due to some old feud. Thalia mentioned there was bad blood between families."

Lish slowed as she passed the cottages, looking for a sign that Gloria and Bernard were around. Their car wasn't in the drive.

Charlie, who'd been unusually quiet on the drive through Seven Springs, finally said, "So don't keep me in suspense. What did the three of you do?"

"Tom and Dick visited their army buddy. I drove around Collingwood then up toward Meaford and back toward Wasaga Beach — passed through Collingwood at least twice on my rambles. I'd packed a lunch and stopped for a picnic at that shale beach you showed me on Saturday."

"Too bad you had to eat alone," Charlie said.

"Not really. I needed some time to myself." Lish turned the car onto the concession road. "You said the other day that you owned land below Delaney's — at the foot of their hill."

"Dad bought one hundred acres of pastureland near the cottages," Charlie said. "It came along with his estate. So, what did you do that kept you away from Granite until last night?"

"Charlie Barnes! You are one nosy fellow."

"I'm just itching to hear about life in the fast lane with the Delaney brothers."

Lish laughed. "The trip was not without merit. You realize that Jeff didn't hang around for the picnic, either. On one of my passes through Collingwood, I saw him and his girlfriend going into one of the real estate offices, probably for a little hanky-panky. A big sign in the window read "Northlands Development."

"Whoa!" Charlie exclaimed. "Are you sure?"

"She had the key. Jeff stood behind her while she opened the door."

"He saw you?"

"No, I'm sure he didn't."

"Well, I'll be," Charlie said. "I knew he wasn't too keen on running a garage. He's not a bad kid, you know, just ill-advised."

"I've only been here three weeks, Charlie. I wouldn't know if he was good or bad."

"I've just had the feeling recently Jeff doesn't want to be stuck in Seven Springs all his life. There's nothing here for him, really. Nothing for anyone if they're young and ambitious.... waul, even if they're old and crotchety. Some years the crops are so poor, many a farmer thinks, chuck it. Then they look around and think, damn it! Give it another year."

"Jeff's your problem, Charlie. Didn't I hear that, because you have no children, you plan to hand the farm over to him when the time comes for you to retire?"

"That *was* the plan," Charlie said.

"If you did give the farm over, Jeff would then own land at both top and bottom of the Valley," Lish said. "That's an interesting situation, given Reginald's attraction to Jeff's father."

"And Delaneys owned the middle," Charlie said.

"They still do own the middle. Nothing's been signed. Tom, Dick, Harry, and WGD are a wary crew. They're as distrustful of Reginald as the rest of you. Tom confided that they are financially hard up. They can't fix the house — can't buy newer farm equipment."

"And when did he tell you this?"

"When we were having supper at a little restaurant last night." Lish turned into Charlie's laneway, then slammed on the brakes.

Charlie threw his hands against the dash. "My God, woman! You almost put me through the windshield."

"Look! Luna!" Lish said. "Over there!"

Luna stopped several times to look back toward the farm, then disappeared into the wildflower meadow.

"She's not carrying a pup," Charlie said. "She's heading for the river."

"That's odd," Lish said. "It looks like she wants someone to follow her. Did she come looking for you, Charlie?"

By the time Lish and Charlie reached the edge of the meadow, Luna had crossed the river and disappeared into the dense bush.

"Don't fret, Lish. We know pooch is okay now. She'll show herself again. You sure you didn't hear anything last night?"

"No. After I came home, I sat with Luna for a while, patted her, and ... well, chatted about Tom, Jeff, Frank. Do you know she licked my hand and whined every time I mentioned Frank?"

"Dogs listen well," Charlie said. "Better than humans, sometimes. You realize that I missed the picnic, too. I drove to Toronto and had a little chat with your landlord."

"Charlie! Why would you do such a thing? If you told him where you lived, and where I might be found. Oh, Charlie ...."

"Now, don't worry, Lish. I pretended that I was looking for an apartment, parked my car two blocks away, and walked to the house. I spoke with an English accent, and dressed the part, too."

"How did you find my city address?"

"I wasn't in the SAS for nothing," Charlie said. "Dino's a nice fellow. He shared a glass or two of homemade wine, and a few stories, with me. He said that he might have an apartment come available in a month or so, depending on what the lady tenant was going to do. He mentioned that he'd be in touch with his tenant if he knew where she was because a couple of crumb-bums have been looking for her. He showed me a pile of mail for her."

"Why Charlie? Why ..."

"For personal reasons, I had to find out whether you are for real or a patsy for Campbell, O'Hearn & Yule — or Rotten Reggie."

"And?"

"Oh, you're for real all right, my girl. Come on into the house. We'll make lunch for Joan. That pile of mail is on the dining room table. As I said, I learned a few things in the SAS that still come in handy. Dino will just think that he misplaced the pile."

"Charlie Barnes! I don't know whether to slap you or to cry."

"A good cry always melts a man's heart," Charlie said, "especially mine when the tears are on the cheeks of the prettiest woman I've *ever* met, bar none."

Mulmur Murmurings by Hugh Dunnit
For the Week of July 7–14

Mercy! Our favourite dog has gone missing, her brood in tow. If you spot her, call the Cagey Farmer, Charlie B., immediately. This is one four-legged resident of the Springs that we do not want to lose.

To add interest to intrigue, signs of a big feline — a bobcat or cougar — have been seen in the Valley. Now, let's not get trigger happy about this. For the first time in nearly seventy years a super cat just might be calling the Springs area home. Leave it be. There is room for everyone around here, including beasts of the four-legged kind.

Regardless how big, or wild, the feline, there's nothing can beat the cat fights in the Springs and Valley. Down Dunedin way, Henriette C took on Josie P the other day over whose laundry was whitest. The dust-up ended in a draw with both lines and dames on the ground. Perhaps the empty bottles seen in Mrs. C's garbage had more to do with the cat fight than the choice of laundry bleach?

Two old bachelor boys were seen stepping out in lively fashion on the arm of the Lovely Damsel. I understand that a good time was had by the boys who haven't been in female company for so long they probably forgot how to act.

It may be that my eyes were deceiving me, but I declare that the prodigal son, the one with dollar signs in his eyes, was recently seen in the Springs. Those who like to push his buttons, duly take note — not aim.

CHAPTER 6
The Week of July 15–21

Monday, July 16

Lish glanced in the dingy office window to make sure that Len was there. He was, seated behind the cluttered desk, car magazine in one hand, a cigarette in the other.

Len looked up as she entered. "If you're looking for Jeff, he went to Orangeville for parts for that Ford taking up space in the garage."

"It's you I'm looking for," Lish said. She put an electric toaster on top of a couple of wrenches on the desk. "This appliance quit this morning. Thalia said before she bought another one I should bring it to you. She said that you're good at fixing things."

Len reached to turn the radio down a bit, butted the cigarette, and said, "It's probably just the cord or plug. Looks like it's been yanked. That's what you ladies do, you know, just yank cords outta plugs without a thought to what you're doing to them." He cleared a spot in front of him and reached for the appliance. "Sit down. It won't take too much time to fix, if that's all it is."

"Thanks," Lish said, wondering what to do with the pile of newspapers she'd taken off the chair.

"Just toss 'em in the box by the stove," Len said. "They'll come in handy first cool day. Before you land, can you hand me that small box off the shelf — over there where the bird carvings are. The box says 'electrical plugs' on it?"

How anyone can find anything around here is a miracle, Lish thought as she retrieved the dust-covered box. It doesn't look like this has been disturbed in some time. "Len, do you do electrical repairs for everyone?"

"I don't make it known that I can fix small appliances," Len said. "But the local folks bring things in — whenever. There's coffee. I'll use a mug. You can drink out of the lid. Georgie washed the thermos this morning when she filled it for me." Len pulled a coffee-stained mug from a drawer.

"Do you want me to wash the mug for you?"

"Nope. It ain't killed me yet," Len said, examining the toaster. "I haven't seen you around much the last week or so, Miss MacPherson."

"Please, call me Lish. I've been ferrying Joan from the farm to Granite. She's taken a bad turn and Charlie's really busy. And Thalia has a ... I'm helping Thalia with her work ," Lish said. Who, she thought, knows that Thalia is an author?

"So, you're Thalia's new secretary. I bet she's working those dainty fingers of yours right down to the bone," Len grinned. "S'okay. I know what Mrs. Logan Russo does to keep a roof over her head. But it is best to be careful who you tell around here these days. So many people are coming in from away, you know."

"It's good that the local people respect her desire for privacy," Lish said.

"She's a good person." Len deftly removed screws from the bottom of the toaster. "A few of us owe her a favour or two." Len's efforts were interrupted by the phone ringing. "The garage ... Nope ... Nope ... Nope ... Yep, I'll tell him."

Lish laughed. "You need an office girl, Mr. Grant."

"Told Jeff that I'm getting too old for the job," Len said. "At my age, I'd rather be sitting in front of a television than in a drafty blacksmith shop."

"Maybe a new garage building would help?" Lish said, looking around.

Len laughed. "Maybe a good fire would solve the problem. Jeff says not to worry. Life won't be this boring for long. He always talks big, you know. Jeff has steak ideas on a ground beef income. That's what Reggie tells him."

"Reggie, as in Reginald Russo?" Lish asked. "Thalia's son?"

Len looked up. "Yep. The one she raised, all right. Reggie himself."

"May I ask a rather personal question?" Lish asked.

"Fire away."

"If Jeff is in his early thirties, like he told Noah, you must have married rather late. I mean ...," Lish stammered, "when you were a more ... mature man."

Len chuckled. "You're being polite now. I married Elizabeth Barnes when I was thirty-five years old. She, God rest her soul, was twenty. I was in the war, you see — that's the First World War — and didn't want to settle down when I got back. I just wandered around for a while to get my bearings again."

"The War, then the Depression," Lish said. "Lots of lives were disrupted by both."

Len pawed through the tools on his desk, picked a screwdriver, and said, "Can you look in the drawer — up there by the animal carvings — to see if there's a driver looks like this should? The box says 'small tools.' The blade's broken on this one. I should have throw'd it out a long time ago, but you get attached to things."

While Len poured coffee, Lish rummaged through the drawer. "I can't help but admire these carvings, Len. Would you consider selling some of them?"

"I guess so, as long as the folks don't fuss about a little dust on 'em," he replied. "I can always make more. I could use the money. I sure wish Jeff had taken up with a woman who don't mind dirt. His current pair of walking legs won't darken the doors of this place."

"I heard he was planning to build a big house for her up on the heights, above the Delaney place."

"Do tell," Len said. "I don't think so. First, he wouldn't have enough money to buy that piece of land. Second, she wouldn't live around here, not for love nor money."

Len doesn't have the look of a man telling a lie, Lish thought. He really doesn't know about the land purchase. "Perhaps I was wrong about the area," she said.

"Once, Charlie did offer him the pastureland for a good price. He figured maybe Jeff wanted to build a new shop ... or house, I suppose. The offer was eventually withdrawn. I can't imagine why Jeff would even think of building a new garage, though. There's more people leaving Seven Springs than moving in. The place is dying. For some young people, crudscape and boxitecture glitter like gold. City lights, you know, blinking dangerous they are for villages like ours."

"You don't like the city," Lish said.

"Yep," Len said, "I don't like the city."

"The other day, I was helping Thalia put names on some of the old photographs for a historical display at the autumn bazaar," Lish said, telling a half-truth. "There weren't any children in the school photos with the last name Grant. Was your family not from around here?"

Len wound the old toaster cord around his hand then laid it aside. "You are a clever lady, Miss MacPherson. I was born up near Midland. That's where I met Frank Russo. He was working on construction up that way. Frank took me under his wing. He helped me get a job — introduced me to his boss and J.D. Boys, oh boys! We were a pair! J.D. wasn't one to marry young, either."

"Well, I've heard that some men do have a penchant for sowing a few wild oats," Lish said.

"Women, too." Len handed Lish a flashlight. "Give me some light so's I can see if there's a broken wire or something. You see, Miss MacPherson, Dad's blacksmith shop was right on the home-place. We're talking about a young buck who'd never been off the farm, if you know what I mean."

"I do understand," Lish said. All too well, she thought. If Len was a randy young buck while hanging around with the Russo brothers, they must have had their spread-the-oats moments, too.

"Afore you ask, after I married Elizabeth Barnes, Thalia gave me an interest-free loan to buy this place, but she never really did collect on the money," Len said. "Now, while I attach a new cord, how be you go to Georgie's for a couple of ham sandwiches and pie. I didn't pack lunch and am as hungry as a hog. Call it payment for a job, hopefully, well done."

"Mustard or mayonnaise" Lish asked.

"Both." Len smiled. "I ain't shared lunch with a young woman in years. Look! How about this. Why don't I finish the job, we test it, and you drive us to Hornings Mill so's we can have lunch out. That's if you're not embarrassed to be seen with me?"

"Len Grant, I'd love to take you out for lunch. How be we pick up Thalia on the way?"

"Just you and me, if you don't mind," Len said. "It's been a long time since I've seen my wife."

"But she died ... didn't she?" Lish asked.

"Yep. Lizzie died far too young — had rheumatic fever when she was a child that left her in poor health all her short, sweet life. I've a few things to chat with her about ...." Len's voice trailed off. "Say! Has Luna come home yet?"

"No. Noah saw her last, a day ago. She wouldn't come when he called her. He said that she seemed to be heading for Granite."

"She's just being cagey," Len said. He pulled the radio's cord out and plugged the toaster into the socket. Len held his hand over the appliance. "You're in the burnt toast business again."

"Thanks," Lish said, gathering her purse and sweater. "Thalia was wondering if you've seen Reginald recently. She was a little disturbed by Friday's Murmurings. She says that the bit about the prodigal son was a reference to Reginald."

"I thought that I saw his car a few days ago, down by Maggie's place," Len said. "But he doesn't stop in so much anymore. We had words, a while ago. He doesn't take kindly to a good buckin'. He's always figured he was right, didn't matter what about."

"Do you recall when Hugh Dunnit started to write Mulmur Murmurings?" Lish asked.

"It had to be after we got the telephone in the Valley," Len said. "That's the only way I figure he can get the information to the paper so quick. He has to phone it in. At the beginning, I figured it was Frank Russo, but the column continued after Frank disappeared. And besides, during his last few years, Frank couldn't have written anything that made sense."

"You think that Dunnit is a he?" Lish asked.

Len laughed. "Look at it this way. There's a 50 percent chance that she is."

"What was Frank Russo like toward the end?"

"We had our fun together," Len said. "But Frank was a sick, angry man by the time he disappeared."

"Is Reginald anything like him?"

"Nope," Len said. "They were as opposite as stone to wood."

Tuesday, July 17

After spending an hour chasing cattle out of the wildflower meadow, Charlie and Noah attempted to fix the breach in the fence, Charlie doing most of the work.

"Noah, you're not paying much attention to what we're trying to do," Charlie said, putting his weight against the fencepost. "I've asked you twice now to pull the wire tight around the post. You're wool-gathering."

"I'm sorry about that," Noah said, twisting the wire with a pair of pliers. "I didn't hear you."

"Kid, you're darn tootin' you didn't. Do you want to take a break?"

"Are you up to giving some advice?" Noah asked.

"Are you up for fielding a few questions?" Charlie countered. "Come on. Let's get a drink from the pasture spring. I saw some rabbit fur and dog tracks around there yesterday. We'll keep an eye out for Luna on the way."

"It's strange how a domesticated animal can adapt to the wild," Noah said.

"The question is, why is Luna doing it? I have to admit I'm a little concerned for her and the pups. If we're dealing with a wild cougar in the area, Luna will defend those pups to her death."

"I don't know what to make of the yowls I hear," Noah said. "Real? Imaginary?"

"One thing for sure, until an animal is seen ... Last one in's a dirty rotter!" Charlie stripped down to naked.

"You snake!" Noah said. "You didn't say anything about a swim." He stripped quickly and they both ran for the river.

After a long, refreshing swim, they lay in the long grass, Charlie with his straw hat over his private parts. "Now, they wouldn't dry like apples on a string," he said.

Noah laughed. "Charlie Barnes, you're one of a kind."

"Dad's theory was that jewels were better fungal than fried. But you just can't be too careful. What if those two snoops are around snapping pictures? You'd look pretty good in some publication with everything hanging out," Charlie said. "Do you want to go first, with our little chat? I'm good at giving advice — as long as no one takes it seriously."

"Come on, Charlie. You've got eighteen years of experience on me. You're nearly old enough to be my father," Noah said.

"Don't rub it in," Charlie said. "So what's bothering you? Take your time. Don't say anything you'll regret later."

Noah watched the ever-changing pattern of the clouds as they drifted overhead, wishing he could sort his problems out as easily as the winds did the nebula. "Have you ever thought about those fellows who circled the earth — Glenn and Carpenter? When they can do that in under five hours, what are a couple of minute specks like us doing down here, taking weeks, months to do the same thing?"

"They didn't leave their lives behind. When they got back to Earth, they had to deal with the same old problems that were plaguing them before they left," Charlie said.

"But the problems on Earth must appear slight compared to what they experienced up there."

"Everything in perspective," Charlie said. "Think about The Mark being your spacecraft. What was eating you that you blasted off to here?"

"I've got to leave soon, Charlie. I've sorted through some of my problems and now realize that I can't put my music on hold forever. The problem is that I've got to find a good excuse for dropping out, then back into that life again — without hurting anyone."

"You regretting your little respite here? When you arrived, you never really said *exactly* how you ended up on The Mark, at least not to me, or Thalia. We just took you at face value."

"It was kind of both of you to do so," Noah said.

"Well," Charlie said, "you eventually proved we were right. You told us about the letters. You hear CAT, if I understand correctly."

"And share the same dream with Lish, Hunter Logan, and a few others," Noah said.

"Most of my dreams are about milking cows, working the back forty, and fixing tractors," Charlie said. "Except for the other night. I had my sights, as in eyeballs, on this big antlered buck that was drinking from Grotto Spring. I'd have to see him in real life to believe the size. Face value does have merit."

"Does it? Or do I just say what people want to hear — things my grandfather spoke about?" Noah said.

"Now, that's what's been bothering me," Charlie said. "Who's genuine and who's not. Take Jeff Grant for instance."

"He's not genuine," Noah said.

"You've been hanging around with him."

"Only to figure out whose back pocket he's living in," Noah said. "I think he is getting money from Rotten Reggie. But why?"

"One star for you!" Charlie said. "Back to your first comment. I agree that if Jason Curlew doesn't want to drop off the charts, he's got to make a reappearance, and soon. You've just got to be careful about how you re-enter the rarefied air of the music business. You've got to be prepared for repercussions — negative and positive."

"I know what it could do for Northlands Development. The beggars flogging that project would take advantage of any publicity generated," Noah said. "We don't want that."

"Darn tootin' we don't," Charlie said. He rolled onto his stomach, but made sure the hat stayed in place.

"Getting a sunburn?" Noah asked.

"Nope. I just didn't want you to smack 'em when I ask my second question," Charlie said. "Hypothetically speaking, if you drew attention to The Mark, then — through ancestral claim to Indian lands — *demanded* your share, you would stand to gain much financially, wouldn't you?"

"I don't want money. But I would like to share The Mark ... with Thalia or whoever she chooses to protect Logan's land — my ancestral land. I'd like to come back every once in a while to get away from pressures," Noah said. "Have you ever stood before an audience who expects perfection? Sometimes I am so tired, so drained, that I just want to get the show over with so that I can sleep."

"Nope. Fer me, it's stressful enough having to take up the collection in church."

"You know where I stand on land ownership. Now, more than ever, the land — Mother Earth — is my spiritual base. It's not a source for anyone's financial gain. It shouldn't be treated as bargain-and-buy real estate."

"We've been through this discussion before. We all know that, in this day and age, nothing's going to change. Certain people chase big bucks and ride the trail, regardless what they trample along the way," Charlie said. "The world evolves, but often not for the good of everyone. On the other hand, there are some people catch the ride and know enough to share the wealth."

Noah gave Charlie a strange look. "You're prophetic, Charlie. You know that?"

"It comes with this territory," Charlie said. "You can't live around Thalia and think normally."

"Then I believe that the person to hold the papers for The Mark must be trustworthy and responsible enough to adhere to the traditional heritage and stewardship of the land."

"Okay," Charlie said. "Two stars for you. You want to be that person?"

Noah took a long time to answer. "No," he finally said. "No, unless I was the last option that Thalia had. I'm not clever enough to handle all the emotional, political, and financial implications, and I don't plan to wed any time soon again. I don't anticipate having any descendants to carry on the responsibility."

"You don't have children now?" Charlie asked.

"No. I was married, but fathered no children," Noah answered.

"So, how are you planning to explain your re-entry into the rat race?"

"I haven't figured that one out yet. I thought perhaps Lish could help me think of something. There's Bernard and Gloria to deal with, sooner or later. It depends on what they want."

"Why so?"

"Some kind of a deal Lish made with them."

"About what?" Charlie sat up.

"I don't know," Noah said. "But I trust Lish. She hasn't blown my cover, or Thalia's."

"Or her own," Charlie said. "Lish has a couple of her own problems to sort out."

"They are not insurmountable," Noah said, "if she knows we all trust her. You do trust her don't you, Charlie?"

"Well, she did drop in on Thalia rather unexpectedly. She worked for some people I do not trust. On the other hand, she's really taken the bit in her mouth about The Mark — asking questions, digging around."

"Charlie! You don't seriously believe Lish has gained our confidence to undermine Thalia. You don't think that she's here to do damage ..."

"Oh, Lish will do damage," Charlie said. "But the question is, to whom? Thalia thinks Lish is indispensable — reminds her of herself when she was young. Thalia says that she's the right person come at the right time."

"Lish is a clever, assertive woman," Noah said.

"I think those sorts of things are bred-in-the-bone," Charlie said. "I like a woman who has a head on her shoulders that's not only pretty but functional. Lish has got what it takes to make skeletons dance. And there are a few hanging in closets in these hills that need to do a jig."

"Have you got any old family bones that are going to get a rattling?" Noah asked.

"Maybe mine just need a slight jiggling," Charlie said. "You know, if we're going to keep the cattle out of the flower meadow, we'd better get back to the job, don't you think?"

They were walking back to the fence line before Noah asked, "Did I pass muster?"

Charlie put his hand on Noah's shoulder. "Let's just say that I learned in the SAS never to take things, or people, at face value. There's always another side to folks when they're under pressure or threatened. You're a good man, Noah Jason Curlew. Try to keep it that way."

"And should Thalia — and Lish — and I trust you, Charlie? You're closest to Thalia. You stand to gain the most."

"Or lose the most," Charlie said quietly. "It's only human to have a few unanswered questions hanging about. I'll admit that I'm as human as the rest of you."

"That's an evasive answer," Noah said.

"Look, if you trust yourself, trust me," Charlie said. "I'll do the right thing for The Mark."

Wednesday, July 18 — The Morning

From Granite, Thalia saw smoke on the eastern horizon when she got up to put the coffee pot on. She thought that she saw flames licking the early morning sky. "Lish! Lish!" she called up the stairs. "Look out your window. Do you see smoke? If you could go to the store, Georgie will know what's going on. If it's a fire, stay around to help where you can."

Lish dressed quickly, grabbed a piece of toast, and drove toward Seven Springs. Down in the valley, the acrid smell of burning wood hung in the air, and a faint mist seemed to drift on the wind. None of the usual characters were lounging on the steps at the General Store. As a matter of fact, Seven Springs seemed deserted. The store was empty but for someone banging around in the kitchen.

"Georgie? What's up? Where's everyone? Where's the smoke coming from?"

Georgie stuck her head around the door. "There's a barn fire a couple of concession roads over, down Stanton way. If you're not doing anything, I can use some help making sandwiches. Len's going to pick them up. The guys will be at the fire for a while. They need to eat. Grab some loaves of bread from the shelf — tins of salmon and tuna too."

"Have you heard how it started?

"It seems that old man Cormack was burning something and sparks flew into the hayloft. I hear that the cows are all on pasture, so there's no livestock lost. Water's a problem, though. The creek's not close to the barn. You butter, I'll fill.

Georgie was a whirlwind — filling, slicing, stashing food in bags. It was all Lish could do to keep up with her.

"By the way you work, you do this often, Georgie."

"Urgent need pushes a few buttons," Georgie replied. "You've got to understand that something like a fire is big excitement around here. Everyone lights out to see the show."

"And to help, I hope," Lish said. "Pity the farmer who's losing everything and becomes a sideshow while it's burning."

"Yes, and that, too. The men will work like machines to save what they can. The women supply the food. Len's been running supplies for the past hour."

The door slammed out front. Georgie looked out and said, "Mrs. MacDonald, just put the cookie tins on the counter. You got your name on them? Good. I'll make sure you get them back."

Lish finished buttering the bread. "Anything else I can do?"

"Find a big box and put all the cookies you can gather into it, including those in the tins on the counter. Len will be here in about ten minutes for the next load."

When Len pulled in, Georgie and Lish helped carry food to his car. "Can you spare some soda pop?" he asked.

"Take what you need," Georgie said. "I'm out of bread, so I can't make more sandwiches. How's the battle going?"

"I think we're gaining on the fire. Charlie and some neighbours are going to take care of the cows."

"Sorry about the sandwich bit." Georgie said.

"Don't worry. Food's coming from Mansfield and Stanton too," Len replied. "Take a break, ladies."

"By jeepers!" Georgie sat at a table and fumbled for her packet of cigarettes. "This is the second barn fire in six weeks. Makes you wonder, doesn't it?"

"What are you going to do when someone like Maggie comes in for her loaf of bread?" Lish asked.

"I'll call my supplier right away. The shelves won't be empty for long," Georgie said. "I just don't know when they'll get paid though."

"You don't get paid for what you give?"

"I don't expect money. Thanks is payment enough," Georgie said. "But I have to tell you, I can't go on forever living on what I'm making at this store. That's why hubby's got a job driving a truck, just so we can stay around here. The old folks expect a store in the village. As far as the young people are concerned, they're leaving. There's no work for them."

"In other words, there's trouble in paradise," Lish said.

"That's one way of putting it. By the way, those two outlanders left an envelope for you. They said they'll be at the cottage today and tomorrow, and will expect to see you."

"I wondered when they'd surface again."

There was no beating around the bush as far as Georgie was concerned. "Why are you even talking to them, Lish? They're bad news for Thalia and that Noah fellow. You know who *he* is, don't you?"

"I needed their help with a personal matter, Georgie. If I can be blunt with you ..."

"Go ahead. I've got a thick skin."

"If someone — say, Reginald Russo — offered you a tidy sum for this store, would you take it?"

Georgie laughed. "I've already turned that madman down twice. I told him that as long as there is a Seven Springs, there'll be a store with me in it."

"And what was his response?" Lish asked.

"Oh, he's smooth-talking, that one. He said that if a ski resort is built, I'd have so much business, I'd have to expand the store. Rather, he'd expand the store because he'd own the building, but I could run the business just like it was my own."

"There could be some truth in what he said," Lish said.

"Think it through, Lish. Say a resort is built. It would surely have a snack bar and restaurant. Who's going to come here?"

"What about groceries?"

"That's an easy one to answer. Those people who'd buy the high-priced chalets would arrive for the weekend and bring groceries with them. Sure, they might run short of milk or bread, but that's about it, as far as using a general store is concerned."

"You're right, Georgie. You're more astute than most. Someone else might have fallen for the sales pitch," Lish said.

"Look at it this way. Someone has to take a stand to try to keep a few of these small villages going. They'll all be as dead as dodo birds in twenty years time, if people abandon them."

"And the rural way of life will quickly follow," Lish said. "That has happened in so many places."

"You have to admit that there's something nice about knowing all your neighbours, helping when you can," Georgie said. "I'll see Seven Springs out to the very end. I keep thinking that there's got to be a way to have it both ways, if you get my drift."

"We'll have to give this some serious thought," Lish said. "Maybe talk to all those who believe like you ... like *we* do."

"Maybe," Georgie replied, not wanting to totally commit to Lish's suggestion. Anyone who would chat up a couple of slick city slickers had to be holding something close to her chest.

"I have to drive to Orangeville," Lish said. "Do you want me to pick up some loaves of bread for the store? Maybe I can get a dozen tins of salmon, same of tuna. And you're out of butter and milk. I'd have to pay the full price, but it's something I'd like to do for you so you won't have empty shelves for those who rely on you."

Maybe I am misjudging the woman, Georgie thought. "Thanks. I'd appreciate that. Maggie and Wee Jimmy usually come in daily for some little thing. As it is now, I can't even make them a sandwich for lunch."

"I'll be back before lunch so you have something for Maggie when she comes in," Lish said. "You won't miss too much business."

"You know, you shouldn't feel too sorry for Maggie. She's not as poor or feeble as she lets on," Georgie said.

"Why, then, does she accept help from Thalia?"

"I don't know. Maybe she doesn't like to say no. Perhaps she likes the attention. She doesn't have to rely on Wee Jimmy to ferry her around. She has a car and knows how to drive it," Georgie added. "I've seen her in Alliston and Cookstown. She gets around."

"Perhaps she's lonely," Lish said. "That's why she comes to the store every day."

"It's more like she's hanging around for the gossip," Georgie said. "I'm always careful what I say in front of her."

"Point taken," Lish said.

July 18 — The Afternoon

Gloria made a tolerable cup of tea and was probably the only one in Seven Springs that still had cookies in her jar. She waited at the door for Lish to get out of the car then led the way to the kitchen, where Bernard had papers spread all over the table.

"You're onto something big here," Bernard said, pointing to various pages. "Some pretty heavy-handed tactics were used to get these properties. Every single one of these people was cajoled into signing. They were old, feeble, suffered from memory loss. In one case, the individual was in a nursing home, for Pete's sake."

"I gather you're not too impressed with the tricks used by some of COY's executives," Lish said.

"Impressed? For the most part, they're a bunch of bloody crooks."

"You didn't seem to have a problem getting information," Lish said.

"In several cases, the families were only too glad to give detailed statements. Some offered to get a letter from a doctor supporting their concerns about their relative's inability to think for himself, or herself, as you can see," Bernard said.

"I'd say that, in at least three instances, valuable land was gotten in a very fraudulent manner. If challenged, the deal might not stand up in court," Gloria said. "The problem is that, in one instance, your name comes into play as a witness to the signature."

"COY sent me out with papers to be signed," Lish said. "I didn't have anything to do with the negotiations and terms of sale. I didn't realize there was a problem, or look into the situation, until I met a very old, confused man."

"The Lord alone knows how a lawyer could twist that information to suit his client," Bernard said.

"I'm not personally going to take this as far as the courts and lawyering," Lish told them.

"I don't think that COY wants this to be public knowledge, either," Gloria agreed.

"What did you find out about your landlord, Reginald Russo?" Lish asked.

"Oh, now the plot thickens," Bernard replied. "Where he was born, we don't know yet."

"It had to be Toronto. Thalia and Frank lived in Toronto after they were married," Lish said.

"There's no trace of him popping into this world in Toronto. That's not to say he didn't, though — sloppy records, you know."

"And doors slammed in our face," Gloria added. "We know that he was raised on the farm, attended school here, went to Hamilton for a while. He disappeared, then surfaced in Toronto in the land development business."

"I gather that he managed to avoid fighting in the war, but only because, even though he wasn't here, he is listed as a farmer," Bernard said. "We can't find out exactly what he did."

"The family was estranged by that time. Thalia thinks that his war contribution had something to do with steel manufacturing in Hamilton," Lish said.

"That's what he possibly told her, but we haven't confirmed that yet," Bernard said. "And here's the strange part: about eight years ago, he started to use another name — Russell Grant. He signs as J. Russell Grant.

"Russell Grant! A tall, balding, paunchy fellow?"

"The one and the same," Gloria said.

"I attended parties sponsored by COY and chatted with a Russell Grant. He showed enough interest in me that I accepted a dinner invitation — *two* invitations to dine with him. That's as far as it went, though. Dinners at an expensive restaurant."

"Well, J. Russell Grant equals Reginald Russo," Gloria said. "Here's a photo of Russell Grant." She handed Lish a small picture. "And here's one of Reginald Russo, both taken not a week ago."

Lish had difficulty believing what she was seeing. She knew the man all too well. A real charmer, he was. He even knew where she lived. Of course, that's where I heard a lot of meaningless rhetoric, including snippets of Reginald's version of Thalia's saga, after the man drank too much, Lish thought. What on earth will Charlie and Thalia think if they find out about my association with Russell Grant, a.k.a. Reginald Russo?

"You're finding all this hard to digest, Miss MacPherson?" Bernard asked.

"I'm shocked by your findings," Lish said. "If I recall, Russell Grant's slick story was that he had business interests in the States.

I've made good friends here. All of them have been hurt to some extent by this man."

Gloria cleared the tables of cups and teapot. "He was probably scoping you out to see if you were a good candidate to get more involved in COY's underhanded property dealings. You'll have to put a good defence together if you're going to tackle that brute," she said.

"I'll have to have a good defence to explain myself to Mrs. Russo, Charlie Barnes, and Noah Curlew," Lish said.

"They're not going to hear it from Gloria or me," Bernard said. "Want some advice?"

"I can use useful advice right about now," Lish said.

"Speaking from experience, people like Grant-Russo always have a vulnerable side. You're just got to find it, and exploit it, without getting bruised."

Gloria, gathering the papers, made an attempt to put them in alphabetical order. "Thanks for the down-payment. Cash is good. Can't be traced. We are looking forward to interviewing Jason Curlew."

"I'll talk with Noah and get back to you with when and where. I'll also pay the balance of what I owe, say tomorrow afternoon?"

"We can trust you to keep your word about Curlew? He's a hot topic right now."

"Trust me. He might even pose for a picture or two," Lish said. "Would you do me a favour? Could you continue to try to find a birth certificate or place of birth for Reginald? May I suggest that you look for the name Grant rather than Russo? Reginald and/or Russell Grant. Perhaps check records in Midland — or up that way."

"We'd be happy to," Bernard said, "for a further small fee."

Lish laughed. "Of course. For the money I'm paying, I do expect confidentiality, you understand."

"Our lips are sealed," Gloria said. "We'll see you tomorrow then? After lunch? You can keep the photos. I've billed them to your account."

July 18 — The Evening

Charlie was scrubbing the milk house when he heard the bell's ringing — one ... two ... three ... four. Before the fifth, he was out the door, running toward the house.

"Don't worry, Joan. I'm sure it's nothing," he called into the parlour while grabbing his jacket and truck keys. "I'm driving over. It's faster than fording the river and climbing the hill."

Joan came to the kitchen door. "Lish wouldn't ring the bell unless it was serious. Listen, the ringing hasn't stopped."

Charlie kissed his sister on the forehead. "There's nothing I can do until I know what the problem is. Lie down again, Joan. I'll be home as soon as I can."

Every possible scenario presented itself on Charlie's mad dash to Granite. Thalia's fallen down the stairs ... she's had a heart attack ... she's tripped on the back step ... she's fallen in the garden ... Rotten Reggie's shown up ...

The Delaney brothers were walking up the Line, and Noah was running down the road, as Charlie neared Thalia's laneway. Bud and Glenn were in their car behind him. Charlie stopped, applied the parking brake, left the truck running, and ran toward the bell tower. "Thalia? Thalia? You're ringing the bell? Where's Lish?"

"She's disappeared," Thalia said. "Gone, just like Frank and Luna. Gone!"

The Delaneys were hiking toward the bell. Bud and Glenn stood by Noah, Glenn restlessly shifting from foot to foot.

Charlie's hand went out to still the bell. No sense in summoning everyone in the Valley, he thought. Not yet, anyway.

"Come back to the house, Thalia." He put his arm through one of Thalia's to help her along. Somehow she'd made the trek to the bell without her cane. Noah took her other arm. The neighbours followed behind. By the time the group reached the house, Georgie's car was coming up the lane.

"Bud, would you shut my truck off?" Charlie asked. "I thought I might have to make a fast trip to the hospital."

Everyone crowded round the table and Charlie helped Thalia to a chair. Georgie pushed through and sat beside her.

"Now, Thalia, tell us what happened." Charlie looked around the kitchen. "Give the woman some breathing room. Move back a bit."

"We had supper," Thalia said. "Then I went into my study to work while Lish cleaned the table. She brought me a cup of tea, and ... I didn't see her again."

"How long before you knew she wasn't in the house?" Charlie asked.

"Oh dear," Thalia said. "Perhaps an hour. I got so busy writing that I lost track of time. Eventually I took my teacup to the kitchen. She wasn't there. I called upstairs, but she didn't answer. Then I saw the dishes ... in the pan."

Everyone looked toward the sink where a pan full of dishes sat, unwashed. An apron had been hastily thrown over several dirty pots.

"Then I noticed the doors," Thalia continued. "Both kitchen and porch doors were wide open. Her beige jacket is gone. And the flashlight — we always kept it on the hook by the door. And rubber boots. She left her shoes where the boots should be."

"What was she wearing?" Noah asked.

"Blue pants. Yellow blouse."

"I'm going to check her room," Charlie said. "Bud, you and Glenn do a quick search of the drive shed."

"Her car's still here," Tom said. "How be we check the barn and house ruins?"

"Good idea," Charlie agreed. "WGD, will you take a look down toward the stone? Pay close attention to the path. It's dusty as hell. Tracks will show up on it, if she went that way."

Charlie took the stairs two at a time. Lish's purse was on top of a large brown envelope on a chair near one of the windows. A pair of binoculars sat on the windowsill. She's either been watching for Luna or keeping an eye on me, Charlie thought. Luna! Does Lish's disappearance have anything to do with the dog? I wonder.

"What did you find?" Georgie asked him.

"Where Lish went, she didn't figure she needed her purse," Charlie said. "Or she didn't have time to get it. Let's wait to see if Bud and the Delaney boys find anything before we decide what to do next."

"Should we call the police?" Georgie asked.

"No. Not until we have to. I think maybe she went for a walk and got lost in The Mark," Charlie said. "If that's the case, it's gloaming. We haven't long to look before dark."

"Charlie, could Reginald be involved?" Thalia asked. "Lish asked some odd questions about him while we were eating supper."

"Why would your son abduct Lish?" said Noah.

"No one's seen him around. But we shouldn't rule him out," Charlie said, "because he's Reggie, and corrupt to the core."

"Why would he abscond with a woman he doesn't know?" Georgie asked.

"Maybe he thinks she's a threat to his trumped-up inheritance aspirations," Thalia said.

"Hush now, someone's coming." Charlie saw figures passing the porch windows.

"She's not in the drive shed." Bud wiped his feet before he came in. "I sent Glenn up the hill where we met her the other day. He can cover more ground in ten minutes than we can in an hour. I told him what to look for."

WGD stepped into the kitchen. "There's fresh prints in the dust on the trail going down to the stone," he said. "There's human, dog, and cat — a big cat. I picked this off a bush." WGD handed Charlie a tuft of tawny-coloured hair.

"Oh my dear!" Thalia cried out.

"Now, now, Thalia. Let's not get carried away. We have to do some straight thinking." Charlie turned to Tom, Dick, and Harry, who'd come into the kitchen. "Anything?"

"No sign of her in the buildings at the old farm." Tom said.

"Okay. Chances are that she's lost in The Mark. I don't want anyone in there tonight, because we'll end up with a couple more lost souls. Lish is smart enough to hunker down overnight. Somewhere she'll be safe. A crevice, maybe."

"If she's thinking, Lish will listen for water, then in the morning, follow the river down to the bridge," Noah said. "She's got her jacket. She'll stay warm."

"And if she doesn't?" Georgie asked.

"Then, we have to assume that the Lovely Damsel is either hurt, or not in the area," Tom said.

Charlie took charge. "Let's all meet here at the crack of dawn. We'll divide The Mark into squares and go over every inch of the place. What's that wailing?"

Bud listened then said, "Glenn's calling her name. It's echoing over the valley. The wife always said he'd have made a good soprano, if he was a woman."

Sounds just like CAT, Charlie thought. He looked out the

kitchen window. "Good lad," he said, watching Glenn rocketing from foot to foot as his high-pitched voice carried over the valley. "Does he do that all the time?"

"Sometimes he stands on the hill on the back forty and lets loose," Bud told him. "No one's around to hear."

"If Lish is around, she'll hear it for sure," Charlie said. "The sound will scare the devil out of Joan. Possibly it will scare a big cat enough to keep it off the prowl too."

"I'll stay with Thalia overnight," Georgie said.

"Do you mind sharing your bed, Thalia? I'd like to bring Joan back with me tonight, but it's too painful for her to go up any stairs today. I've got to go home to arrange for Len to milk the cows. Jeff can join the search, if he's around. The last I heard he went to Toronto."

"How be that we meet here at four a.m," Tom said. "We'll check our bush tonight, cause we know it like the back of our hand."

"Keep your eyes open for something that wears a lot of this." Charlie held up the tuft of hair. "And thanks, boys."

"Yes, thank you," Thalia said. "I've not ..."

"Now's not the time to dredge up past differences," Dick said. "We'll bring ropes and flashlights with us."

"Bud, will you stick around for a while with Glenn? Let him call until I get back with Joan?"

"Will do," Bud said. "I'll bring a first-aid kit with me in the morning. There's a stretcher in the church hall that used to belong to the first-aid group. And you don't need to worry about Glenn. He's as sharp-eyed as an eagle, but it'd be best if he stayed near the house if we're doing a square search."

"I'm not at all worried about Glenn," Charlie told him.

"If you don't mind, I'll check the road up toward the cabin again," Noah said. "She might come out on the road tonight."

"I'll go with you," Harry said. "We'll check the path into the cabin."

"If we don't find her by noon hour tomorrow, we'll call in a few more people," Charlie said.

"And the police," Georgie added.

"Them too," Charlie said. He waited until the men left the kitchen and Georgie went to find some bedding before he spoke quietly to Thalia. "You sure you didn't hear anything? A car door slamming ... Luna growling or barking ..."

"Luna. Of course, Lish went to look for Luna," Thalia said.

"My thoughts exactly," Charlie said.

"I'm sure that I saw Luna this morning, the other side of the bell. It was just a fleeting glimpse, mind you. I was out on the front porch looking at the smoke. You realize that was a serious comment I made about Reginald's possible involvement."

"I'm not sure there *isn't* some connection between Rotten Reggie and Lish," Charlie said. "What sort of odd questions did she ask?"

"Where Reginald was born, if his second name is Russell, if recently I've talked to some old fellow seated outside the General Store at Stanton, if I'd ever visited Midland, where my marriage took place ..."

"And? Go on," Charlie said.

"I'm afraid that I was rather sharp with Lish. She shouldn't be asking such questions."

"Why not?"

"She should mind her own business," Thalia snapped. "And so should you, Charlie Barnes."

Core! Has Lish uncovered a skeleton that needs an airing? My Bird on the Hill is sure hiding something, Charlie thought. "I'm going to chalk that testy response up to worry," he said. "Either that, or ..."

"Charlie, I am so sorry that I spoke to you, and Lish, in such an offensive way. Please forgive me. I'm just so old, and tired, confused, and worried."

"Now, Thalia," Georgie said, coming down the hall. "Let's get you into bed. I've made one up on a couch in the parlour for me so I'll be close to you all night. When Charlie brings Joan back, I'll tuck her in with you. What's your plan, Charlie?"

"I'll wrap myself in a blanket and sit by the bell just in case Lish calls or tries to signal with the flashlight," Charlie replied.

"You can't stay awake all night," Georgie said.

"Done it before in the SAS —a few years ago, mind you. For Lish I can do it again."

Georgie laughed. "Charlie Barnes. You're falling for Lish MacPherson."

"I've already fallen — big way, big time." Charlie smiled, then left for home.

Thursday, July 19

Lish slowly opened her eyes, but could see nothing. Of course, she remembered. I followed Luna ... climbed the high pile of scale-rock at the foot of the bluff ... reached the top ... bent to enter. My rubber boot slipped on a large piece of rubble, then ... tumbling. Yes, I tumbled ... down ... down ... dark. I'm in the pitch-black of a cave on the other side of the rock pile with something warm lying beside me, licking my hand. "Luna?"

Luna whined.

Lish reached to touch the dog. Pain shot up her left arm. Her side throbbed. She tried again, this time with her right hand. Not so much pain there, she thought. She touched Luna and felt for the pups. "I didn't fall on you, did I?" Lish's voice echoed round the walls of the cave.

Luna moved enough that Lish knew she was okay. The pups were having a good meal. Lish raised her hand to her forehead. "Ouch. Big lump there and sticky. Blood. I must have knocked myself out." She felt her left shoulder. "Extremely painful, but I can move my arm and hand. I can wiggle my toes, move my right leg. Oh! The left one's taken quite a knock, but I can move it."

Lish let her hand rest on Luna's neck. "Okay, girl, we're all in one piece. I'm just going to close my eyes for a moment to calm the pain and give some thought to what to do next."

Bad situation, she thought. No one knows where I am but Luna. I'm a bit bruised so I'm not going anywhere for a little while. How long did I follow Luna? What will Thalia do when she realizes that I'm not in the house or on the property?"

Luna's head went up. She whined, growled, whined again, and licked Lish's hand.

"What is it, girl? An animal? CAT? I don't hear anything. No, wait. I do hear something, very faint. Yowling?" Lish closed her eyes again. Her head throbbed with pain. Charlie will look for me. Thalia will call Charlie. She can't! She doesn't have a phone. She'll ring the bell. Did Luna hear the bell?"

Luna got up. Her claws scraped the rock as she climbed the rubble.

Lish placed her hand on a pup. How long Luna was gone, Lish didn't know, but the dog eventually returned and lay beside her again. The flashlight, Lish thought. I tripped when I reached for the light. She felt in both jacket pockets. It was in neither. If I fell on my left side, it must have fallen out. "Sit up, Lish MacPherson. Careful now. There's nothing broken but, something sure as Hades hurts." With great effort, Lish managed to get into a seated position.

Luna moved, then sat on her haunches.

Lish felt around in ever widening circles as far as she could reach in a seated position. "Ah, there it is, wedged between two rocks.... Dented ... but the switch works."

The ceiling of the cave was more than thirty feet above her. One jagged limestone wall was three feet away, the other at least twenty feet to the left. She'd landed on hard-packed dirt. The two pups slept, tangled together by her right knee. Luna's eyes glowed yellow as the light reflected in them. But for a wide slash at the top, a huge pile of rocks, which over the centuries had scaled off the cliff face, filled the cave's entrance.

It's dark outside, Lish thought. No one will find me until dawn. I'll have to somehow climb the rock pile then shout for help. Not now. When I can see light in the morning. In exasperation, Lish said, "Why did you leave home, Luna? Why hide your puppies here? Why did you lure me to this hellhole? Was my chatter so boring that you needed some excitement? After all, we were only talking things over. COY, Rotten Reggie, Thalia, Frank Russo. A lot of ruminating about Frank." Lish turned the light on Luna. "Good Lord! I just said *we* like you could talk back, Luna."

Luna whined and walked away from Lish toward the back of the cave. She stopped, turned, whined again.

"What now, girl? You're doing the same thing you did to lure me here. You want me to follow you? I can't. It's too painful. Maybe later." Lish aimed the light beyond Luna. The cave didn't appear to be too deep. At the back the ceiling sloped to form a shallow crevice.

What's that? At the far end? "Luna, come girl. I can't see for you standing in the way."

As Luna trotted toward Lish, the light fell on a pile of what looked like rotting cloth. Brown coveralls ... red plaid shirt ... wide braces ...

Lish squinted and lifted her arm to aim the beam of light toward the odd-looking debris. "Oh my Lord! A skull!" She turned the flashlight off. "Don't scream. No one will hear you. You'll only scare yourself to death, Licinius MacPherson. Do not SCREAM."

Luna sat beside Lish again.

Despite the pain shooting from her left shoulder, Lish hugged the dog. Who is it? Red plaid shirt. The old man at the Stanton store? No. Could it be Frank Russo? "That's why you brought the pups here, Luna. *We* were talking about Frank and you went to find him. No, you knew where he was all along, didn't you, and you brought me to find him."

"I've got to get out of here *now*." Lish slid on her backside to the cave's blockage. The pain in her left side was excruciating, but she managed to pull herself onto her knees. With great effort, she tried to crawl up the pile. Each move sent pain through shoulder and rib cage. "I can't do this. I'm going to pass out from the pain. A little rest.... The morning ... I'll try again in the morning."

Lish curled into a fetal position at the bottom of the rocks. "Not now. That thing's not going to hurt me. At the crack of dawn, I'll climb out. What's that? Sounds like my name. No, like the yowl of a cat — a big cat. There it is again ... far away. Lish put her arm over Luna who'd come to lie beside her. "Did you hear it, Luna?"

Lish fell into a dream-filled, restless sleep. When she opened her eyes again, the pups were sleeping next to her chest but Luna was gone. A bright band of light defined the cave's high access slit.

"Lish? Lish? Are you in there?" a voice called. Luna barked. Claws scraping on rock announced the dog had returned.

Friday, July 20 — The Morning

Bud saw Luna running through the bush. "We're not looking for you today," he called. "But, dog, I'll remember where I saw you."

Noah and Dick caught only a glimpse of something four-legged in the distance and wondered between them if it was a bear cub or cougar.

Tom and Harry saw nothing. They were checking the deep pools in the river.

WGD was on the square next to Charlie, crawling through dense undergrowth.

Glenn was at the bell calling Lish's name, Thalia seated beside him.

"Lish might like to hear a song," Thalia said. "You can sing, Glenn. I've heard you."

"I know 'Down in the Valley,' ma'am."

"Yes, Lish would like that song very much. Sing it, please."

Joan insisted on helping Georgie make sandwiches in the kitchen. "Glenn is only trying to help, but thank goodness he changed his tune."

"Yeah," Georgie said. "I was going to feed him again just to get a break from his yowling. It's a wonder that Luna doesn't howl back."

Luna heard Glenn, but paid attention only to smells as she ran through the forest. As soon as she found the scent of her master she barked, then, nose to the ground, set off in the direction of the scent.

"Luna," Charlie called, picking his way carefully along the boulder-strewn base of the escarpment. "Luna, girl. Show yourself." Sounds like she's up near the waterfall, Charlie thought. "I'm coming, Luna. I've got to be careful here or I'll break an ankle." Looking down, Charlie spotted tracks. Not dog, he thought. Something big and feline. Heaven help me. I'm into something here! And I was blaming Glenn for the yowling we've heard.

Luna saw her master, barked once, and stood still. When he was close enough that he could see her, Luna turned and moved away. She stopped, looked back to make sure he was following, then led again until she reached the base of the scale-rock obscuring the cave. She waited for her master to catch up.

"She's in there?" Charlie asked. "Up we go, Luna."

Luna was beside Lish by the time Charlie made the top of the rock pile.

A flashlight shone on the cave's ceiling and then down on Lish. "Lish, my girl. You're safe. I'm coming." Small rocks rolled ahead of Charlie as he descended the pile to reach her.

"Charlie? Charlie! My Cagey Farmer," Lish said.

Charlie knelt and cradled Lish in his arms. With Luna by his side, and the woman he loved next to his heart, Charlie figured he'd conquered the world.

"Hush now. Dry those tears. I found you. You're safe now. Everyone's looking for you. We'll get you out of here soon enough. He kissed the top of her head, her unbruised right temple. We really have to stop meeting this way." Charlie smiled at his joke.

"Charlie. Charlie, please listen." As emotional as it was to see Charlie and have his arms around her, Lish needed to tell him about the skeleton.

"What is it, my girl?" Charlie asked.

"Stop kissing my head and shine your flashlight into the crevice — back there. I'll turn away. I can't look."

Charlie flashed his light where told. "Good Lord!" He walked to the back of the cave for a good look at the bundle of rags. "Holy Mackerel Snappers! It's Frank Russo — been here a long time, I'd say." Charlie bent to examine the remains. Damp-cave mouldy.

Bones chewed on, after death. Big and little teeth marks.

Charlie came to sit beside Lish. "After all these years," he said, "and so far along the escarpment. This cave is way beyond Grotto Spring. It's close to the glen and The Mark's boundary. How did the old fellow make it this far?"

"We have to tell Thalia. We've got to alert the police," Lish said.

Charlie was quiet for a few minutes then said, "I know that you're hurting and you want to get out of here, but listen a moment. Maybe, just maybe, we should talk this Frank thing through."

"What do you mean?"

"Think about it, Lish. Thalia spent a long time looking for Frank. When the seven-year period was up, Thalia's lawyer had Frank officially declared dead so that she could collect his insurance. What will it do to Thalia to know that Frank was mouldering in a cave on The Mark, all the time?"

"Give her some sort of peace of mind," Lish said.

"On the contrary," Charlie said. "Very much on the contrary. It looks like his skull is ... well, let's just say he *may* have been struck by something heavy."

"Murder? He was murdered?"

"Maybe," Charlie said. "The Police just might think so. And in that case, who would be under most suspicion?"

"Thalia, if she got a *large* insurance settlement," Lish said. "Reginald?"

"I'd think the police would deduce quickly, but not accurately, that Thalia, aided by Rotten Reggie, did him in," Charlie said.

Lish remembered the cigarette holder. She'd tell Charlie about it later, when she could show it to him. That would implicate Reginald. "What do you think we should do?" she asked.

"Here's my plan," Charlie said. "I'm going to shift some rocks back that way to make a blind. Not put them on top of him, mind you; I'm just going to do something that looks a little natural, to hide him away from prying eyes. Then, I'm going to get you out of here. I'll take you and the pups down the way a bit. We don't want anyone to climb in here for a look-round. Do you hear me, Luna? You and the pups gotta go home."

"Someone might eventually stumble across the remains, just like I did," Lish said.

"Not because we'll say anything. We must not *ever* talk to anyone about what we found."

"Not ever?"

"If there *ever* needs to be an exception, we must agree on the circumstances before the deed is done. Do you understand? It's just you and me, in this together."

"If he was murdered, there's one other person knows," Lish said.

"But that person won't know that we were in the cave and found the body. *He* or *she* or *they* won't suspect anything is awry. That's why we must say nowt to anyone."

"If it was murder, and whoever did it knew that we saw the remains, our lives could be in danger," Lish said.

"Ah, you understand the situation, very well," Charlie said.

"Could we possibly discuss it later with Thalia?"

"No," Charlie said. "If the police got involved later, what would they say about you and me not contacting them now?"

It took Lish a moment to comprehend what Charlie was getting at. "They'd think you had something to do with Frank's disappearance because you're so close to Thalia. They'd figure that you did the deed and hid the body."

"A most astute observation. If we're in agreement, I'll move a few rocks then I'll carry you out of here."

It took a half-hour for Charlie to build a somewhat natural-looking blind and another fifteen minutes for him to carry Lish out of the cave. He moved her far enough away from the area that no one would suspect where she had sustained her injuries. Luna, mouthing one puppy, followed him. The other was nestled in Lish's good arm.

July 20 — The Afternoon

Charlie sat on the edge of his bed, a bowl of soup in his hand. "Doc Johnson tells me that there's nothing broken. He says you're badly bruised, but that after you've had a bit of soup and a good rest I can take you back to Granite in the car, not in the back of the truck like you arrived here. Georgie's going to ask her mother to help Thalia and Joan and you for a few days."

"I told the gentleman that a piece of Blue Heathen tripped me up on The Mark, and that I tumbled down some scale rock just as we discussed. I feel like a criminal now, Charlie."

"Don't. That's exactly what happened, in a sense," he told her. "How be I shovel and you swallow? Before she went back to the store, Georgie said that if I can give a bottle to a calf, I can spoon soup into you. Doc says WGD did a good job of bandaging that bump on your forehead. It was lucky that he had the first-aid kit and arrived right after we started hollering, and Luna set to barking."

"Where is Luna?"

"She's on a blanket in the kitchen, keeping WGD company. I guess we'd better start to call the fellow Joe. Joe's cooking up a storm, heating cans of soup for the fellows, making coffee, too. He says that he learned first aid and cooking from his mother. Apparently, he does all the cooking for his brothers when they're not at Georgie's place."

"And Noah?" Lish asked, savouring a spoonful of soup.

"He's at Granite taking care of Joan and Thalia. The rest are downstairs, eating through the pile of sandwiches Georgie left. While Doc was up here, we were all doing some reminiscing about the war years."

"I believe in Farmglish, that would be chewing the cud," Lish said.

Charlie laughed. "Try chewin' the fat."

"Well, as long as they are not chewing on each other. How am I going to thank them for what they did?" Lish asked.

"We'll have a party. Soon's you're feeling better, we'll throw a huge evening get-together: music, dancing in the barn, food. That hasn't happened in the Valley in a while," Charlie said. "Why, I might even invite those two snoops that showed up."

"They came here?"

"Yep. Looking for you, just after we arrived back at the house. Noah kept out of sight. Bud told them you'd had a little accident while out looking for the dog."

"What did they say — or do?"

"Bud said that they were quite sympathetic. He was to tell Miss MacPherson to get better and that they'd see her in a week or so."

"If my accident has achieved anything, it's drawn people together," Lish said. "Thalia wasn't talking to the Delaney brothers. Glenn is made fun of so much that Bud keeps him out of sight most of the time. Len sticks pretty much to his shop."

"You noticed that, under the veneer, Seven Springs is coming unstuck at the seams," he said. "Thalia tries to be the glue that holds them together."

"But you're wrong, Charlie. They all just need a cause. They came together for a stranger: me. And to help with the fire."

"You're not a stranger, Lish. You're almost family."

Lish blushed. "I hope you meant that in a communal way," she said. "I am in your pyjamas, in your bed."

"Yep," was all Charlie said. He spooned the last of the soup. "Do you want another bowl?"

"No thanks," Lish replied. "As good as it is, leave it for the fellows. They must be hungry, and tired."

"I was thinking," Charlie said. "I'm going to ask Joe if he'd like to help me around the farm. I could use a second hand around here. Len's not a young buck. I can't continue to rely on him all the time to get me out of a jam."

"It seems to me that you need to plan ahead, Charlie, to think about starting your own family. Time's just a flyin' by in Farmglish terms."

"You proposing som'pin interestin'?" Charlie gave Lish a strange look.

"Men propose. Women assume," Lish said. "I'll rest now then you can haul me home like a heifer fer fattenin'"

Charlie laughed. "It's pigs fer fattenin' and heifers fer milkin' ... eventually," he said. "That's som'pin farm wives gotta know, for sure."

"I'm a fast learner," Lish said.

"Lordy love a duck's egg. I love Farmglishees in training."

Lish smiled. "I hope just one at a time."

CHAPTER 7
The Week of July 22–28

Tuesday, July 24

Lish was dressed and seated by the window with papers spread before her on the sill when Georgie's mother, Mary, appeared at the bedroom door. Heavy footsteps on creaky wooden floorboards announced her arrival.

"It's a hot day," Mary said. "Good clothes-drying weather, but we're going to get a dousing-hell rain before dawn. I know what Doc said about taking it easy, but do you feel like doing some work today? I can handle the laundry, but I'd appreciate some help with the dishes and meals. Thalia says she has some pages you can type."

"That I can do," Lish said. "If my left arm gets too sore, I'm pretty good at typing with my right hand."

"You got the note and the parcel Georgie sent with that Noah fellow? He was sure interested in the return address on the box," Mary told her.

"I did, thanks," Lish said. Not that the note answered any questions, she thought. At least Bernard and Gloria were still working on the case. They did want to know if anything had been arranged regarding the meeting with Noah. She'd have to speak to Noah soon. On the other hand, the parcel from

Port Arthur held all sorts of little gems of information.

"Charlie's coming for supper," Mary said. "That's the fourth time in as many days. It appears that Thalia's running a restaurant around here."

"Charlie doesn't like to eat alone," Lish said. "I appreciate your coming to help us."

"You'll be spending some time downstairs tonight?"

"I will. I feel much better today."

"Good, because I've got to be back in Creemore tonight. Do you think you'll be able to handle the meals from now on?"

"I'm sure that I'll be okay," Lish said. Although the bump on her left temple was an ugly purple sore, and she'd have to remember not to lift anything heavy, Lish was determined to put some sense of normality back into her life. "Perhaps Joan can help me a bit."

"Don't count on Joan to do too much," Mary said. "It's a bad thing she's got. It's good she's staying here now. Charlie can't farm and nurse too. I imagine Joan put on a good show to the very last before she admitted defeat. Her mother died of the same thing: disease in the bone."

"When I arrived, I wouldn't have imagined Joan was so ill by looking at her," Lish said.

Mary smiled. "There are a lot of things about this place and these people that defy the imagination. By the way, you asked about an old fellow that you saw at Stanton Store."

"I did," Lish replied. "Noah saw him, too. I just thought that you know so many people around here and in other villages that you might know him."

"Well, I know him, all too well," Mary said.

"Who is he?"

"Frank Russo's brother, J.D. He lived near Elmvale. He doesn't get over this way much. You know, the first time I laid eyes on the man I thought that he was Frank. They're like peas-in-a-pod, 'cause they're twins."

"And he never visits Seven Springs?"

"He used to visit a lot," Mary said. "I hadn't given J.D. much thought lately. Then I was driving past the store, maybe three weeks ago, and saw him and Reginald."

"Reginald Russo?"

"Yes. Reginald was helping him into a big black caddy."

"You didn't happen to notice in which direction they went."

Mary laughed. "I'm that nosy that I did. I looked in my rearview mirror. They headed up the road toward Mansfield."

"And possibly Seven Springs?" Lish asked.

"They were headed in its general direction. I remember now. It was a Sunday. I was driving down to Hockley to see my sister. J.D. likes sitting out in front of stores, even if they're closed."

"Of course, Lish thought. Thalia would be in church. Rotten Reggie could spy on Granite from the barn ruins for a couple of hours before anyone returned from Seven Springs. But why is he spying? And why bring J.D. Russo?

"Just one other question," Lish said. "Does J.D. Russo have a scar like Frank's?"

"Frank's scar was gotten in a fight, so I wouldn't think J.D. has one like it," Mary said.

July 24 — The Evening

Evening breezes that wafted through the front porch provided some relief from the relentless heat for Charlie and Lish, who sat on the side steps away from the front door so that Thalia couldn't hear the drift of their conversation. They also kept their voices low so that Joan, in her upstairs bedroom, wouldn't hear either.

"I've had this cigarette holder since Glenn found it the day I met Bud on the hill. I was going to give it to Thalia, but thought better of it as her story began to unfold. I felt you were the person who should know about it," Lish said.

Charlie turned the case in his hand. "You think Rotten Reggie has been spying on Granite — on Thalia."

"That would explain why Glenn found the case in the old barn ruin," Lish said. "And it might also explain something a bit more sinister, if Frank Russo had it in his pocket the night he disappeared."

"And Mary saw J.D. hanging around with Rotten Reggie," Charlie added. "Why the chummy relationship between those two now — other then the obvious uncle and nephew connection?"

"A better question is, why did Reginald start to use another name around the time his father vanished?" Lish asked. "J. Russell Grant — Jeffrey Russell Grant."

"He had a fixation for Len's shop," Charlie said. "Using Len's last name might just be the next step by a warped brain. But to take on Jeff's persona? For what reason?" Charlie gave the holder back to Lish. "Are you going to tell Thalia, or talk with Len?"

"Not right away," Lish said.

"I won't either," Charlie said. "I'll let that information settle on my brain for a while."

"I'd appreciate that. Charlie, I should tell you that I know Reginald Russo as Russell Grant. I met him in business situations. I had dinner with him on several occasions. The man knows that I worked for COY. I wasn't here on the Sunday that Mary saw him pick J.D. up at the store, so he wouldn't have seen me that day. But if he's spied before ...."

"Now don't jump to conclusions," Charlie said. "Even if he did recognize you, he hasn't been in touch, has he?"

"No."

"Rotten Reggie knows that his mother regularly attends church. He knows that I accompany her. That's me and her out of the way. He is also aware of the fact that the Delaney boys usually go to church. He possibly parked at their place and walked across the field to the old barn. That way his car wouldn't be seen on the road. He'd leave before I returned because he knows that if I ever saw his car, I'd go looking for him."

"Reginald would wonder about Noah. If you recall, Noah stayed around Granite that morning fixing Thalia's back door. I wonder: if Noah hadn't been here, would Reginald have entered the house, possibly to look for something?"

"Maybe he knows Noah," Charlie said. "We never thought of that connection."

"I can't imagine Noah collaborating in any way with Reginald Russo," Lish said.

"I can't either, but the possibility is there."

"Charlie, you obviously didn't see Reginald at that one meeting you attended in Toronto."

"No. He wasn't there. Can we forget about the Rotter for a little while and talk about us?"

"Sure," Lish said. "What's on your mind?"

"Have you given any thought to our little party?"

"Not yet. I'm sure it will be the event of the year in Seven Springs if you have anything to do with its planning, Charlie."

Charlie reached for her hand. "Did you really mean what you said the other day, Lish; or was it the giddy realization that you had been rescued by the strongest, handsomest man in Mulmur, who just happens to have a soft spot for you?"

Lish stroked the big, calloused hand. "I meant every word, Charlie."

"Lish, there's such a difference in our ages. I'm an old man, for Pete's sake."

Lish chuckled. "I've always been partial to older men."

"I'll have teenage children when I'm more than sixty years old," Charlie said.

"I'll be in my forties and will handle them," Lish said.

"We've known each other for such a short period of time," Charlie said.

Lish laughed. "Dad used to say that time is only hands on a clock. Hearts beat forever."

Charlie squeezed her hand. "We're old enough to realize that there is a lot of puffin' between hot coals and a fryin' fire," he said. "I don't think that we should make it common knowledge that we're sparkin' until we know for sure we're going to do some serious cookin.'"

"Agreed," Lish said. "There are a few things that need to be cleared up before anyone makes a lifetime commitment around here. First things first."

"The first thing we have to do is make sure that someone stays around Granite when Thalia is away," Charlie said.

"That isn't a problem," Lish said. "You've noticed that I'm not a regular churchgoer. Noah can help, too."

"I don't think Noah is going to be around too much longer. He's getting itchy feet. Says his music needs tending to." Charlie slipped his arm around Lish's waist.

"Perhaps he's trying to avoid a messy confrontation with his wife," Lish said. "That wouldn't be so good for his career. I don't think I ever read that he was married."

"Come to think of it, that could be the biggest reason for him hiding on The Mark."

"Part of the reason," Lish agreed. "He does believe in saving Hunter's Mark. He is really closest to the legend and believes that he hears CAT."

"Or Glenn Henderson, depending on your point of view,"

Charlie's hand crept from Lish's waist to her chest.

"Charlie Barnes! Are you always this forward with women?"

"I wouldn't know," Charlie said. "Last time I handled one was in 1945."

Thursday, July 26 — Fergus

Lish, with Noah by her side, stood in front of a modest-looking headstone in Belsyde Cemetery. Afternoon sunlight, sifting through mature spruce trees, danced across the lettering: "Jessie Whitefish MacPherson, 1911–1933." Instead of the usual rest-in-peace sentiments, one line was engraved in large lettering beneath the dates: "The Cougar is Forever."

"Dad wrote Peggy that he saw the design of the headstone in a dream."

"Lish, I've been thinking about the dream that we share. I figure that its message is that everyone has an obligation to share something worthwhile. I've still not figured out why I'm riding a deer, or where I'm travelling from, but what I'm sharing is my music — my songs."

"Perhaps the journey is about finding ourselves, and CAT is about finding our creativity — our special talent," Lish said. "Before she died, Mother found her voice. The package that Peggy sent to me contained lots of stories and poetry that Mom wrote, personal notes, greeting cards."

"This woman — Peggy — knew your mother?"

"Mom worked in one of the restaurants in Port Arthur and boarded at Peggy's house. Apparently, the two were like sisters. Peggy was kind enough to sort through some things that Mother left behind when she and Dad moved south," Lish explained. "After Dad wrote that Mother had died, Peggy tucked them away in a closet, thinking that, someday, some-one might appreciate the information."

"Intuitive woman," Noah said. "How did you find Peggy's address?"

"Among the few things that I took from Dad's room, along with the memory jar, was a card box, full of correspondence. I thought that it was important because he mentioned the box several times to me during the week prior to his death."

"Your father loved your mother and embraced her heritage," Noah said.

"That he would have Mother's tombstone inscribed in such a way proves to me that he knew about The Mark and believed the legend," Lish said.

"I do find it odd that he didn't tell you about your Indian heritage."

"He knew that his mother would be left with the job of raising me. But maybe in his own way Dad tried to give me clues," she said. "I vaguely recall details of trips that we made during the summer when he felt well enough to travel. I also remember terrible arguments between Dad and his mother before and after those trips."

Noah squeezed her hand. "You've been given time to think through everything now."

"Although Grandmother wasn't an ogre, she was strict and had her own way about her. She was cold, but raised me properly," Lish said. "Her way was not the way I'd bring children up, but that's another story."

"She did raise you properly, but not truthfully," Noah said. "If, like a lot of people, the lady harboured a prejudice against Indians, her son's choice of wife — an Indian woman — would have angered her. She justified her prejudice with the belief that she had to protect you from your mother's heritage."

"Referring rarely to my mother was her strategy," Lish said. "I understand now why I wasn't made executor of her estate. She was afraid of what I might find among her papers."

"Prejudices slip easily from one generation to the next. If Granny had passed hers along, you'd not be the free, caring, accepting person that you are today."

"I hope that I inherited Dad's ability to accept everyone, regardless of their ancestry. We can talk more about this over lunch. I packed sandwiches and a thermos of coffee. Let's sit on the hill in that park we passed on the way in."

"It's good that you brought food," Noah said. "I'm a little shy about being seen in public after that rattling on the radio."

"I appreciate your offer to drive today," Lish said. "My left arm still aches terribly when I use it too much. I hate to tell Thalia that I can't type her manuscript."

"It's my pleasure," Noah said. "How's Thalia's latest book coming along?"

"I have to admit that I'm having as much fun as she is working on this book. Thalia encourages participation and accepts suggestions really well."

"I had an ulterior motive for coming with you today, Lish. I needed to talk to you."

"And I have to talk with you — about Bernard and Gloria," Lish said.

They had no sooner made themselves comfortable on a blanket, their backs against a tree, than a group of teenaged boys arrived to play pickup ball.

"If you don't mind, I'll toss manners to the wind and wear my hat and sunglasses," Noah said. "Those guys would be the first to recognize me."

Lish spread the contents of the picnic hamper on the blanket. "The more I see of this village, the more I remember. You see that two-storey house on the other side of the highway? It was a tourist home. I'm sure that Dad and I stayed there."

"But you don't recall your dad bringing you to the cemetery?"

"No. I don't remember visiting a grave," Lish answered, pouring coffee for Noah. I may as well take the big leap, she thought. "I understand that you're planning to leave Hunter's Mark soon, Noah."

"Charlie's been talking to you."

"He has," Lish said. "He says that you want to get back to your musical career. I think that before you took the next big step — Nashville, and all that entails — you came to the conclusion that you had to deal with your Indian heritage and your wife. A divorce perhaps?"

"It was probably stupid of me to disappear, but The Mark gave me time to think through both situations," Noah said. "Now I have to ease myself back into the reality of the business. I need to give good reasons why I walked away from my concerts. And I must sort things out with my wife. You understand that it's a big step — to take my career from Ontario to the big time in Nashville, Tennessee."

"How would Charlie put this in his brand of Farmglish?" Lish said. "It's showdown time in the ol' corral."

Noah laughed. "You've got a real hankerin' fer that fella."

"Undoubtedly. I've never met anyone like him. He is one of a kind," she agreed.

"My agent can let the media know that I'm back in the music business. But I need reasonable answers to questions that are going to be asked." He squeezed a cookie and tossed the crumbs toward a nosey grey squirrel that roamed near his feet.

"Noah, sometimes a person has to go out on a limb to get the best fruit. Tell the truth."

"I don't want anyone rushing to Seven Springs and ruining

the solitude of The Mark," Noah said. "Publicity like that will only help Northlands to sell their development."

The squirrel walked up Noah's leg to reach a big crumb. "Someone must be feeding that beggar. He's not afraid of me."

"He's taking the high road," Lish said. "You should, too. Don't involve your agent, to begin with. Meet Bernard and Gloria at Georgie's store. Let them take pictures of you. Tell them, in honesty, that you had to give serious consideration to two situations."

"What might these situations be?" Noah asked.

"The first is your culture. You stress that you appreciate the fact that your many fans accept your Indian heritage and you want to thank them for being astute enough to realize that cultural differences shouldn't be an issue in this day and age — despite what some may have heard, or read."

"Making a public statement like that could break my career as well as make it. I have always assumed my fans don't know that I'm Ojibway Cree." Noah said. "The reporters will want to know why I've never publicly divulged the information before."

"That's a simple question to answer," Lish replied. "Explain that you only realized a problem might exist when one insensitive person accused you of hiding your Indian heritage for career reasons. You state that you want to make it perfectly clear you are proud of your ancestry and culture. Emphasize that you know your fans are too."

"You might be onto something, Lish."

"Be charming. Be yourself. Nothing has changed your musical ability. You've just added another layer to your mystique."

"Point one taken," he said. "What's the second?"

"To explain why you went into seclusion. That, due to the deteriorating relationship with your wife, you needed private time to sort out the situation."

"Make it common knowledge that I'm married?" Noah said.

"Why not? The hounds will dig around and find out anyway. Beat them to the punch. Do you want your fans to hear the sordid story from you — or your wife — or read about it in some sleazy tabloid?" Lish asked.

"You're right. There is an underbelly just waiting to be scratched. I doubt that my wife would cooperate. When she left, she promised not to mess up my career. But someone close to her might embellish the story if money is involved," Noah said.

"Is the marriage over?"

"Yes," Noah replied. "There is no way we can mend the fences. It was one of those quicky marriages that shouldn't have happened. We both realized our mistake. I've got to do what's right for her, now."

"Don't mention divorce. Let her do that if she so desires."

"How do I explain *where* I've been for nearly two months?"

"You chose to stay with friends who respected your need for privacy. Emphasize how much you appreciate the quietude of Seven Springs, and the fact that the area hasn't been discovered."

"I can't say that," Noah said. "Those comments are guaranteed to bring hordes of people here. That's not good for The Mark."

"But it is good for people like Georgie who can barely exist on what she's making in the store. She can decorate the place with your memorabilia. Noah, if your fans visit the area they won't stay around. They're buying your records, not land."

"Another point well made. But people like Len won't like it one bit. He values his privacy."

"You've seen Len's carvings. They're overflowing the shelves in his office. He's a consummate whittler. Len's quite willing to sell his carvings. He needs the money and can create more when necessary. If he doesn't want people wandering around the blacksmith shop, Georgie can display them at the store. Other local folks could profit too if they realize the benefits of catering to visitors."

"What about Northlands feeding off the publicity?"

"Let the chips fall where they may," Lish said. "If we plan this right, it will take the wind out of their sails, so to speak. You can allude to the fact you've heard rumours that some group is trying to ruin your paradise. That's all you need to say. No names, no details. *Paradise* is the key word."

"What you're saying is that if I cooperate with Bernard and Gloria — if nothing is made public until their story breaks in whatever publication buys it —"

"We gain the upper hand," Lish said.

"It's a brilliant plan, Lish!"

"It's not without some risk. Don't mention that you've taken up painting again. That is a private and special passion, the pictures to be shared only when you choose to do so," she said. "Painting is something that you can retreat to when you feel like the world is on your tail."

"I can schedule regular breaks, and take them at Hunter's cabin — if Thalia will let me continue to use it."

"I'll talk to Bernard and Gloria. Can I tell them you'll see them within the next two weeks? I will make it clear that you'll give them an exclusive interview. If they blab, everything's off and you disappear — to reappear in Toronto with your agent at a very public event."

"What do I have to lose?" Noah said. "We must *never* show them Hunter's cabin or let them know what Thalia Logan Russo does for a living."

"Mum's the word from now until the meeting. If you don't say anything, no one else will. The next thing that has to happen is that everyone involved in Thalia's vision for The Mark and Seven Springs has to be persuaded to gather for a little chat, preferably just before you meet with Bernard and Gloria."

"I don't trust Jeff Grant."

"Let me talk to Jeff," Lish said. "It's better that what has to be said to him comes from a lady. The person I don't trust is the one who is penning Mulmur Murmurings."

Friday, July 27

Lish had the paper spread on the table by the time Thalia came into the kitchen for her first cup of coffee. "This Murmurings column is addictive," she said. "I missed it last week."

"Because it wasn't in the paper proves that whoever is responsible was involved with the fire — or looking for you," Thalia said. "Are we narrowing the field of prospective suspects?"

"Not by much," Lish replied. "Listen to what Dunnit says about the absence of the column.

Mulmur Murmurings by Hugh Dunnit
For the Week of July 22-28

Ladies, gentleman and all the others, too. Apologies are in order for the lack of Murmurings last Friday. The Valley and Springs were jumping with events of the most extraordinary kind that couldn't be ignored.

Fire destroyed the Cormack barn, one of the oldest in the area. Twenty milk cows were herded five miles to the Barnes farm for keeping by the Cagey Farmer. Charlie B rode herd on Juniper like he was a character out of a Zane Grey novel. It was something to see, folks: the old man riding the old nag. The ladies can't be forgotten for their generosity and aid. We should never forget the contributions of all the communities around. Before you go vigilante, the fire was caused by a fella puffing in the hayloft because his wife wouldn't let him smoke in the house. She has, no doubt, learned a hard lesson.

The bell tolled more than thrice, leading some in the Springs to think the Bird on the Hill had fallen off her perch. Instead, it was the Lovely Damsel who left the castle in haste. A search was mounted and I am pleased to announce that the lady was returned to the fold. Her foray into the wilds netted a raft of nasty bruises, our favourite dog, her pups, and an appreciation for chicken noodle soup. We will not mention in what circumstances the Lovely Damsel consumed that soup.

The rare curlew bird has once again been seen in the Hills. To what do we attribute its appearance and when is it going to fly away home? Its nesting ground is in the Arctic is it not? Or at least in northern reaches. Has it been blown off course by a lot of hot air?

Is marriage in the air? Has David H finally proposed to Mildred A? She sincerely hopes so. A nine-year courtship is a bit long-in-the-tooth for a woman who's already missing a few.

"Whoever is writing this column knows a lot more about Noah than most people around here. Who is aware of his true identity besides us?" Thalia asked.

"Jeff Grant, for sure. Len, if Jeff tells tales out of school. Georgie has known for a long time, too. Who was at Charlie's the day I was found?"

"Everyone that had been looking for you. Len, Jeff, Joan, and I were here," Thalia said. "But everyone in the Springs and Valley is aware of your layabout in Charlie's pyjamas. Did I tell you that I'm having a telephone installed?"

"You did," Lish said. "I think that it's a wise decision. You don't have to answer it if you don't want to. A phone will give you some assurance that if you *are* in trouble and *can't* get to the bell, you can alert someone."

"Having to ring the bell to summon people to find you made me realize just how archaic some of my ideas are. I'm the past. You're the future."

"Thalia, you are unlike anyone I've ever met. You're a breath of fresh air in a world gone stale. Please continue to be yourself. Don't change too much, too soon. I don't want the life-force that is Thalia Logan Russo to lose its glow. No one does."

"Calling me a life-force is just a pleasant way to say I'm eccentric and unconventional," Thalia said. "I've been called crazy, loose-of-brain. I've been accused of an incapability of being serious about anything."

"Some people can't understand, or tolerate, anything that's not considered normal behaviour," Lish said. "But who sets the standards for what's normal and what's not? Not you, or me, I hope."

"Well, I never want to be known as a traditional, run-of-the-mill woman," Thalia said. "Frank used to shake his head and say that there was nothing he could do for me but pray that a couple of men didn't show up one day to take me away in a straightjacket."

CHAPTER 8
The Week of July 29–August 4

Sunday, July 29

Lish was in the middle of preparing a breakfast tray for Joan when Thalia appeared at the kitchen door and struck a pose in a pale-blue 1920s suit with matching hat.

"I was so disheartened when I woke up this morning that I almost dressed as though it really is 1962," she said. "Then I remembered our little talk. Do I meet your expectations?"

Lish laughed. "You have exceeded expectations, Thalia. You look radiant."

"I can see by the way you are dressed that you're not going to join the group of gloverlied grannies and sloe-eyed slops in church this morning."

"I'm neither gloverlied nor sloe-eyed," Lish replied. "The bump on my head would get far more attention than the minister. My side is paining a bit, too, which leads me to believe that sitting in church wouldn't help the situation. A wooden pew can't do your hip much good either, Thalia."

"I will admit it is painful on occasion. For the past number of years I've never missed Sunday service — except when I was laid up with the broken leg or when church had been cancelled due to weather."

"To be perfectly honest, I don't feel like answering questions today and I'm sure that well-meaning people will have a few."

"Prying eyes show no mercy and loose tongues hurt." Thalia laughed. "Or should that be the other way round?" She gathered her purse, gloves, and cane. "If you'll help me to my garden chair, I want to enjoy the morning air before becoming a prisoner — by choice, mind you — in church. How is Joan this morning? I called up to her but can't make the stairs."

"Worn out," Lish said. "She's going to have breakfast in bed. I've encouraged her to spend at least the morning resting. The bedroom windows are open so she can enjoy birdsong and breezes. Doctor Johnson left some pills that are supposed to dull the pain."

"A month ago Joan wouldn't have taken them," Thalia said. "Poor dear. She never lets on just how ill she is. Come on now to the garden to wait for Charlie. Scat, cats. You're bound to trip me up, aren't you? We need Luna around here to keep these two felines in line. You must spend some time in the patch this morning, Lish."

Lish carried Adam and Eve to the blanket by the stove. Before she reached the door with Thalia, they were underfoot again. "You spoil them, Thalia. They want to cuddle with you in the sun."

Thalia was right. From a chair in the middle of the vegetable garden, Lish could survey the kingdom. She had a good view of the treetops in The Mark, of Charlie's farmhouse, of two sides of Granite, and most importantly, a good stretch of Lavender Line before it disappeared behind the lilac bushes. Because the road petered out a quarter mile past the lane, the only thing that Lish had to watch for was cars coming up the road. The past several days had been dry and hot. Vehicles would leave a telltale trail of dust. Periodically, Lish glanced up at Joan's bedroom window. Joan promised to call if she needed anything.

She wasn't sure what she was watching for — possibly a black car? Reginald sneaking up on the place on foot? Did the man know that Joan was in residence? If he was as rotten as Charlie made him out to be, he probably wouldn't let an invalid stand in the way of any planned devious deed.

As the soft colours of the morning settled on the landscape, Lish once again understood why The Mark held a special place in everyone's heart. Charlie was right. As beautiful as the Hills of Mulmur were, nothing could match The Mark for rare primordial wilderness.

"Dreaming of things to come?" a voice said. Jeff walked around the back of the house, a haversack in his hand.

Lish looked for his car. "How'd you get here?"

"I parked down by the bowstring and climbed the hill. I was going to do some fishing, then decided to hike up to see you instead."

"How did you know I wouldn't be in church?" Lish asked.

"If you weren't here, I thought I'd visit Joan."

"Do you have permission to walk into Thalia's house when she isn't home?"

"Who needs permission?" Jeff said. "She knows me."

"I think that, in the future, you mustn't come to Granite when Thalia is away," Lish told him.

"Who says but you? And who are you to tell me what to do?"

Lish shrugged. "Let's sit on the front porch." He won't know what bedroom Joan's in and I'll talk loud enough that she'll hear, Lish thought. There's no way I want anyone to think that I'm cooperating with this cad.

Lish led the way, around the house, not through it, to the porch.

As soon as Jeff sat down he pulled a beer from his sack. "Want one?" he said.

From Jeff's attitude, he's already been into the booze, Lish thought. "No thanks," she said. "Isn't it a bit early to imbibe?"

"Anytime's a good time for beer," he said. "So, how long are you going to stick around here, Lish?"

Jeff wastes no time beating around bushes, Lish thought. "As long as I'm needed."

"You've certainly made an impression on a few people, my father included," he said. "It's Miss MacPherson says this, Miss MacPherson says that, like you're some sort of guru."

"I spend time listening to your father. He has a lot to offer me — and you, Jeff."

"Well, Dad and I haven't had much to say to each other recently," Jeff said.

Lish hoped that Joan was awake and listening. "You certainly didn't mention the purchase of Bud Henderson's acreage to your father. You haven't mentioned that your girlfriend works for Northlands Development in Collingwood, either."

"How do you know about her?" Jeff raised his voice. "My girlfriend, and what she does, are none of your business."

"When I first met you in June, I never imagined a girlfriend of yours *would* be my business," Lish replied. "She is now."

"What if she works for Northlands? What if I own land around here?" Jeff said. "There's nothing written says that I can't."

"What if you are a good friend of Reginald Russo, who is very much involved in Northlands," Lish replied. "I venture that you're working on his behalf. You've fallen for his rhetoric. He bought your loyalty. He gave you the money to purchase Bud's land."

Jeff tossed his empty bottle off the porch and reached for another beer. "You don't get it, do you? Half the people in the

Valley and Springs don't get it, either. They are stupid enough to buck Northlands. They're living in the past, just like Thalia. She's the one who influences or finances them. Like mother, like son, I'd say."

Ah, Lish thought. Jeff just confirmed that Thalia has the support of quite a few people in the area, not just those she assists financially. "There's a big difference between what mother and son are doing with their money," she said. "Perhaps, you don't get it. All you see are dollars. You're not using common sense. Those closely involved with Northlands will be the only ones to come out of this venture with money in their pockets if the project comes to fruition. You're being used by Reginald Russo."

"You sound just like my dad," Jeff said. "You're both wrong, dead wrong."

There's no grey area for Jeff, Lish thought. People like him are as dedicated to money as a rat is to cheese. It's time to introduce a little dissension into this man's life. "Did you know that Reginald Russo also uses the name Jeffrey Russell Grant? Now, why would Russo do a thing like that but to impersonate you when he feels it necessary not to reveal his real identity? Did he buy your name, too?"

By Jeff's look, Lish knew he wasn't aware Reginald had assumed a name-of-convenience. "At one time he apparently spent a lot of time with your dad."

"Stop right there," Jeff said. "I don't have to listen to this claptrap."

"No, you don't," Lish said. "But there is one more thing you should know. Charlie and I are aware of the fact that Reginald has been spying on Granite. I think you know his movements, too. He crosses the land that you own to reach the barn. He, just like you, is looking for something. What is it, Jeff? What has Thalia ever done to you that you'd turn against her to the point that you'd go through her possessions when she's not home?"

"It's none of your damn business," Jeff said.

"Then I suggest that you leave now, Jeff. Pick up the empty bottle on your way."

Lish watched until Jeff disappeared over the hill, then went to Joan's bedroom, where she kept an eye on him as he walked the trail toward the bridge and his car.

"I heard everything," Joan said. "You were so forceful ... professional, like you've done similar before. What on earth are those two looking for?"

"I haven't a clue," Lish replied.

"It has to have something to do with this land," Joan said. "That seems the only thing that Reginald is interested in. Thalia does keep a file of important documents."

"If you're well enough to spend some time downstairs tonight, let's ask her if I can see it," Lish said. "Jeff's just driven away. I'd hate to be in Len Grant's shoes today."

"I think that the question is, when will Jeff confront Reginald?" Joan said. "I'd like to be a spider on the wall for that meeting."

"I doubt that he'll approach Reginald right away. He'll not want to upset his personal bank, ol' moneybags himself."

"I think that he'll talk everything over with his girlfriend before he confronts his father," said Joan.

"The problem is that when Jeff mentions my name to Reginald, he will know who I am. He will definitely question how I know he's using another name — two names, as a matter of fact. I'm not looking forward to that encounter."

"Charlie will help you if he can," Joan said. "I'm sure that Thalia doesn't know Reginald is using Jeff's name on occasion."

"Perhaps we should keep that bit of information to ourselves until we find out why he's doing it."

"I hate keeping things from my best friend, but under the circumstances, I couldn't agree more," Joan said. "There will be an appropriate time and place to tell her."

"Or for her to tell us — at least part of the story," Lish said.

July 29 — The Evening

A cool east wind kept the ladies in the house after supper, but a light rain didn't stop Thalia from asking Lish to open the parlour windows. Thalia sat opposite Lish in her favourite chair, with several photograph albums open on a table in front of her and an encyclopedia on her lap. Lish shared her knee with Eve and a thick folder of papers. The copper pot gleamed in its glass case on a lamp table beside her. Joan, knitting on the afghan, sat between them on the settee, pillows behind her back, a plaid woolen throw across her knees. Adam lay on her lap taking occasional swipes at the yarn and knitting needles.

"The nicest time to enjoy this parlour is during a winter blizzard," Thalia said. "That's when Granite comes into its own as a solid, comfortable home. It doesn't matter how strong the wind, it's never heard within these walls. During the worst storms, Frank would light the oil lamps and put a fire on the hearth. We'd wind up the Victrola, read, and chat."

"Now you have electricity," Joan said.

"But no Frank," Thalia said. "There are occasions when the power goes out during the winter that I must go to Charlie's place. He doesn't trust me to stay alone here."

"He just wants you to be comfortable," Joan said. "As long as Frank was here and thinking properly, Charlie didn't worry."

"Did Reginald enjoy that sort of domesticity?" Lish asked.

"Heavens no," Thalia said, moving a bookmark down a page.

"He was not a child to read. We kept a jigsaw puzzle on the go. He would tolerate working on that for a while. The best times that Frank and I enjoyed were *after* he left home. Lish, did you know that the name your mother, or father, bestowed on you is Roman? Licinius. How unusual."

"It is a man's name," Lish said. "Grandmother didn't like it and told people that 'Lish' was a short form for Elizabeth, which is my middle name. Dad had an appreciation for ancient cultures. Some of the books he read were on Roman history. When I finally found out what my given name was, I thought it was exotic, and probably suitable. By that time, I was more tomboy than prissy girl."

"How about this fellow: Flavius Galerius Valerium Liciniamus Licinius, Emperor 308–324. Oh dear, he did have some unpopular vices and was eventually assassinated."

"Don't most heroes die in some horrible way?" Joan said. "Consider Joan of Arc. I'm sure that Dad named me after her. He had a fixation with her story and owned two books about her."

"Then we have to put Hoshaphat in that category, too," Thalia said. "He was a warrior, a brave man who died for a cause he believed in."

"Who had the pot placed under glass, Thalia?"

"My grandfather," she said. "My father had the little plaque put on the side."

"I don't see it," Lish said.

"Turn the case.... Slowly now, it's fragile. Now ... there it is."

Lish squinted in the low light to see the lettering.

Before she could read it, Thalia said, "The Cougar is Forever. There's a piece of paper in the pot with a poem of sorts on it."

"I don't have to see the paper to know what it says," Lish said. "The same words are engraved on my mother's tombstone."

"The last time the pot was out of the case was the summer Jimmy Curlew came to visit. I don't know who wrote the piece," Thalia said. "It does embody the beliefs that Jimmy held. He could recite the words by heart."

"Why a copper pot?" Lish asked.

"I can explain that," Joan said. "I read that the Ojibway held natural copper in the highest esteem. A copper pot would be a most acceptable receptacle for a golden idol that they wanted to revere or appease."

"Hunter Logan thought the pot important enough that he kept the Mishoomis Gazhagayns deed in it," Thalia said. "He mentions that in his journal but didn't quote what was on the paper."

"I wonder what happened to the original document," Lish mused. "Have you seen it, Thalia? It isn't in this file."

"I don't have it. Father didn't have it," Thalia replied. "That's why I wrote to Jimmy Curlew. I wanted to know if Manchild took it with him when he left Hunter's Mark."

"Charlie thinks that the paper was buried with Mishoomis Gazhagayns. By then Hunter had received his land allotment from the Crown for being a Loyalist," Joan said.

"The Crown document is in this file," Lish said, "along with deeds and wills, including that of your father, Thalia. I wonder if the bit of prose *is* what Mishoomis Gazhagayns wrote — or said. Perhaps the original paper deteriorated so much that the sentiments were copied many times over the years?"

"And Mishoomis means 'grandfather,'" Joan said. "That information was in the journal."

"The thought has crossed my mind that CAT represents the land. Gazhagayns resides forever near the stone. The cougar is forever ... The Mark must be forever. The idol is on this land — forever free. Many possibilities exist."

"Mother had a copy of the prose. Noah knew the words. Jimmy Curlew knew the words. It's something that was important enough to be passed down through the years. Another legend?" Lish ventured.

"I guess that we'll never know for sure," Joan said.

"There are important papers not in the folder you're looking through, Lish. My current will and testament is in the hands of my lawyer. Charlie has the man's name." Thalia told her. "There is also a copy in my personal file that no one sees."

"I assume that's where you keep Hunter Logan's original journal too," Lish said.

"That would be the logical place for it," Thalia said.

Thalia's personal file must be what Reginald is after, Lish thought. There's nothing in this particular folder that would help his cause.

Thalia, leafing through a photo album, chose photos and handed them across to Lish. They depicted Thalia and Frank, Frank and Reginald as a child, Reginald as a young man, Thalia in her garden, Thalia at the old barn. "Frank was quite the photographer. He owned an expensive German model camera. I've still got it in a trunk in the attic."

Could it be photographs that Reginald is after? Lish thought, looking at each as it was given her. But why would he want them?

"Joan, we mustn't forget that Len is going to pick us up early tomorrow morning for our doctor's appointments," Thalia said. "Lish is going to stay here to do the laundry. The weather should clear by then. There's no harm hanging clothes on the line during a rain, though. It just gives everything another soft-water rinse."

"I do apologize for not driving you to Collingwood," Lish said.

"Did I tell you that Charlie is also coming early tomorrow morning to take a look at the butler's pantry?" Thalia said. "You can't continue to climb the stairs, Joan. I don't need a pantry, but you do need a downstairs bedroom. It will be cosy and warm and right next to the bathroom."

Joan stopped knitting. "It isn't necessary to restructure Granite to accommodate me, Thalia."

"Charlie says that the wall cupboards can probably be removed without too much damage to them. They can be stored in an upstairs room, or put along a wall in the dining room. With lace curtains, several throw rugs, a nice lamp, your own comfortable bed ..."

"Thalia, we're two lame ducks," Joan said. "You can't look after me. I can't take good care of you."

"Have you both forgotten about me?" said Lish.

"Perhaps you won't stay at Granite," Joan said. "If I recall, you said that you had three months before you had to ..."

"If I recall, I mentioned that I needed time to sort a few things out. I've paid three months in advance on my apartment," Lish told them. "I have a few weeks left on that rent. As far as sorting things out, I think my life has gotten more complicated."

"Charlie," Joan said.

Lish smiled. "Yes, indeed. Charlie."

When Lish was tidying the parlour after Thalia and Joan retired, she leafed through the photo albums. Although there were many pictures of Reginald, she saw none of him as a newborn babe. That's odd, Lish thought. If Frank was the avid photographer that Thalia described, the most important pictures he'd snap of his heir — his son — would be very soon after Reginald's birth. And where are Thalia's wedding photographs? There is not one picture of her and Frank in their wedding finery.

What's this? Lish looked closely at several pictures, turned a few pages, then came back to the two photographs. She slipped them out of the album and tucked them in a pocket.

Monday, July 30 — Early Morning

Charlie appeared at the kitchen door, Luna by his side, a pup under each arm. "Every time I head for the truck, she beats me to it. Luna's here to stay for a while. She won't run away again as long as you don't mention F-R-A-N-K too much in her presence."

"I see that she's already chased Adam and Eve off their blanket," Lish said.

Charlie put the pups on the floor. "That pair are a handful. They'll give the cats a run for their money. I've got a list as long as my elbow of people who want them, but I want to keep one. You can choose which one it's going to be." Charlie chuckled. "They're both female, in case a city girl like you didn't notice."

"I noticed," Lish said, pushing hair off her damp forehead with a wet hand.

"I bet that days like this make you wish you were back in an office in the city," Charlie said, coming to stand beside Lish. He found his handkerchief, wiped Lish's brow, then kissed it.

"If that's what you think, you've misjudged me," Lish said. "I'm settling into country life quite nicely, thank you."

While she finished the laundry, Charlie busied himself measuring cabinets and walls. The pantry's amenities were so beautifully built that he didn't want to dismantle them completely. The room was part of what made Granite so special.

"Have you had breakfast?" Lish asked, looking round the door. "I can't imagine you cooking bacon and eggs."

"Joe made 'em," Charlie said. "He's turned out to be a pretty good hand around the place. I could use a cup of coffee, though."

As soon as Charlie sat down, Adam was on his knee.

"Can I ask a serious question? And I do expect an honest answer." Lish sat next to him, a notebook in her hand, her purse on the table.

"Go ahead," Charlie said.

"Are you responsible for Mulmur Murmurings? Are you Hugh Dunnit? You know everyone — everything."

Charlie laughed. "I've been asked that question so many times. Why don't you just put a little tick beside my name in that little book of yours. Maybe it's Thalia."

"It can't be her," Lish said. "She doesn't have a telephone — yet. That's the only possible way the news can get to the paper so soon after it happens."

"Are you going somewhere?" Charlie poked the purse.

"While you're here, I thought I'd chase down Bernard and Gloria. They're supposed to be at the cottage today. I'll be back before noon. Then I'll fill you in on my little encounter with Jeff."

"Joan managed to get a couple of sentences in before Len came," Charlie said. "Now, will you be honest with me?"

"Of course."

"When you get back, will you tell me what on earth you're doing canoodling with those two snoops?"

Lish laughed. "Canoodling. Cagey Farmer, you are something else." Impulsively, she leaned over and kissed Charlie on the cheek.

He returned the favour with a long, tender kiss on her lips. "Yes, I am. Now, an answer: *yes*, you will tell me, or *no* you won't tell me."

"Yes, Charlie. I promise to tell you even if they think that you're Hugh Dunnit. I place a great deal of trust in you."

Charlie sat back in his chair. "You asked them to find out who Dunnit is?"

"Maybe," Lish said. "I'll see you before lunch."

"Waul, I'll invent a few jobs to keep me busy around here while you're away," Charlie said.

"The cold-water tap is leaking in the bathroom," Lish said. "For variety, there are some papers in a brown envelope on my dresser that I'd appreciate your opinion on, if plumbing isn't your forte."

"I'll tackle the papers," Charlie said. "I don't have the time to get into a big plumbing job today."

The Cottage

Bernard and Gloria were expecting Lish. They had everything laid out on the table. Their suitcases were packed and sat next to the back door. The refrigerator was empty, its door open. Gloria met Lish as soon as she heard the car door slam.

"Under the circumstances, we could do nothing but wait for you to feel better," Gloria said. "We appreciated your telephone call."

"Thanks for your patience," Lish said. "I hope you didn't mind the extra work."

"Patience does pay off." Bernard pointed to the table. "Ten days ago we didn't have this information. If you hadn't asked a few pertinent questions, given us some direction, we'd have run into a brick wall. You're an astute observer, Lish"

"I learned to be at Smith & Jones," Lish said.

"You worked for Smith & Jones?" Bernard asked.

"Until they closed their Toronto branch," Lish said. "I was offered a job in their Detroit office but decided not to make the move. You know — different laws, more dangerous territory."

"Let me shake your hand," Bernard said. "I applied — twice — but didn't have what they were looking for. You must have been good."

"You understand that no one knows of my association with S & J. I was hired by COY on bank references," Lish said.

"Understood." Bernard said. "I bet that working for Mrs. Russo, and hanging around Seven Springs, must be the most mundane thing you've ever done."

Lish laughed. "On the contrary," she said. "What do you have for me?"

Gloria gave Lish a small white envelope. "Everything is here. There are a number of possibilities. You'll have to sort it out — make up your mind." Gloria handed Lish the bill. "It's not as much as we could have charged because of the Jason Curlew arrangement," she said. "That coupe will pad our pocketbooks nicely."

Lish motioned toward the suitcases. "You're leaving then, as we discussed? You agree to all the conditions?"

"What did you expect," Bernard said. "For an exclusive interview with Curlew, including posed photos, we'll agree to living in a cave, if necessary."

Given certain circumstances, that would be quite rewarding, too, Lish thought. "Noah will see you on August 11, at eleven a.m. at the General Store. You leave him, and Seven Springs, alone until then. You say absolutely *nothing* to anyone, bring no one with you ..."

"This lady is good," Gloria said.

"This lady wants what is best for Seven Springs and Noah Curlew," Lish said.

"I have to admit that it is a special place. You know, the other day I could have sworn that I saw a large cat," Bernard said. "I was driving across the bridge, coming into the valley, and noticed a big tawny-coloured animal near that odd-looking stone below the Russo place."

CAT, you've done your work again, Lish thought. "Dunnit mentioned in Murmurings that one was sighted," she said.

"Cougars are scarce as hen's teeth. They've been hunted to near extinction," Bernard said.

"Then this one is best left alone," Gloria said. "Live and let live, I say. You mentioned Dunnit. About that other little job ..."

"How far did you get?" Lish asked.

"Not far. The paper won't divulge its sources. No one in Seven Springs will admit that they know the perpetrator. We figure it's a man by some of the comments," Bernard said. "I haven't ruled out Charlie Barnes."

"I asked him outright," Lish told them. "He didn't exactly give me a straight answer."

"You never know," Gloria said. "Don't discount Georgie. That woman knows everything. How about that Len fellow at the garage? He's got plenty of time on his hands, and a telephone that never stops ringing. Or Wee Jimmy. He's one for gossip, I'll tell you, and he's got a telephone. Plus, he used to write for a farm paper."

"I'm still working on Len and Maggie," Lish said, glancing at her watch. She'd have to hurry if she was going to get back to Granite in time to make Charlie lunch. How domesticated I've become, she thought, that I worry about the Cagey Farmer's stomach.

"Before you go, you should know that Reginald is out of the country," Bernard said. "When I gave notice about vacating the cottage, his secretary said that he was in New York City for a few days, then going to Connecticut."

I wouldn't count on that being the case, Lish thought. "You called COY?" she asked.

"No," Bernard said. "Northlands Development, their Collingwood office."

"The lady was quite chatty, but she wouldn't divulge where he was staying in New York. She did say that he was driving down and back, and that he'd be away until at least August 9."

"Bernard, you are thorough," Lish said.

"That's a compliment coming from someone — especially a woman — who worked for Smith & Jones Investigative Services. Thanks."

Noon Hour — Granite

Charlie chewed through a half dozen ham sandwiches and two pieces of cake before he settled in to discuss the papers.

"It appears to me that COY's business practices border on criminal activity," he said. "That's why you left the company, isn't it? You hired Bernard and Gloria to confirm your suspicions?"

"More or less," Lish agreed.

"Are you going to do anything about it?"

Lish busied herself clearing the table. "At first I was, but the situation has become very complicated. There's still much to take into consideration."

"I'll stand behind you, whatever decision you make," he said. "Someone has to stand up for those who can't act for themselves."

"Charlie, you are the most decent person I've ever met," she said. "How can I help but love you?"

He wrapped his arms around Lish and drew her to him. "There are no secrets between us, Lish, my girl." He began a slow dance round the kitchen, keeping step with a tune on the radio.

"But Charlie, there are," Lish said.

"Nah," he said. "Don't you believe that, not for one minute. Trust me."

"There's one thing I'd like to prove," Lish said. "We know that Reginald Russo is involved in Northlands Development. How is he connected with COY? I personally know that he socializes in the same party circles as the bosses at COY. Maybe if people find out that he's part of a firm that makes shady land deals, the project could be derailed."

"None of the papers in the brown envelope carry the names of Reginald Russo or Russell Grant," Charlie said. "This Campbell, O'Hearn & Yule.... Have you seen Campbell?"

"Yes, I've spoken to him face to face on many occasions. He spent a lot of time in the office."

"What about O'Hearn?"

"I never met the man, never heard his voice on the phone. I never saw a picture of him. He was the silent partner."

"Yule?"

"Yes, Yule was in the office. He was the one that fired me."

"Is it possible that there is a connection between Russo and O'Hearn?" Charlie asked.

"It was always my understanding that O'Hearn spent most of his time in the States. Guess where Reginald is supposed to be for the next few days, according to Bernard."

"The good ol' U.S. of A."

"New York and Connecticut," Lish said. "That situation needs looking into."

Charlie waltzed Lish around the table. "Speaking of 'situation,' how about our party?" he asked. "I figured that August 11 would be a good night fer some jiggin' in the hayloft."

"I think that's an appropriate date," Lish said. "Would you ask Noah if he would play a few songs as Jason Curlew?"

Charlie held Lish at arm's length. "You mean that? Noah

would agree? You've talked with him?"

"Yes to all three questions. But keep the information under your hat, Cagey Farmer — and I mean that seriously. No talking to anyone about Noah."

"I swear on Logan's grave," Charlie said.

"There are a couple of other things need doing too that demand absolute secrecy. I have to rely on you to do them, Charlie."

Charlie snuggled Lish close to him again as the next song came over the airwaves. "What are they, Commander MacPherson?"

"Everyone who supports Thalia, or who believes that North-lands Development must be stopped, needs to get together — August 10. The evening."

"A meeting of the minds," Charlie said. "Where should this meeting take place? At Granite?"

"The meeting of *some* minds," Lish said. "Thalia mustn't be present. We can't have an open discussion with her in attendance because no one will want to hurt her feelings ... alienate her in any way. The group has to meet somewhere else."

"You're not planning an overthrow of the Bird on the Hill?"

"On the contrary. I'm trying to preserve The Mark and help Seven Springs to survive."

"What place do you have in mind for the word-chow?"

"A place where no one would think to find a group of people," Lish said. "I'll leave it to you to sort that one out."

"I was thinking: Noah could take Thalia for a long drive on August 10. They can have dinner out," Charlie said. "I know these people. Noah is from away. Valley folk are an insular lot. They have to come to their own conclusions, solve their own problems."

"You're right on that summation, Charlie. Noah is part of the solution, but shouldn't be at the gathering. I'm sure that some of the people will think I'm interfering in things that I shouldn't. I won't let that attitude bother me. I'll explain everything when I get back."

"You're going somewhere?" Charlie stopped dancing.

"I've got a few things that I have to clear up," she said. "I'll be back either this Friday evening or Saturday morning, Charlie."

"You're not going to tackle Rotten Reggie, are you? I won't let you do that by yourself. I'll go with you if you're thinking of confronting him."

Lish took Charlie's face in her hands. "Charlie, I promise that you and I will tackle Rotten Reggie together. I've got to make arrangements to vacate my apartment. If I'm going to be housekeeper ... and a few other things for the Cagey Farmer ... I don't need a den in Toronto."

"Do you mean that, Lovely Damsel?"

"With all my heart," Lish said. "This may sound like something, or someone has bitten my brain, but I'm now part of this place forever sweet, where dreams and legends just might come true."

Wednesday, August 1 — The Morning

The town of Midland was not one of the names on the label of the memory jar. It was not a place that Lish remembered visiting. Nevertheless, the town was important to the ongoing saga at Granite.

Bernard and Gloria provided the names of two women who might be able to contribute useful information about Reginald. It was surprising that both were still alive. They were midwives who had worked throughout the area around the time of the First World War.

Before Lish booked into a small motel on the highway, she drove around to familiarize herself with the town. As she passed Martyr's Shrine and Wye Marsh, Lish thought it ironic that Reginald's life may have begun in an area with so much Indian history.

After lunch, Lish knocked on the door of a tidy cottage on Hugel Avenue.

"She's not home," a neighbour called. "Shell be back in fifteen minutes, though. She's out for her afternoon constitutional and went to the grocery store."

While Lish waited for Miss Andrews to return, she sorted through her notes. What she knew for sure was that Reginald's birth didn't take place in Toronto. As a matter of fact, nothing was found to indicate that he'd been born in Ontario. Finding that information was a stroke of luck. Yesterday, when she contacted the appropriate agency, Lish spoke with someone that she'd worked with at Smith & Jones. Five hours later, when she made a second call from a payphone in Orangeville, Lish had her answer.

T. Eaton Company payroll records were harder to gain access to, but the problem was not insurmountable. The records indicted that Thalia quit before she married Frank Russo. She worked for the company for two years and eleven months, beginning in 1911. Her name appeared as Miss T. Logan on all records.

From her notes, Lish knew that Bernard and Gloria ran into a dead end when they checked the property on Bloor Street. Unfortunately, the house where Thalia said that she and Frank lived had been taken down to make way for an office building. No one was found who had owned the property.

Lish watched as a short, stocky woman, pulling a child's wooden wagon full of brown paper bags, shuffled along the sidewalk. This must be Miss Juliette Andrews, she thought. Lish waited until the elderly woman reached the side door of the cottage before getting out of her car.

"Hello there. Let me help you with your bags," Lish said.

Miss Andrews turned dull, watery eyes toward Lish and tried to focus on her face. "If you're selling something, go away," she said.

"I'm not selling anything. I'm trying to complete a family history," Lish said. "Someone said that you might be able to help me, Miss Andrews. I understand that you delivered scores of babies around here."

"Hundreds, it seems like, from 1899 to 1932. After that, most women wanted to have their babies in a hospital," Miss Andrews said.

"How good is your memory?" Lish asked.

"For an eighty-four-year-old, it's pretty sharp. If you'd carry the bags into the kitchen please? Put them on the table. What name were you looking for?"

Lish picked up two bags. "The name is Russo. The family lived out in the country — close to Elmvale."

"Russo? I know the name, but only because Ettie Mackie talked about them. Ettie was a midwife, too. She lives three streets over — big red brick house. She married, I didn't. Her husband died in a storm on the lake."

"Do you recall the Logan family from over near Seven Springs? Was their name ever mentioned?"

"Logan. That name is familiar, but only because there's a woman lives over that way by the name of Logan that some people say is touched in the head. I say live and let live. Everyone's got odd ways about them, don't you think?"

"I agree with you," Lish said.

"Did you drive, or take the bus to get here?"

"I drove. My car is parked at the curb."

"Would you give me and my little red wagon a ride to the library? It's a bit far for old legs, you know. I don't mind walking back. On the way, I'll point out Ettie's place."

Ettie Mackie's two-storey red-brick house sat well back from the street. Rose gardens lined the walk. Comfortable rocking chairs graced the wide front porch. Music wafted through the latched screen door.

Lish knocked. When no one answered immediately, she called out. "Mrs. Mackie? You have company. Miss Andrews sent me."

There was movement in the hall — a shadow, footsteps. A big raw-boned woman with a quantity of snow white hair pinned into a bun at the nape of her neck looked at Lish through the screen.

"I'm tracing some family members. Miss Andrews thought that you might be able to help me."

"Come in," Ettie said. "How is Juliette?"

"She said to say hello and that she'd walk around to see you soon," Lish told her.

"This house is far too big for one person, but Juliette is too independent to live with me; not that the invitation hasn't been extended. We have a lot in common," Ettie said. "What's your name?"

"Lish MacPherson."

"I don't recall birthing any MacPherson babes after 1921," Ettie said. "We'll sit in the parlour. Don't mind the quilt frame. Quilting's really a winter job but it's so cool in here during the summer that I keep the frame up. I may as well stitch while my eyes are still capable of seeing to do it. I was working a row when you knocked."

Ettie sat at the frame and took her needle to hand. "Who are you looking for?" she asked.

"The Russo family," Lish said. "In particular, the birth of Frank Russo's son."

Ettie drew her needle through the quilt. "You're talking about the Russo clan from the Elmvale area?"

"That is the family," Lish said.

"There's a strange story connected with that tribe. They were a rambunctious bunch," Ettie said. "Talk about hellions, especially J.D., the son of the first wife. Are the Russo's your relatives?"

"They're connected in some way," Lish said. Little white lies often lead to big black truths, she thought.

"Well, just hope that you didn't inherit any of their nastier traits," Ettie said. "You mentioned that you were looking for information on the birth of Frank Russo's son?"

"That's right," Lish said. "A birth that took place in 1914, if my information is correct."

"Well, I can tell you that, to my knowledge, Frank Russo was not the father of any baby that I delivered. That is not to say that he didn't possibly father a child though, if you get my drift."

"You don't recall attending the birth of a baby that was born after the marriage of Thalia Logan to Frank Russo?"

"I don't recall hearing that Frank Russo married," Ettie said. "I do recall being midwife to an unmarried woman who had a baby boy. The birth was normal. The circumstances afterwards were unusual. When it came time to register the baby, she wouldn't make up her mind who the father was."

"You don't say!"

Ettie smiled. "I just did say. She worked the needle through the material. "I'll make a cup of tea. That'll give you time to mull that information over."

"Can I help you?"

"No dear, just enjoy looking around the parlour. My husband collected things on his travels around the lakes. He had very eclectic tastes."

Oh, what a tangled web is spun with every interview, Lish thought as she watched Ettie leave the room. The Reginald Russo story is taking bizarre twists, worthy of any mystery novel.

Ettie returned with a tea tray and placed it beside Lish's notebook on a side table. "I'm looking forward to your questions," she said. "You came prepared to take notes."

"Was the girl from Midland?" Lish asked.

"Margaret Deacon came from the Elmvale area. Her parents were poor as church mice. They didn't have two pennies to rub together. There were seven children: six boys and one girl — Margaret. She was the eldest and was used just like a slave at home, if you know what I mean. She never ate properly."

"What did Margaret look like?" Lish asked.

"Petite and delicate of frame. She wasn't the prettiest woman around. But she had a nice smile. She did seem to be a bit morose, even theatrical, but given her past I could understand the way she felt on occasion. I could feel sorry for her one minute and want to slap her the next."

"Perhaps it was her home life that got her involved in the oldest profession in the world," Lish said.

"Not to begin with," Ettie said. "The only job that Margaret could find when she came to Midland was in the office of a chandlery near the docks. She was in her mid-twenties — not a young woman. That's where she met a few unsavoury characters who eventually wore down her resolve to be a good, virtuous woman."

"I imagine that after the home life you described, Margaret was ripe for adventure," Lish said.

"J.D. Russo worked around the docks. He introduced Margaret to his brother Frank who hung around with a young man by the name of Leonard Grant."

"Let me guess," Lish said. "The inevitable happened."

"When Margaret found out that she was with child, she didn't know what to do. She couldn't go home," Ettie said. "One of the ladies at my church approached me. Could I take her in as a maid? she wondered. My husband captained a lake ship. He was away so much of the time that I couldn't see there would be a problem."

"Margaret worked here while she was pregnant," Lish said.

"She was a guest," Ettie said. "Frank Russo paid for Margaret's room and board — probably felt he should atone for the indiscretions of both his brother J.D. and his friend Leonard."

"Both claimed parentage?"

"Both men apparently had reason to do just that," Ettie said. "Margaret didn't deny that she'd fiddled around with both."

"I'll assume that the baby's birth was never properly registered," Lish said.

"Not that I know of," Ettie said. "She called the child Reginald only — never introduced the poor thing with a last name."

That lets a grown man invent any story he wants to, Lish thought.

"The most unusual circumstance is that Frank Russo eventually took full responsibility for raising the child. He persuaded Margaret that he could do an adequate job. She agreed — I believe that a certain amount of money was involved. The boy was six months old when Russo took him away. I don't imagine it was an official adoption."

"What happened to the mother?" Lish asked.

"Margaret was, without a doubt, devastated after handing the child over," Ettie said. "I kept in touch with her for a while after she left. She eventually married a man from the Paisley area. After a while I lost track of her. I don't know where she is now, or even if she's still alive."

"How many years has it been since you heard from her?" Lish asked.

"Forty years at least," Ettie replied. "Has any of this information helped with your family research?"

"Immensely," Lish said.

"You should talk to J.D. Russo," Ettie said. "During the summer, he's always down on the dock fishing. You'll know him by the way he dresses. Watch for his diamond-patterned braces. They are his trademark. Apparently, someone from the States sends them to him."

"How is his health?" Lish asked. "I mean, he must be an elderly gentleman. Is his mind good?"

"I heard rumours about him — or was it his brother? You know how rumours are embellished in the telling," Ettie said.

"Frank Russo disappeared eight years ago," Lish told her. "There was mention of it in the papers."

"J.D. batched it on the farm until he moved to Midland. He has a room down by the docks," Ettie said.

"J.D. never married?"

"Who'd have him?" Ettie said. "He's had a reputation for years as a lady's man. Frank was the decent one. Oh, he didn't mind going out on the town and having a good time, but he wasn't a womanizer. Margaret spoke highly of Frank."

"Have you heard from Margaret's son?" Lish asked.

"Not recently," Ettie said. "Just after the war, in early 1946, I got a letter from him. He was living in Connecticut at the time. He was trying to establish details about his birth for government forms. Whether it was Canadian or American forms, he didn't say."

Now the plot does thicken, Lish thought. "You were able to help him?"

"Of course. I always kept my records accurate and accounts up-to-date. I sent his mother's name, his birthdate, and the place of birth. I didn't mention the problem of dual fathership. That was Margaret's story to tell, her problem to solve. I wrote that his mother gave him up for adoption, but didn't say to whom. Unfortunately, by the time he wrote to me, I had completely lost touch with his mother."

Ettie took the tea tray. "Would you like to see his letter and my reply?"

"I certainly would," Lish said.

"Better still, would you like to *have* the letters and Margaret's records? I'm to the point where I don't need to keep that sort of information at hand. I'm not a government agency."

"Ettie Mackie, you're a gem," Lish said.

"I've been called much worse but no better," Ettie said. "Come along. The files are in an upstairs bedroom. It'll take a bit of digging to find the right box. My goodness, my mind is slipping in old age. I referred to Margaret as being a Deacon when she lived here. Deacon is the surname of her official husband. Her maiden name was O'Hearn."

The Afternoon — Granite

Charlie was surprised to see Luna, the pups, Tom, Mary, and Joan walking down Lavender Line, near the lane to the Delaney farm. When Joan waved him down, Charlie stopped and said, "Mornin' Tom. Is it that bad that you all have to leave home?"

"We told Thalia not to bother you," Joan said. "She wouldn't listen."

"We decided to meet you on the Line to warn you that she's in rare form," Mary explained. "She was impossible to live with all morning. We made sure that she had lunch, then left, and are staying clear of her while you're there."

"Charlie, I've never seen Thalia so angry and miserable. She's had small temper fits before when things have bothered her, but she's never been like this," Joan added. "Why she called you, I don't know."

"Maybe it's because she knows that I'm the only one can handle her," Charlie said. "The Bird on the Hill has met her match."

When Charlie strode into the kitchen, Thalia was waiting for him. "It took you long enough to get here," she snapped.

"Waul, it's just fortunate that Joe had to go back to the drive shed for some tools and heard the phone," Charlie said. "He ran back to the field to tell me that you chewed him out. What's this all about?"

"You should know," Thalia said. "You're the one fraternizing with Lish MacPherson."

"What of it?" Charlie said. "That shouldn't be a reason for you to get your scuzzies in a knot."

"The woman is not to be trusted," Thalia said. "She asked the most personal questions and then she just up and left me in the lurch without so much as an adieu."

"Lish arranged for Mary to come help you while she is away," Charlie said. "She will be back by the weekend."

"That's what she says. But will she come back or is she somehow connected to Reginald, and maybe working for him?"

"What makes you think that?" Charlie asked.

"It's the questions she asks. Did I have any enemies?... What year was I married?... Did Frank and Reginald, or Reginald and Maggie, fight all the time?... Did Frank's brother J.D. visit often?... Were my personal papers in a safe place?... Did I pen the Logan journal?"

"They are all good questions," Charlie said. "I hope that you answered Lish — and truthfully."

Thalia took a step toward Charlie, wagged a finger, and said, "We've been through this before. Certain information is none of her business, and none of yours either, Charlie Barnes."

Charlie turned a kitchen chair to face the angry woman. "Sit down, Thalia."

"Don't tell me what to do," she said. "Show some respect for your elders."

"Thalia Logan Russo. You will listen to me," Charlie said. "It's about time there was some honest talk between you and I. Now, sit down!"

Charlie waited until Thalia did as she was told, then pulled up a chair and sat facing her.

"I trusted her, Charlie. I invited her to stay and she immediately began to cause trouble for me," Thalia said.

"By 'she,' I assume that you mean Lish," Charlie said.

"Who else might I be referring to?"

"I could list a few people, starting with Maggie Webster, but I won't," Charlie said.

"What do you know about Maggie?" Thalia asked.

"Not as much as I'd like to," Charlie said. "But my middle name's patience. Time will tell all, I'm sure — if you don't."

"I will not tolerate this insolent behaviour." Thalia struck the table with her hand.

Is it frustration or fear I detect? Charlie thought. "You won't tolerate insolent behaviour? That's like the pot calling the kettle black. Thalia, listen to me. You spoke so harshly to Joe that I had to drop everything to rush over here to see what the hell was up. You owe Joe an apology."

"Apologize to WGD?" Thalia said. "He's a Delaney. And why is Tom hanging around Granite?"

"If you recall, years ago Tom Delaney was sweet on Mary Thomas," Charlie said. "And Joe's a good man. Leave bygones be bygones. Stop visiting the sins of the fathers onto the sons. It shouldn't matter now what happened more than one hundred and sixty years ago."

"I didn't think that the man would pass the message along. He said that you were a bit busy and if it wasn't too important ..." Thalia said. "I told him that I was the one to judge the urgency of the situation because, perhaps, he wasn't capable of doing so."

"That's contemptuous talk, Thalia. I've never failed you. No one has. We all drop what we're doing to be at your beck and call, including the Delaney boys."

"Some people need to show a little gratitude," she said.

"And they do," Charlie said. "But not without grumbling about it occasionally. Thalia, you're only the Queen of the Hill. You're not ruler of the County. You have to understand that people like Lish and myself — and yes, the Delaney boys — help because we care about you, not because you're paying us to do so."

"Those are harsh words, Charlie."

"They were meant to be," he said. "You've no reason nor right to take a snitty-fit just because Lish decided to take a few days off."

"What is she doing away?" Thalia asked.

"I've no idea, but obviously you're worried about what Lish is up to. You're afraid she's — to put it bluntly — digging up the past."

Charlie was unprepared for the flood of tears that followed. Thalia never cried. Not when Frank went missing, not when she broke her leg, not in front of Rotten Reggie or Joan. He didn't reach to comfort her, but did rummage in a pocket for a handkerchief and handed it over. Let her cry, he thought. The dam has finally burst. Now we'll get somewhere.

It took some time for Thalia to compose herself. Her voice broke as she said, "I just don't know where to turn next, Charlie. I woke up this morning so frustrated and took my feelings out on anyone I could find."

"Or call," Charlie added. "Maybe the telephone wasn't such a good idea if you're going to use it to chew folks out."

"That phone hasn't stopped ringing since it was activated this morning. Where did people get the number? Why are they calling just to say hello?"

"It's big news in the Valley that the Bird on the Hill has finally got another perch to sit on," Charlie said. "At least you can't blame Lish for talking the number around. She's away."

"Perhaps I distrust Lish because she's lured my most dependable and honourable compatriot away," Thalia said.

"But you will gain a wonderful woman who will be devoted to you and The Mark," he said. "And I'm hoping that you just might have several babes to spoil, if you don't drop off yer perch too soon after we take vows — or not take vows, if that be the way it works out."

"I'll pretend that I didn't hear you say that, Charlie Barnes."

"You have to promise me that regardless of what Lish finds — what she says, what she asks — when she comes back, you must answer her questions. Do you understand that, Thalia?"

"But there's so much she shouldn't know," Thalia said. "Things I haven't told anyone. Things that no one must know."

"Like the fact that you never married Frank Russo," Charlie said. "That's a good 'un. Let's talk about that." The look of confusion, anger, and surprise on Thalia's face was an adequate reward for his question.

"Where did you conjure up that lie?"

"It's not a lie," Charlie said. "It's the bare facts. I've ways and means of sorting fact from fiction. There's no marriage certificate, nothing written in the family Bible, nothing in local church records." Charlie didn't mention the phone call from Lish late last evening.

"I was married in Toronto at City Hall," Thalia said.

"Now, Thalia. Let's tell the truth, beginning right now," Charlie said. "Your official papers are signed Thalia Logan. Remember, I pick up your mail occasionally. The publisher addresses their envelopes to one Thalia Logan. I bet that their cheques are cashed by you under the name Thalia Logan. That's why you have your accounts in banks that are miles away from Seven Springs."

"Who knows?" she asked him.

"Probably no one but you, me, and Wee Jimmy. You're paying him to keep quiet about your lack of nuptials, aren't you? He was one of Frank's closest buddies. He lived in Toronto for a while, near you on Bloor Street."

"Wee Jimmy tattled," Thalia said.

"His mouth is zipper-tight," Charlie assured her. "You don't realize that, even if the information was common knowledge, folks around here wouldn't care, Thalia. They appreciate you for who you are, not for what you didn't do years ago. A friendly 'how-de-do' counts for far more than an 'I do' these days."

"Marriage vows counted when I was young," Thalia said. "I was living in sin."

"Waul, if that's the only thing that you're atoning for, there's nowt to be concerned with. Now, if you told me that you had som'pin to do with Frank's disappearance, I'd worry."

Thalia fidgeted with her brow. "I did have something to do with Frank's death," she said. "I'm sure I did."

This is something that I might not want to hear, Charlie thought. "While you're in a confessing mood, you'd better tell me," he said. "Out with it afore Tom, Mary, and Joan get back from their walk."

"I frightened them with my bursts of anger, didn't I?" she asked.

"They were like scared rabbits and took Luna for a walk just in case she mistook your outbursts for an outright physical attack."

"I'll apologize," Thalia said.

"You'd better. Now, tell all," Charlie said. "You mentioned the word 'death,' not disappearance."

"I woke up at three o'clock this morning and thought, 'Frank is *dead*.' I never thought of him in that term before. Disappeared, yes. Dead, no. Dead is so final that I hid the word in the back of my mind for years. Then it struck me that not only was he dead, he possibly committed suicide — somewhere on The Mark. I lay awake the rest of the night, so angry, so resentful."

"It's taken eight years of denial before your mind finally switched to the right way of thinking," Charlie said. "So, what did you do that you feel contributed to his death, by whatever means?" Charlie couldn't take the brow-beating any longer. He reached for Thalia's busy hand and drew it down to the table.

"The day Frank disappeared we had a terrible fight," Thalia said.

"I didn't think that Frank was coherent enough to have a meaningful conversation, let alone a significant argument," Charlie said.

"Neither did I. His demands were so unusual, so thoroughly thought through, that I knew it couldn't be Frank that dreamed them up."

"What were they?" Charlie asked.

"He insisted that J.D. live on The Mark — to help me and him."

"Frank asked if J.D. could move in with you?"

"Frank demanded that J.D. live here or at the cabin. He insisted that J.D. assume control over his property — not that he had any, mind you. Frank wanted his brother to have signing authority — I believe that it's called power of attorney?"

"What did you say — or do?" Charlie asked.

"I lost my temper. Given what I knew about J.D., I told Frank that hell would have to freeze before I'd allow the man to live on The Mark or at Granite."

"What do you know about J.D. other than the fact that he's Frank's twin?" Charlie asked.

Thalia evaded the question. "The point is that after the fight, I avoided talking with Frank about anything. He stayed in the parlour, playing one record over and over again. I kept to the kitchen."

"Was there anything of importance in the parlour that he could destroy?" Charlie asked.

"If you're thinking personal papers — bank books and such — no there weren't. After the little episode with Reginald, those were placed well out of his reach," Thalia said. "When Frank began to lose his faculties, I took special care to tie up a few loose ends — financially and personally — as far as The Mark and Granite were concerned."

"What happened next?"

"We ate supper in silence," she said. "While I did the dishes, Frank went for a walk with Luna. He did that twice a day — down the lane and back again. I usually watched him from the porch just in case he strayed. I didn't that day."

"Then you didn't see anyone meet him? J.D. or Rotten Reggie?"

"No, but Frank was a little longer coming back. He looked upset but said absolutely nothing — just puttered around the kitchen for a while, then went off to bed with not one word spoken between us since the argument."

"Let me guess," Charlie said. "He didn't sleep in his regular bed."

"Oh, he did," Thalia said. "I was still very angry with him. I slept in a different room. That's why I'm responsible for his death. I should have slept in the same room. If I'd found the bed empty sooner, Frank might have been found." Thalia burst into tears again. This time Charlie reached to console her.

"I doubt that Frank wanted to be found," Charlie said. "He knew every inch of The Mark and the escarpment for miles each way. Even in his bewildered state, Frank could vanish without a trace if he wanted to."

"Well, he did disappear, didn't he? And I was left with a real mess to sort out."

"Through all, you managed to keep that indomitable spirit of yours alive, Thalia. That's what people love about you," Charlie said. "You attract people, demand their attention, make them laugh."

"Not Noah," Thalia said.

"What about Noah?" Charlie asked.

"He tells me that he's leaving soon. He wants little to do with The Mark, save have the privilege of using the cabin on occasion."

"I hope that you wished him luck in the real world and graciously agreed to his request to use the cabin," Charlie said.

"I expected more of that young man," she said. "I was counting on him to help me save his ancestral land."

"Noah will help you, though not perhaps in the way that you think he should," Charlie said.

"In way of thank you, Noah has proposed that I go to Collingwood with him next Friday for dinner and a movie," she said.

"You *will* go. You're too much a lady to refuse that sort of invitation," Charlie said.

"I'll think about it."

"If I have to hog-tie you and toss you in the car, you'll accept

Noah's invitation," Charlie said. "That's the least you can do for all the trouble you caused today."

"If you're that adamant about it," Thalia said, "I will agree to accompany him."

"I am. Look, I'm trying to run a farm. There's a tractor in the back forty still needs fixin'. I gotta go work for a livin'. Thalia, you will apologize profusely to Tom, Mary, and Joan. And in the future, show some respect toward Tom Delaney when he comes a-courtin'. Promise me."

"I promise," Thalia said. "I apologize for bothering you, Charlie."

"Glad that I could help," Charlie said. "This might seem an odd question, but do you think that Frank might have given J.D. his cigarette holder if he decided to ... to do himself in?"

"He could have done so," Thalia said. "J.D. visited him the morning that we had the argument."

The Afternoon — Midland

Midland's docks bustled with activity. Summer visitors lined up to purchase tickets for the boat tours that cruised the bays and islands. Dockside tie-ups were in short supply as seasonal cottagers boated from their island retreats into town to buy supplies. Although a number of men fished from the docks, there was no sign of J.D. Russo. Lish finally resorted to asking a few people if they knew the man, and where he might be found. One pointed in the direction of a small bayside park some distance away from the dock area. "He was over there the last time I saw him. He hates crowds."

J.D. was seated on a bench, his fishing gear beside him, a sturdy cane hooked over the side of the seat. Lish watched the man for some time before approaching him. J.D. wore the telltale diamond-patterned braces over a blue plaid shirt. There was a rip in his right pant leg. One shoe lacked a full lace. A fringe of hair around his balding head needed a trim. Ill-fitting glasses hung on the end of his nose.

J.D. glanced her way once, pushed his glasses up his nose, and went back to watching the gulls fight for bits of bread that someone had scattered on the ground.

As Lish walked up to the bench, she took a good look at the man's face. It was creased with age and weathered from years of working outside. A two-day stubble made it difficult to see if he had a scar on his cheek.

"Mr. Russo? J.D., isn't it?" Lish asked.

J.D. adjusted his glasses again and squinted to see who was talking to him.

Lish realized the problem and moved to create a shadow so that the man could see her in diffused light. The shift allowed her to ascertain that he didn't have a scar. The remains in the cave were definitely those of Frank Russo.

"We've met before, haven't we?" he asked.

"We have. The last time our paths crossed it was a by-chance meeting. This time I've made a deliberate attempt to see you again. May I sit down?"

J.D. pushed his gear to one side. "I never say no to a purdy woman," he said. "You're the lady that talked to me at Stanton Store some time back."

"I am," Lish said, putting a brown bag on the bench.

"I remember you because you were looking for Hunter's Mark."

"And I found it," Lish said. "Would you like a honey-dip donut? A little bird told me that they're your favourite snack."

J.D. reached for a sticky treat. "Now, here's a woman who definitely knows the way to a man's heart."

"The donuts come at a price," Lish said.

"I figured as much. What are yah lookin' fer?"

"Information."

"Thalia sent you?"

"I guess that you could say she did, in a roundabout way."

J.D. finished the donut, licked his fingers, and reached into the bag for another. "You didn't happen to bring some coffee to wash these down?"

Lish pulled a thermos from her bag, undid the lid, and said, "Smell this."

J.D. took a whiff. "Who persuaded you to juice the java?"

"A casual acquaintance of yours," Lish replied.

"We're going to have a serious chat, aren't we, young lady? You don't ply a man with booze unless you want something. Women are different, you know. If you want something from them, you give 'em flowers and candy — lots of candy. They'll do anything for a pound of chocolates."

Lish smiled. J.D. was indeed a womanizer. Someone like Margaret O'Hearn would be impressed.

"I figure that you can't be bought by a few trifles," J.D. said. "By the way, what's your name?"

"Lish MacPherson. And yours?"

"James Douglas, but only on government forms. My friends still call me Randy."

I bet they do, Lish thought. "I think that I'll stick with J.D.," she said.

J.D. poured a wee dram and offered the cup to Lish.

"I'll pass," she said. She waited until J.D. downed the whiskey, then said, "I was talking with Ettie Mackie about Margaret O'Hearn. She was kind enough to give me a few details about Reginald's birth."

"You're one to get right into the fine print," J.D. said. "So you know that the child Thalia raised is my son. It was Frank figured out the solution about the babe."

"I gathered that," she said. "I assume that you enlisted shortly after the birth to avoid possible responsibility for the child."

"You could say that," J.D. said. "I knew that I was not a man to raise a kid."

Lish took a donut and passed the bag. "Reginald didn't know that Frank and Thalia weren't his parents?"

"That was part of the deal. He was never to find out," J.D. said. "Problem is that something went wrong when he was around sixteen years old. Someone told him that he was adopted — not who his real father was though."

"Who would tell him?"

"I figured that it was his mother. She was working at Granite at the time. She promised not to, but maybe she blabbed."

"Who was working for Thalia at the time?"

"Maggie Webster ... who was Maggie Deacon ... who was Margaret O'Hearn. Do yah mind if I have another tipple?"

"Go ahead," Lish said. Of course, that's the reason Maggie gets a payoff, Lish thought. "What makes you think that she broke Thalia's trust? Perhaps Reginald found out from someone else — or from something that he read."

"Well, don't look at me. I wouldn't rat on Frank and Thalia. I was al'ays welcome at Granite. We had good times. Uncle J., Reggie called me. We tramped The Mark, played games, laughed a lot. Then along came Maggie and I had to curtail my visits."

"Eventually Reginald left home," Lish said.

"When he was eighteen, he left Seven Springs. By then he was a nasty bit of business, al'ays carried a chip around on his shoulder. A couple of times I wanted to knock it off, I'll tell you. By then he spent as much time with Len Grant as with Frank and Thalia."

"And he must have spent time with you, too," Lish said.

J.D. laughed. "I didn't see him much. I was farmin' the home place. Reggie wanted nothing to do with farmin'. That doesn't mean that I didn't see Thalia and Frank. I visited often, even after Frank began to forget things. Thalia always kept life interesting for him. I was welcomed until complications arrived."

"Where did Reginald go?"

"He disappeared for a while, then showed up in Hamilton. He vanished again right after the war and turned up in the States." J.D. poured himself another shot. "Are you sure you don't want to join me? I hate to drink alone. I was surprised to hear from him again maybe ten years ago. That's when I told him that I was his father, not his uncle."

"How did he take the news?" Lish asked.

"It was almost a joke to him," J.D. said. "He keeps in touch, takes me fer little drives, mostly around Seven Springs. I don't say no cause I get to see my daughter that way."

"Your daughter?"

The young woman who owns Seven Springs General Store. Oh, I gotta be careful around her. She doesn't know that I'm her dad. Mary worked fer Thalia, you see ..."

"J.D. Russo! You are a man of few morals and a loose zipper," Lish said.

"Do yah see a halo? No one will tell you that I'm a saint. I'm not one to turn down a lady's attentions," J.D. said. He refused a donut, but poured another wee dram.

"So, you think that Reginald and Georgie are half-brother and sister," Lish said.

"But they don't know it. Mary said that she never told Georgie who her father was. I hope that she never does. Reggie's not a fella you'd want to be related to."

"Coming from you, that's an interesting comment," Lish said.

"I didn't realize how devious he was until he egged me on about moving into Granite to help Thalia with Frank," he said.

Amazing the information one can extract from a few shots of whiskey, Lish thought. She waited until a noisy motorboat passed on the bay then said, "Obviously, his plan didn't work."

"The day that Frank asked Thalia to let me live at Granite was the last time that I saw my brother alive," he said. "It's so clear in my mind. We were sitting in the old barn foundation waiting for an answer. Frank walked down the drive and told Reggie that Thalia said I wasn't welcome."

"That would be around eight years ago."

"About that," J.D. said. "Oh, there were words! Poor Frank was so bewildered that I had to step between them and send him back up the drive. That dog — Luna — was ready to attack Reggie. He kicked her. Terrible scene — just terrible."

"Frank didn't happen to give you his cigarette holder that day, did he?" Lish said.

"Frank give anyone, including his brother, his fag holder? Not on your life. Thalia gave him that silver baby as a birthday gift. It was his good-luck charm. He carried it with him everywhere. Why d'you ask?"

"I just thought that if Frank knew he was going to ..."

"Spit it out," J.D. said. "Commit suicide."

"Yes. That he'd maybe give you something to remember him by."

J.D. began to gather his gear. "I daresay that the thought of doin' himself in might have crossed what Frank had left of his mind. He always fretted about Thalia having the responsibility of caring for him. By the look of those clouds, we're gonna get wet if'n we stay here. My room's a block away."

"I'm sure that you gave Frank a few presents," Lish said,

"including a pair of those nice braces that you like to wear."

"Sure, we were twins, weren't we? Frank liked the braces just as much as I do, so I kept him supplied. Boy, that bugged Reggie — to see a gift that he gave me on Frank's back."

Lish carried the thermos and J.D.'s tackle box while he hobbled along with his cane in one hand and fishing pole in the other.

"I feel badly, fathering a son like Reggie," J.D. said. "I know what side o' the family the nastiness sprung from, though: my mother's. Her father was the devil incarnate. Thought nothin' of taking a birch whip to his wife, kids, and grandkids, too."

"J.D., I'm going to burst your fatherly bubble," Lish said. "At the same time you were courting Margaret with flowers and candy, she was also intimate with Len Grant. Because she couldn't decide if you or Len was Reginald's father, his birth went unregistered."

"You mean to say that Len and I were both bedding the woman?"

"I am saying that Reginald Russo goes by the name Jeffrey Russell Grant when it suits his purpose."

"Well, I'll be damned!" J.D. said. "I'm being used by the man."

"It appears so," Lish said. "I don't know for what reason, but I have the feeling that the moment you are of no further use to him, he'll foist you off like an old shoe."

J.D. opened the door to the room he called home. Its furnishings were sparse — a bed, wardrobe, dresser, table, chair, small fridge, hot plate, radio, and telephone. "Only thing I don't like about this place is that I gotta run down the hall to the john," J.D. said.

Looking around the dingy room, Lish thought there should be better for a man who sold his farm. "You moved here? What happened to the money that you got when you sold the home farm?"

"I can't sell the farm. The deed's in Frank's name. He handled all the important papers, made sure the bills were paid. I never bothered to do anything about getting things sorted out after the seven years ... you know, the court thing. The township says that as long as the taxes are paid, they won't fuss. I manage to scrape money together for the taxes and this room."

"No one's renting the land?"

"No. It's sitting fallow. Reggie says that he wants it. He had a hard time believing that the deed wasn't in my name." Reggie says that he'll pay for my room, the taxes, and a lawyer to get everything cleared up. But I won't accept money from him. He's not a man to get involved with where money's concerned, especially when he's handing it out."

"If Reginald has no interest in farming, why does he want your land?" Lish asked.

"Aggregates: sand, gravel, black muck," J.D. replied. "Same reason he's tryin' to buy all the land around Seven Springs. It ain't fer a ski resort. That's a smoke screen. Them hills, The Slope and that valley is the motherlode. There's big money to be made in aggregates, with all the building going round the province these days, according to Reggie."

"Well, you shouldn't have to live in a hovel like this," Lish said.

"The latest thing is that Reggie's trying to get his hands on Frank's papers. He called the other day and said that we'd go see Thalia next Wednesday afternoon about the deed fer the farm. I don't like the sound of that."

"Neither do I," Lish said. "Don't go."

"Other than declaring that I won't take money from him, I'm afraid to buck Reggie. He'd hit a person as quick as shake their hand," J.D. said. "I'm a little old fer a punching bag. I had too much of that as a kid. You're telling me that after all these years of me thinking that I was his dad, I might have been barking up the wrong family tree?"

"Why do you think that Reginald is using the name Grant but to hedge his bets?" Lish said. "I'm worried about you, J.D. If this situation takes a turn for the worst, you could be in danger. Is there anybody you can visit for a while?"

"I figured that there was hanky-panky when Frank disappeared. I've al'ays wondered if Reginald had something to do with his vanishing act. I couldn't prove anything, so I kept my trap shut."

"A good strategy for you to take, given Reginald's purported temper," Lish said.

"And the Sunday morning we spent sitting in the barn foundation gettin' up to no-good ..." J.D. pulled an old carpetbag out from under his bed. "I'm leavin' town," he said. "I wash my hands of the bugger. Now, I'm downright scared of him."

"Where can you go that Reginald won't find you?"

"I've an old army buddy who lives near Huntsville — out in the bush off the Muskoka Road. He's been after me to stay with him. His wife died and he's lonely, you see. You're gonna drive me there, young lady."

"On one condition," Lish said. "You leave a key to this room with me. I'll meet Reginald here next Wednesday."

"Oh, I wouldn't do that," J.D. said. "You're asking fer trouble."

"I'll have backup," Lish said. "Charlie Barnes. Be sure to pack any letters from this army buddy just in case Reginald turns up before Wednesday. I bet that he has a key to this room."

"Bet yer shirt and I'll get to see far more of Lish MacPherson than she'd like me too," J.D. said. "Reggie just walks in here any time he feels like it."

Mulmur Murmurings by Hugh Dunnit
For the Week of July 28–August 2

The Valley and Springs are charged this week, and the power isn't travelling through hydro lines. Stay tuned.

The Lovely Damsel was seen leaving the Valley with not so much as an adieu. Perhaps she heard that cagey old bachelor farmers are hard to train, especially in the budwar.

Speaking of the Cagey Farmer, he's holding a hootenanny on August 11. You're all invited. The fun starts at gloaming at Charlie B's. Bring what you can. It'll be a hungry bunch. Leave the booze at home. Stragglers get to milk the cows next morning. Gorgeous G at the General is putting her annual order in for Niagara peaches by the bushel. If you don't get your licks in this week, you're not going to have peaches on the table this winter 'cause she's only going to get one delivery this year and she wants to make it a good one. GG one doesn't mind floating credit, but you gotta pay for last year's peaches before you get this years — and that means you, H.C.

There was a buzzing good time in the Valley this week when Timmy B tried to get some sweet treat for Jenny K. He tackled a wild bee tree and was rewarded with more then a trickle of honey. The production line declared war. Timmy made a line for Jenny's house with the revenge-seeking buzzers in hot pursuit, aiming for all uncovered parts. Miss B saw them coming and slammed her door, leaving no choice but for Timmy to run the quarter-mile to his place — in record time. Advice for Timmy: Never wear shorts when you're gonna rob a bee tree. Sit on soft cushions. Share the honey.

To end on a sour note, the United Church belles are in a pickle and hope you'll soon be, too. Their preserves table at the annual bazaar was a dilly last year. They relish more of the same this time around. Get pickling, ladies. The cucs are like nukes this year: they're proliferating.

Friday, August 3, Very Early Morning — Seven Springs

The phone call came late last night but the information the Lovely Damsel imparted was well worth the aggravation of being wakened from a deep sleep. Charlie was away early, with his first stop at Delaneys, where Harry agreed to help Joe at the farm for the day.

"About the other little request?" Charlie asked.

"We talked it over and agreed to everything. It'll take a bit of work, but we'll be ready," Tom said.

"Good. Thanks. By the way, Joe, did you receive an apology from Thalia?"

"The Bird was most contrite," Joe said. "She's an old lady, Charlie."

"Age doesn't matter. Thalia has to understand that she can't chew people out on the telephone. I'm off, then. See you later this afternoon, Joe, Harry."

Charlie's next stop was at Wee Jimmy's cottage. The elderly man, still in his pyjamas, opened the door. Charlie handed over a small piece of paper and waited while Wee Jimmy retrieved his glasses to read it.

"What's this all about, Charlie?"

"I can't blab, and neither can you," Charlie said. "Do you understand my drift? Do you need a ride?"

"No. I'll be there and bring Maggie with me."

"Maggie isn't invited," Charlie said. "Not to this one, anyway. And not a word to her, Jimmy."

"You must have your reasons," Wee Jimmy said. "I'll keep your secret."

"You'd better," Charlie said, "or I'll have your hide on that wire fence."

As he drove to the store, Charlie justified his decision to leave Maggie Webster out of the loop by reasoning that blood is thicker than water; a mother's love can start a war as well as stop one.

Charlie banged on Georgie's door until she answered.

"Keep your pants on, Charlie. I don't open till eight and you want breakfast?"

"Yep," Charlie said. "I needed to get to you early."

"To do what?"

"To talk to you. I've got a lot on my mind today."

"What do you want to eat?" she asked

"Three eggs, same of sausage, same of bacon, four pieces of toast, strawberry jam, and coffee," Charlie said.

"Why didn't you just say 'the usual'?" Georgie disappeared into the kitchen. By the time she returned with a cup of coffee, Charlie was reading a section of folded newspaper. "Part of yesterday's rag," he said.

"It'll make more sense right way up," Georgie said. "At least that was how I was taught to read."

"Waul, I brung it with me because there's a letter about a woman who's lookin' fer her dad," he said. "I thought about you. I al'ays wondered about your dad."

"You wondered?"

"Fer yer sake." Charlie slipped the paper into his coveralls.

"Don't think on it another minute, Charlie."

"You don't want to know who your dad is?"

"I don't care," Georgie said. "Why should you?... Unless we're blood-related."

"Believe me, we're not," Charlie said. "Bring my food and then we'll chat."

Georgie sat facing Charlie while he ate. "So, spill the beans, Charlie."

"The way I understand it, your mom lived in Creemore, in a cottage that she inherited from her father."

"That's right," Georgie said. "Then she saw an ad that Thalia needed help. Creemore isn't far from Seven Springs and Mom was looking for a bit of adventure, so she applied."

"She got the job," Charlie said.

"Mom rented the cottage and moved into Granite. She drove back to Creemore on her days off because she had a couple of beaus there. Obviously, from what happened, I'd say that she got real sweet on one. When Mom found out that she was pregnant, she moved back into her little cottage."

"How'd you end up here?" Charlie asked, holding his cup out for more coffee.

"Mom rented the cottage again soon after I was born and moved down here to run the General Store. She wanted to raise me away from her home town because she said I'd have a rough time of it, being a bastard child, you know."

Meaning that Mary moved closer to Granite so she'd see J.D. occasionally, Charlie thought. She probably figured that he'd regret his errant ways and marry her. "I assume that Thalia gave her a financial boost," he said.

"No. Mom had the rent from the cottage to help here. When I married, she moved back to Creemore while hubby and I took over the store."

Charlie glanced at the clock above the counter. He had exactly twelve minutes before Georgie opened for business.

"I gotta ask the next question," he said. "You'll understand why in a few minutes."

"Fire away," Georgie said.

"Rotten Reggie's breezed through a couple of times recently. Has he ever stopped in to see you?"

"Are you kidding?" Georgie said. "He wouldn't be welcome. He did let that Russo fellow out once to hang around while Reggie went about his various devious diversions. He probably didn't want J.D. to know what he was up to. I know that the old fellow is Frank Russo's twin. That's why, when he looked at me, I felt really sorry for him — you know, the way Frank disappeared and all."

"Did J.D. talk much?" Charlie asked.

"Heavens, no. It was a Sunday. The store was closed. I found him sitting at the checker table outside. I had a smoke with him, made him a cup of coffee. The guy's so unlike his brother — I do remember Frank."

"Did he mention Frank?"

"When he did say something, it was about fishing, and the war, and Midland." Georgie began to clear the table. "Another day, another dollar," she said.

"Afore you get busy, read this," Charlie said, handing Georgie a small piece of paper.

Georgie read quickly. "You're kidding, Charlie. There?"

"Yep. There," Charlie said. "I can check you off my list?"

"I wouldn't miss this for the world."

"Absolute secrecy, Georgie. I don't want Dunnit to catch wind of it."

Georgie ripped the note into small pieces, put them in the ash tray, and lit them with her lighter. "Evidence burned. Details committed to memory, sir," she said.

And so it went for Charlie all morning. He had to return twice to Bud's farm before he found him at home.

"Bring Glenn with you, both times," Charlie said. "When you're at Granite, you're keeping watch for Rotten Reggie. Glenn can play with the pups. Just don't tell him what's up about the meeting. I need him to watch the Line."

"Understood," Bud said. "This is just like the good old days, Charlie."

"Waul, the summer's sure got a spark to it this year," Charlie said.

"Charlie, is everything okay between you and the Lovely Damsel? I mean, she just up and left, according to Dunnit."

"She'll be back later tonight," Charlie said. "And I'm gonna be at Thalia's to meet her."

Charlie left visiting Len and Jeff until last. Jeff, who was working on a motorcycle, saw Charlie and called out the garage door, "Hey, I want to talk to you. Don't go anywhere fast."

Charlie stepped into Len's area, then stood in the doorway between the garage and office. There was no door to close for privacy, so Charlie had to use his bulk to block Jeff's view.

"Morning, Len, read these." Charlie handed two small notes to his brother-in-law. "Don't say much. Nod if you understand."

Len read the notes, nodded, folded them, and tucked them in the hide-a-buck area of his wallet.

"You might want to tune in to the next conflab," Charlie said. He turned and strode into the garage.

Len rolled his chair into the doorway.

"Jeff, you wanted to see me?" Charlie kept the bike between himself and his nephew.

"That woman you're so hot on is stirring things up," Jeff said. "Tell her to keep her nose out of Valley business."

"Afore you go beatin' some more on Lish, I'm gonna ask you a question or two. Do you know that the house you're planning to build for your future wife will stand at the edge of one of the biggest gawd-dang gravel pits in the area?"

"I don't know what you're talking about."

"I didn't think so. And did you know that when Rotten Reggie is talking ski resort to some folks, he's using your name? But when he's talking gravel extraction to his buddies down country, he's using his own name?"

"Which means?"

"Which means that when a ski resort doesn't materialize, and a big honking gravel operation does, you know who the sucker investors will come looking for," Charlie said. "You. It's the old switch-the-name, bait-the-game trick. Your name will be muddied for years."

"People around here will know," Jeff said.

"I'm not talking about local folks," Charlie said. "You look a little pale under the gills, kid. Do you know what I think you should do?"

"The past week hasn't been the best that I've lived," Jeff said.

"Then take a holiday. Soon. Like, beginning tomorrow. Lodge a complaint with the police — both the Ontario Provincial and Collingwood Police — about the use of your name for fraudulent purposes. Dump that girlfriend without so much as a 'goodbye sweetie.' During that holiday, you find a job that keeps you away from Seven Springs for a while. Never contact the Rotter again. Keep in touch with your dad. Course, I'll expect a Christmas card."

"If I don't take your advice?"

"You're in deep manure, Jeff. Dig yourself out afore it's too late. I'm leavin' now. I hope I don't see you around for a while. Len, by the way, someone left this for you at the farm." Charlie handed Len a thick brown envelope.

Len nodded. "Thanks, pal. See you at the church meeting."

"I'm around if you need anything," Charlie said, putting his hand on Len's shoulder.

Late Afternoon — Toronto

Lish took one last look at the cosy apartment that she'd called home for so many years. She'd miss Dino Dimato even more than she would his second-floor flat.

"Are you sure that you want to do this?" Dino asked. "You met the guy less than two months ago."

"I'm sure, Dino. Even if I hadn't met Charlie, I'd have given up the apartment. The last few weeks have made a big difference in the way I think about things. You're the one who preaches about sitting in the forest for a day and coming out a changed person."

"You've lived here since you came to the city," Dino said. "You're like family, Lish. Maybe if I met the guy you're going to marry I'd feel better about it. I'm a pretty good judge of character."

Lish smiled. "He's a good fellow, Dino. The type you'd share a few glasses of vino with. The two of you have a lot in common, including age."

"I'll have to take your word on that," Dino said. "So, you want these few boxes put in your car?"

"Yes," she said.

"And the large boxes need to be stored in a dry place until you can arrange to have them picked up."

"They are full of clothing and some bedding," Lish said.

"The rest you sold to me: the furniture, the drapes, rugs, kitchenware — everything."

"I've gone through the apartment. There's nothing left that has any meaning for me — no family connection. I can let go of everything without too much pain."

"It's good quality stuff," Dino said. "You bought the best."

"You'll be able to rent a furnished apartment faster than an empty one, Dino. You're so close to the university that someone will snatch it up within the month."

"No students," Dino said. "They're nothing but trouble. It's too bad that English gentleman didn't leave an address. He said that he might be back. I liked him. If this Charlie fellow that you've fallen head over heels in love with is anything like him ..."

Lish laughed. "You just never know, Dino. He might be."

"Did I pay you enough? I feel that I got the best of the deal," Dino said.

"More than enough," Lish said.

She was behind Dino on the stairs when he said, "You know that big shot in the black caddy? He's dropped in at least twice — just to talk to you, he said. The last time was about a week ago. That guy gives me the creeps. I told him that I had no idea where you were."

Reginald Russo / O'Hearn / and sometimes Grant suspects something, Lish thought. "Remember, you still don't have any idea where I am," she said. "I'm not leaving a telephone number or address. You have my permission to scare the hell out of him if he appears again. I know you can do that very well."

"I've got some mail for you," Dino said. "There was another

pile, but I can't find it. It must have slipped off the desk into the waste basket. Sorry about that."

"These things do happen," Lish said, glad that she was behind him. The situation was so absurd that she couldn't keep a straight face.

"You know my kitchen like the back of your hand," Dino said. "We've spent enough late nights in there sorting out the world. You make the coffee — strong — while I put the boxes in your car. I'll use the fire escape. It's faster than the stairs."

"That's a deal," Lish said. "Are you doing anything special next Saturday night?"

"No. Why do you ask?"

"No particular reason."

Late Friday Evening

There was no one more relieved than Charlie Barnes when Lish's car pulled into Thalia's lane. He hurried to meet her and took her in his arms as soon as she stepped from the vehicle.

"I missed you, Cagey Farmer."

"And I missed you, Lish MacPherson," Charlie said, showing exactly how much by smothering her face with kisses. When he finally noticed that the back seat of Lish's car was full of boxes, he said, "You plannin' on goin' somewhere, Luscious Licinius?"

"I'm coming, not going," Lish said. "Your place would be better than Thalia's for these boxes. They contain a few things from my apartment that I just couldn't part with."

"I'll leave my truck and drive your car home tonight," Charlie said. "The boxes will be safe in one of the bedrooms until ... well, you know ...."

"Charlie? Charlie? Lish?" Thalia called from the back porch.

"Come on, Lish girl. Thalia, Joan, and Mary have baked, cleaned, fussed, worried. All evening they asked, 'Are you sure she's coming, Charlie? Are you sure?'"

"And were you one hundred percent sure, Charlie?"

"Two hundred percent," Charlie said. "How about you?"

"I've come home, Charlie. I'm here to stay. Through thick and thin, hell and high water, you've got me."

CHAPTER 9
The Week of August 5–August 11

August 5 — Sunday Afternoon

Luna and the pups were sprawled on the blanket on the back porch. Charlie, Joan, Noah, and Mary were off on a countryside jaunt, which left Lish and Thalia alone to talk. They were closeted in the parlour, Lish with her notebook on her lap.

"Let's talk about Maggie first," Lish said.

"After Frank found me in Toronto, we decided to remain in touch. He spent a lot of time working on construction upcountry, so I didn't see much of him. When he came to the city we sparked."

"You courted, after a fashion," Lish said.

"We had a pleasant, unconventional arrangement," Thalia said, "until he told me about Maggie and her little predicament. He asked me to marry him so that the baby would have a proper home. You have to understand that I liked Frank, enough to marry him, but I said no."

"You were thinking of The Mark," Lish said.

"That's right. I didn't mind raising a child, but I didn't want it to have any supposed claim on this land later in life."

"You agreed to return to Granite looking like husband and wife with babe in arms — only the babe was at least six months old."

"It was time for me to return to Granite and The Mark. I was an only child. I had obligations here that couldn't be ignored."

"Wouldn't one of those obligations involve having a child — or two — to pass the responsibility of The Mark along to?" Lish asked.

"A child of my own flesh and blood," Thalia said. "An heir who could claim the land by a blood connection to Hunter Logan or Hoshaphat. Unfortunately, as it happened, Frank had a condition that meant he couldn't father children. That's why I knew that Frank was not the father of the baby."

"What did your parents say about the arrangement?"

"Dad was dead. I didn't have to deal with his wrath. Mother was a different story. She didn't mind having the babe around, didn't ask questions, just acted the perfect grandmother."

"For all intents and purposes, you looked like a happy family."

"At the beginning, Reginald was a joy to have around — a robust, happy child. We fell into the family routine. I even began to rethink my position about blood lines."

"But Maggie entered the picture," Lish said.

"Many plots in my novels reflect Maggie's life. She left Midland, found a job in Walkerton, straightened up, married a nice fellow from Paisley — Mr. Deacon. Frank and I were so happy for her."

"What happened?"

"Maggie had a baby girl early in 1918. She lost both husband and the child to that terrible influenza outbreak early in 1919. Peter Webster befriended her and asked if she'd housekeep for him. He was forty years her senior. Eventually she married the man, against the wishes of his children."

"That's a recipe for a family feud," Lish said.

"For a short period of time, Maggie found security and happiness again. When Peter died, his family kicked up such a fuss that she packed and left. She knew they'd fight tooth and nail for everything the fellow had. Maggie came here, penniless and desperate. Is that Luna barking?"

"I'll be right back," Lish said.

The object of Luna's attention was Bud, who'd backed his vehicle into Thalia's lane. Lish glanced at her watch. He was right on time. She waved, and propped the porch door open so that Glenn would be able to get to the pups. It would be interesting to see who would wear whom out soonest.

"Is there a problem?" Thalia asked.

"Bud brought Glenn over to run with the pups," Lish said. "They won't disturb us. Bud won't let them come into the house — or Glenn near the bell. We were talking about Maggie."

"Of course, we took Maggie in, although there were times when I did regret the decision. She had quite the temper, you know," Thalia said.

"Did you not foresee problems?"

"We felt at the time that Maggie had been through so much in her life, she needed a home and people who would take care of her. After all, we did have her child. But Frank and I made Maggie promise that while she lived here she would never tell Reginald that she was his mother."

"You were generous and trusting," Lish said.

"Maggie was destitute and ill. For a few years Granite ran like a well-oiled machine. Frank worked hard to put money in the bank. Maggie and I raised Reginald."

"Who did Reginald think that Maggie was?"

"He called her Aunt Maggie and knew that she was definitely not a servant," Thalia said. "She was never treated like hired help — more like a sister. Sometimes she did accuse us — me — of being a little patronizing. She could be so dramatic!"

Glenn whizzed past the window, calling to the pups.

Thalia smiled. "At the beginning we had such good times. We laughed a lot, cried and worried together. Even J.D. behaved himself. Those were the happy days."

"What changed?"

"I don't know. One day — oh, I remember it so clearly — Maggie was at the sink. I was seated at the table. Reginald, who would have been sixteen years old, barged into the kitchen and demanded to know if he was adopted."

"There was no forewarning about this?" Lish asked.

"He'd been broody for a few days," Thalia said. "I answered truthfully. I said that he was our chosen child. What the boy did next was totally unpredictable. He screamed, picked a platter off the table, and threw it against the wall, narrowly missing Maggie. He reached for another dish and shouted 'my mother's an easy sleep-around, a real floosy.'"

"What was Maggie's reaction?"

"She turned from the sink with a cooking pot in her hand. She swung it and struck Reginald on the side of the head. She said, 'Don't you dare say that about me.' Reginald was shouting so that I very much doubt he heard her."

"What did he do next?"

"He left the room. As quick as he stormed in, he stormed out. He wouldn't let Frank near him to see if he was hurt."

"When might Reginald have found out that he was not your blood child?"

"I honestly don't know. I thought that possibly he'd found my personal diaries. I trusted that he would respect privacy. I possibly shouldn't have. Maggie had become so unmanageable that she could have told him."

"What did Frank do?"

"Frank was furious with the boy. He never laid a hand on Reginald, but he made it known that his irrational behaviour would not be tolerated again."

"When did Reginald start to hang around Len Grant?"

"He got in with a couple of bad boys from school. Whenever they could, they were at Len's place, where there was an ongoing poker game. After Reginald failed his grade, he quit school, pumped gas, tinkered around the cars."

"Do you think that possibly Len enlightened Reginald about his mother?"

"No. Len was Frank's best buddy and he would also protect Maggie. He had more feelings for her than J.D. He was just an easygoing fellow who didn't ask much of Reginald, but a bit of tinkering. Len probably thought that he was doing us a favour by keeping Reginald busy."

"What about J.D.?"

"He might have, but I doubt it. I know that he didn't say anything to Reginald when the boy lived here."

"Did Reginald say anything about leaving home for good?"

"No. He was here for supper and gone the next morning. You know the rest of the sordid tale, Lish. I hate to say it, but when Reginald left, it was a great weight off our shoulders. Maggie left shortly afterward. We gave her money to buy her little isolated cottage in Seven Springs. It wouldn't surprise me if Len and J.D. didn't give her money, too."

"I have to talk to you about J.D," Lish said.

"What a man. He never learned by his first — or second — mistake. He's as eccentric as I am," Thalia said.

"I agree. There is one difference though, Thalia. He's dirt poor and has to rely on others for everything. He hasn't accepted money from Reginald. He doesn't trust the man. He can't sell the farm because it's still in Frank's name and he hasn't got money to pay a good lawyer. Someone needs to help him." Lish said.

"And that someone is going to be you?"

"If I can, I will."

"There is a file. It's with my personal papers. I'll get it, *if* you promise not to follow me."

"I won't leave this chair," Lish said.

Glenn rushed past the windows, howling like a wolf, the pups skittering across the wooden porch floor after him.

"That young man needs to be hitched to a windmill," Thalia said, rising from her chair with great difficulty. "He'd pump some water!"

Lish listened. Thalia's climbed the stairs and entered my room.... She's walking across the room toward the south window.... Silence.... Thalia's retracing her steps.... Now she's going into Joan's room.... Now down the hall to the back bedroom.... Silence.... She's coming down the stairs again. Clever lady!

"I'm giving you this file because I trust you and want to help J.D. too," Thalia said, entering the parlour. "I agree. He's had a horrible life. It's time that this was cleared up."

There were only two items in the file: the deed to the Elmvale farm, and a handwritten note dated 1936, well before Frank's dementia began to take hold:

> In the event of my death, or the deterioration
> of my mind, title of the land as described in
> the deed shall pass to Thalia Logan, who will
> oversee its sale, invest the income, and provide
> a modest monthly income for my brother, James
> Douglas Russo.

"Thalia, this should have been taken care of years ago. I'll see a lawyer tomorrow," Lish said. "I know a good one in Toronto. Did Frank have a premonition about his dementia?"

"His mother's mind went the same way; his grandfather's,

too. From what Frank could understand of their history, their disabilities began around the same age that Frank noticed he was forgetting too much. You're going back to the city?"

"Only with Charlie in tow, if he'll come along for the ride," Lish said. "There is one more thing that I have to ask you about." Lish handed Thalia the two photographs that she had removed from the album.

Thalia held them near the lamp to see them better. "This is your father, isn't it?"

"It is," Lish said. "When I was putting your album away I found the photographs. You must have known him."

"I didn't, Lish. I was away the day that he visited — a meeting with my lawyer. It was in late September, if I recall."

"There's no name written on the pictures," Lish said.

"When I returned, Frank said that he'd met a man who said that he was connected by marriage to the Curlew family. Apparently, your dad drove in the lane and asked if he was at Hunter's Mark. When Frank said yes, the fellow asked if he could look around."

"This would be a year before Dad died. If he visited during the week, I'd be in school."

"Frank got his camera and off they went to the cabin and Knob — Frank never went anywhere without his camera. You can see that one photo is of your father standing in front of the cabin. The other appears to be him standing near the Knob."

"Frank never asked his name?"

"When I asked what the fellow's name was, Frank couldn't remember. He said that the fellow promised to return with his little girl."

"I assume by the time Dad got around to making his memory jar, Frank was beginning to experience memory loss — and then Dad got quite ill and gave up driving."

"Lish, just think: if your father had stayed here until I returned, and told his story, you might have ended up here on The Mark. I would have taken you in a minute if I knew that you were related to Jimmy Curlew."

"The way that life evolves, I guess that we weren't supposed to find each other until this summer," Lish said.

"But we eventually did find each other at the most appropriate and important time in our lives," Thalia said. "Charlie would agree with me wholeheartedly on that statement."

Sunday Evening

Charlie and Lish snuggled on the bench at base of the bell tower, wrapped in a blanket to ward off the dampness as the dew fell. Overhead, a velvet moon rose in a sky of endless twinkling stars and coruscating Milky Way. In mirror image, fireflies danced in low-lying areas throughout the valley. Spirit Rock glowed in the moonlight as though highlighted by a spotlight. The only man-made interference came from a single yard-light at Charlie's farm.

"On a night like this, you understand why the valley and these hills are so special." Charlie spoke in a hushed tone.

"It's magical, Charlie," Lish whispered.

"Sanity Hill and my Thinking Stones are seven miles away as the crow flies," Charlie said. "Someday we'll link the two and claim paradise."

"If it were only that easy, Charlie."

Charlie's keen eye picked up movement near Spirit Rock. "Hush now. Watch the stone," he whispered into Lish's ear. "Look sharp. Coming from the right, slinking along the rail fence. Do you see it?"

A dark shadow, the size of a very large dog, slunk to the darker side of the rock. It stopped, looked around, and then moved silently to the moonlit side of the rock.

Lish clutched Charlie's hand and squeezed it. Charlie wrapped his arm tighter around her waist.

The animal's size and colour were easily seen now. The cougar sniffed the base of the rock, then rubbed its jowls against Blue Heathen, a number of times, marking its territory. Several times the cougar looked up the hill toward Granite before it stretched, then slunk into the bushes to the left of the rock — once again a shadow in the night.

"It's magnificent," Lish said. "Our own cougar on The Mark."

"It's probably heading for Vale of CAT," Charlie said. "I found its tracks in there the day that I was looking for you. If I'm not mistaken, there could be more then one."

"Has Thalia seen it?"

"Noah and she sat out here on Thursday night. They both saw it."

"This is so significant for the Valley," Lish said.

"Some people won't think so if it — or they — don't stick to the wilder areas of the escarpment," Charlie said. "I can see the headlines now: 'Lock up your children. There's a four-legged carnivore in our midst.'"

"Then, we mustn't tell anyone," Lish said. "If word gets out that we've got a cougar, the Valley will be overrun by people looking for it."

"Hugh Dunnit already made mention," Charlie said. "We'll let the scenario play out. There are plenty of small animals around The Mark. Adam and Eve should be safe — for a while. But it is significant that the animal is brazen enough to come so close to a dwelling."

"We'll have to think up a far different strategy if the cougar is seen frequently in the area," Lish said.

"You bet. We don't want Ministry officials tramping around here, sticking their noses in every crevice and cave in The Mark. Let's hope that CAT is clever enough to set its boundaries ... tight. If it doesn't, the cat just might be master of its own demise."

"You could put up some 'No Hunting' and 'No Trespassing' signs around The Mark's boundaries — and your farm, too," Lish said.

"My neighbours won't think that's a friendly gesture," Charlie said.

"Speaking of neighbourly gestures," Lish said, "Ettie Mackie would love to have us as houseguests on Tuesday evening — and before you salivate all over your clean shirt, it's separate bedrooms."

"Darn," Charlie said. "And I was thinking about gettin' up to a little hanky-panky."

"There'll be enough of that on Wednesday," Lish said. "Charlie, tell me when you found out that I worked for Smith & Jones?"

"Waul, you told Noah and Thalia, but they didn't pick up on the significance of the name. I really pinned it the day that I talked to Dino Dimato," Charlie said. "He let the cat out of the bag. After I left him, I visited an old chum of mine from the days of the SAS. He just happened to work for Smith & Jones too. You might know him: Jake Wilson?"

"You are a never-ending source of surprises," Lish said. "I do know the man."

"Jake says that you were one of the best investigative people the company had. He said that you were observant, astute, thorough, possessed integrity. You apparently always caught your man — or woman."

"Did Jake ask why you wanted the information?"

"Yep. I told him that you were the woman I was going to marry. And you are."

Lish laughed. "You're called Cagey Farmer for good reason. Can I invite Dino to your party on Saturday evening, Charlie? You won't mind having your cover blown?"

"I'd like to pay Jake another visit tomorrow," Charlie said. "I don't think that we should leave Granite unattended during our little shindig on Saturday evening. Jake would be a good man to have around while we're cuttin' a rug. Luna can back him up."

"That sounds like a very good plan, Charlie. I'm worried about leaving Granite with no one to protect it, after what we have planned for Wednesday."

"There's still a skunk in the works at this end," Charlie said. "We'll set a live trap for the beggar. With all this covert activity going on, I'm not getting much farm work done. I'll view this jaunt as my vacation. Thank goodness for Joe and Harry."

"The Delaney boys are satisfied with the arrangement? Do they need help getting the house cleaned up?" Lish asked.

"You're talking about Friday evening, now?"

"The meeting," Lish said.

"That'll be an affair, for sure," Charlie said. "I can hardly wait for folks to come face-to-face with the Delaney residence."

"It was a brilliant decision on your part to choose that location."

"If I do say so myself." Charlie hugged Lish to him. "Life is only dull when you don't see the humour in it," he said. "If we're going to get an early start tomorrow, I'd better get you tucked in for the night."

"That's wishful thinking on your part, Charlie Barnes. Save your strength for our wedding night. You'll need it."

"I'm eating my wheaties," he said. "Do you want to hear what I dreamed last night? I was riding this big antlered buck around the Valley, and was handing out baby nappies and bottles to anyone who happened to get in my way. Doesn't that just take the cake?"

Wednesday, August 8 — Midland

J.D.'s small room was electric with anticipation. Conversation was kept to a minimum so that any movement outside the door could be detected. Charlie and Lish had one false alarm as someone shuffled down the hall to the common washroom. Sitting on J.D.'s bed, Lish had a good view of the parking lot without being seen at the window. From what she had found out during the trip to Huntsville, J.D. expected Reginald to arrive around the noon hour to take him out for lunch. The room's door was locked. For double security, and to ensure that they wouldn't be surprised, Charlie had installed a hook and eye.

As J.D. mentioned, a slender address book was tucked in a drawer below the phone. It held a bonanza of telephone numbers that Charlie immediately put to good use.

"I haven't had such fun in years," Charlie said as he made the first phone call — long distance to Connecticut. The conversation took place with Charlie in full-blown British accent.

"Yes, could I speak with Mr. O'Hearn. Mr. Reginald O'Hearn. Yes, thank you."

Charlie put his hand over the receiver. "The company is called O'Hearn Property Management," he told her. "I've been passed along to Mr. O'Hearn's secretary."

"Yes, ma'am. Could I speak with Mr. O'Hearn?... I see ... I've missed him.... Can you tell me when he's expected back in the office?... At the end of the month.... I'd prefer not to.... It is a personal matter.... Could I reach him at home, speak with his wife?... My mistake, I do recall now that he mentioned he isn't married.... Leave a message?... No. I'll try again at month's end.... August 29.... Yes, thank you."

Charlie sat at the table, hands behind his head. "Well, we know that he owns a well-established business in Hartford, Connecticut, that he maintains a residence in the state, and that he isn't married. He also plans to hang around Ontario for the next little while."

"Not if we can help it," Lish said.

Charlie used a broad southern accent when he called Campbell, O'Hearn & Yule.

"Could I speak with Mr. O'Hearn please?... I see.... He's not expected in the office. Can I reach him in Connecticut?... Yes, I'll do that.... I have your number also listed for a Mr. Russo.... Can I talk with him?... I should call Northlands Development.... Is it possible to speak with Mr. Grant?... Russell Grant?... Contact Northlands.... You've no one that works at Campbell, O'Hearn & Yule by that name.... I'm only in Canada for a short period of time, you see, doing some investigative work.... You'd be pleased to take messages and make sure that Mr. O'Hearn and Mr. Russo receive them? That's kind of you, but I'd prefer to talk with Mr. Russo or Mr. O'Hearn myself. If you could give me the number for Northlands.... Toronto or Collingwood Office? Both please."

When Charlie hung up, he said. "We've now established links between Northlands and COY, and between COY and O'Hearn Property Management. It's your turn at the phone."

Charlie traded places with Lish while she dialed the office of the Collingwood newspaper.

"Good morning. Could I speak with the editor?... Yes, sir, let me explain. I'm a widow who was left a bit of money by my husband. I invested it with a company that has an office in Collingwood, Northlands Development. I understood at the time that I was investing in a ski resort.... You're familiar with the company?... Yes, well I hear now this company has no intentions of opening a seasonal resort. Their main interest is in gravel — aggregates, I believe my friend said.... Where did I hear this information? From a gentleman who lives in Hartford, Connecticut, and who is involved with a company down there by the name of O'Hearn Property Management. I think that you should investigate. There must be more poor widows who have been duped into investing in this bogus plan.... Yes, there is a big difference between a ski resort and a gravel pit.... You will look into the allegation. Thank you, sir.... My name? I'd prefer not to give it.... Thank you, I appreciate that."

"Well done, Lish," Charlie said.

"And back to you, Charlie. Just don't let Farmglish creep into this one." Charlie's last telephone call gave him the most satisfaction. He called Northlands' Collingwood office.

"Susan? I've an urgent message from Reginald Russo.... Yes, I know that he left your office three-quarters of an hour ago. Reginald said that you must put everything away, clear your desk, and leave immediately.... Why? It's obvious that questions are being asked.... You don't know what I'm talking about?... Yes, just do as I say. Put the files away and lock the cabinets. Clear all personal items from your desk. Leave. Lock the door behind you. What should you do with the key?... Put it through the mail slot.... Paid? Of course, you'll be paid.... Reginald will be in touch.... He does have your home phone number.... Good.... Who am I? Did I not say where I was calling from? Campbell, O'Hearn & Yule.... Yes, that's right.... Good bye."

"Charlie, you're missing your calling by mucking cows," Lish said.

"I don't know," Charlie said. "I'm getting a bit old for espionage. Anything yet?"

"No action in the lot," Lish said.

"Are you ready for your part in this little escapade?"

"I sure am," Lish said.

"I don't know how long I can stand behind the door," Charlie said. "I'll make sure that Reggie's stepped well into the room before I close it. Keep the table between you and him. I'll stay behind him. I won't let him get near you, Lish."

"If Reginald left Collingwood when Susan said that he did, it won't be long now before he shows up," Lish said. "I just hope that he's astute enough not to pick a fight. Heads up! A Cadillac has just pulled into the lot."

Charlie slipped across the room to take a look. "It's Rotten Reggie, by himself, all tarted up. Take your places. Lights! Cameras! Action!" Charlie unlatched the hook and stood so that, when the door opened, he'd be hidden from view behind it. He'd taken a mirror, which might have given his position away, off the wall opposite the door when they arrived.

The doorknob turned. There was a pause. A key was inserted in the lock, turned, and the door opened. "J.D., why lock the door? You knew I was coming." Reginald stepped into the room and squinted in the low light. "What the hell! Who are you? Where's J.D.?"

"Come a little closer, Mr. Grant ... or is it Mr. Russo?"

Reginald stepped closer to the table. "Well, well, if it isn't Miss MacPherson. I heard you were in the area, causing a few problems."

"No doubt you have, from Jeff Grant ... Jeffrey Russell Grant, a man whose name you banter about as though it was your own," Lish said. "We do need to talk — whoever you are today."

"I've no intention of talking to you," Reginald said. He turned to leave.

The door slammed shut. Charlie stood in front of it, blocking Reginald's exit. "You will talk to Miss MacPherson, or you'll talk to me," he said. "At the moment, I'd rather punch than chat. Sit down Reggie."

Reginald stood his ground. "Where's my father?"

"If you're thinking of J.D., he's enjoying a nice long holiday. If you're referring to Len Grant, I imagine that he's at the garage," Lish said.

"Are you going to sit down, or shall I wrestle you into that chair?" Charlie asked. "Like Miss MacPherson said, she wants to chat with you."

Reginald took a look at Charlie's clenched fists and decided to sit down. "I assume that this won't take too long. This little charade isn't going to get either of you anywhere but jail," he said. "I've friends in high places ..."

"I've a few good contacts in both high and low places," Lish said. "They would be very interested in what I'm going to say."

"Obviously you're acting on behalf of Thalia Russo," Reginald said. "You've fallen under the old hag's spell."

"Thalia Logan," Lish said. "She never married Frank Russo, so that avenue was closed to you some years ago as far as any claim to The Mark through J.D. is concerned."

"Oh, you have done your homework, Miss MacPherson."

"In spades," Lish said. "Charlie and I represent a number of people who intend to stop your plans to destroy the Valley and surrounding area."

Reginald laughed. "That's the most absurd comment I've heard recently. You can't stop Northlands Development. Give up now. Your weeping and pleading will get you nowhere."

Lish smiled. "I've no intention of weeping or pleading.

Charlie and I are going to present cold, hard facts."

"Evidence, I'd call it," Charlie said. "Information that could land you in jail for a few years, Reggie."

"Do tell," Reginald said. "What are you two playing at? Barnes Detective Agency?"

"Smith & Jones Investigative Services," Lish said. "Does that name mean anything to you? It should. Their U.S. headquarters are in New York City."

Reginald looked from Lish to Charlie. "I've heard the name," he said, drumming his fingers on the table. "What garbage have you two dredged up?"

"Let's begin with a number of land transactions completed by Campbell, O'Hearn & Yule," Lish said. "At least a half dozen are now documented with signed statements from the relatives of senile elderly people, that the property was vastly undervalued and signatures were gotten under duress."

"That has nothing to do with me."

"It certainly does, Mr. O'Hearn, President of O'Hearn Property Management of Hartford, Connecticut," Charlie said. "You're the silent partner in COY."

"I spend most of my time in the States — in Connecticut. I am not made party to all that takes place in Toronto between Campbell and Yule," he replied.

"I would suggest that you are very much involved and informed," Charlie said. "I'd say that you are the brains behind the brawn."

"Perhaps we should discuss Connecticut and the name O'Hearn," Lish said. "I'm sure that U.S. Immigration authorities would be interested to know that you weren't born in Midland, Michigan — or North Carolina, or Texas, Maryland, or Ohio," Lish said. "I have Ettie Mackie's file. Unfortunately, when the lady wrote her note in 1946, she simply wrote 'Midland,' making it easy for you to doctor the document so that you could establish the U.S. as your place of birth. She's quite willing to swear an affidavit that Midland, Ontario, Canada is where you were born."

"How long have you claimed that you are a U.S. citizen? By my tally, at least eighteen years," Charlie said. "I wager that you gave officials a cock-an'-bull story about your father being killed during the First World War and your mother dead by 1946."

"On the contrary, my mother is alive."

"But Maggie Webster would lie for you, wouldn't she?" Charlie said. "She'll do anything you ask."

"Maggie promised Thalia and Frank that she wouldn't divulge the truth, but she did," Lish said. "She held her tongue for a while, but eventually everything spilled out — in a most vindictive fashion. The more Maggie stirred the pot, the more hateful you became."

"I don't have to sit here and listen to this rhetoric." Reginald pushed his chair away from the table.

"Not so fast," Charlie said. His hands landed on Reginald's shoulders. "You haven't been excused, Reggie."

"Get your filthy hands off me."

"Put your hands on the table where I can see them," Charlie said. "There's one other thing that should be discussed — just a little point needs clearing up."

Reginald started to drum his fingers on the table again. "What is it?" he asked.

"There is the situation connected to this item." Lish flashed Frank's cigarette holder. "Frank Russo had it on him when he disappeared. You lost it in the barn foundation not long ago. Murder is a serious offence, Mr. Russo-Grant-O'Hearn."

Reginald stopped drumming and put his hand out for the holder.

Lish slid it into her pocket. "I think I'll keep this as evidence."

"You'd need a body to make that allegation stick," Reginald said.

"If we choose to look for a body, say in one of those back-country crevices, don't think that we couldn't find one with a little help from Luna," Charlie said.

"I don't see any documentation to back up your allegations."

"Information is in the hands of my lawyer," Lish said. "We're clever enough not to give you the opportunity to destroy evidence by laying it out on this table in front of you."

"What's the point of this meeting?" Reginald turned his head to look at Charlie. "What are you planning to do now?"

"That all depends on how far you go and how long you stay," Charlie said. "If you so much as show your face around Seven Springs again, the appropriate authorities will be notified, if they haven't already been alerted."

"You haven't contacted anyone. That's why I'm sitting here," Reginald said. "I think the most appropriate word to use about this situation is 'blackmail.'"

"A fair assessment. You're astute enough to know what has to be done," Charlie said. "Back off on your little campaign to destroy the Valley. You've no claim to The Mark. Leave Thalia Logan alone."

"Why should I leave her alone?" Reginald said. "What did she ever do for me that I should be grateful for?"

"She gave you a good home, befriended your mother, treated her as family, and still assists her. Thalia tried to raise you properly," Lish said.

"Some home. My mother was considered a servant. I was left out of everything. I wasn't good enough to be party to any

Logan business. I was expected to work the land, but not to inherit it."

"After your mother began to spew her venom, did you give Thalia and Frank any reason to trust you?" Lish asked. "If you'd given them half a chance, you'd be a better man for it today."

"Ah, the lady spews Thalia's brand of half-truths."

"I can't understand your logic, Reginald. You managed to invent a new life for yourself in the States. Why get involved here?" Lish asked.

"Hate combined with greed makes an unusual alliance that knows no boundaries," Reginald said. "Where there's money to be made by any means, there are people like me who'll do it."

"If your mother hates the Valley and Seven Springs so much, why didn't you relocate Maggie to Connecticut?" Lish asked.

"Her, leave the Valley? She's been waiting years to even things up with Thalia Logan. She can hardly wait to knock that looney dame off her perch."

"Enough chatter, Reggie. I expect to hear in the next week or so that Northlands Development is dead, that you're back in Connecticut, and that some changes have been made at Campbell, O'Hearn & Yule. If not ...." Charlie backed up and opened the door.

"Before I take my leave, I always give the lady the final word," Reginald said.

"If I were you, Reginald, I'd consider your options very carefully. You don't want to throw everything that you've accomplished away for one more moment of stupid revenge," Lish said.

"Revenge can be sweet, under certain circumstances," Reginald said as he backed out of the room.

Charlie and Lish watched from the window until Reginald drove away.

"Imagine Reginald's surprise when he finds the Collingwood office locked up," Lish said. "He knew that we had enough evidence to back up three serious charges against him."

"I expected more of an argument," Charlie said. "I'd like to say that our mission is accomplished, but I think that Rotten Reggie just might have a trick left up his sleeve."

"If you're right, Charlie, it's time we went home. He might show up there before we do."

"It's okay," Charlie said. "I know a shortcut or two. We can call Mary and have her keep a sharp lookout for the beggar. Luna's at Thalia's, too."

Mulmur Murmurings by Hugh Dunnit
For the Week of August 3–10

Just to remind folks that the Cagey Farmer is holding a good ol' fashioned evening of stompin' and chattin' tomorrow night. If you want to eat, bring food. If you play a musical instrument, bring it along too. Chest pianos are permitted. Leave the booze at home. Don't forget your dancing shoes. Practise your do-si-do's.

Is Lavender Line turning into Lover's Lane for old bachelors? Tom D was seen walking the Line hand in hand with Mary T, proving that sparkin' isn't only for the young-at-heart.

Bob and Judy V had company this week when their six grandchildren descended for a summer holiday. Whether the old folks enjoyed the visit depends on which adult you speak with. Is it my imagination or are rugrats a little harder to handle these days?

If you see Maggie W. driving her car, run the other way or jump for your life. Yesterday, she nearly ran over Len Grant, who was leaving Gorgeous G's store. She says that she had a weak spell. He says that she aimed the car's hood ornament right for him. Maybe someone should hide her car keys?

By eyeballing this week's Murmurings, can't you tell that not much happened around the Valley and Springs during the past seven days?

Friday, August 10 — The Evening

People began to arrive at the Delaneys' early. Tom and Harry directed as many cars as possible to park close to the house and barn. The last to arrive had to park on the side of Lavender Line. Glenn was instructed to watch the Line and told to run to get his father, or Charlie, if anyone tried to drive up Thalia's lane.

Charlie met everyone at the front steps and directed them to go around to the kitchen door. From the appearance of the porch, with its rotten boards and sagging roof, it was a wise decision. Lish and Mary were ready inside with plates of cookies and a continuous supply of hot coffee.

The boys had scrubbed the kitchen floor, but had done nothing about the paper peeling off the walls or the large cobweb sculpture behind the woodstove. Dick and Joe gathered chairs from around the house and set them at the table. A note tacked on the hall door indicated where the bathroom could be found — outside, near the woodshed.

Charlie came into the room on the heels of Wee Jimmy. "We've got twenty-seven people here," he said to Lish. "I'll swear that half of them came just to see the Delaneys' house, but that's why I chose the place. Are we ready to begin?"

"I think so," Lish said.

Charlie rapped his knuckles on the table and waited for the chatter to die down before he spoke. "I'm glad that you could all come tonight, and I thank Tom, Dick, Harry, and Joe for the use of their house."

There was polite applause.

Charlie scanned the room. "Before we begin, I just want to say that if any information about what transpires at this meeting appears in Mulmur Murmurings, I'll know who-done-it, for sure. So watch what you write, Hugh Dunnit."

Everyone glanced at the person beside them, watching for an acknowledgement, or nod, but Dunnit didn't give himself — or herself, away.

"You all know why you were invited to this little gathering, so I won't keep you long," Charlie said. "We ... No. I should say that Lish — Miss MacPherson, the Lovely Damsel — found out this week that Northlands Development has nothing to do with a ski resort but a lot to do with a gawd-damn aggregate operation — excuse my language, ladies."

A murmur went through the group.

"That would change the face of the Valley and Hills if it was allowed to happen," Len said.

"Look what happened down-country. The escarpment was chewed up real bad," someone at the back of the room said. "Gravel pits would ruin this area for everyone."

Dick, who was lounging against a cupboard, came to stand beside Charlie. "You're talking the truth. How do we stop it, Charlie?"

"We've got to pass the word to those folks who weren't invited to ensure that we're all fighting the same battle," Charlie said.

"I'm sure that most of those who are ambivalent about Thalia's efforts to save The Mark would not support a gravel operation."

"I don't know, Charlie. There'll be a few see the benefits of selling their land," Wee Jimmy said. "There's them at the top of the heap in the township that would think it's the best thing to happen here since sliced bread arrived at the General Store."

"No doubt," Charlie said. "We'll have to work around that one by talking about all the trucks that will use the roads, and the waste of good farmland. It'll be a struggle. But, if we stick together, we're up to the challenge. The battle might be half-won."

"We'll have to keep on top of this situation," one of Charlie's neighbours said. "We need to schedule a regular meeting to discuss strategy."

"A great idea," Charlie said. "Why not hold it bi-monthly, say at the store, after hours. Would that be all right with you, Georgie?"

Georgie put her hand up. "It's okay by me. You know that stopping a pit operation might solve Thalia's immediate problem, but it doesn't help people like myself who are trying to make a living in Seven Springs. Have you any suggestions about what we can do to get more business after ... tomorrow?"

"What's so different about tomorrow?" someone asked. "It's always twiddle-thumb days around here. I want to live here but there's no job for me. I've got to drive twenty miles to work every day."

"I have no solution for that situation," Charlie said. "I understand what you're saying, but if you don't farm, there's few jobs. Maybe you have to balance the quality of life in a small community with the inconvenience of driving to your job."

"There's need for someone to fix cars and farm machinery," Len said. "Jeff's gone, so I've got an empty garage that someone can use — and gas pumps to operate too. At least that would provide jobs for a couple of people, if they're willing to work."

"What we need is more people driving through," Georgie said. "Once they see how beautiful the area is they might come back for another visit, and bring friends with them."

"Have you thought of putting better signage at the highway?" Lish said. "There's only one small sign that is difficult to see. How about a large one —'Welcome to Beautiful Seven Springs'?"

"We're planning to fix up our sugar shack and go into maple syrup production again," Tom Delaney said. "We could sell the syrup at Georgie's store and at a roadside stand out at the highway. Why don't we all share a big farm stand out there with fresh vegetables, syrup, and honey? Georgie, you can display some stuff and have a handout about your store."

"I was thinking of cleaning out one of my storerooms and putting in some local items," Georgie said. "Len's going to give me some carvings. I've got several ladies who are willing to display their quilts. Isn't there someone who's making pottery that lives a couple of concessions over?"

"I figured that Christmas trees are something to get into," Bud said. "What do you think, folks?"

"That's a good one," Wee Jimmy said. "That'll keep you busy and put some money in your pocket in a few years."

"There is a need for overnight accommodation," Lish said. "Does anyone feel like opening a tourist home?"

"How about a summer hootenanny with real good country music," Joe said.

"Perhaps we could advertise our autumn bazaar a little further afield — make it into something really big," Reverend Harrison suggested. "We could attract people from Collingwood, Thornbury, Meaford, Midland, and Elmvale to see the autumn leaves."

"Advertising costs money," Georgie said.

"You can get free publicity if you know how to go about it," Lish said.

"What about a fund — say a cooperative effort." Charlie reached into his pocket for his wallet. "I'll contribute twenty dollars."

Lish reached for her handbag. "I'll give twenty dollars too, and help with writing the advertisements."

"We should meet and talk about what we're going to do to attract visitors," Georgie said. "Is everyone in agreement about that?"

A general discussion followed that produced more interesting ideas and a few solutions.

Charlie smiled at Lish. This is precisely what they hoped that those who were invited to the meeting would do: help themselves.

Charlie rapped the table with his knuckles again and waited until the room quieted down. "I think we're well on our way to doing something good for the Valley and Springs," he said. "But there is one thing that needs to be discussed. Look around you. When you're finished ogling, listen to me."

Everyone took a good look around the kitchen.

"There's people that could always use a little help," Charlie said. "I say that we should put work parties together after the harvest, when we have a bit of time on our hands. Wee Jimmy's cottage needs a new roof. The front porch and roof of this house need rebuilding."

"I could use help getting wood in for the winter," Jimmy said. "But I can't afford to pay anyone to do the job."

"We've forgotten what it's like to be neighbourly," Charlie said. "It's time that we got back to basics. Let's say that if folks can come up with the cost of the materials, we get down to work. We set up a work co-op. We get hours back for hours worked."

"Agreed," Reverend Harrison said. "There is one person in this community who has demonstrated over the years what neighbourliness is all about. Unfortunately, she isn't here this evening, but we all can learn from her example. I am referring of course to Thalia Logan Russo."

"Here! Here!" someone shouted.

"Thank you, ladies and gentlemen," Charlie said. "We'll see you at Georgie's store, say August 20, eight o'clock in the evening?"

Saturday, August 11 — The Evening

Charlie's party was a resounding success. On the front lawn, ladies in flowered dresses hovered near two tables that were laden with food. A third table held a washtub full of fruit punch with a dipper tied to a handle and a copper wash boiler full of hot coffee that bubbled on a campstove. As friends and neighbours chatted about crops, machinery, weather, and politics, word spread quickly about the ski resort that turned into an aggregate extraction operation.

The threshing floor had been swept and the large doors swung open so cool breezes could circulate through the top of the barn. A handwritten sign on one door spelled out in no uncertain terms what would happen to anyone who was caught smoking in the barn. A second sign warned that anyone imbibing liquor would be tossed off the property.

"You know that I don't mind a tipple of the uisage baugh," Charlie told Lish. "But when you get a crowd like this, you've got to be tough. There're too many young'uns who don't bide the rules. They're welcome, but an eye will be kept on them. That's Bud's specialty — tossing teens."

An impromptu group of musicians played for the crowd. Their numbers increased, or decreased, depending on who wanted to play, and who wanted to eat. Thalia sat in a comfortable chair that Charlie moved from the parlour for the occasion. Joan sat beside her like a lady-in-waiting, a bright smile on her face.

"Have you seen anything like it?" Charlie said, as he waltzed Lish around the floor. "They both lap up the attention."

"It took Thalia half the day to choose what to wear," she told him. "She decided that she wanted to have something Edwardian, which meant a trip to the attic. That place is a virtual museum, Charlie."

Tom Delaney nodded and smiled at Lish as he waltzed past with Mary.

"Where did he learn to dance properly?" Charlie said.

Lish laughed. "Mary and I have been working on his technique. He's a fast learner. Dick's the one with two left feet."

Dino Dimato arrived at the farm early, buoyed by an invitation to spend the night as a guest of Thalia's. As Charlie and Lish waltzed past Thalia for a third time, he was crouched by Thalia's chair, having an animated discussion with both women.

"Dino is quite the fellow," Charlie said. "Fortunately, he saw my ruse as a joke, after you explained the situation to him. What did you say that he does for a living?"

"He teaches mathematics, but his hobbies are hiking and saving trees. He's associated with a group of people who are dedicated to establishing a trail along the escarpment from Niagara to Tobermory, which means that it could pass right through The Mark if he can persuade Thalia, as the landowner, to agree. Completing that trail is a passion with him."

"A genuine tree hugger," Charlie said. "He's a good fellow to have around."

"He's a fifty-five-year-old man who cares about his sur-roundings," Lish said. "I bet that he and Thalia are discussing preserving The Mark."

When the musicians took a break, Charlie and Lish headed for the punch table. They passed Bud on the way.

"How's it going," Charlie asked him.

"It's real quiet. I checked everyone who arrived. Most seem to have gotten the message. A couple of mickeys were handed over. What do you want me to do with them. Pour them in the punch?"

"Give 'em back to the owners when they leave," Charlie said.

"Where's Glenn?" Lish looked around the yard.

"When Charlie brought the pups home, to free Luna — well, you know why — Glenn tucked himself in with them. He's in the kitchen cuddling the collie-looking one. I've never seen him so quiet. I told him not to let any of the kids past him, but he should let the mothers in to check their charges every once in a while."

"Have you had an opportunity to dance?" Lish asked.

Bud smiled. "Don't worry about me. Widow Jamieson's guarding the food. We've got a thing goin'"

"William Henderson! You're courting," Lish said.

"It must be som'pin that's been sneaked into the water that's making all the bachelors around here randy," Charlie said. "If you'll excuse me, Lish, I've got a couple of things need to be done."

Lish found Georgie and Hank sitting at a table in the orchard. "Do you think that we accomplished anything this morning?" she asked. "Noah did an excellent interview. He said all the right things. Bernard and Gloria were suitably impressed. You did a great job of decorating the restaurant with Noah's pictures."

"Time will tell," Georgie said. "Noah says to keep the pictures up. He'll bring some memorabilia the next time he visits Thalia. I'm going to serve a Curlew burger and play his music when there are visitors around. Hank got me a record player for the store."

"I told Georgie that I know people who'd drive miles out of their way to visit a place that Jason Curlew raved about," Hank said.

"I'm going to sell Noah's records. And I decided to tuck a book rack in a corner, too," Georgie said. "I figure that I'll lend books out, along with selling a few. That'll bring people in. They might exchange a book and buy something else."

"That's a great idea," Lish said. "Have you seen Noah — or should we be calling him Jason now?"

"He said that he'd be here," Georgie said.

"Girls, he's already here," Hank said. "He sneaked in the back way. He's in the house, making a few telephone calls. He has to head back to the city tomorrow. Apparently he's on the road again next weekend."

Charlie found Lish near the front gate talking to several neighbours who were leaving.

"It was nice of you to come," he said.

"We're leaving because we promised to have the sitter home by midnight," the woman explained.

"You should have brought the little one with you," Charlie said. "Last count there were fourteen of 'em sleeping on blankets on the parlour floor."

While walking back to the barn hand in hand with Charlie, Lish said, "Did you notice that most of the lights are on at Granite?"

"I did," Charlie said. "Don't worry, Lish. Jake can handle any situation. Luna won't let him down. Joe's doing some scouting over that way, too. We know that Rotten Reggie headed south late on Wednesday evening. We just have to worry about one other person, 'cause she's not here tonight."

"Neither is Jeff," Lish pointed out.

"Okay, that's two unaccounted for that are connected to the Rotter."

A familiar baritone voice wafted out the barn doors.

"It's Noah," Lish said. "He's in the barn, ready to sing."

Excitement spread through the crowd as word circulated about who was going to perform. People began to gravitate to the barn, drawn by Noah's chatter.

"Good evening. I am thrilled to be invited to sing on this very special night. It's Jason Curlew, if you don't know who's speaking." Noah stood with the local musicians, a guitar in his hand. "I'm going to sing a few songs and then I've a special announcement to make." Noah launched into his first song.

As Charlie gathered Lish in his arms and danced around the floor, Thalia and Joan moved closer to the musicians. Some people danced. Most listened with rapt attention to Noah's / Jason Curlew's fine vocals.

Noah took a break after his third song. "Now, ladies and gentlemen, it's time for that special announcement. Where are Charlie Barnes and Lish MacPherson? Could you show yourselves?"

Charlie took Lish by her hand and threaded his way through friends and neighbours to the front, where Joan, flush with excitement, held Thalia's hand.

Noah smiled at the couple. "Charlie, I do believe that you have something to say to Miss MacPherson? Now Cagey Farmer, don't let us down. This is not the time to be at a loss for words."

"What's going on, Charlie?" Lish turned toward Charlie, who was red-faced and fumbling in a pant's pocket.

The people who pressed forward to see the show had never seen Charlie Barnes so flustered.

Charlie pulled a red plastic chicken's leg-band from his pocket, got down on one knee, took Lish's left hand in his, kissed it, and said, "Lovely Damsel, will you marry the Cagey Farmer and live with him happily ever after?"

Lish looked from Thalia, to Joan, to Noah, to Charlie, to the improvised ring. She laughed and said, "Of course I'll marry you, Charlie Barnes, as long as you promise that life will always be this unpredictable — and that the wedding will be soon. I do hate long engagements."

A cheer went up. The crowd clapped. Noah launched into the Hawaiian Wedding Song.

Wee Jimmy turned to Dick Delaney. "Ten dollars says the wedding will take place on Thanksgiving weekend."

"Nah," Dick said. "My money's on the Saturday before Christmas."

"I bet it'll be on the first Saturday in November," Harry said.

"That's way too soon," Len said. "I'm in for mid-February."

* * * * * *

The cougar, disturbed by the unusual sounds that drifted across meadow and river, didn't visit the stone as was his usual routine. Instead, he growled and slunk deeper into the Vale of CAT, heading for Grotto Spring. He stopped several times, sniffed the air, listened, then rubbed his jowls against the nearest tree. As he approached the spring, the cougar, mystified by the sound that still followed him deep into the forest, turned to look back toward the river. Frustrated, he yowled loudly a number of times.

The cougar's protestations startled a large buck that was picking its way down the old Indian trail. The buck leapt away, swam the river, then stood in the wildflower meadow looking back toward the forest and bluff.

The big cat stood for a moment near the spring, trying to catch the scent of prey, or enemy. Satisfied that he was alone, the cougar approached the Grotto cautiously, then bent to drink. As the cat lapped, the moonlight shone on the water and penetrated its depths. One beam struck a small, odd-shaped object wedged between two rocks. The object shimmered in the lambent light and mirrored refulgence into the cougar's eyes. The cat, mesmerized by the display, stared for several minutes into the depths of the spring. Then he sat on his haunches and splashed at the water with a paw. The ripples caused the shimmering to defuse and disperse.

The cougar licked his wet paw, yowled loudly at the moon, then slunk along the base of the escarpment toward the waterfall and a deep crevice, where he had detected the scent of a female of his own species.

Various Gleanings from Mulmur Murmurings
by Hugh Dunnit

For the Week of August 11–17, 1962

Strange things happen when the moon shines bright. While folks were enjoying themselves at Charlie B's party, Maggie W was up to no good. Jake W, a guest of the Cagey Farmer, was out for a walk with our favourite dog when he found Maggie emptying her gas can on the Bird on the Hill's back porch. Although she doesn't smoke, Maggie W had a cigarette lighter along for the walk. We wonder why. When needs dictate demand, the woman has proven that she can be a real little trotter. Firebug Maggie lit out for her car on Lavender Line with Jake W and our favourite dog in hot pursuit. She soon found out that Joe D had locked all the car's doors and was sitting on the hood just waiting for her to show up. The lady — can we still call her that — is now in a place where the only fire she'll be allowed to light will be the spark of recognition if someone chooses to visit her.

A note for the Cagey Farmer: the next time you propose, try putting a real ring on the finger of the Lovely Damsel. She's not a chicken, Charlie. But the lady sure does have a sense of humour.

And who is going to be the proud owner of one of our favourite dog's latest batch of pups? Glenn H. who will surely teach the pooch a thing or two about yowling and running. Nisko is the name of the black pup that the Cagey Farmer's wife decided to keep.

For the Week of October 6–12, 1962

Great news for the Valley. The Cagey Farmer and the Lovely Damsel finally tied the knot — Wee Jimmy wins the bet. The deed was done at the home of the Bird on the Hill. A good time was had by all.

The cottage that Maggie W lived in for so many years has been sold to a young couple from away. Let's welcome them to the Springs with a smile and a handshake.

The United Church's Autumn Bazaar had the biggest crowd ever to attend. Pies were sold out by noon hour — darn it. The new quilt auction raised $1,115. Where can I learn to quilt?

For the Week of December 8–14, 1962

If you're looking for the Delaney Four, you'll find them at the Cagey Farmer's house. The roof fell in on the home farm. As Charlie B and his wife are residing with the Bird on the Hill, the arrangement suits everyone. The Farmer can still farm; now he has an extra eight hands to help him.

Would the person who stole Mrs. B's fancy new broom off her front porch please bring it back? How do you expect the lady to get around without her conveyance?

For the Week of August 10–16, 1963

Did you know that there's something in the Valley a lot older then Wee Jimmy? This fellow who occasionally visits the Bird on the Hill has a theory that some of the cedar trees on Thalia's Mark are more then five hundred years old. They could be almost one thousand years old! Dino D. says that, because the escarpment through The Mark was never cleared, the area might be home to some of the oldest trees in Ontario. If you believe that, folks, I've got a bridge to sell you.

In the same vein, the Bird on the Hill is taking steps to make her little bit of heaven declared a nature preserve.

From reports coming from Gorgeous G at the General, I think that our wildcat has found a mate. Someone up the line says that they saw little ones roaming the uplands.

For the Week of August 24–30, 1963

A foot-stomping good time was had by all at the first ever Valley Jamboree. Cars were lined up for a mile coming into the Springs. The Cagey Farmer's lower pasture was used for parking, and farm wagons ferried folks to River Bend Park where the rare Curlew and his friends twittered all day. Boy, those birds can chirp! Anyone who was clever enough to set up a booth to sell anything — and there were plenty of local people asked for a spot — made a killing selling everything. Gorgeous G at the General put tables outside and couldn't keep up with orders. Her hubby was reduced from driving big trucks to serving pie. Even Reverend Harrison got into the act and flipped burgers — better that than handing plates around, as in collection. The second Valley Jamboree is already being discussed, with the need for more thunder shacks high on their list of gotta-haves.

For the Week of October 19–25, 1963

The Valley is reverberating with the news that a bouncing baby boy has joined the family at Granite. Hunter David Barnes will have a lot to live up to, being the son of the Cagey Farmer and the Lovely Damsel.

The Valley's big cat was spotted near the bowstring bridge again. Eyeball it only. The only trigger that you should be thinking of pushing is the shutter release on your camera.

Word is buzzing up and down Township concession roads that Maggie W expired near Hartford, Connecticut at the home of a relative. As we've no way of confirming or denying the rumour, we'll put a tick against her name and take the rumour as being true. Let's hope she took a lighter with her to her final reward, just in case the fire goes out.

For the Week of December 21–27, 1963

Wouldn't you know it, on the most blustery day this December, Mary and Tom D were presented with a baby girl. The stork survived the trip. Mother is doing fine. The father is still recuperating from the shock, as are Uncles Dick, Harry, and Joe. Did I not mention that Mary and Tom were married on an equally blustery day in February of this year? We are talking about the union of a nearly-to-the-top-of-the-hill woman, and a well-over-the-top-of-the-hill fuddydud — who proved not to be a dud after all. This little family is living in one of the three cottages on the road into the Springs that we understand belonged at one time to the prodigal son with the dollar signs in his eyes.

Mary and Tom D will have two interesting neighbours. The Curlew bird, who is spending Christmas at Granite, has purchased the second one. Two months ago Jake W purchased the third home in the row.

Speaking of that prodigal son, he hasn't been seen in the Valley and Springs since July 1962. No one's complaining about his absence. The feeling around here is that if you do see him, shoot first and ask questions later.

For the Week of October 10–16, 1964

All those interested in helping frame a building, show up at the Delaney Four's farm on October 17, bright and early in the morning, with necessary tools in hand. There's a load of lumber coming in, ready for a banging good party. The Lovely Damsel and Bird on the Hill expect everyone to show up for chili, buns, and cake when the lunch whistle blows.

For the Week of November 6–12, 1965

Charlie B and his wife are excited about the arrival of a daughter, Elizabeth Thalia Barnes. The Bird on the Hill is overjoyed that she has another babe to spoil, but cautions the Cagey Farmer and Lovely Damsel that she's running out of bedrooms.

For the Week of June 11–17, 1966

Joan Barnes, the youngest sister of Charlie B, died in her sleep on Wednesday past. For a number of years, this kind lady has suffered from a debilitating bone disease. She will be missed by everyone in the Valley and Springs.

The first book by Licinius MacPherson, a murder mystery that's set in our Valley, is now

available at Gorgeous G's store. You can borrow
the book or buy your own copy. A word to the
wise: sit in front of a mirror when you read this
book so you can see who's sneaking up behind
you. It's a real page turner. By the way, you're
going to be surprised when you find out who
Licinius MacPherson is!

For the Week of May 29–June 4, 1971

It is with deepest regret that I have to break the
news that the Bird on the Hill has fallen off her
perch. The grand old lady was born eighty-seven
years ago in the same house where she died on
Tuesday past — a place that everyone who knew
and loved her referred to as the cottage of lilacs
and laughter. Thalia had been in poor health for
the past year, so it is fitting that she lived to see
her beloved lilacs bloom one more time. Her eu-
logy, delivered by Noah Jason Curlew, included
a salute to the lady's heritage. The gentleman
said that Thalia Logan lived her life to the fullest,
giving something unique of herself to everyone.
He mentioned that Thalia never compromised
her ideals and eccentricities. She danced with
both the bear and the wolf, outlasting one, and
outwitting the other. Mr. Curlew's final words
were that Thalia Logan proved once again that
the cougar is forever.

www.ingramcontent.com/pod-product-compliance
Lightning Source LLC
Chambersburg PA
CBHW031059030726
47496CB00002BA/294